HUNTING ZOE

AND OTHER TALES...

Steve Gerlach

Probable Cause Publishing

Published in Australia by Probable Cause Publishing

steve@stevegerlach.com

stevegerlach.com

Typeset in Adobe Garamond Pro

ISBN: 978-0-9578641-5-3

To:

Everyone who kept her alive for so long.
This one's for you.

And a special thanks to the "Gerlach 69 Girls".
May your membership continue to grow…

TABLE OF CONTENTS

7   When Fantasy Met Reality:
An Introduction by Brett McBean

11   Hunting Zoe:
An Introduction by the Author

15   Hunting Zoe

183   Broken Cookie

189   Schism

201   Cellcandy

221   Dead of Night

241   Jungle

257   White Christmas

281   Down on Katie - The Ninth Day
An extract from *The Modern Days of Sodom*

291   Prey

319   Amber Rising
A short sequel to *Lake Mountain*

333   Steve Gerlach: On The Edge
An Interview by Ron Clinton

WHEN FANTASY MET REALITY

AN INTRODUCTION
by Brett McBean

We all go a little crazy sometimes...

Writing is a strange affair. We writers are in the business of making up stories and populating these tales of fancy with make-believe characters. But in order for our tales to be successful, we have to create worlds that are real and characters that live and breathe. We have to convince the reader to care about these fictional people, and that this world we have created really does exist.

It's an amazing process, but it's also a grim, sometimes disturbing, process, especially for those who work in the arena of dark fiction. For those of us who write horror, we frequently inhabit a world of pain and terror, where bad things happen to good people, and good things happen to bad people. We are forced to plunder our deepest fears and tap into those skeletons that we wish so much to keep safely locked up, never to see daylight.

But, if we want to create truly memorable works, then we have to reach in and access that darkness. We have to live, sleep and breathe death, evil and pain.

It's dangerous territory, there's no doubt about that. But when an author is successful in harnessing that darkness, something magical happens—there's a fusion between writer and reader, a bond, an understanding if you like. The work grows into something more than just ink printed on paper; it becomes a very real thing, a palpable experience that doesn't end when the reader reads the last line and closes the book.

Sometimes, if we're lucky, we get a character that's truly memorable, one that takes on a life of their own. They seem as real as any living human. We think we know them intimately—their fears, desires, the way they look, smell, and feel. We wish they were real so we could talk to them, know them, hell, maybe even be their friend.

Or lover. Or sex-slave.

Or all of the above.

Folks, welcome to the world of Steve Gerlach. Welcome to Zoe's world.

* * *

I first met Steve back in 2001. I had conversed with him over email and chatted with him on various message boards, but it wasn't until the unfortunate passing of Richard Laymon that we finally met in person.

It wasn't the happiest of circumstances. A group of Melbourne Laymon fans had organised a memorial to the late writer, as our small way of paying homage to his writings, and a way of saying goodbye with people who understood where each of us was coming from.

We were both relatively new writers at the time. I had only a few short stories published; Steve had already published *The Nocturne* and would soon publish *Love Lies Dying*. We talked a lot that night about our hopes and dreams, which essentially amounted to the same thing—to be successful writers. To reach people the way Richard Laymon reached us, and for our work to live on for a long time.

It's amazing to think that, all these years later, we are both still writing, and that Steve has written a semi-sequel (or 'addition' if you'd prefer) to *Love Lies Dying*. A story borne out of his ever-growing number of fans' love for Zoe.

Which is testament to the power of Steve's book, and I think most people would agree, his writing has indeed touched people.

* * *

We all go a little crazy sometimes…

Zoe was paraphrasing *Psycho*'s Norman Bates when she

spoke this line in *Love Lies Dying*, and it's appropriate that Gerlach has Glen, the main protagonist of *Hunting Zoe*, repeating this line numerous times throughout the story. Not only is it in keeping with Glen's fascination with Zoe, but it's a wry statement, given the lengths the characters in the story go, to live out their fantasy.

But the Hitchcock allusions don't stop there. I know Gerlach is a big Hitchcock fan and aside from the *Psycho* reference, he pays homage to one of the master's greatest films, *Vertigo*. Much like Jimmy Stewart's character in the Hitchcock film, Glen wants to transform his girlfriend into his idea of female perfection (in this case Zoe), high-lighting the principal theme of both the Hitchcock film and Gerlach's novella—obsession.

Because that's what is at the heart of *Hunting Zoe*—a fan's obsession over wanting to live out his favourite book. To find his leading lady, the woman that has haunted his mind and heart for a long time.

And it's this blurring of real life and fiction that makes *Hunting Zoe* so potent. Gerlach knows that in order to create a work as engaging as *Love Lies Dying*, it requires the author to go a little mad, and he's aware the effect its story, and in particular the character of Zoe, has had on his legions of fans.

You wouldn't be holding this book in your hands if it didn't.

We're all guilty of holding a woman, or man, up on a pedestal, whether it's an actor, musician, or model; we've all fantasised about meeting that person, having a relation-ship with them. Even though we know deep down that if we were to meet them in real life, we'd be bitterly disap-pointed that they didn't meet up to that fantasy. And for most of us we're happy to leave it at just that—a fantasy.

But what if you were to become so obsessed with some-one that your life was consumed by them? Would you go to any lengths to meet them?

And what would you say to them if you did find your-self standing face to face with your fantasy?

Well you're about to find out.

Let Gerlach take you to that place where reality becomes fiction and fiction becomes reality.

Are you ready for the madness?

I hope so. Because Zoe is.

Brett McBean
Melbourne, Australia, 2007

HUNTING ZOE

AN INTRODUCTION
by Steve Gerlach

Hi there. Need a lift?
Sure, no problem. How far you headed?
Climb in. I'll take you where you want to go.
Throw your stuff in the back. There's plenty of room...
Seat belt on? No? Ah, to hell with it then, let's take our
chances.
We're ready.
Welcome to *Hunting Zoe*.

It's good to see you here, eagerly anticipating what lies ahead. Call this introduction a map, or a guide, if you like, for both the seasoned and first-time travellers among us who'll be walking this path. Let me shed some light on where I'll be taking you, and why...

You see, this little trek serves two purposes. The first is for those of you who have read my novel, *Love Lies Dying*. You've met Zoe before. So you know what she's capable of and, yet strangely, you're back for more. Still, I can't blame you. If it weren't for you, none of us would be here today. You're the ones who wrote to me requesting a sequel to *Love Lies Dying*, and I thank you for the kindwords, dedication and persistence. To you people, this is it! Your sequel! Well, *sorta...*

You see, this journey is not really a sequel to *Love Lies Dying*, believe it or not. For one thing, it's way too short to be classified as a novel. No, this is a novella, a short side-trip, a brief trek, a quick stroll into the world of *Love Lies Dying*. Think of it as a campfire story, a teaser, a bit of fun between you and me, giving you more information about the history of the original story and of Zoe herself. After all, that's what you wanted, right?

More Zoe?

Of course!

And hidden along the path ahead may be some hints as to what's still to come, as yet untold...

Hunting Zoe is a story that can be enjoyed equally by those who read the original novel, and by those of you who are here for the first time. My aim was to give readers who had read *Love Lies Dying* more thrills and chills, while also providing those readers who are new to Zoe a taste of what they've been missing. For you new readers, this first taste will be sweet indeed. And you will— hopefully—wish to avail yourselves of the main course after finishing with this mere nibble.

Oh, but there was that other purpose too. I almost forgot. And that reason is to get Zoe out of my head. As readers of *Love Lies Dying* will know, she's a persistent gal, is our Zoe. And I found even after writing *Love Lies Dying* and closing the book on that tale, she wouldn't leave me alone. She's like that, you see.

She stayed with me, as she stayed with my readers too. She whispered to me at night, curled up against me with her warm skin and glowing smile, strands of blonde hair escaping her ponytail and falling across her face. She giggled and told me wicked, horrible things. Things even I didn't know about. I was shocked...and just a little bit scared.

And that tale is contained within these pages...

Alfred Hitchcock said a director must fall in love with the leading lady of each of his films, to better capture them on celluloid. And I think that's true of writers as well. They must fall in love with their leading characters. As I fell head-over-heels for Zoe.

So, dear reader, in your hands you have the outcome of those late night conversations between Zoe and myself. In this very special limited edition, you have the story she wanted written, the story she told to me in her own words, and you have—I hope—a fitting "addition" (not sequel— *don't* say "sequel") to *Love Lies Dying*.

Let's pray she's satisfied now and will leave us all alone. Although, I don't like our chances of that happening anytime soon…

Enjoy it.

Zoe did.

You ready?

Sure?

'Cause there'll be no stopping until we get to the end.

Don't look so scared. I told you, you're safe with me.

For now…

Here, you hold the map. Make sure you get the directions right and don't get us lost. I don't want to get stuck out here at night, okay?

Ready?

Let's go…

Steve Gerlach
Melbourne, Australia, 2007

HUNTING ZOE

LUST

ONE

"We're getting close."

"You sure?"

"Yeah, can't be far now."

The long lonely road stretched out in front of them. They hadn't seen a car for at least twenty minutes. Glen Eloy didn't think they would see many more cars at this time of the afternoon, not when they were so far out in the countryside. For a second, he took his gaze off the road in front of them and turned his head to look across at Mark Webber.

Only Mark would agree to do this with him.

Only Mark.

Mark was his best friend. Always had been and always would be. They'd lived next door to each other growing up, they'd gone to school together and they'd stayed the best of buddies through thick and thin.

No matter what.

Even when others would say Glen's ideas were crazy, Mark would stand by him.

As he turned to concentrate back on the road, Glen knew that they were friends for life. They had something others didn't, a brotherly bond.

He smiled.

"What do you think?" he asked.

Mark lifted his head from the newspaper article he was reading. "Impressive stuff," he said.

"I told you I'd come through with the goods."

"Yeah, but I didn't know you had so much material. Where did you find all this?"

Glen smiled. "The internet's a big place."

"But you didn't find all this stuff online," Mark said as he rifled through some more of the dozens of pages in the fat, bulging manila folder.

"No, that's true. I had to become a real little sleuth to find some of that stuff. It wasn't easy, that's for sure."

Glen took one hand off the steering wheel and leaned across to Mark. His eyes wandered from the road as he reached into the folder and pulled out a piece of paper with a red Post-It note attached to the top.

"Read this one," he said, placing the photocopied news article on top of Mark's pile. "When I found that article I almost blew my load."

Glen straightened up and placed his hand back on the steering wheel. The mid-afternoon sun was behind them now, throwing a long shadow of the Jeep out in front of them.

As they drove through some low-lying areas, Glen spotted the first wisps of fog that would blanket the area at night. He cranked up the heater one more notch, even though it wasn't so cold, knowing if they took too much longer, the evening air would seep through the cloth top of the Jeep and envelop them.

Gotta make sure we arrive before nightfall.

"We should be doing this at night," he said.

"Nah, we can't," Mark replied. "We'd probably miss a turn and get lost."

"Yeah, you're right. But to make it as realistic as possible, we should be doing this at night."

Mark laughed. "You've got it bad."

"Huh?"

"How much more realistic do you want it? We're in a red Jeep, it's a Saturday afternoon, we're on the right road…"

"Still, at night would be cool."

"Look, I'll do a deal with you," Mark said. "If what you have in this folder is correct—"

"Oh, pal, it's correct alright."

"And we find what we're looking for…"

"We will, I promise you."

"Then we can always come back and do the whole thing properly, okay? You know, come back next weekend and set off on Saturday evening when it's dark and arrive before midnight. We'll know where we're going and what to keep an eye out for."

Glen thought about it for a second and then agreed. "Okay, deal."

He turned to smile at his friend, but Mark had returned to reading the newspaper article.

Focusing back on the road, Glen mentally patted himself on the back for the good job he had done.

I can't believe we're here, on this road, and doing this.

We're actually fucking doing this.

It had taken so much work, so much time. But it was all paying off now.

He listened to the sound of the Jeep's engine and the low whistle of the afternoon air as it collided against the soft-top. The plastic handcuffs swung from the rear-view mirror to the rhythm of the road.

This is going to be so cool, Glen thought.

A hush fell between them as they travelled further into the countryside.

"Wow," Mark said as his eyes lifted from the newspaper article.

Glen turned to look at him, but Mark was staring out through the windshield.

"Amazing, huh?" Glen asked.

"Sure is."

A bend in the road appeared in front of them and Glen turned the steering wheel to compensate. The Jeep skidded slightly as it turned to the left.

"Murder Two…" Mark whispered.

"I know," Glen replied. "Hard to believe, isn't it? There's just so much more to this than *anyone* knows about."

"Was he convicted?"

Glen shook his head. "I don't know. That's what frustrates me so much. That's the one thing I couldn't find out."

"But if they reported on this, I mean like in the newspapers, then they must've reported on the trial." Mark began to shuffle through the papers in the folder.

"I couldn't find anything. I looked forwards and backwards on those damn microfilm rolls until I thought I was going to be sick, but I couldn't find anything. The whole story just vanishes."

"You've got a goddamn goldmine in here."

"I know." Glen grinned again. "And *we're* the only ones who know about it."

"I just wish we knew if he was convicted."

"I tried. Believe me, I wish I knew too. But I couldn't find it anywhere. I even called the court and they couldn't find any record of the trial either. It's so damn strange. You don't know how hard I searched to find that out. In the end, for us, I guess it doesn't matter. But I tried to find out anyway."

Mark turned and reached to grab the novel from the back seat. He sat back in his chair and opened the book in his lap.

"How many times have you read this now?" he asked.

"Thirteen."

Mark laughed. "Unlucky for some."

"Not for me."

"And I thought I was addicted having read it *five* times."

"You've got a long way to go to catch me," Glen said.

He turned his head and eyed his dog-eared copy of the novel.

It all started there, he thought. *On page one. On line one.*

The spine of the oversized paperback was broken in countless sections. Some pages were dog-eared, but most contained a Post-It note or two, or three. All in different colour combinations, all denoting a different part of the book, a different fact to check, a different idea to follow up. He could see some of his notes scrawled in black pen across the Post-Its. He'd worked all night on countless nights to dig and find that research, just to make sure he was on the right track.

Glen had always wished he'd bought more than just

one copy of the book, but it sold out so damn fast he never got the chance. He reminded himself to look on eBay when they returned home, because he didn't feel like waiting until the US limited edition was released in two years time.

Fuck that, I can't wait. eBay. I might get lucky and find one there, he thought.

"I'd have done it with her straight away," Mark said, his eyes lifting from page one.

"*Oh yeah*, me too. Although he was married, I still would've done it."

"Yeah, you can't say no when she's like that."

"She'd be so good," Glen said.

So good, he thought.

He could feel his cock start to pulse and grow.

Just imagine fucking her all night. In every way. In every position. In every hole.

His cock pushed against the inside of his boxers and he could feel the tightness in his jeans.

He glanced across to Mark, but Mark had gone back to reading the novel.

Glen concentrated back on the road.

If a girl like that turned up at my place and was there like she was, I'd say yes straight away, no matter what. Fuck the world and everyone else in it. You don't get chances like that every day. Just think, to hold her and feel her naked against my skin and to slowly have her slide down and lick and suck me. To shoot my cum all over her face and tits and gorgeous pussy...

Glen moved in his seat, trying to get comfortable and reposition his hard cock.

Imagine bending her forward and seeing her gorgeous ass and, just below it, that smooth shaved mound of beauty. And I'd spread those cheeks and slip inside her and fuck her until we both collapsed exhausted on the floor. But she'd come back and want more, much more, lots more and we'd go all night. We'd fuck and fuck and become one. She'd be mine forever.

Glen's forehead furrowed as he tried to think of something else.

The silence between them continued, filled only with the constant white noise of the air rushing against the Jeep.

Glen peered through the windshield. Any sign of civilisation had disappeared long ago now. All around them were trees and bushes; there were no other cars or signs of life. Just a road that stretched on in front of the Jeep for what seemed like forever.

This really is a back road that no one uses these days.

He wondered if they were doing the right thing.

Of course we are. This is what you've been working towards for almost a year now.

Glen shook his head.

A year? Is it almost a year?

He remembered when the book first arrived. Just before Valentine's Day. He'd planned everything. He was going to show Jodie a real cool time out on the town, but he'd started reading the book the day before and hadn't wanted to put the damn thing down until he'd reached the end.

It had that effect on you.

So he called Jodie and told her he was sick.

He didn't think she really believed him. She knew he was lying. She thought he didn't want to go out and spend the day with her. He did. But the book was more important.

Who cares anyway? That book changed my life.

Glen stared at the road and watched as it stretched out before them. He looked for anything different in the surrounds as they sped by, but it all looked the same.

All the same, mile after mile. Just like life, day after day. Until something comes out of the blue and changes your life forever.

Mark lifted his head from the book and sat back in his seat.

"She's so fucking *hot*," he moaned.

Glen laughed. "No need to tell me, man. I'm well aware of that."

"Who do you think would play her in the movie, if they made one of the book?" Mark asked.

"Way ahead of you, pal. That's an easy one. Leelee Sobieski."

"Nah," Mark said after giving it some thought. "She doesn't do nudes."

"Really? *Fuck!* You sure?"

"Yep, I read that somewhere once. She wouldn't do all the sex scenes and, hell, I don't think you'd even get her naked in front of a camera in the first place."

"Shit." Glen was disappointed. "I really wanted her in the role. She'd be great in the film."

"How about Asia Argento?" Mark asked.

"Are you kidding? Asia's a brunette."

Mark shrugged his shoulders. "Yeah, that's true I guess. Well, she could dye her hair or wear a wig or something."

"Sure." Glen gave the idea some thought. "They do that all the time these days in movies. I didn't think of that. She'd be really cool. But I don't know, I think it has to be a real blonde. Someone like Leelee."

"The teenage girl from *24*?"

"Nope, not beautiful enough."

"Anna Kournikova?"

Glen broke out laughing. "She's a tennis player, not an actor."

"Who the hell cares?" Mark muttered. "As long as she's in it."

They both laughed.

"Anyway, if the actress wasn't a real blonde, we'd find out in the first few minutes of the film." They both laughed again.

"No we wouldn't," Glen said. "Because she's shaved down there. We'd never know for sure."

They both watched the road stretching out before them.

"Have you ever seen a real shaved pussy in a film?" Mark asked. "Not, you know, a bikini line. I mean a real shaved pussy?"

Glen thought about it. "I don't think so. Not in mainstream stuff. I mean, in porn films, yeah, all the time. But not in any Hollywood blockbusters."

"Japanese films?"

"Nah, the Japs like 'em bushy. So do the Europeans for some strange reason."

"Well, they'll never make *this* book into a mainstream film."

"Hell no, even an R rating would make the film too tame. It'd have to be an underground film. Or an unrated direct-to-DVD film like all those old European films you can buy at Amazon that are really porn films but are being sold as 'high art'."

Mark returned to the book. "Good point. I didn't think of that."

Glen was glad they'd had the conversation. It had taken his mind off her and his erection had subsided. He was comfortable again and could concentrate on the road once more.

Mark turned in his seat and threw the novel into the back of the Jeep.

"I could read that again and again," he said.

Glen nodded. "I know what you mean."

"Did you ever contact the author?"

"Nope." Glen shook his head. "I tried to track him down, but no one can find him. He used to have a website or something, but I can't find him anywhere. No one knows where he is or if he's done anything since."

"That's weird."

"Everything connected to that book is weird. Some people say the author's dead or that he just disappeared under mysterious circumstances."

"Really? Did he write anything else?"

"A couple of novels, but I think they were written before this one and they were just polished up for release afterwards."

"I hate it when they do that," Mark said as he turned his attention back to the folder of articles.

Glen checked the fuel gauge. They had more than enough gas to get there and back without refilling the tank. He'd made sure of that before they left because he didn't know how much exploring they'd be doing.

"The countryside's a big place," he'd told Mark as they

had pulled into the gas station. "I don't want to be stranded out there. No one will be around and I don't want to get stuck without any help."

"We've got our cell phones," Mark said.

"I don't think there's coverage that far out."

"Oh, okay. Better check the tyres too."

He had. All were fully inflated. Even the spare.

The girl behind the counter at the gas station looked okay, Glen remembered. The uniform didn't do much for her, but her hair was in braids and he liked that. He'd never given it much thought until he read the book, and now every girl who looked sexy and fuckable made him think of Zoe and wonder whether this real girl measured up to her.

Few do, he thought. *No, scratch that. None do.*

I wish I had a Zoe in my life.

Mark's voice brought him back.

"Are there many sites on the net?" he asked, holding up a printout from one of them.

"There's dozens. All fan sites though. No official sites. Just some people who have read the book and want to make sure she lives on."

"It's a weird place, the internet," Mark added. "I'm glad I keep away from it."

"You've got no idea. There's discussion boards and email lists just on her. They discuss *everything* to do with her. It's amazing. There's everything you ever needed. Fanfiction and more. There's even a site where people can upload photos of girls they think look like her."

"Now that *is* weird."

"Like I said, everything connected to her is weird."

Mark turned and smiled at him. "But we're the *first*, right?"

Glen nodded. "Oh yeah, we've cracked the code alright."

"This is *so* cool."

"So *fucking* cool!" Glen drummed his fists on the steering wheel. "We've cracked the code and were going to be the first."

"You're sure?"

"Absolutely."

"You haven't fucked up anywhere?"

Glen shook his head. "Nope. Trust me. I'm right. I've checked it all. I've looked at all the facts. I'm right, I know I am."

"I sure hope so. I don't want us coming all this way to be wrong."

Glen steered around another corner. "Don't worry so much. Hell, you read the newspaper article, it literally says it all in there."

"Yeah, but the guy's name is Daryl."

"Don't worry about that. Authors do that all the time. You know, 'The names in this book have been changed to protect the innocent' and all that."

"He wasn't innocent."

Glen laughed. "No, but they *changed it* anyway. Probably to make sure he didn't sue or something. The main point is look at *her* name, look at it again if you have to. It's just like the name at the start of the book, in the dedication."

"But her surname wasn't printed in the dedication, just the first letter of it."

"Ah, but some early advance reading copies did have her surname in full. That's why it *has* to be right. It *has* to be her."

Mark's eyes skimmed the article again. "Yeah, I guess you're right."

"You *know* I am. That article gave me the proof. It was the start. And all the other facts check out. Sure, the place names and character names are different, but that's what authors do."

"You're a regular little Sherlock, huh?"

"For this, I had to be. But they can't fool Glen Eloy for long. I found all the hidden clues."

Silence filled the car again. Their surrounds blended into one long dry and barren landscape. The only sound was of the motor and the wind against the canvas.

So exciting, this whole thing, Glen thought.

And he was glad his best buddy was with him.

It was hard to believe it was just a week ago that he'd finally worked it all out. When the maps had proven he was right and he could plot the whole drive in three easy steps, he'd called Mark straight away.

"Pal, I *got it*."

"Huh?"

"I've fuckin' *done it*."

"What?"

"I've cracked the code. I've worked it all out."

"No way."

"I have."

"You *serious?*"

"Deadly. I'm sitting here with it all. I've worked it out. It all makes sense and we can do it. It's easy."

"I can't believe it."

"You better. It's all here, in black and white. I've got it, I've photocopied it and I'm ready to roll."

"You really want to *do* this?"

"Yes."

"All of it? Like we said?"

"*Fuck* yeah!"

"When?"

"Next weekend. How about we leave on Saturday afternoon?"

Mark had chuckled on the other end. "Saturday, huh?"

"Yep, what could be better?"

There was a pause for only a second before Mark had agreed. "Okay, deal."

"Cool, I'll pick you up, okay?"

"Yep, that's fine. You sure you've got this right?"

"More sure than I've been about anything else."

"Okay, see you then."

Glen smiled as he thought about that conversation. Turning his head, he checked on Mark. He was reading another article. Glen knew all the facts were there. He knew that if he just let his friend digest it all, there'd be no doubt in his mind either. The facts spoke for themselves.

The author was smart, he'd hidden a lot, but not everything.

"You know some guy on the internet is trying to write a sequel," Glen said after a few more minutes of silence.

Mark looked up from the article. "Bullshit."

"No, it's true. He's trying to re-create her in some spin-off thing."

"That sucks."

"Yeah, it sure does," Glen agreed. "It'll never be as good, even if he manages to write it at all, which I don't think he will. Sequels are never as good as the originals."

Mark scratched his chin. "You're right. Except for *Psycho II*."

Glen thought for a second. "Yeah, *Psycho II* was cool."

"And *Stepfather II*, that was a cool sequel too," Mark added. "And people think *Mad Max II* was better than the first, but I'm not so sure…"

"Yeah, well, *anyway*," Glen continued, "we're talking about books here and book sequels never work."

"Except like the *Beast House* series…"

Glen nodded. "Well, *mostly*, most times, sequels don't work."

"Yeah, you've got that right." Mark said as he returned to the articles.

But imagine if it did *work,* Glen thought. *To spend another 500 pages with her would be like heaven on earth. Even just 200 pages. But it will never happen.*

He didn't think Jodie ever really understood what it was all about. He'd tried to explain it to her, but she wouldn't listen. She saw his infatuation with a fictional character as a threat.

Stupid bitch.

He'd tried to get her to read the novel, so she could see for herself what he was talking about. He'd tried to explain it to her, but she wasn't interested.

"Do you love *me* or your fucking precious little *Zoe*?" she'd screamed at him.

Shouldn't ask a guy a question like that when you're having an argument.

"Well she sure gets me to cum more often than you do!" he'd said.

Bad move.
Real.
Bad.
Move.

Of course, he didn't really mean to say it. He'd said it to get back at her. He'd said it to hurt her. To cut deep.

And it worked.

Well fuck you anyway, Miss Precious. I don't need you. I'm out here and I'm going to follow my dream and you can go fuck yourself.

He thought he'd feel better after that.

He didn't.

"Don't take this the wrong way…"

Glen's thoughts were interrupted. "What?"

Mark closed the folder and turned to face him.

"You don't think that maybe, just a bit, you might be taking this whole Zoe thing too far?"

Glen's eyes darted to his friend and his jaw dropped. He didn't know what to say.

"I'm just asking," Mark said.

"Why would you say that?"

"Well you know…" Mark's voice trailed off.

"No, I *don't* know." Glen's eyes narrowed.

"Well, this file full of clips and notes. The book covered with comments and stuff…"

"And?"

"And? You want *more?"*

"I don't see your point," Glen said.

Pal, don't ruin this before we're even there.

"I don't want to seem unkind or anything. I mean, I'm really glad you asked me to come along with you on this trip. I just think that maybe you're a bit too obsessed by the whole thing."

"Really? Obsessed?" Glen was shocked.

"I'm just asking what you think, that's all. Some people might find all this pretty weird."

Like Jodie.

"I don't think so," Glen answered quickly. "There's plenty of weirder people out there, especially on the net.

Don't worry about me, I'm as sane as the next guy. I can walk away from this at any time. Drop it all at any time if I need to or want to."

"Really?"

"Yep."

"So, if I said we should turn around and head home…?"

Glen's eyes checked the road before darting back to Mark. "Are you *serious?*"

"I'm just *asking*, I'm not saying we *have* to."

"I've done all this work, all this research to get us here today. You were all for it, you said yeah let's do it when I told you about it last weekend, you said you'd come along. Don't go all chicken-shit on me now."

"I'm not, I just wanted to know what you thought."

"Look, this is it, okay? This is the last puzzle piece. We've found out all the stuff we needed to find, we discovered all the hidden clues, it's all done. Once we return from this weekend, it's all over. Our lives can move on, but we've got to see this through to the end, and now. We have to be the *first!* We have to close this once and for all so we can look back on it in years to come and say, yeah, we did it and we were the first. Okay?"

"But you know…" Mark pointed to the handcuffs hanging on the rear-view mirror.

"So what?" Glen said. "You want me to put fluffy dice up there or something? Or an alien? Or some fucking Indian dream-catcher feather bullshit or a stupid plastic dancing fucking Elvis?"

Mark pointed at the silver studded black wristband on Glen's right wrist. "The wristband. Just like the dog collar Zoe used…"

"It's a *wristband*. A fashion item. Nothing more, nothing less. Let's not spoil this great weekend with this argument. It's just stupid. Okay?"

Mark looked at him for a second but then nodded his head.

"Yeah, okay."

Glen smiled. "Cool. I knew you wouldn't let me down." His eyes returned to the road.

What was all that about? He's starting to sound like Jodie. And another one of her I don't need. Why do people always have to stamp all over your dreams the moment you lay them out in front of them—when you're at your most vulnerable, when you're most sensitive to attack? I thought he understood why we're here.

Glen shook his head.

I'm glad I never told him about the cock-ring, that might've thrown him right over the edge.

He was never sure about the cock-ring either. Doing the research on the net was easy, but once he started calling around to tattoo parlours and piercing salons to find out prices and procedures, he felt a bit out of place.

Not to mention letting another guy hold your cock and fondle it before sticking a fucking great needle through it.

And it hurt like fuck too.

Then he had to clean the non-stop discharge seeping from the two holes for about a week before they cleared up. And he couldn't have sex for months. Still, Jodie was gone, so it wasn't like he was having sex with anyone anyway.

Was it really just three weeks ago I had it pierced?

That means Jodie's been gone five weeks.

He wondered if her leaving had given him the strength to get the piercing done.

I'll show her, he remembered thinking.

Even masturbating was too hard. He'd have to wait for the Prince Albert to heal completely before he could try it out again.

But, man, that first wank was fantastic, even through the pain.

He thought he'd cum for hours.

If only Zoe had been there to drink it all in. To suck me dry and to make me cum hour after hour.

If only...

If only I could find her...or someone like her.

He knew now that she existed. The newspaper clippings proved that to be true. They matched with the dedication at the front of the book. The names were the same.

No doubt about it. What had happened in the book had happened in real life. She was real, more real to him now than some of the people he'd known for years. He knew girls like her were out there.

I just have to find them.
And I will.
After this weekend.
Nothing matters until after this weekend…

He was proud of the research he had done. Proud that he was able to decode the hints in the book and work out exactly where the real events took place. Once he found out where the author lived, working from there hadn't been so hard. He discovered the author had lived in Glen's home town and that some of the events had taken place just a few blocks away from where Glen lived.

Almost as if I were destined to be the first to find out the truth…

There were many stories on the net that the author was really the main male character of the novel, but Glen wasn't so sure about that. And when he found the article about the trial, it all started to fit together nicely. The locations all existed and they were exactly the distances apart as described in the novel, but the author had changed the town names as well as the names of the characters.

All except Zoe. She stayed the same.
But I worked it out.
I found Zoe.
Well, not yet. But I will.

He just wished he had been able to find a follow-up article that answered the questions about the trial. He needed to know if the guy was found guilty or let off. But he hadn't been able to find anything. He'd even tried to track him down by doing searches of voter registries and on the internet, but he couldn't find him. The guy didn't seem to exist.

Unless he was the author.

"Did the other girl stay with him?" Mark asked.

Glen looked across to him.

"Huh?"

"The other girl, did she stay with him?"

"I don't know," Glen replied.

"I liked her too."

"Oh yeah, she was great. Just imagine her and Zoe together." Glen smiled.

"I am."

Aaaah, Glen thought. *So you* are *as turned on by this as I am.*

The road stretched out in front of them.

Glen checked the trip clock on his dashboard. The miles were churning over fast.

"We're getting close," he said.

"Really?"

"Not long now."

"Cool," Mark said.

Glen stared out the windshield and relaxed, letting the feel of the road and the sound of the air calm him.

I've waited so long for this.

Nearly there.

They'll stop laughing at me once we come back with the proof. They won't be able to say shit once we prove it to them. I'll wipe the smirks off their stupid faces.

"The internet's fucked," Glen said.

"I know," Mark replied. "I don't know why you spend so much time on there."

"I don't."

"You do. You're always on it."

"I was *on it* to find out all this stuff so we could get here *today*, remember?"

"Yeah, yeah." Mark buried his head in another article.

"We wouldn't be here if it wasn't for all the time I spent on the net finding this stuff out and researching..."

"And downloading porn."

"And trying to find out information..."

"And downloading porn."

"And trying to contact people and get the facts so we could get here."

"And downloading porn!"

"Whatever."

Porn's no good when you've got a bolt through your cock and it's seeping green pus…

He hadn't seen it appear on the horizon. He didn't know if the argument had distracted him for those vital seconds, but now there was a car on the road, heading their way.

"Hey, looks like we've got company." Glen pointed at the car.

Mark lifted his head and squinted into the distance.

"I thought this road was supposed to be empty."

"Maybe not."

"Says so in the book," Mark replied.

"Well, the author lied. *Again.*"

"Still, one car in half an hour isn't exactly gridlock."

The car was a black Ford.

It was getting closer.

And fast.

"Our friend's in a hurry," Mark added.

The Ford sped closer. It swerved into the centre of the road, then pulled itself back into its lane.

Glen took his foot off the accelerator. He studied the car.

It was beat-up with long scratches across the hood. The front fender was bent at a weird angle and it had a broken headlight.

"What's that on its windshield?" Mark asked, peering closer.

Glen narrowed his eyes to focus harder.

"It's a pattern of some kind," Mark whispered.

"Huh?" Glen turned to look at his friend.

"Like it's painted on or something…"

Mark screwed up his face to concentrate harder. Then his face went white with shock.

"Fuck! Quick!"

He dived for the steering wheel.

Glen's eyes darted back to the road.

Saw the Ford.

Almost upon them.

Saw the shattered windscreen.

Clear in his vision.

Saw the Ford cross into their lane and charge to meet them head on.

Mark's hands were on the wheel, spinning it violently as Glen's slipped and fumbled for grip.

Glen pushed hard with his foot, slamming on the brakes and Mark pulled the steering wheel savagely to the right. The tyres screamed and the world became a blur. The engine of the Ford was as loud in their ears as the screams in their throats.

The Jeep swerved and shuddered onto the shoulder of the road. It spun wildly and jerked up onto its right wheels. Glen reached out to grab hold of something to steady himself and found Mark's arm.

The Jeep skidded along the gravel shoulder, rebalanced itself with a sickening thud and threw up a dust cloud around them. They skidded and spun for what seemed like an eternity and Glen waited for the impact of the Ford or the trees on the side of the road, or both.

Eventually they skidded to an abrupt halt.

"FUCK!" Mark screamed. "Did you fucking *see that?"*

Glen tried to nod, but couldn't.

He couldn't speak.

"What a fucking lunatic." Mark turned to stare out of the back of the Jeep. "And the fucker just kept going. He hasn't even stopped. He's sped off and left us for dead."

"Did you see it?" Glen whispered.

"See it? How could you miss it? What a fucking *ass-hole!"*

"Not the car." Glen stared at the steering wheel, trying to get the image out of his head. "The windshield."

"Huh?"

"Did you see the *windshield?"*

"What about it?"

"It was shattered."

"So?"

"Completely shattered."

"Well, if that's the way that idiot drives, I'm not surprised. He's probably taken out five pedestrians in the last mile." Mark shook his head and turned back to face the front of the Jeep. *"Fuck.* But at least he's gone now. And we're both okay."

Glen closed his eyes and tried to wipe the image from his mind. He was sure he saw something else too.

Something about the beat up Ford, the windshield or who was behind it...

Or was it something to the side?

It was a blur, but I'm sure I saw it.

He just couldn't quite work it out.

He was driving so fast. And he aimed right at us.

The lunatic.

Right at us...

Looking out of the Jeep, Glen discovered they had come to rest on the side of the road. The Jeep was pointing at an angle to the road and there was no one in sight.

He turned his head to look out the back of the Jeep. He could see the long skid-marks left by the Jeep's tyres and what remained of the plume of dust their slide had created.

The Ford wasn't in sight.

Fucking maniac.

Mark punched him on the shoulder. "Hey, don't worry about it anymore. He's gone, okay? And your dream's about to come true."

Mark was smiling and pointing at something in front of the car.

Glen turned back to follow Mark's pointing finger.

He smiled.

Fuck that lunatic. He's not going to spoil our weekend.

"There it is, pal." Glen gripped the steering wheel once again.

"We're close. Aren't we?"

"Yep. Our first stop in hunting Zoe."

Glen checked for traffic both ways before he pulled the Jeep back onto the road. The tyres slipped on the gravel for a second before taking hold.

They sped quickly past the sign:

DAYLESFORD
15 MILES

TWO

After they passed the sign to Daylesford, it didn't take them more than a few minutes to reach the outskirts of the town.

"Here we go," Glen muttered to himself as he saw the town in the distance. "The payoff begins here."

The bushes and trees started to thin as the road they were on suddenly broadened and became paved. A couple more cars passed them, driving out of the town.

They drove down the Avenue of Honour, a long strip of road planted with elm trees, one tree for every local who had lost their lives in times of war.

That's a fucking lot of trees, Glen thought as he watched them all flash by.

Soon after, they turned onto Main Street.

"Only Street, more like it," Mark commented.

Glen checked the dash as soon as they turned onto the street. His mileage count was correct and his timing was off by only three minutes.

Almost perfect, he grinned to himself.

Main Street was wider than a usual street, to account for the parking spaces that ran up the middle, like a giant metallic spine. They found a space halfway up and quickly pulled in. For a few minutes, they sat amazed at the size of the town.

"Wow," Glen said.

"Yeah." Mark looked around him. "This is so totally different."

It was only then that they climbed from the Jeep. Glen walked to the front of the Jeep and knelt down, handkerchief at the ready.

"That's truly sad."

"What?" Glen looked up at Mark.

"The licence plates."

Glen looked back at the licence plate and started to wipe the dead bugs from it. He was amazed how many had collided with the front grill of the Jeep and splattered the last seconds of their puny little lives across his hood. With a bit of spit and rubbing, they came off easily enough.

"Hey, no one else has a Jeep with these licence plates."

"I know."

Glen stood up and wiped the dust from the knees of his jeans. He was proud of the licence plates. They were unique. He'd been worried he wouldn't be able to get hold of them, that someone else would already have had the idea and got in before he had a chance to, but no one had.

Ahead of the pack, once again.

They finished the Jeep off perfectly. He didn't care if no one knew what they meant. There were some people out there who would, but most wouldn't. He didn't care. *He* knew and that's all that mattered.

"They're unique."

"A-huh," Mark's eyebrows raised and he nodded his head slowly.

"I'm unique," Glen continued.

"You're not wrong there. Maybe that's why Jodie left you."

That hurt.

Deep.

Why would he say that?

"This has *nothing* to do with Jodie."

"Really?"

"Nothing at all."

"You don't think maybe, just maybe she thought you were going overboard when you bought a red Jeep you couldn't afford?"

"It was a lifestyle choice."

"And then paid *more* money for red licence plates with LLD on them?"

"Some people just don't understand genius," Glen said

as he turned away from Mark and looked further up the main street of Daylesford.

"I guess they don't," Mark muttered from behind him.

Glen slowly ran his eyes up and down the main street.

It's different from how I imagined it.

There were many more stores here than he expected. In fact, there was more life in the town than he had been prepared for.

It wasn't that way in the book.

He walked back to the Jeep and opened the driver's door. Reaching in, he grabbed his copy of the novel and flipped through the pages until he found the description he was looking for.

> *He had looked out the window as the town passed by in the hope of seeing some form of life. But all the house and shop windows were dark and there was no sign of anyone. The general store was the only building with a light burning in the night, and it was blinking on and off. Even the local hotel and bar was closed. And then, within seconds, they had left the town and were continuing along the lonely road.*

He ran his hand through his ruffled hair as he read the paragraph.

It doesn't say there weren't other stores. It just mentions two of them.

He threw the book back into the Jeep and closed the door. Turning to look back at Mark, he said, "Bigger than you expected, huh?"

Mark agreed. He was still standing in front of the Jeep, looking up the main street with his arms crossed in front of him.

"I expected it to be smaller than this," he said.

Glen locked the Jeep door, hooked the silver key ring to the belt hook on his right hip and walked to join his friend.

"Well, that's the author playing with you again. He only mentioned a couple of stores to make it seem more scary and he didn't tell us about all these others."

"I guess so."

"I *know* so." Glen set off down Main Street. "Shall we?"

"Are we looking for anything in particular?" Mark asked as he followed him.

"The book only mentioned the general store and the hotel and bar. Let's find them, check them out and then continue on to our *real* goal."

Glen smiled.

This is working out perfectly…

Main Street ran up a slight rise. Glen couldn't see one end of the street from the other end, as it rose up and over the small hill and out of sight. He was amazed, as they walked down the street, to find how many different kinds of stores and businesses were here.

None of this is in the book.

Why didn't he put it in?

This ain't no quiet sleepy ghost town.

No way.

They passed a grocer, a fruit merchant, a video store, antique store and bank. On the other side of the main street was a bookstore, a fast food restaurant, hardware store, butcher and baker.

But no candlestick maker…

Most of the car spaces were filled with cars, and those that weren't were quickly taken by those driving into Main Street. Glen was sure some people were looking at them, checking them over, watching them out of the corner of their eyes or over the top of newspapers.

All country people do that. That's not unusual. Don't let it get to you. They know everyone who lives around here and when strangers come to town, they know about it straight away. They're probably already talking about us.

Well, let them.

Glen ignored them and continued to walk down the street.

Let them stare.

"This place is huge," Mark said as he walked beside him.

"Not that huge, but bigger than I expected," Glen agreed.

"You sure this *is* the right place?"

"Of *course* I am."

"Well, it's just not like it was in the book. What if you've got the wrong country town?"

Sighing deeply, Glen stopped walking and turned to face Mark. He took a step closer and whispered to him so no one around could hear him.

"I've *told* you about this already. In the book the town is called Hepburn Lakes. Well, there's *no town* called Hepburn Lakes *anywhere*, okay?"

"Okay."

"But there *is* a small place called Hepburn *Springs* just outside of here, just a couple of miles along this road. And Daylesford, the place we're standing in right now, has a *lake* nearby."

"I know this," Mark said. "You've *told* me this."

"So the author changed the name to throw us off, and he merged the two into Hepburn Lakes for the novel. Get it? This *is* the right place, I guarantee it."

"But it's so big and there's so many people. I just can't believe this is it."

"What about that article? What did it say? You remember reading *that*? It pinpointed here as well, remember?"

"Yeah," Mark looked around him. "You're right about that. And that's too much of a coincidence."

"*Exactly.* It's facts, man. Facts don't lie. Even though authors do."

They stood at the low end of Main Street. Glen shoved his hands deep into his pockets as a cool wind blew around them. He glanced above them to see a clear blue sky, but the sun was much lower now. The shadows in the street were starting to grow.

We're running out of sunlight. And time.

Gotta move on soon.

He wasn't interested in antique stores or cruddy fast food outlets, or anything else in Main Street, except for the general store and the hotel with its bar. He had to find them first before they could move on.

"Come on, let's walk back up and check out the other end of the street."

"Okay."

They turned around and retraced their steps.

"You got the camera?"

"Yep," Mark tapped the pocket of his black jacket. "The film's in and ready to roll."

"Cool."

They passed a few people as they walked back up the slight incline along the street. Glen smiled at them as they passed, but the people didn't smile back. They looked at him, checked out his clothes and then stared right through him.

Some people can be rude. Who the hell gives a shit anyway? I'm not here for them.

But he did feel uneasy. Out of place.

Watched.

Should I be doing this?

Fuck, yeah. I've worked hard on this and I deserve the payoff. No one's stopping me now.

He walked faster, his eyes scanning the street in front of him on both sides, looking for what he knew was here.

It's got to be here. It has to be.

After walking a few more yards, he spotted it on the other side of the road.

DAYLESFORD GENERAL STORE.

Jackpot.

A-grade fucking legend.

That's it. That's where she shopped.

I am soooo cool.

So.

Fucking.

Cool.

Glen stopped in his tracks and pointed at the store for Mark.

"What did I tell you?"

"Wow," Mark said. "You're right. Shit, that's *it.*"

Glen ran his eyes further up the street. Three stores

along from the general store was the Daylesford Hotel.

He nudged Mark's shoulder. "Look, just a bit further along."

Mark followed his line of sight again. "Fuck! The hotel."

"Yep."

"*The* hotel."

"Exactly." Glen was more excited than he thought he'd ever been in his whole life.

This proved he'd been right all along.

"Still think I've got the wrong place?"

Mark shook his head. "No way. This is it, alright."

"I *told* you it was."

"And I believe you."

"Yeah, *now* you do."

Glen checked the road was clear and then sprinted across the street to the other side. He ran towards the general store, his eyes taking in every detail of the old building. He didn't want to miss anything.

We should've brought a video camera along with us. Not just a normal camera.

Didn't think of that.

Still, we'll be back next weekend and we can film it all then, and at night too. Much creepier.

Damn it if I'm not shit-hot for breaking this open and working it all out. They won't think I'm so stupid anymore when I prove to them I was here. I'll put the photos online and tell them to check it all out.

Glen stopped at the front door of the store to catch his breath. He turned around to look for Mark, who was slowly walking across the road, still a long way behind him.

"Come on." Glen waved at him to walk quicker.

Turning back to look at the store, Glen tried to commit every detail to memory. The large sign above the building was old and its lettering was fading. There was some kind of country scene painted on the sign, but the years of weathering had taken their toll. He could see a large mountain and a stream, and what looked like a female shepherd guiding something to drink at the stream. Sheep?

Cattle? Half of the scene was missing, so he had no chance of working it out.

He dropped his eyes lower.

The two large windows took up most of the storefront and he could see the glass was dirty and grimy and hadn't been cleaned for a long time. He looked inside the windows. They were packed with an odd assortment of knick-knacks and antiques. There were old dolls and scooters and a skipping rope, hammers and saws and a large anvil, even an old wind-up gramophone with a broken speaker.

Weird.

The front door was weather-beaten just like the sign above. It was made of wood that had gone grey with age. The door looked flimsy, as if it were about to fall apart. The hinges were old and rusty and the metal mail slot at the base of the door had been welded shut years ago.

You could get through that door in no time.

An old faded sign hung on the door.

Operating Hours:
Mon, Tues, Wed—11am to 3pm
Thurs & Fri—CLOSED
Sat & Sun—12pm to 4pm

They *were* strange operating hours.

Just like the book said.

The doorhandle was an old brass gargoyle of a kind Glen had only ever seen reproduced in some gothic stores in the city.

The kind of reproduction people who thought they were cool would buy for lots of money.

The eyes of the gargoyle were made of red stones, set deep into the brass, and they reflected the light, making it look like they were following him. Glen wondered why no one had ever tried pulling the eyes out.

Probably just glass anyway...

He noticed the handle pulled down out of the gargoyle's mouth, so he had to place his hand in its mouth and tug on the tongue if he wanted to open the door.

Putting your hand in to be bitten.

Still, it could be worth a bit of cash if it's made of real brass.

It was only held on to the door by three small screws.

I'll have a closer look at it next weekend. Must remember to bring a screwdriver. They'd go mad if they saw I took this and kept it at home as a memento. They'd shit themselves.

As he looked closer he saw thin scratches all across the surface of the gargoyle.

Damn, that would bring the price down.

No, it's been used for years. Makes it more real that way. It's not new. It's used. Perfect.

His eyes dropped to the bottom of the door where he noticed the paint had peeled away.

Peeled? Or scratched?

The bottom of the door was scratched badly. Some of the scratches were deep into the wood, and some splinters of wood had been pulled off or fallen away.

That's weird too.

Glen bent down to run his fingers across the scratches.

"Someone's got a big dog," Mark said from behind him.

"Huh?" Glen stood and looked at him.

Mark pointed. "Those scratches. Probably a Rottweiler. My aunty has the same trouble with her dog. It tears the door apart to get inside and I always say to her, Aunty Flo, don't tie the dog so damn close to the back door."

"Yeah, it obviously wanted to get inside real bad," Glen agreed.

"Exactly, and they'll just keep scratching the fuck out of it until they do."

"Just like here."

"Yep, no doubt about it."

Mark took a step back and took in the whole building. "This is cool."

"I know," Glen nodded. "She shopped here."

"And now *we're* here."

"Exactly."

Mark walked towards the road and pulled the camera from his pocket.

"You ready?"

Glen stood next to the front door and crossed his arms over his chest.

"Hang on!" Glen shouted as he pulled the sunglasses out from his pocket and slipped them on. "Okay, fire away!"

"No problem. You just stand there and I'll take a couple of photos close up and then a couple to get the whole store in shot."

"Cool." Glen recrossed his arms and showed his best side to the camera.

They're not going to believe this when I show them. They're not going to know whether to shit or go blind. This'll blow them away and no one—no fucking A-grade asshole—will be able to say shit about me anymore.

As he stood there for the photos, he peered up and down the street through his sunglasses, watching the people as they walked by, watching the cars slow down as the drivers glanced first at Mark and then at Glen.

Maybe we're making waves. Maybe they know about the book and are trying to keep it secret and they know we've cracked the code and know all about it. They'll be talking about us for quite some time to come.

Let 'em.

So take a long hard look, people, because we're the ones who are going to tell the whole world about your dirty little secret here.

I'm the one who found it all out.

I'm the one who'll get all the credit.

I'm the one...

"Done," Mark smiled next to him.

"Already?"

"Yep."

"All of them?"

"Yeah, three close ups and three long shots. Even one on an angle to make it look all weird. They'll be cool."

Glen smiled. "Well done. You want some photos taken too?"

"Nah, doesn't matter. You discovered all this, you should have all the pics and all the credit."

"Thanks, pal." Glen took off his sunglasses.
Of course I should…
And I will.

THREE

The tongue of the gargoyle pushed down easily and Glen heard the snap of the latch.

The general store was dark and musty as they stepped through the doorway.

Glen's eyes took a moment or two to adjust to the darkness, but he could soon make out the rows upon rows of items, all crammed into the small confines of the store.

"Wow, they really do mean *general,*" Mark whispered from behind him.

And he was right.

It looked as if every item imaginable were on the shelves. From useful products like candles and buckets and spades and crowbars, to stranger items like lanterns and old wheels and rocking chairs and air raid sirens. Half the store seemed to be a functioning general store and the other half was like a dumping ground for bad antiques. They were jumbled together all over the place and there was very little room to walk through it all.

"This place is crazy," Glen said.

"You can say that again," Mark replied by his shoulder. "Look." He picked up a broken china doll, half its head missing. "Who'd buy stuff like this?"

"Obviously no one." Glen wiped a thick layer of dust off a nearby stuffed barn owl.

They inched forward, being careful not to knock anything from the shelves. A handwritten sign hung from the ceiling: FOOD THIS WAY.

No way I'm eating any food from this dump.

Glen stared further into the store, but he couldn't see the counter or the end of the room for the junk that was piled high above their heads. He listened for any sounds, but could only hear his own breathing and their footsteps on the floorboards. The smell became more dank as they moved further down the aisle. The sunlight through the windows diminished and the overhead fluorescent tubes mostly flickered on and off.

Something smelled foul.

"I can't believe she shopped here," Mark said.

Glen shrugged. "It had everything she needed, I guess."

They walked further into the store.

"Have we seen enough?" Mark asked.

"I think so."

"Wanna get out of here?"

"I think so."

They turned to leave.

"Almost closing time," a voice boomed from nearby, making them both jump.

They looked at each other, their eyes wide.

"You've only got five minutes," the voice said, closer to them now. "I shut this place at 4pm."

How does he know where we are? He can't see us.

Glen pointed in the direction of the door.

"Quick, let's go," he whispered.

And then the man stepped out in front of them.

They stopped dead, frozen to the spot.

"Can I help you?" he asked.

The man was tall and fat and wearing a checked shirt that looked three sizes too big for him. He had a ruddy complexion and a big white beard that made up for the lack of hair on the top of his head. He was chewing something that cracked and snapped in his mouth.

"Ah, nope, it's okay, we were only looking," Mark said in a quivering voice.

"Lots to look at around here."

The man continued chewing.

"I think we've seen everything," Glen added, taking a step forward.

"Tourists, huh?" the man asked.

"Ah, yeah," Mark said. "Just driving through."

"You like my store?"

Glen looked for a way out, but the man took up the whole aisle. There was no way they could get past him. They'd have to go further into the store and double back down another aisle. But there was a risk of getting even more lost in the process.

"Yeah, it's cool," Mark said.

How can he be talking to him like this?

"A little cluttered, maybe..."

That's it, pal. Provoke the guy.

"I like it like this." The man smiled, still chewing, surveying the items in the aisle. He reached over and picked up a small hatchet hanging near Mark's head. "If you can't see them in the street, they can't see you."

Mark tried to laugh. It was unsuccessful.

"That way, no one knows you're here," the man continued, running his thumb across the blade of the hatchet.

"That's true." Mark's voice sounded unsteady.

The conversation was dying.

"Well, we better be going," Glen said quickly.

"Not yet." The man put out his other hand to stop them. "You're not from around here."

Good going, Sherlock. Jeez, you're fast.

"No, as we said," Mark said a little slower this time. "We're just passing through."

"Good photos?"

"Huh?"

"The photos you took of my store. Out the front? Good shots were they?"

"How did you know about that?" Mark asked. "I thought you couldn't see the street."

"I can't from back there," the man pointed past them. "Doesn't mean I can't watch from somewhere else though. It pays to watch and take in every detail, you know."

"Yeah, fine, whatever..." Glen was fed up with the conversation. He walked up to the man and pushed past him.

As he did so, the man grabbed at him. His large hand wrapped around Glen's right wrist, holding firm and spinning Glen around, stopping him in his tracks.

Glen let out a cry as the studs from his wristband bit into the skin on his wrist. He wondered about the sharp end of the studs poking into the man's palm.

Can't he feel them?

The man looked straight into Glen's eyes, boring down into his soul.

"Careful how you go," he whispered. "There are some delicate things around here."

Glen tried to pull away but the man's grip held firm.

"Take in every detail. Watch for anything," he whispered. "And everything..."

Glen pulled harder and the man finally let go.

"Understand?" the man whispered.

"Yeah, uh, whatever... Thanks for that," Glen said as he stumbled down the aisle, rubbing his wrist.

"Anytime," the man said. He smiled at Mark as he walked past him. Twirling the hatchet in his hand, he turned and disappeared back into the darkness.

Mark dashed to Glen's side.

"Are you okay?" he asked.

"Fuck," Glen whispered as he continued rubbing his wrist. "He was a strong fucker."

"And scary." Mark's eyes darted around, keeping a lookout for the man. "Let's get the hell out of here."

"You won't get any argument from me on that." Glen said.

They headed for the door.

FOUR

Glen placed the studded wristband on the bar and looked at the red welts on his wrist.

"Shit, he must've put a hold on you real tight," Mark said as he drank his beer.

"He did." Glen continued to massage his wrist.

Mark shook his head. "What a scary fucker."

Glen looked around the inside of the bar.

Once they'd left the general store, Glen knew he needed a drink and needed one fast. His heart had been pounding in the store and he needed something to calm him down.

They'd walked up to the hotel and found the entrance to the bar.

He knew this was the rendezvous in the book, but he didn't care. He just wanted to sit down and give his heart enough time to calm down and get over what had just happened.

All of a sudden, he didn't want to be in this place anymore. He wanted to be in the safety of the Jeep and driving out to their next stop. He needed time alone, time to think, and to calm down.

But I'm not letting some hairy moron scare me off. No way. He's not going to stop me. No one is.

The bar was small and compact and claustrophobic and half full. It had that cheesy '70s look about it, as if the owner were stuck in a time warp or just never had the money to refurbish. The insides were drab and painted in browns and yellows and oranges. It looked like someone had been sick and they'd painted the walls with it.

They'd walked straight up to the bar and ordered two beers. Glen had thought about taking a side-table, but he didn't want to be trapped in a confined space or corner like they had been in the general store.

Not twice in one day.

So they'd decided to drink the beer standing at the bar. When they were finished they'd return to the Jeep.

I just want to be out of here as soon as possible.

Mark pulled the map out of his back pocket and spread it out on the counter.

"Where next?" he asked.

Glen snapped the wristband back on his wrist and focused on the map.

"We're here," he said, pointing to Daylesford. "We've got a ten minute drive out from here to a place called Franklinford."

Mark nodded. "Yep. I remember now. What's it called in the book?"

"Redlingford," Glen said.

"That's right."

Of course it's right.

"He didn't hide that one too well.".

Glen laughed. "No, he didn't."

"And that's where the church is?"

"Yep, we leave here and head to Franklinford and in ten minutes we'll be at the church."

"Wow."

"Exactly," Glen agreed as he drank the last of his beer. "We're almost there. Can you believe it? We're *sooo* close now."

I'm almost there. It's so close now I can feel it.

"It's not there, you know."

Glen put down his glass and looked at the barman. He was leaning on the bar a short distance away.

"Excuse me?" Glen asked.

"I said, it's not there, you know."

"What's not there?"

The barman put down the magazine he was reading and slowly moved closer to them. He was tall and thin and young, but he wore heavy-rimmed glasses that made him look like an old man.

"What you're looking for, it's not at Franklinford."

Mark and Glen exchanged a quick glance.

Fuck, it can't be blown now...

"Sorry, I didn't mean to overhear you," the barman said as he stopped in front of them and leaned towards them. "But I was close enough to hear most of the conversation, and it's a barman's duty to eavesdrop."

No!

"I don't know what you're talking about," Glen snapped back.

The barman stifled a laugh. "Fine, okay by me. I'm not stopping you going to Franklinford, but you'll be wasting your time."

He pushed away from the bar and walked off.

Mark and Glen looked at each other again. Mark then darted his eyes to the barman.

"What if he's *right?*" he whispered.

"He can't be."

"You sure?"

"Of course I am."

Am I?

"Ask him."

"No!"

"He could tell us something we need to know. We can't *not* ask."

Shit. Damn it to hell.

"We *have* to."

"Okay, okay," Glen agreed. "He might know something, I guess."

Glen turned to look at the barman. He was reading his magazine again. Slowly, they walked down the bar to him.

"Ahh, so you're interested now?" the barman smirked without looking up from his magazine.

"My friend and I have had a chat and decided we should listen to what you have to say," Mark said.

The barman looked up over his glasses and stared at Glen.

"He's right." Glen was unable to mask the disappointment in his voice. "We'd like your help on this."

The barman put down his magazine and leaned closer. "Show me your map," he said.

Mark handed the map to him.

The barman looked it over and picked at his nose with his little finger. "Yeah, I see where you're heading but you're wrong."

"No, we're *not,*" Glen countered. "I've done the research, and this *is* right."

The barman shook his head. "Nope, you got close, but you fucked it up."

Fucked it up? Me? I did not!

"Really?" Glen said in a sarcastic tone.

"Yes, really," the barman replied.

"Look—"

Mark's hand quickly grabbed Glen's shoulder.

"You have to excuse my friend." Mark smiled to the barman. "He hasn't had much sleep lately and he's just had a run-in with one of your townsfolk and even though he seems a little on edge he'd really like to know what you have to say."

Mark smiled at the barman and then turned to smile at Glen.

Glen stared blankly back.

I want to punch the fucker. Rip out his tongue for saying I fucked it up. Who the hell does he think he is?

The barman took a pencil from behind his ear. Glen noticed that part of the barman's ear was missing. The top was completely gone, sliced off, leaving behind a ragged, uneven tear.

"You'll find nothing at Franklinford," the barman said as he started to draw on the map. "What you're after is on the other side of town, past the lake."

Glen and Mark focused on the map.

"Follow Main Street out this way and around the lake," the barman said, continuing to draw on the map, the line leading out of town in the opposite direction and into the middle of nowhere.

I can't've been wrong. There's no fucking way.

"Follow this road, and then this side road for seven

more miles and you'll find it there." He drew a circle and then an arrow pointing to it. "Just before Rocklyn. *That's* where you'll find what you're looking for."

"You're kidding, right?" Glen asked.

The barman shook his head. "Nope. That's where it is, I'm telling you."

"How would you know?" Glen slammed his hand on the bar and pointed to the map. "*I've* done the research. *I* know everything there is to know about this."

"Suit yourself," the barman shrugged. "I'm only trying to help and save you some disappointment. If you'd gone out to Franklinford and found out for yourself, you wouldn't've known where to look next and you'd've gone home all disappointed. And I get the feeling you don't want that to happen. You *want* to get there. You *need* to. Right?"

"Who the *fuck* do you think you are?" Glen asked, keeping his voice low and steady.

"Hey, take it or leave it. I don't give a damn. I'm just trying to help."

Yeah, trying to help alright.

"How do you know that it's what I came to see anyway? It's probably totally different than what I actually came to see."

"Because I've lived here all my life. I *know* where these things are. When you're a kid you explore out here, there's nothing else to do. So you go camping and trekking and you *find* these things, you *discover* them. *That's* how I know."

The barman put the pencil back behind his half-ear, picked up his magazine and walked off.

Glen watched him go.

I'm not wrong.

Am I?

I can't be.

But what if he's right?

Does it matter? Check it out anyway. No one needs to know I got this section wrong. No one will ever know. Mark won't tell anyone either. If the barman's right, I'll take the credit anyway.

Yeah, that'll show the fucker.

I'll win anyway.

"He could be wrong or just joking around with us," Mark said, close to Glen's ear, a worried look on his face.

"No, I don't think so," Glen replied.

"Huh?"

"I think the barman's right."

Mark looked surprised. "But you've done all the research and everything."

"Don't worry about it," Glen shrugged his shoulders. "He could be right. We have nothing to lose by checking it out anyway. So let's go."

"You sure?"

"Yep, I'm sure." Glen pointed at Mark's half-full glass. "Drink up big, pal. Then we can get out of this crazy town and head for the church."

"Wherever it is," Mark smiled.

"Yeah, wherever it is."

We'll find it. I know we will.

We're so close now. I can almost smell her.

I'll show them.

I'll show them all.

FIVE

The sun was lower in the sky as they walked back down Main Street. There weren't as many parked cars as before, and the number of people in the street had halved. Glen noticed as they walked past the General Store that it had a large CLOSED sign sitting in the window.

He's crawled back down his burrow for the rest of the evening.

The glowing red eyes of the gargoyle followed him as they walked by the store.

It would serve him right if I came back and stole it, took it home with me and kept it for good.

"What is *that?*" Mark asked as they walked back towards the Jeep.

"What's what?"

Mark pointed at the Jeep.

As they walked closer, it all became clearer.

"What the…?" Glen said as he picked up his pace. "Fuck, *no!*"

"Who would do that?" Mark whispered from behind him.

"In this town, probably anybody."

Glen reached the driver's side of the Jeep and knelt to the ground.

Fucking local country fucks. Fucking hillbillies.

He ran his hand along the deep, jagged groove torn through the paintwork and into the metal of the Jeep. It stretched from just above the front tyres, along the driver's door and all the way down to the taillight. It wasn't just a straight line, it rose and fell, like someone had done it as they walked past. And done it hard.

Why is everyone always so jealous of others?
Why are they so jealous of me?

"But why key the Jeep?" Mark asked, his voice sounding strange as he looked around the street slowly.

"It's a fucking *big* key, man." Glen's thumb slipped in and out of the groove as he traced along it. "It's bigger than some little stupid key. Someone's *attacked* my car with something else."

Why? Why do it to me? I haven't done anything...

Glen stood and turned to look all around them. He eyed the people in the street and in the cars. There weren't that many of them around anymore, but Glen searched them out and studied them all. The guy in the car, the woman with the kid in the pram, the family on the park bench, the butcher looking out his window, the girl and the guy kissing in the van and the old guy with the black dog. These were some of the same people who were so interested in them before, but now they were ignoring them completely. Too tied up in their own little world to pay any attention to Glen and his car.

Or were they?

"Fucking hillbillies!" he yelled at them.

No one took any notice.

"I'll get you for doing this to my Jeep! I'll get each and every one of you fuckers! You hear me?"

The old guy looked up at him when he said 'fuckers'.

That hit a nerve, didn't it, old man?

The guy and the girl weren't kissing anymore. They were looking out the van's windshield at him. The girl had a weird look on her face and the guy was staring intently at Glen.

"What are you looking at?" Glen yelled at him as he gave the guy the bird. "You wanna make trouble, man?"

The guy just shook his head and turned and said something to the girl.

She laughed.

"Oh, yeah, that's it, laugh. Go ahead, *laugh* at me! You think you're that tough?"

Mark was by his side, unhooking the key ring from

Glen's hip and unlocking the door to the Jeep.

"Come on," he was saying as Glen continued to yell. "Let's get you out of here so you can calm down."

"You can't stop me, you know!" Glen turned to point at the old guy, then swung around to stare at the family on the park bench.

But they had gone.

"No one can! Least of all you country throwbacks!"

Before he knew it, Glen was sitting in the Jeep, pounding the steering wheel and screaming, "Why? Why? *Whywhywhywhywhy?*"

Mark climbed in the other side and handed him the car keys.

Glen snatched them from his fingers.

"Feeling better now?" Mark asked.

"Only slightly."

"You went a little crazy out there."

Glen smiled. "We all go a little crazy sometimes."

"Let's get out of here, okay?"

Glen sat back in the seat and leaned on the headrest. He closed his eyes and tried to blot this place from his mind.

He couldn't.

All he could see was the jagged tear all the way down the side of his Jeep.

My Jeep.

Why would they do that to me?

"What do you think?" Mark prodded.

Glen opened his eyes and looked at him. "Huh?"

"I said, let's get out of here."

"You won't get any argument from me on that," Glen said as he leaned forward and put the key in the ignition. "Let's blow this shit-hole."

He put the Jeep in reverse, looked behind him and backed the Jeep—

My vandalized Jeep.

– out of the parking space. He didn't look for other traffic, didn't stop to check, he didn't care.

Let them ram me. I'll beat up on some of their cars and

see how they like it.

He stopped in the middle of the lane, blocking three cars wanting to drive through.

Let them wait.

Slowly, he put the Jeep in gear and then sped out of town, the tyres screeching on the pavement. He didn't look back.

"Attacking someone else's property. It's unbelievable. Some people need to get a life," Glen muttered.

"I know," Mark replied. "There're some sick people around who just delight in other people's misfortune and agony. They don't like what you have so they try to destroy it."

"I know. Those people are sick."

"Not much you can do about it."

"No. Nothing. That's what gets me so mad."

"Glen, don't let this ruin your weekend."

"It's hard not to."

"Try. Just focus and remember why we're here and what we're here to do. After all, we're not far from our goal now."

"True."

"So just keep that in mind."

"I will, pal. Thanks."

"No problem."

He tried. But he couldn't.

"It was that fucking *barman*," Glen spat. "Had to be."

Mark shook his head. "I don't think so. He was in the bar when we left and we walked straight to the Jeep. I can't see how he had the time to leave the bar and do it before we arrived back at the Jeep."

"Whatever. I still think it was him. Creepy little shit."

The town was soon well behind them and Main Street narrowed and turned back to dirt. To their right, the lake quickly came into view and the road curved to skirt it.

Call that a lake?

The water looked murky, almost black. An old rusted shack sat by the lake's edge, but half of it had fallen down and the other half was covered in weeds. Further along was an old boardwalk that was missing most of its wooden flooring and looked as if it were about to topple to one side. The only boats moored at the boardwalk were weathered and old and looked as if they'd been there for centuries. One had already sunk. A piece of rope was tied from the boardwalk to the bow, but most of the boat was underwater.

While the road skirted this side of the lake, a large hill rimmed the other side of it. Glen could see a few houses dotted through the trees on the hill. The houses had a good view of the whole town, and the lake, but they looked like they had fallen into disrepair as well.

They sped along for a few minutes in silence as the road curved away from the lake and headed into the countryside.

When I find out who did that to my Jeep, their life won't be worth living. How dare they destroy something of mine that I worked so hard to get. Who do they think they are?

I won't miss that sorry shit-hole of a place once I leave here. They can all rot in hell for all I care.

"You know we're heading *away* from Franklinford," Mark said.

Glen smiled.

"So you think the barman is right?"

Fucking barman with his fucking glasses and stupid fucking smirk.

"No, I don't," Glen said. "We're going this way to prove *I'm* right and *he's* wrong."

"Okay."

"Then, when we know that, we can turn around and head back to Franklinford where I *know* the church is."

Okay, whatever you say."

They lapsed into silence again.

The road deteriorated some more. Large potholes marked the surface, forcing Glen to slow down and pick his route carefully. He gripped the steering wheel hard and turned it from left to right, making sure to miss as many holes as possible.

This road will slow us down even more, damn it.

"Do you think he came out here?" Mark asked.

"Who?"

"The author."

"I guess so. He'd have had to do some research out here. And he lives in this state, or at least used to, so he probably travelled on all the roads we've been travelling on. You'd have to, so you could write it correctly for the book."

"Yeah," Mark didn't sound convinced. "It's just the description of Hepburn Lakes in the book isn't like the real Daylesford. And he said the church was at Franklinford, or Redlingford in the book, but it's not there. It's in the other direction."

"We haven't proved that yet," Glen interrupted.

"True. It just seems weird, that's all."

"Everything's weird out here. Aren't you convinced of that yet? After what we've just been through? Having the Jeep keyed and talking with the barman and that weird guy from the General Store."

"You're right."

The guy from the General Store.

He had a hatchet.

The fucker had a hatchet.

"Damn it," Glen punched the steering wheel.

"What?"

"The guy in the General Store. *He* had a hatchet in his hands."

Glen watched as Mark worked it out for himself.

"You think so?" he asked.

"It's gotta be. You saw how deep that scratch is. What else could it be?"

"Fuck!"

"Exactly. See what I mean? You and me, man, we're the only sane ones out here."

Mark laughed at that.

"What?" Glen asked. "What's so funny?"

"You and me."

"Why? Don't you think we're sane?"

"We're out in the middle of nowhere, trying to hunt

down a fictional character from a book we're obsessed about. Doesn't sound like we're too sane if you ask me."

"The book's *based* on a true story."

"Yeah, yeah."

"It was in the newspapers."

"I know. But it's still pretty crazy if you stop to think about it. Maybe we fit in with all those weird people in the town more than we'd like to admit."

"I don't think so."

"Don't you think maybe you've taken this a little too far?"

Now he's *saying it too.*

"I don't think so," Glen said through gritted teeth as he drove across a pothole by mistake, causing the Jeep to shudder and lurch to one side.

"You sure?"

"Positive."

Don't you think maybe you've taken this a little too far?

Jodie had said those exact words the very last night they were together. He knew she wasn't interested in the novel or the true story behind it. He knew she thought he was spending a lot of time searching for the facts, too much time, but he truly believed she at least supported what he was doing.

Like a lover should do.

But that night he realized she wasn't on his side either. Never had been. She was just like all the others. She was waiting for him to trip up and embarrass himself and fall flat on his face so she could turn to him with that snide look of hers and say, "See? I told you so."

There's more to life than some dumb book.

She'd said that too.

Like her life is so wonderful anyway. With only a crappy desk job and no career prospects, coming home every night to the same one room apartment like any of it really mattered. Not having any dream to dream or goal to chase. Not trying to better herself in any way.

Like she could talk.

And that was the last straw. After all he'd given her,

after loving her so much, she could just turn around and cut him so bad, so deep.

There's more to life than some dumb book.

Really, Jodie? Show me? 'Cause you sure as hell aren't it.

It proved she had no idea what he was really about or who he really was. She had no idea about him as a person. She didn't want to know. She was only interested in herself. What she could get out of him and out of life.

The fight had been long, big and ugly, and she'd walked out.

She'd picked up her handbag and her shoes and stormed from the room, slamming the door as she left. He could still hear the door slamming in his head, over and over again.

They hadn't spoken since.

Five weeks.

"Turn here," Mark said, looking at the map.

"Huh?" Glen refocused on the road.

"To the right here, turn," Mark showed him the map and pointed at the barman's line.

Glen nodded and turned right.

The countryside was bare now, with very little vegetation anywhere. The land was flat and dry and dusty and sometimes it was hard to see where the dirt track ended and the countryside began.

Dead, hollowed-out trunks of trees were the only landmarks, and they were scarce as well, scattered across the landscape like ghostly reminders of a prosperous age. Most of the trunks were black, as if a fire had totally destroyed the area years earlier and life had never returned.

"This doesn't look too promising," Mark muttered.

I knew it.

"How many miles?" Glen asked.

"He said to drive for seven miles along this track."

Glen checked the dash. "Six to go. Keep looking and see if you can see anything."

They both peered through the windshield at the road ahead.

Flat, desolate and empty.

It can't be out here. It just can't be.

This is nothing like the book. There were trees, lots of them. Almost like a forest. This is totally wrong.

They drove on further.

Three miles.

Then six.

Nothing. A-grade fucking nothing.

Glen brought the Jeep to a halt. He wound down the window and looked all around them.

Flat.

Dead.

"Nothing," Mark said, mirroring Glen's thoughts. "The fucker lied to us."

"Damn it."

"Why would he *lie* to us?"

"I have no idea. But I never believed his stupid story anyway. There's nothing out here. I knew I wasn't wrong about this."

Mark shook his head. "I have to admit it, you were right. I'm sorry I doubted you."

Glen smiled. "No problem, man."

Just don't do it again.

"Now, let's get going and make it to the church before the sun goes down," Glen added. "And let's prove to these country fuckers that they can't fool us for long."

"Yeah, let's do it." Mark grinned.

Glen swung the Jeep off the road and around in an arc and started driving back down the track.

If I ever see that barman again I'll rip off the rest of his ear, and the other one too. Then I'll shove both of them down his throat and make him choke on them.

They travelled quickly down the road.

Trying to make me lose face in front of my friend. Shit, he almost had me thinking I was wrong. And I know that was exactly what Mark thought too.

Glen looked out of the corner of his eye at Mark. He couldn't see him clearly, but Mark was sitting forward slightly, and wasn't moving at all.

"Pal? What is it?" he asked.

He peered over to Mark. But Mark was looking past him and out of the driver's window.

Mark pointed. "What the hell is *that?*"

Glen slowed the Jeep and turned his head to follow Mark's gaze. He couldn't see anything to begin with, but as his eyes searched the dusty horizon, he saw what Mark was looking at.

"I have *no* idea," Glen muttered.

"I just can't work out what it is."

Glen squinted. With the low angle of the sunlight and the bare landscape, it was hard to make out. There was some kind of structure sitting on a small mound in the middle of the countryside three hundred feet away from them.

In the middle of nowhere.

"What do you think?" Mark asked.

"I don't know."

"Should we?"

"Well, we're out here, we might as well check it out."

"It's not a church."

"Doesn't look like one to me. Certainly not the one from the book."

Glen turned the steering wheel. They left the road and drove across the field towards the structure.

Maybe the barman was right after all…

It didn't take them long before the features became clearer.

"This is weird," Mark said.

"I know. Why would this be all the way out here?"

"Beats me."

"It's not like anyone's just going to stop by and take a look. It's miles away from everything."

The Jeep pulled alongside the small, circular dirt mound. Glen wound down his window and looked out at it. It rose ten feet from the surrounding earth. It was wider and taller than the Jeep and on the very top sat an obelisk made of granite. Long and thin, it tapered to a point at the top and looked like it had been chiselled years ago by someone who didn't have the right tools for the job.

Glen opened the door and climbed from the Jeep. He looked up at the obelisk and guessed that with the monument on top, the whole structure was probably twenty feet high.

"It's like a small version of the Washington Monument," Mark said.

Glen turned to his buddy as he climbed from the Jeep too. "Yeah, but why? What's it for?"

"No idea. It can't be a memorial, not all the way out here."

"I know," Glen agreed.

He slowly walked around the mound, checking it over and trying to work out its purpose. But it was just a large mound of dirt, totally unremarkable except for the fact that it was there and had a weird obelisk on the top of it. As he walked, he kept his eye on the obelisk too. He was looking for any writing on the granite, any inscription or any symbols. Any words chiselled into it that would give him an idea as to why it was here.

Nothing.

Glen returned to the Jeep after walking all around the mound. Mark was leaning against the hood, taking a picture of the obelisk.

"What are you doing?" Glen asked.

"Pissing on a pig. What's it look like I'm doing? I'm taking a picture of it."

"Why?"

Mark shrugged. "No reason."

"It's not in the book."

"That's okay. I think it looks cool."

"Well, still, it's *not* the church."

The fucker played us for fools.

"Yeah," Mark agreed. "It sure ain't."

Glen walked back to the Jeep.

"Asshole."

"Don't let the guy get to you," Mark said. "He's getting the reaction he hoped he would get."

Glen climbed back into the driver's seat. "I know, but he fucked with us and I don't like that."

Mark took one more picture and then walked back to climb into the Jeep.

"Still, what do you think it's for?"

"No idea," Glen said. "From what I can see, there's no writing on it anywhere. Nothing to give an indication as to what it's for. But I guess it doesn't really matter. It doesn't concern us."

"Yeah, you're right." Mark agreed.

Glen gunned the engine, swung the Jeep around, and headed back to the road.

Bastard.

He was trying to keep his anger in check. He didn't like being screwed over. Not by anyone. And certainly not by a complete stranger.

They're probably all laughing at us back at that bar now. See the city slickers make fools of themselves by driving out into the middle of nowhere. They probably do it to everyone who stops by. The obelisk is probably a memorial statue for stupid city people who followed their directions and got lost out there. A-grade fuckers, the lot of them.

"He's wasted our valuable time," Glen said as he drove, peering out at the setting sun.

"Don't worry so much about it."

"I have to. We've only got like an hour or so of daylight left."

"We'll get there. We just have to get back to the town and then in ten minutes we'll be at the church."

"What if we miss the turn-off?"

"We won't."

"What if I'm wrong?"

"You're *not*. You've just proved that."

Yeah, I'm not. Thanks for believing in me, man.

You always have.

You've always stuck by me.

Not like Jodie.

He wondered what she was doing now. It had been five weeks since they'd had the big argument and they hadn't spoken to each other since. He'd wanted to call her, to see what she was doing, but he didn't want to be the weak one, the one who called first. That was up to her. She was the one who walked out, so she had to make the first move.

And she hadn't done it.

Bitch.

And she said she loved me.

Yeah, right. They all say that. First they screw you and then they screw you.

"Do you think I should've called Jodie?" Glen heard himself ask as they turned back onto the dirt road.

"That's up to you," Mark said.

"I know, but you'd think she would've called me by now, right?"

The potholes became fewer, and the trees and bushes slowly returned.

"Well, maybe she's giving you some space so you could get this whole business out of your system. Maybe she'll call once we're back home."

"But she doesn't know we've driven out here."

"Well, you can call her next week and say you've done it all and you proved you were right. Then you could say that you're ready to move on and you want to see her again."

"Do you think that'll work?"

Mark paused before answering. "Nope."

"Me neither."

They both laughed. It helped ease the tension.

"I just don't understand why she went all psycho on me," he continued.

"Yeah. I know."

"Why do women change so suddenly? Why can't they be normal like you and me?"

"I know."

"I never hurt her, I never hit her. I was good to her. We were good together. She just went all weird after a while."

Mark stifled a laugh. "And I guess buying your girlfriend a specially made leather bondage outfit just like the one in your favourite book has nothing to do with it either?"

Damn, forgot about that.

"Hey, I spent a lot of money on that suit. I didn't just

go and buy her one from some leather store, you know. I read the book and designed it all and got it specially *made* for her. It cost me a *fucking fortune!* How was I to know she wouldn't wear it?"

"Can't imagine why she wouldn't," Mark shrugged his shoulders.

"She was weird anyway. I only wanted her to try it on once or twice - she might've *liked* it. Hell, how the fuck did she know she wouldn't like it until she actually *tried* the damn thing on? I begged her to wear it. I told her it'd make her look sexy. But she just stood there with her hands on her hips and stared at me like she hated me all of a sudden. She wouldn't go near the thing."

"And then there was the hair thing..." Mark added.

Glen nodded. "Yeah, she was *strange.* "

The lake came back into view.

"I tell you one thing," Glen said as they both glanced over the lake to the houses on the other side. "I won't miss this place one bit once we leave."

"That makes two of us."

Let's just get in, get the evidence we need and then get the hell out of here.

That's all I want to do.

"How much do you think it's going to cost?"

Mark turned to look at him. "What?"

"To fix that *fucking gash* in my paintwork."

"A packet, probably."

"A *fucking* packet. More money gone. I've still got the bondage suit in my wardrobe. What the hell am I supposed to do with that?"

"Wear it yourself?"

"Fuck, no!" Glen said, almost choking at the thought. "I don't think I have the right equipment to fit in the sections of *that* little number."

"Well, you'll just have to find a girl willing to wear it."

"Yeah. But where the hell am I going to find her?"

He pushed the accelerator further to the floor and the Jeep sped along the side of the lake and towards the town. The road widened and became paved, and Glen didn't take his foot from the pedal.

"I'd like to mow down the whole town right about now," he whispered. "Show them they can't fuck with us."

"Take it easy." Mark grabbed at the dash. "Don't do anything stupid. We want to get to the church in one piece, right? We want to reach the goal, don't we?"

Glen nodded and lifted his foot. "Yeah, you're right."

As they entered Main Street, they noticed it was nearly deserted. Only the old guy and the dog, and the girl and guy kissing in the van were still around.

"Maybe she'd wear it," Mark said, pointing at the girl in the van.

"Don't think so," Glen replied. "Anyway, I don't date bush pigs."

They sped down the Main Street hill and were out the other side of the town within seconds.

"Fuck them all," Glen muttered as they left the town. Then he wound down his window and stuck his head outside. "FUCK YOU ALL! YOU FUCKING COUNTRY MOTHERFUCKERS!"

He sat back in his seat and laughed.

I feel better now.

They continued on in silence as they took a side road just outside of town.

You can't trust anyone these days. You have to pick and choose so carefully. Friends, family, even total strangers who don't even know you. You never know who might turn against you at any time. Even those you sleep with, they can turn quicker than anyone else.

Just like Jodie.

"I just can't believe she wouldn't do it for me," he said.

"What?"

"You know, the hair thing. Was it too much to ask?"

Mark thought about it for a few seconds. "Well, *she* thought so."

"But, pal, couldn't she understand? I mean, I liked her hair the way it was. It was nice and long and curly and brown and all that. It was fine. But it got *boring*, you know? It was the same. There's nothing wrong with change, is there? But could she see that? Could she see it through my eyes? *No!* If she straightened her hair and dyed it blonde, couldn't she see that I would love her *more* for it? I'd find her even *sexier?* Why couldn't she see that?"

"Maybe she thought you were trying to make her into a version of Zoe," Mark said, rubbing his chin deep in thought. "Like she had to become Zoe to keep you happy, or something like that."

"Yeah, she did, that's *exactly* what she said."

"I'm not a little version of your sick imaginary fuck fiend," she'd said.

"But she was wrong. *Sooo* wrong. All I was asking was for her to become more beautiful, *more* perfect. It makes sense, right? That way I could love her even *more*. Give her more. Want to be with her more. You understand, don't you?"

"Well, kinda."

"But she didn't see it that way. She just thought I was using her and sleeping with her while I was wishing I was with someone else. She just couldn't understand."

"I can't imagine why..."

"It's not unusual, is it?"

"What?"

"You know, when you've been with someone for a while, to close your eyes and think about doing it with someone else while you're doing it with them."

"No, I don't think it's unusual."

"Exactly. They say an active fantasy life is normal for anyone. So what if when we did it with the lights out I was thinking about Zoe and pretending Jodie was her? There's nothing wrong with that."

"I sure don't think so. I think about Zoe all the time."

"At night, when I held her, it was almost like I was holding Zoe. She could've *been* Zoe, but only with the lights out."

Only with the lights out...

"Anyway, I'm better off without her. She could never be Zoe anyway. She's nothing like her, not in her league, that's for sure. She was a dead lay, a cold fuck. Boring as hell. She even went off at me when I asked her to shave her pussy."

"I don't do that," she'd said.

"Most girls do," I said.

"Well I'm not most girls."

She was right about that, unfortunately.

"She wouldn't be here on this trip with me, she wouldn't support all the research I did to get us here today. She was only interested in herself and no one else. She wouldn't stand by me."

"Nah, she wouldn't," Mark agreed. "Did you ever ask her about piercing her bellybutton?"

"Nope, never got around to it. She wouldn't've done it anyway."

"Probably not."

"Selfish bitch."

"I guess so."

"I don't need her."

"No, you don't."

"No one does."

The road deteriorated once more. It turned to dirt and new potholes appeared.

Forget her. Forget about all of it. I'm just ten minutes away from my goal.

Yeah, ten minutes. And no one's going to stop me now.

No one.

"I think it's just over the next hill," Mark said as he looked up from the map.

The Jeep shuddered along as the tyres bit into potholes and bumps.

Glen spotted it first.

"Look." He pointed through the windscreen to the side of the road. "We're almost there!"

They sped past a small rusting sign that read FRANKLINFORD.

Almost there.

It's all happening.

This is it. The most important event in my life.

I'm here.

And this is it.

Glen slowed the Jeep down and began looking from side to side.

"It's around here somewhere," he mumbled. "Gotta be careful with this one. It's tricky. Don't want to miss it."

"I'm looking," Mark added. "We should be able to see it better now than at night, though."

"Yeah."

I just hope I'm right.

Then he spotted the turn off to the left.

"There!" he said, trying hard to hide the excitement in his voice.

"Hey, well spotted. You know your stuff."

"Well, you still have to read the book a few more times before you know as much as I do."

He was sure that if they hadn't been looking for the road, they would have driven straight past it just like everyone else.

Well concealed from everyone.

"We're almost there." He turned the steering wheel and drove on.

He wanted to get to the church as soon as possible. He needed time to look around while there was still light. They'd brought two flashlights with them, but he wanted good photos, excellent proof that he'd been here.

You can't see enough at night. People won't believe me if I show them night photos.

But they'll have to now. All of them.

Even Jodie.

As he stared out the windshield, he pictured being with her again. He wondered where she was now, what she was doing.

Who she's with…

He wished she could be here with him, that it was her and not Mark in the Jeep with him, that she was as excited by this as he was. They could get to the church and break in and lie down on the floor and take off their clothes. He could mount her and slide deep inside her and fuck her all night.

But try as he might, his thoughts of Jodie slipped from him.

What if Zoe were here? What if I were here at the church with her?

What if we were inside the church together, just me and her?

Zoe's totally naked on the sofa, her legs apart. So tantalising. Her shaved pussy wet and glistening.

He wanted to taste her so bad.

"I just want to help you, Glen," she would whisper.

He remembered her pierced bellybutton and the diamond that sat inside it, and the way she would giggle. And he wished she would catch him in the shower, while he had an erection from thinking about her, and suck down all the cum he had to give her.

His cock began to pulse again; he could feel his ring moving across his balls.

Just imagine if she were here with me now. Sucking me off as we drove towards the church, making me cum in her mouth again and again and again.

Calm down, pal. Get a grip.

Concentrate.

You don't want to miss a second of this.

They crested the hill and Glen put his foot on the brakes.

"I think it should be here on the right somewhere. From what I remember, you can't see the church from the road, but there's a steep driveway somewhere."

Slowly, they continued driving, peering out the windows, looking for the driveway.

There's no turning back now.

Mark spotted a gap in the foliage ahead.

"There," he pointed. "Is that it?"

A grin broke out on Glen's face. "I think so."

He stopped the Jeep and stared up the dirt driveway.

"Well," Mark prodded. "Should we?"

This is it.

Glen's eyes darted back and forth up the driveway. He wanted to take it all in slowly. He knew at the other end was what he'd spent so long searching for.

I've made it.

"You're not having second thoughts, are you?" Mark asked, a worried look on his face.

"No, no." Glen shook his head. "I do want to go up there. I'm…I don't know…just trying to get my thoughts in order."

"Come on, we've hit paydirt."

"You're right."

No turning back.

"Good." Mark rubbed his hands together. "So let's get up that driveway and check out this church while we still have enough daylight left."

"Deal."

"This is it. This is what we've been waiting for!" Mark yelled at the top of his voice, his hands drumming the dashboard.

Glen grinned. "Let's do it."

The Jeep accelerated towards the driveway.

Glen stared out through the windows, checking both sides of the Jeep and trying to take in everything at once. He didn't know what he was looking for, but he didn't care. He had to see everything. But other than large clusters of trees and bushes, there wasn't that much to look at.

The Jeep shuddered as it climbed the steep unsealed weed-strewn driveway.

"Nearly there," he said, his voice vibrating with the vehicle.

I'm nearly there…

REMAINS

SIX

Glen realized he was holding his breath and bracing himself.

This is it. Everything I've been working towards...

They reached the top of the driveway. The ground levelled out. Glen turned to look at Mark. He was staring out the windshield, an excited look on his face.

He's just as excited as I am.

This is history in the making.

And I'm making it.

The driveway curved slightly and Glen took his foot off the accelerator. He could see something through the trees.

That's got to be it.

They drove closer.

Yes, it's the church. It has to be.

And the closer they got, the quicker Glen's heart sank.

No!

No, this can't be right!

It's not like this in the book.

"Oh, shit," Mark muttered, turning to face Glen. "Can you believe this?"

Glen just stared and shook his head as the Jeep drove up the last few feet of the driveway and rolled to a stop.

They were parked just outside the small brick church. Or what was left of it.

This can't be right.

It can't be.

He turned to stare out the other windows, looking around for something, anything, to prove this was wrong or couldn't be happening.

He discovered they were sitting on the top of a small, well-forested hill. Trees and bushes were closely packed all around them, but the area directly around the church was cleared of everything, leaving only dirt. Long shadows stretched across the earth as the sun began to set.

Glen stared out through the trees and could see the bottom of the sun sitting on the horizon.

It's all gone wrong.

And the light's about to go too.

He turned and looked up through the windshield at the wall of the church.

It looked small in the surroundings, smaller than he had imagined, but was probably a normal size for a brick church that was built maybe a century ago. The wall they were facing had to be the side where the altar used to be, as he could see the outline of a brick cross built into the wall. The cross stretched from the ground to what used to be the roof, and the bricks were a darker colour, making the cross look as if it were standing out against the wall of the church.

A third of the wall was blackened and burned; he could see where the fire had licked. The wood shingles that used to be the roof were strewn everywhere, some burnt, some not, some laying on the ground near them, having slid from the roof. Others were still attached to the burnt rafters, while a few blew in the wind as they hung from the spouting.

He couldn't see any windows, but as he dropped his eyes lower, he found the door. Or where it used to be.

The hinges were still attached, and part of the old wooden frame was still hanging from them, but only the doorway was left.

"Fuck," he muttered as he turned off the engine.

"Should we take a look around?" Mark asked.

"Is there any point? The whole place is gutted."

Mark shook his head. "Look, we haven't driven all this way out into the middle of nowhere just to turn back again without getting out and at least having a look around."

"But check it out." Glen pointed.

"I know. Not like in the book at all."

"It's fucked, man."

"I know. It must've been a huge fire that roared through here."

"Yeah, some fire alright." Glen turned and stared at the trees and bushes that surrounded them.

All green.

There was no sign of a fire in the trees. Their trunks were green and brown, not charred black like the church.

No sign of a fire at all.

Except at the church.

"Do you think this is the right one?" Mark asked.

Glen nodded. "Yeah, it's the right one. You can still see the outline of the brick cross built into the wall."

"I noticed that too."

"Just like in the book."

"Exactly the same."

"I just can't believe it's almost totally destroyed."

They sat and stared in silence for a few minutes.

"Okay," Mark finally said. "I'm in your hands. What do you want to do?"

Glen rubbed his chin and realized he hadn't had time to shave that morning.

I'd been so excited about all this.

So excited.

For a pile of burnt shit.

And then his mind flew back twenty-four hours. He'd wondered at the time if they were doing the right thing. But, of course, by then it was too late to turn back. He'd already told Mark and they'd decided to come. He'd already been online and gone to the message boards and discussion groups. He'd started a flame war by telling them all where he was heading and what he would come back with. None of them had believed him. They all thought he was lying.

I'll show them.

I'll jam it all the way up their asses and twist. I'll make 'em eat their words and grovel and apologise to me, the assholes.

They won't talk to me like that again.

Fucking brainless net-obsessed fuckers.
He couldn't go back empty-handed now.
He had to see this through. No matter what.
But none of this was what we expected.
None of it.
"Alright," he finally said. "We're here, so we might as well get a look at the place. It *is* the real church after all, even if it is in ruins. We can still take photos and prove we've been here."

"Exactly," Mark agreed. "We're *still* here, this is *still* the church. Let's get what we came here for."

Glen opened his door. The cool night air rushed in at them.

"Going to be a cold night." Mark shivered as he opened his door and stepped outside.

Glen climbed from the Jeep and took a good look at the pine trees surrounding them.

They haven't been burnt at all. None of them.
Which means someone burnt down the church.
Fuck, yeah.
The church has been torched.
But who would do it? And why?
He walked over to the doorway to join Mark, who was rubbing his hand on the wall.

"Soot," Mark whispered. "This place burnt really well."
"The church was over 100 years old."
"Yeah."
"Would've burnt really easily."
"I guess so."
"All that wood."
"Yeah."

Glen pushed what was left of the wooden door-frame aside. The hinges creaked and the wood gave way in his hand, disintegrating in his grip and falling to the ground.

He walked through the doorway.
Darkness greeted them.
He stood and waited for his eyes to adjust, spending the time thinking about the layout of the church and how it was described in the novel.

It's all so sad.
So ruined.
Slowly, he could begin to make things out.

The interior was dark, but not from lack of light. Most of it was burnt black.

He stepped forward into the church. The air was musty and cold. The dying light from the setting sun seeped through the large charred holes in the roof, illuminating most of the centre of the church but leaving the corners in darkness.

Glen walked down a short step and into the main hall. Three of the four corners in the church were in a murky, unsettling darkness. There was no far right corner, part of the wall had given way, and Glen could see outside to the trees beyond.

How did this happen?

As he walked forward the burnt wooden floorboards sagged under his weight, a couple of the boards creaking loudly in the silence and threatening to give way underneath him.

He could make out what was left of a large, heavy wooden table off to one side of the church, where the pews probably once sat. It lay on its side, two of the legs charred and the other two missing completely.

How intense was the fire to cause all this damage?

"Is *that* the table?" Mark asked behind him. His voice was loud in the silence and it startled Glen.

Glen walked over to the table and knelt down to check it out. It was burnt and charred and the heat had bubbled the varnish on the top.

Is it varnish?

He ran his hand along the top and could feel the deep grooves in its surface. They were still there. He rubbed away at some of the blackness and soot, widening the grooves and making them deeper.

The fire didn't hide everything.

His hand came away black.

"I think so," he said.

"Shit. That's it!" Mark sounded excited. "If I was tied

down on that old table, I wouldn't have minded one bit."

Glen laughed. "That makes two of us."

"You want me to take a photo of you standing beside it?"

"Nah."

"Why?"

"I just don't want to."

Mark looked surprised. "But this is *the* table!"

"I know, but it doesn't matter."

Glen didn't feel like having any photos taken right now. Even the photo he had dreamt about taking—the one where he was handcuffed to the front of the Jeep, with the church in the background— just didn't feel right now. Nothing was as it should be.

Sure, it's the church, the right church, the church from the book, but it's just so sad. It's destroyed. There's nothing of worth here. This isn't the same place, the right place. Even though I know it is.

He turned to look at what was left of the small kitchenette. Straight away he could make out the melted remains of the stove.

That fire was hot. It melted metal.

The bench that separated the kitchenette from the rest of the church was a pile of ash and debris now. Burnt wood and plastic melted into a morass of nothing.

Just behind the kitchenette was a doorway that was blocked by fallen rafters and other beams from the roof.

I should check back there. That's where the bath and toilet were.

That's where she took him.

But he just shrugged. He couldn't be bothered.

What's the point? It'll just be a ruin anyway.

He turned back to face the rest of the church. Mark was kneeling down at the table, running his hands along the grooves and shaking his head.

Glen walked past him, stepping over the holes in the burnt floorboards.

At the other end of the church should have been a wooden railing that separated the far section from the main room. From what he remembered the railing was semi-circular in shape and cut across the room. In the middle of the railing was a gap just wide enough for a person to walk through.

There was no sign of the railing now.

Fucking fire. It's ruined everything.

Glen could make out what was left of the two beds that sat behind the railing. He could see a torn piece of material and probably the remains of a pillowcase or two. To one side was a small metal wheel, melted into the floor. But nothing else caught his eye.

Just ash and black shit.

Nothing more.

Ashes to ashes…

My plan is fucked.

He turned around.

Halfway down the right wall of the church was the fireplace.

Maybe that's how it started. A spark from the fireplace.

But neither the fireplace nor the wall surrounding it were black or scarred by fire. Compared to the rest of the church, that section looked as if it had survived without being touched by flame.

That's a damn irony.

The bricks were covered in dust and a thick cobweb hung across the fireplace entrance.

On the other side of the fireplace were two weird-looking metal statues. Glen walked closer to them and bent down to check them out. They weren't black like the rest of the church, and he reached out and ran his hand along the cold surface of one of them.

It took him a while to work out what they were. Or what they once were. Metal chairs. The fire had melted them into freakish globs of metal.

That's one seriously hot fire.

Slowly, he walked around the church, unable to shake the feeling that this had all gone wrong and that someone, somewhere was laughing at him.

Again.

Why do they always laugh at me?

He checked the two dark corners at the far end of the church for anything. But there was nothing, just more piles of ash and burnt wood and debris. As he walked, he glanced out the old broken stained-glass windows. They were set into the two side walls at regular intervals; there were four on each side. But not one of them remained intact. All had been broken and destroyed, either by the fire or something else. Nothing remained of any of them except for some shards here, some melted glass there.

They would've looked so beautiful once.

Glen peered through the windows to the trees. The cool air rustled his hair. The sun was half-set.

Time's running out.

He walked down the church again and through where he guessed the gap in the curved wooden railing dividing the main room would have been. He stood where the two beds were once positioned. The area smelt musty and mouldy. The wall here had crumbled. The black bricks had fallen away, leaving a large hole to the outside, bigger than a normal entrance. Weeds and grass had begun to push up through the destroyed floorboards and Glen could see out to the ring of trees just beyond the church. He looked up and out through the holes in the roof.

This side of the church didn't look too stable, so he backed away quickly, just in case.

He turned and stared down the church to the front doorway. Mark was struggling towards the door with some large pieces of wood in his arms.

"What are you doing?" Glen asked.

Mark stopped and turned around to face him. "These are the legs from the table. I'm going to put them in the Jeep."

"Why?"

Mark looked strangely at him. "So we can take them home with us. These are *the* legs from *the* table!"

Glen wished he felt as excited as his friend. All of a sudden this whole thing just seemed like a giant waste of time.

Maybe they were all correct.
Maybe Jodie was right.

"Drop them, man. Throw them away."

"Are you *serious?*"

"Look, no one's going to believe us if we show them burnt shit. They're just gonna think we picked them up anywhere, on the side of the road or from a dump or something. Hell, *anyone* could grab a burnt bit of wood and say it's from the table. No one's gonna believe us if we show them crap like that."

Mark thought about it for a moment and then nodded in agreement. "You're right. I'll put them back then."

Glen's eyes lifted to the far wall where he spotted the large brick cross that he had also seen outside. It was at least 20 feet tall and ten feet wide and took up most of the wall inside too. Fire had licked at its base, but almost all of it seemed to have escaped the heart of the blaze.

He remembered that below the cross was supposed to be a small platform and lectern built out from the wall and raised above the floor of the church.

It wasn't there now. There was only a pile of black ruins and destruction.

That's probably what's left of it.

It was this pile of rubbish that was blocking the door to the bath and toilet.

There was supposed to be a small spiral staircase near the kitchenette as well. It was connected to one side of the platform, Glen remembered. But he couldn't see it.

Melted too, probably.

The sounds of wood and metal scraping together turned his attention back to Mark. He was kneeling near the kitchenette now, fossicking around in another pile of remains.

This is sick.
I can't believe we're doing this.
It's just not right.

When Glen had begun his search for the real church and the real story behind the book, he'd thought it would be cool to find the real places where the events took place and to become part of the events as well. Part of the history. But he'd expected it to be exactly like it was in the book.

But as he stood in the carcass of his dream, he suddenly realized how stupid it all was. And how stupid he'd been. He'd risked so much on this trip. He wanted the thrills, the excitement, but every step of the way it just continued to go wrong.

It's all ruined.

And now he knew that standing here, being here, would diminish his memories, would sour the good times and all the fun he had reading the book and researching the real story.

This ruined it all.

Nothing would be the same again.

I wish I'd never come now.

Glen thought about asking Mark whether he was ready to go, but he looked as if he were concentrating hard on sifting through his pile of black destruction. Glen didn't want to disturb him.

At least someone is still excited by what's left of my dream.

He shivered as he realized just how cold the church had become.

I can't stay here.

He walked towards the doorway.

"I'm going to take a look around outside," he said.

"Okay," Mark replied without turning around.

"I won't be long."

"Okay."

Glen watched as Mark's hands feverishly dug through the remains. He pulled small pieces out, tried to rub off the blackness and stared intently at each piece he held, as if willing them to speak to him, to tell him what they were.

The guy's obsessed.

"If you hear me screaming, that's just me dying," Glen smirked.

"Okay," Mark continued to focus on the debris.

Glen shook his head.

"I'll be back in a few minutes."

"I'll be here," Mark said.

"I have no doubts about that."
No doubts at all.

SEVEN

The sun had disappeared by the time Glen stepped outside the church. He looked up into the sky and he could tell that night would fall soon, and quickly.

No security floodlights out here like there were in the book.
Lucky we bought the flashlights.

Glen walked to the Jeep. As he did so, his eyes followed the long gash in the metal that ran down its side.

Country throwbacks.

Unhooking his key ring from his right hip, he unlocked and opened the back door. Reaching inside, he grabbed one of the flashlights. The metal was cold in his hand.

He turned on the flashlight as he closed the door and hooked his key ring on to his hip.

He took one last look at the church.

My dream's destroyed. Just like this place.
Things can only get better.
I have to save this weekend from total disaster. I have to go back with some sort of proof. If I go back a failure now, they'll just laugh even more.
That can't happen.
I won't let it.
I'll come back with something. Something better than burnt wood.

He stared out into the trees and bushes that surrounded the church. The flashlight beam was weak in the twilight. He listened for any kind of noise, but the night was quiet. Almost unnaturally quiet, except for the cool breeze rustling through the pines. But there was no sound of any animals.

Weird.

The only sounds he could hear were his own footsteps in the dirt and gravel and the occasional cooling sounds of the Jeep's engine. He walked by the Jeep once more, his fingers tracing the gash along its side.

It's so deep. It'll cost me a fortune to fix.

He slowly began to walk around the church. He walked down the long right side wall first, the path getting darker as he walked, the light from the flashlight guiding his way. He kept his eyes focused on the church. He could see where the flames had licked and spread, he could see the path of destruction the fire took.

He climbed over some of the fallen roof beams and shingles, his feet crunching on broken glass. As he passed one of the window frames where the stained-glass windows once were, he peered inside. He could clearly see Mark, still in the corner near the turned over table, still scouring for anything.

It's a waste of time, pal. Get over it.

He heard a noise from behind him, like a muffled snap.

He swung around, the flashlight beam sweeping into the pines.

"What the...?" he muttered.

The beam cut into the growing darkness behind the trees, but there was no one to be seen.

Don't go crazy on me now.

Calm down.

The mind can play tricks.

It was at that moment he realized he didn't have a weapon or anything to protect himself with.

From what?

From who?

Damned if I know.

Suddenly he felt a little vulnerable, but he wasn't going back into the church to look for a weapon or club.

What would Mark say to that?

Exactly.

Just don't let the night get the better of you.

The only way for him to go was forward.

He reached the far end of the church having seen or

heard nothing suspicious. With every step he took, he felt more confident and more self-assured. He smiled.

Me and my imagination…

Glen paused at the corner of the church. He ran the flashlight over the outside wall, checking the bricks and the hole where the wall had given way. This side of the church looked slumped, like it had sunk into the earth and was leaning over, getting ready to topple completely. The fallen bricks from the wall were spread around on the ground, all black and charred, like black ants going nowhere.

The area behind the church was cleared too, but more so than anywhere else. About thirty feet away and down a slight decline was a smaller building, built to resemble the church. But this building was made of wood.

No. It can't be!

Quickly, he ran over to the building and began to inspect it.

It has to be.

It is!

It fits the description and everything.

It was half the size of the church and the paint on the wooden walls was peeling. While it resembled the church from a distance, up close he could tell it was nothing more than a storage or machinery shed.

This is exactly like in the book.

The description fits.

There was a double doorway and one window, both set into the front wall.

Just like in the book.

Glen swept the flashlight back and forth as he inspected the area. The trees and bushes began again directly behind the shed, but they had been cleared on both sides.

It's exactly the same.

Glen's hopes and dreams started flooding back. Maybe there was a way to save this weekend and return home the hero. Maybe he could still make them eat their words and apologise.

This is soooo cool.

Wait until Mark sees this. He's in there playing with dirt while I'm finding the real stuff. He'll shit himself!

Glen turned around to call to his friend.

Then he changed his mind.

Not yet. I have to see what else is out here.

Glen cupped one hand around his face as he pushed up against the window and shined the flashlight in with his other hand. The shed was empty, he could see that much, but he didn't care.

It's the shed. Just like it was described in the book.

Jack-fuckin'-pot!

I wonder what else is out here?

Maybe it all is. That would be fucking fantastic!

Smiling to himself, Glen turned and jogged alongside the wall on the other side of the church.

I just have to check to be sure…

The scorching from the fire wasn't as bad on this side. The church looked almost untouched except for the broken windows and half-destroyed roof.

Weird the wooden shed didn't burn to the ground.

Maybe they put it out in time?

Yeah, maybe.

In the shadows halfway down the side of the church, his flashlight beam hit it.

"Yes," he whispered. "That's *got* to be it."

A paved path headed off into the pines.

I'm so fucking right…

He stopped by the path and ran a hand through his hair. He turned back and looked at the church.

Mark really should be part of this.

He really should be…

He turned to look at the path again.

But I got us here. It was my research. My discoveries. I really should be the one to find out what's down here. I should be first.

I should be alone.

He turned and carefully walked down the path.

He did this in the novel too. Except when he first walked down here, it was dark. He didn't have a flashlight.

Glen turned off the flashlight.

Night surrounded him.

It got dark so fast.

This is sooo cool.

Screw Disneyland.

The silence closed in around him and the cold night air made his breathing heavy and damp.

He took a step forward, then another. Then a couple more.

How long can I push myself? How long will my nerves hold out?

I can do it. I can hold out as long as I need to.

He took a few more steps.

Then a few more.

And then the hand touched his face.

"FUCK!" he screamed as his fingers fumbled for the flashlight switch. He couldn't find it. The flashlight slipped from his hands and fell. He reached for it, but grabbed only air.

He heard it hit the ground.

"Jesus, *no!"* He fell to his knees, his eyes wide but seeing nothing, his hands fumbling in the dirt and grass.

Then he felt the cold metal. Grabbed at it and lifted. Turned the flashlight back on.

He swung the beam around above him, his eyes wide, his heart thumping, his breath fogging in the night. He stood quickly, sweeping the flashlight from side to side, around him, all around him.

But no one was there.

Just an overhanging tree branch with leaves that were at the level of his face.

He laughed then. Or tried to through the deep breaths and the thudding of his heart.

Fucking idiot.

Scared of a stupid tree.

He bent over to catch his breath.

He laughed harder.

Hope Mark didn't hear me yell out. But imagine if he did? He'd be scared shitless right now.

He laughed again.

Fucking trees.

He straightened back up and shone the light in front of him.

The path ended just in front of him and opened out into a large and mostly empty rectangular space.

This has to be the old tennis court.

He looked around once more before he took a few steps further and shone the flashlight in an arc.

It is.

I'm right.

This is the old tennis court and the gazebo used to sit right in the middle of it.

According to the book, the large circular gazebo was painted in greens and creams, and directly behind the gazebo were sets of wooden seats.

But the area was empty.

Of course, it's empty now.

He took a few tentative steps out into the area and looked around. The ground underneath him was not paved, but it wasn't dirt either, it was clay.

He looked around once more and nodded his head.

No gazebo and no wooden seats—not any more.

That's right.

This is it.

There were two large piles of broken timber sitting on the opposite side of the court. One pile had overbalanced and fallen down, spreading its contents across some of the court. Both piles were covered in green moss.

Been like that for a while, Glen thought.

His flashlight then glided across the large, deep grooves that ran almost the length of the court.

He swung the flashlight from side to side, wanting to take it all in as quickly as possible.

Just like the book described.

Glen was starting to feel better now. Maybe the weekend could be saved after all.

There's more to this story than just a burnt-out old church.

The lines that had been painted on the surface of the court were now worn away by the weather, but he could just make out fragments of them here and there.

No one's played tennis here for a while, he thought as he stood in the centre of the court.

But they played other kinds of games.

He smiled to himself.

The wind swirled around him as a shiver sliced down his spine.

He wondered what Mark was doing.

And Jodie.

She should be here with me, supporting me like a real girlfriend would. But, no, it's all too hard.

"I don't care about your stupid book," she'd said.

"Or your stupid fantasy fuck," she'd also said.

I told her not to call Zoe that.

Didn't she realise that if she'd helped me it would've brought us closer together? That's what love's all about. Doing what the other person wants to do, being with that person. Wanting to be with that other person, no matter what.

She just didn't understand.

All she had to do was wear the clothes, dye her hair and be with me.

We could've been together forever if she'd just understood and agreed to do what I asked her to do.

I wasn't beating her. I wasn't fucking her hard and making her scream. I wasn't tying her up and putting clips on her nipples and twisting them hard. I just wanted her to be more like Zoe.

Is that too much to ask?

But she'd said no.

Stupid bitch.

Now she's home alone and sad and lonely, while I'm out here, finding it all.

She should be here. But she isn't.

He turned to take one last look around him.

I've got to get back, he thought. *Mark will wonder what's happened to me.*

As he walked towards the path to take him back to the church, something triggered his memory.

He stopped in his tracks and turned his head sharply

to the right and took two steps backwards. He shone the flashlight in the direction he was looking.

It's gotta be around about...there!

At the end of the tennis court, just past the treeline, he spotted it at ground level, shining back at him.

Yes. It's gotta be.

My God, it is!

Slowly, he turned and walked towards it.

The flashlight reflected off the large metal cross, half-buried in the ground.

Now this is fuckin' amazing.

If I can't take something from the church back with me, maybe I can take a cross or two.

The flashlight beam bounced from the first cross to the next cross, and then to the one next to that.

It's gotta be the path to the cemetery.

He turned his head from side to side and realized there was a whole row of crosses bordering the edge of the old tennis court.

And directly in the middle of them was another path.

Just like in the book.

Soooo cool.

He stepped over the crosses and onto the path.

Forget Mark. He can see this for himself after I have.

He walked down the path, which was lined with metal crosses on both sides. They were all evenly spaced apart, one every four feet or so. Some still stood erect, while others had toppled over and were lying sideways.

I found all this.

I'm the one who'll break this wide open.

They'll HAVE to believe me now.

I did it.

I'm the first.

I'm the one they'll follow.

The further down the path he walked, the more claustrophobic it became. It was almost as if the trees had moved closer and the darkness was swallowing the flashlight beam.

How far does this path go again?

I can't remember.

Just as he started to think about returning to get Mark, the path terminated at an old iron gate in a half-standing wire fence. The gate was rusted and had fallen off its hinges. Glen lifted it out of his way to continue.

He stopped just inside the fence and shone the light out in front of him.

"Fuckin' hell," he whispered as he dropped the flashlight and fell to his knees.

His world spun out of control.

EIGHT

He couldn't believe what he had just seen.

He shook his head. "No."

It's not possible.

Just not possible.

The dark closed in around him as the flashlight rolled to the side of the path.

He tried to get his thoughts in order, tried to get his mind under control, but it was too hard.

I couldn't've seen it right.

But I did.

There's no mistake.

One way to find out…

Reaching down, he picked up the flashlight and pointed it at the graves again.

The small metal crosses gave way to large stone ones that sat atop the concrete graves. He surveyed the area and could count over two dozen graves, most with stone crosses, but some with wooden ones and others with gravestones as well. There were other graves here too, but they were without headstones. The graves were arranged in two semi-circles, both facing the gateway he had just entered.

The earth smelled different here; the air seemed dank and colder than before. Glen rubbed his arms to keep himself warm as he peered around the crosses and headstones, looking at each one and reading what was written on them.

The chiselled inscriptions had long ago faded, but the graffiti had not.

"This can't be right," he whispered as he moved the flashlight from one headstone to the next. *"How* could this be right?"

Zoe gives good head!
I am Zoe
Fuck me hard!
For a good time, call Zoe 6969 6969
Zoe & Elvis still live!
Live on the edge, fuck on the edge
Johnny loves Zoe
MD & LF fucked here
Fuck me, I live!
Fuck today, die tomorrow
Blow me, blow me hard
Open up & say cum
Zoe lives! Have my lovechild!
Suck on this, bitch
I am Zoe, I live
Kill all men
Fuck all men
Zoe will never die

The graffiti was in different colours, and written in different styles. And it was everywhere. From the headstones to the metal crosses, the writing was spread and sloped over almost every grave. Some headstones were almost completely covered in overlapping graffiti, leaving nothing of the original engraving to be seen. Only those graves without headstones or crosses were spared the vandalism.

Glen's heart was beating hard, his breathing was fast.

This can't be happening.

"No. Why? How could they do this? Who would do something like this?" he said to himself. *"Noooooo!"*

His scream echoed into the night.

I was the first.
I had to be.
I was sure of it.
No one knew.
Only I worked it all out.
Me.
Just me.
I had to be first, not these fuckers. Not these vandalising assholes!

No one can beat me to this.
How did they know?
How did they get here first?

He swung the flashlight in an arc again, checking out the graves once more. The more he looked, the more graffiti he found sprayed on the headstones.

She came, she saw, she fucked
Harder, Harder, yeah baby, harder!
Ride me til I bleed, Fuck me til I die
Zoe is the best
Suck, gargle and swallow
Live on the edge, die on the edge
I did it for us. Both of us.

For Glen, the excitement had gone, and so had the shock. There was an emptiness in his heart and mind now as his eyes moved from one headstone to the next.

He wanted to wish it all away, he wanted to take a step backwards and never enter the cemetery, never know what had been done here.

They're doing it again.
They're taking away my dream.
I won't let them.

The anger was building now. Fast and strong.

Fuckers destroying the place like this, leaving their shit sprayed all over the place. Who do they think they are? Getting here first and then parading it in front of everyone, writing their sick shit all over here.

Destroying history.
Destroying the evidence.
Sick fuckers.

The flashlight danced to the furthest part of the cemetery. The beam slid over them once, then again. He noticed the two stone angels on the last two graves at the very back of the graveyard. They were so far back that they actually sat between some of the trees that bordered the area.

Both of the ornate angels sat on marble columns that were covered with ivy. The angels were holding harps and looking up to the sky. They were mirror images, facing each other and smiling sweetly for the rest of eternity.

From where Glen was kneeling, one of the angels looked as if its head were too small. It certainly didn't have the same size head as the other one, although its features were still the same. The other angel had large black marks all over it, but Glen couldn't work out what they were.

He stood and looked around him once more.

This is starting to get way too creepy.

It's weirding me out.

Go back.

No way. Not yet.

Slowly, he stepped between the first row of graves in front of him and walked closer to the angels.

He moved the flashlight from side to side, making sure he wouldn't miss anything. And also making sure there were no unexpected surprises.

Like a corpse or two.

Or anyone. Waiting.

There's no one here.

Someone could be watching.

Who?

And why?

Everything looked darkly charred, but he wasn't sure if that was a trick of his mind or whether the earth around the cemetery was actually burnt. He bent down and ran his hand over the dirt nearby. It came away black and sticky.

Weird.

He straightened and walked the last few feet to the angels.

He noticed the ivy was entwined around both marble columns, and the area around these two graves was not burnt at all. It was the opposite, so overgrown with ivy that it was hard to see the mounds of the two graves that were at his feet. There were no gravestones on the two graves, just the marble columns with the angels sitting on top.

Glen ran the beam of the flashlight over the first angel. It was missing the side and back of its head.

That explains why it looked smaller.

The angel's smiling cherub face still beamed happiness and love, and from the front it was hard to notice it had been vandalised. There was only one small crack visible from the front. It started at the angel's hairline and ran across its left eyebrow before disappearing in the eye. From the back though, most of its head was missing, almost as if someone had attacked it with a heavy blunt implement, smashing it until portions of the head broke away.

Why bash half the head in without going all the way?

Why not knock it off completely?

Glen turned and ran the beam over the second angel.

It had been vandalised too, but in different ways. Long dark ugly lines had been drawn all over it. They ran across its chest, down its arms, and around its feet and wrists. Its face had been changed from a happy, loving smile to an evil look of terror. The eyes had been darkened into black swirling circles and the smile was now a dark scream of terror. Someone had drawn a cock between its legs too.

Animals.

Why would they do all this?

These are graves.

People are just fucking sick.

He traced the flashlight beam down along the second angel's marble column. He was looking for any sign of an epitaph or message engraved anywhere on the column.

Something has to be written somewhere.

He bent down, but the ivy was wrapped tightly around the bottom of the columns. Putting the flashlight on the ground, he pulled at the ivy. Slowly, it started to tear away from the column.

Something…somewhere.

And then he heard the footsteps.

Running.

He grabbed the flashlight once more, stood and turned to look back across the cemetery to the old iron gate and further up the path.

The footsteps were coming closer, he was sure of it. They were getting louder.

He quickly knelt down behind the nearest headstone, turned off his flashlight and stuffed it down the back of his jeans. The twilight that had surrounded him now turned into pitch black. He grabbed the top of the headstone and peered over it into the darkness towards the gate.

The footsteps continued.

The beam from a flashlight came into view, swinging wildly.

The figure charged towards the fence, but it pulled up quickly as the flashlight beam landed on the first of the graves and their headstones.

"*Fuck.*"

The whisper carried across the cemetery to Glen.

The figure slowly walked through the old iron gate, its breath steaming in the night. It knelt down at the nearest headstone, shining the flashlight onto it.

Glen could just make out Mark's features as the light reflected from the headstone.

Thought so.

Knew so. But I had to be sure.

Glen smiled.

Now this is going to be fun.

I shouldn't do it.

But I can't resist.

Slowly, he crept from his place behind the headstone, trying hard not to breathe or make any sound that would give away his position. He stayed hunched over as he softly walked, following the trees that bordered the cemetery and making his away back towards the gate. And Mark.

He kept an alert eye on Mark and his flashlight.

Don't move, man.

Just stay right where you are.

Mark's beam danced from one headstone to another, his eyes wide as he read each of the messages left in black or red or purple. He shook his head back and forth.

I know, pal.

I felt the same way.

Glen moved closer. His smile widened. It was hard not to laugh.

Mark swept the flashlight beam further back into the cemetery, to another row and along the line of graves.

Glen froze. The beam narrowly missed him.

Stand still, or he'll see you.
He held his breath and didn't move.
The beam swung in the other direction.
That was close.
He crept closer.
Closer.
He was behind Mark now, coming at him from the side.
This'll be so cool.
Closer.
Mark's beam was searching the furthest corners of the cemetery. It was sweeping back and forth, across the graves and headstones, up to the angels at the very back and then down across the headstones again. He was totally absorbed in what he was doing.
Totally oblivious to what's happening around him.
If I were some homicidal maniac escaped from an asylum, he would be a dead man right now.
He should always be on his guard, no matter what. Like I am.
Glen was only five feet away.
Just before he pounced, he stopped and stared at his friend, watched him in the night, savoured the moments before attack.
His smile grew wider.
So fucking exciting.
He raised his arms out in front of him.
Prepared to spring.
He heard Mark's sharp intake of breath and saw the flashlight jiggle in his hands. He watched as Mark took a step backwards and turned off the light.
Huh?
Darkness surrounded them.
What the…?
The night was deadly quiet.
All Glen could hear was Mark's heavy breathing.
"Fuck, what *was* that?" he heard him whisper.
Glen dropped his arms. His smile vanished. His eyes turned back to the cemetery, trying to remember where

Mark's beam had been pointing before he turned it off. But it was no use, it was too dark to see anything.

I wonder what freaked him out?

The angels?

They weren't that scary.

They both stood in the darkness.

Still.

This is crazy.

Then Glen smiled.

No it isn't.

The bastard, he heard me. He heard me and now he's trying to freak me out.

Sick asshole.

It almost worked too.

Almost.

He won't get away with this. No way.

I'll show him.

"Mmmmmaaaaaaaarrrrrrrrrrrkkkkkkkkkkk!"

He started softly at first, but quickly he raised his voice higher and louder.

He could hear Mark fumbling in front of him.

He heard him say, *"Shit."*

And then the flashlight beam was on again, whipping around and finally coming to rest on Glen's face.

"Asshole!" Mark reached out to grab him.

Glen broke into laughter and jumped out of his way. He couldn't help it. It was so funny.

Mark's face was dead white, a look of terror still there, slowly turning to anger.

"What the fuck are you doing?" he yelled. "Trying to scare me to death?"

Glen leaned against a gravestone, his arms wrapping around his sides, trying to hold in his laughter.

"Sorry, pal," he said between breaths. "It was just *soooo* funny. I couldn't resist."

"You scared the *shit* out of me," Mark said, walking closer.

Glen nodded. "I know. You should've seen your face. Talk about a Kodak moment. I should've had the camera with me."

"Oh, *very* fucking funny."

"Yeah, it sure was."

"And I came to save you and everything."

"Huh? Save me?"

"Yeah."

"From *what?* The bogeyman?"

Mark shook his head.

"Come on, *tell* me!"

"I heard you scream and I came looking for you, that's all. I thought you were in trouble."

"I didn't scream."

"Yes, you *did.* I heard you. More than once."

"I might've yelled a couple of times, but I *don't* scream."

"Whatever. I *heard* you. I thought you were in trouble. So I came looking. It wasn't until your last scream that I worked out where you were."

"I *don't* scream."

"Yeah, well, whatever. Wish I hadn't bothered now."

Glen walked over to Mark. "Okay, look, I fucked up and I'm sorry, all right?"

"Yeah, whatever." Mark played with the flashlight.

Christ, he's worse than a woman sometimes.

"Jeez, man, I said I was sorry. Just let it go, okay?"

Mark turned to look at him. "Okay."

"We're cool?"

"Yeah, okay."

"Great."

The things I have to do for a little fun around here…

"You *did* scare the shit out of me," Mark laughed.

"Like I said, I couldn't resist."

"You bastard."

"That's me."

They laughed again and Mark swung the flashlight beam across the cemetery once more.

"Ain't this freaky?" he whispered.

"Yeah, I know what you mean. I was walking through here when I heard you running."

"And all this shit written everywhere."

"I know."

"It means we weren't the first."

"I know."

"Or maybe they're just local kids who know the story and come out here to get scared or something."

Didn't think of that.

"It doesn't mean we're not the first to break the code and make it out here to see all this," Mark continued. "Maybe it's just local idiots playing around."

"Good point. Or the barman could've done all this."

"Yeah, perhaps he's one of the kids who did this when he was younger. You never know. That's why he sent us to the other place, he didn't want us finding this. Ruin his secret and everything."

"You could be right," Glen agreed.

"Still, it's disappointing."

"I know. I thought this would be a really cool place. But all this graffiti shit just makes it all so sad."

They stood in silence, watching the beam as it danced across the graves.

"You still going to?" Mark turned to face him.

"Going to what?"

"Take a headstone."

Glen shook his head.

Another part of my grand plan gone wrong.

"Why not?"

"There's not much point, is there? They're all ruined."

"Maybe if we took one we could scrub the spray paint off and get it like new again."

"Naaah, it's too hard, and we might destroy what's underneath. Anyway, look at those headstones, they'll be way too heavy to lift back to the Jeep."

"I guess you're right. What about the crosses?"

"Nope."

"You sure?"

"This whole place, it's just so disappointing. If I took one, it'd remind me of what we found here. Even if we cleaned it up, I'd still know what it looked like when we first saw it. You understand?"

"Yeah, I think so."

"Come on, pal," Glen said. "I think we've seen everything there is to see here. Let's go back."

Mark nodded.

He swept the flashlight in one last arc of the cemetery, his eyes searching across the gravestones and into the night.

"Yeah," he muttered. "There's nothing here."

They turned and walked back up the path.

NINE

"It's fucking amazing," Mark said, his voice in awe.

"No doubt about it."

"I mean we're here. This is it!"

"It sure is."

"And it happened about here?" Mark asked.

Glen looked around the tennis court, remembering how it was described in the book.

They were standing in the middle of the court, their flashlights sweeping all around them.

"You're standing in the right spot."

Mark beamed. "It's so amazing. This is *the* spot."

Glen smiled.

He's getting more of a kick out of this than Jodie ever would.

She's missing it all.

Serves her right.

She'll wish she'd come along once I tell her what we did.

And Mark will have the same story.

She'll have to believe us then. Both of us.

Everyone will have to believe it's true.

"Do you think that wood is all that's left?" Mark pointed to the two piles of mossy wood to the side of the tennis court.

"Probably," Glen said. "Who knows how long it's been sitting there."

"This is such a great place. I'm so glad we came."

Glen watched as Mark splayed his feet and raised his arms above his head. He lifted his face to stare out at the night sky above them and he smiled wildly.

"*Zzzzzzooooooooooeeeeeeeeee!*" he yelled at the top of his

voice.

The sound bounced all around them, echoing into the night before being swallowed by the darkness.

"You okay, pal?" Glen asked.

Mark grinned back at him. "That's what she used to do, call out in the night."

"I *know* that."

"It was in the book."

"I know. I read it too, remember? Thirteen times."

"Just thought I'd give it a try. It's cool. Try it?"

"Nah."

It's stupid.

"Try it. Go on. I won't tell anyone we did it."

Glen's smile widened.

What the hell. Who gives a fuck anyway?

"Ready?" Mark asked. "We'll do it together."

"Okay."

"Cool. Get in position like me."

Glen shook his head from side to side.

"This is *sooo* fucking ridiculous," he said. But he did it anyway. He moved his feet apart and lifted his arms above his head. He looked up into the night sky at the stars overhead.

So fucking ridiculous.

"Ready?"

"Yep."

"Let's do it."

"Zzzzzzoooooooooeeeeeeeee!" they yelled into the night.

It felt so good.

They did it again.

"Zzzzzzoooooooooeeeeeeeee!"

Now they were laughing.

Zzzzzzoooooooooeeeeeeeee!

The night swallowed each cry.

"It would be wonderful if she called back," Mark said.

"I don't think that's possible."

"I know." Mark turned and walked over to the piles of wood. "It'd still be amazing though."

"Well, I think our chances are pretty low."

"Can't hurt to dream." Mark crouched by the fallen pile of timber. "Do you ever close your eyes and think about her? Think about what she would be like?"

"Oh yeah, of course. All the time."

"Yeah, me too. It'd be so cool if we knew her. If she was part of our lives. I've wished for that so much."

"Wishes like that don't come true."

"I know."

"Anyway," Glen replied as he swung the flashlight around the tennis court again, "the author probably just made all that up. There's no proof that Zoe ever called out into the night like that."

"I know. But when I see a girl like her, with the same build and the same hair and smile and beauty, I always wonder if that's really her. I can't help thinking that way. If she's walking on the street, or driving past me in a car, or maybe I see her in a restaurant or she serves me coffee, I always wonder if she's really Zoe."

"I know. I do too."

Glen was sure the darkness was heavier, his beam not reaching as far as it had before.

Maybe the batteries are dying.

He shone the beam across the tennis court and back up the pathway towards the church.

We should be getting back soon.

Other things yet to do.

"Oh my *fuck!*" Mark said from behind him.

Glen swung around.

Mark's back was to him. He was crouching over the fallen pile of wood. Some of the wood had been moved to the side.

"What is it?" Glen asked.

Mark was shaking his head. *"Fuckin' fuck.* You're *not* going to believe this."

"Believe *what?*" Glen walked towards him.

Mark slowly stood up. He turned around to face Glen, his hand held out towards him.

Glen moved the beam of his flashlight to Mark's hand.

It reflected in the light.

"Fuck *me*," Glen whispered.

"Exactly."

"Fuck me straight to hell."

It was a gold half-heart pendant.

"It's *Zoe's*," Mark whispered.

Glen stared at it, taking it from his friend's hand.

It was just like the one described in the book. It was a gold half-heart pendant, swinging on a thin gold chain.

It's Zoe's.

It has to be.

Just like in the book.

Just like he'd seen in all those cheap jewellery stores he'd looked through when he was dating Jodie. He'd always planned to buy one for her. She would wear one half of the heart, and he could wear the other.

We'd be together forever, he remembered thinking. *As true lovers should be.*

Yeah, how wrong was I about that?

It had been a cool idea, but he hadn't even told her about it. He knew she wouldn't wear it if she found out he'd gotten the idea from the book. If he never told her the idea was from the book, and she never read the book, then no one would ever know. It was a safe bet. He'd always meant to buy her one to show her how much he loved her.

Meant to...

And every time he saw it around her neck, it would remind him of Zoe.

It would've been perfect.

But he never got around to it.

Would've been wasted money on her anyhow.

Totally wasted.

But now he had something better.

Now he held one in his hands.

And not just any one.

Zoe's.

A-grade fuckin' Zoe's.

"Can you *believe* this?" Mark was saying as he danced around in the night. "Can you believe we *found* this? Just like that?"

Glen turned the half-heart pendant over. He let it sit in the palm of his hand and become a part of him.

It was dusty and discolored, a myriad of black spots dotting its tarnished surface.

Blood?

It felt light and cold. It felt powerful too.

This was hers. She wore this.

It said so in the book.

It rested on her skin. Rubbed against her chest. Felt her.

Was a part of her…

"Where did you find it?" he asked.

Mark turned around and pointed. "I was just moving a few planks of wood, from the pile there, the one that's fallen down. I moved, like, three planks and this was sitting under them, half-buried in the clay. I saw the chain first and then when I pulled the heart came out and I just couldn't believe it. I still can't."

"I can't either," Glen whispered.

I wish I'd found it.

But he found it.

It's his.

Fuck.

"This is the proof we need, right?" Mark was jumping with excitement. "It can't get any better than this. This is *all* we need. It's her fucking *pendant!*"

Yeah, it sure is.

And he found it.

"Hang on," Glen said, throwing it back to him. "You can pick these pendants up anywhere. You can find them in every shitty jewellery store across town. They're everywhere, man. All over the place. It doesn't prove anything."

"Huh?" The excitement drained from Mark's face. "Are you *serious?*"

Glen signed deeply and shook his head. "We could've just picked one up at a store and said we found it out here."

"But we *did* find it out here. It's got clay and dust and dirt and shit all on it. It's *hers!*"

"I know that, and *you* know that, but no one's gonna believe us."

Mark's eyes fell to the pendant. "You think so?" he asked, disappointment in his voice.

"I do. I'm sorry. It was a neat find. But not important enough for what we want. Don't worry, we'll find something else of more value. I'm sure of it, okay?"

And I'll find it this time.

"Come on. Don't go all quiet and depressed on me. Let's head back to the church and keep going."

"What's the point?" Mark threw the pendant onto the ground.

Glen watched where it landed.

"What do you mean?"

Mark looked up at him. "What's the fucking point? We've come all this way and found all this stuff, but no one's going to believe us anyway. No matter what we take or what we tell them, they're going to think we're lying."

"Not necessarily."

"It's true. It's a fucking waste of time unless we can prove we've been here and this is the real place. If the pendant isn't good enough proof, then I don't know what is."

Glen put his flashlight on the ground and walked to Mark.

"Now you listen to me. No one, *no one,* has been with me every step of the way on this journey like you have. You've been there no matter what. You've stood by me while others have laughed and told me I was crazy and told me to fuck off. Hell, you stayed by my side even when my *girlfriend* told me I was insane and to take a flying fuck off the end of the planet. I *didn't* come all this way to go home empty-handed. We *will* find something that proves we're right. We *will* succeed. You understand?"

Mark nodded.

"Say it."

"I understand."

"Say it like you fucking mean it, pal."

"I understand!"

"That's better."

Mark smiled at him. "You're right."

"Of *course* I'm right. I'm always fucking right."

He led Mark towards the path.

"Sorry about that," Mark muttered as they walked. "I went a bit crazy there."

"Don't worry." Glen smiled. "We all go a little crazy sometimes."

They walked from the tennis court and onto the path to the church.

"Where to next?"

"Our last stop," Glen said. "Strangways. We're almost there."

"Ah, that's right. That's where the real farmhouses are meant to be. Right?"

"Exactly. Just ten minutes drive to the north of us."

"Cool. I hope we find what we're looking for there."

"We will. I'm sure of it."

They walked on in silence.

"Shit."

Mark stopped to look at him. "What is it?"

"I've left my flashlight at the tennis court." Glen held up his empty hands.

"Okay, let's go back for it."

Glen shook his head. "No, no. We don't both have to go back. I can find my way."

"You sure?"

"Yeah. Why don't you head back up to the church and I'll meet you there in a minute."

"Okay. Don't get lost."

Glen laughed and slapped his friend on the back. "No chance of that. And if I do, I'll just call Zoe's name."

Mark smiled. *"Zzzzzzooooooooooeeeeeeeee!"*

"That's the one."

Mark laughed as the echo died away.

"See you at the church," Glen said as he turned and walked back down the path.

"Yeah, okay."

Glen walked slowly away from Mark, taking his time and letting Mark get further into the distance.

Easy.

Underneath his feet, he felt the path end and the clay

from the tennis court begin.

Almost there now…

There was a small glowing rim of light on the other side of the tennis court.

So easy.

Like taking candy from a baby.

He walked over to where the flashlight was sitting globe-down on the surface of the court. The rim of light escaping from the sides of the flashlight was all the guide he needed to help him return to the right spot.

He looked over his shoulder.

The night was dark. No sign of Mark anywhere.

Too fuckin' easy.

He bent down and picked up the flashlight. He swung the beam left.

It's here somewhere.

I know it is.

It only took a few seconds for the beam to find the half-heart pendant on the dusty clay of the tennis court. It reflected the light back at Glen.

He reached out and picked it up.

Found you.

And you're all mine.

So easy.

He stood and swung around, the beam heading across the tennis court and up the path to the church.

No one was there.

Glen smiled.

Some people are so fuckin' gullible.

He slipped the pendant into the back pocket of his jeans and smiled into the night.

And I'm sooo fuckin' cool.

TEN

Strangways, here we come.
In ten minutes we'll be there.

Glen walked alongside the wall of the church, his flashlight moving from side to side on the path in front of him.

Just one more place to visit and then this is all over.

Overall, it hadn't been such a bad trip. And even though it hadn't gone exactly to plan and had been spoiled by a few people, and the graffiti in the cemetery, he still knew that he'd cracked the code and was ahead of the pack.

People will have to believe me now.
They've got no choice.
I've got the gold half-heart pendant.
I own it.
Pulled it from the ground on the tennis court.
They'll be in awe.
I'll be a legend.
A damn legend.

He thought about what life would be like when he returned home. No more researching, no more wondering or dreaming. He'd been on his personal quest. He'd dreamed about this for so long, and now he was living it. Living his dream.

How many people get the chance to do that?

He knew his life would never be the same again.

He turned the corner of the church.

Nothing will ever be the same again.

Mark was squatting by the back of the Jeep, his flashlight pointing to the ground. He looked across at Glen as he approached.

Glen smiled and waved a hand at him.

"I'm *baaack.*"

Mark stood slowly.

"Sorry I took so long."

"Why'd you do it?"

"Huh?"

"Isn't this *enough* for you?" Mark took a step towards him. "We're out here in the middle of *fucking nowhere* and we're doing what *you* want, but that's not enough, is it?"

"Hey, man, hold it a minute…" Glen came to a halt between the Jeep and the church.

"Is this place too *boring?* Not exciting enough?" Mark marched towards him. "Do you have to go and make it even *more* exciting?"

Mark was standing close to him now, glaring angrily into his eyes.

Does he know?

"Pal, calm down."

"I'm getting sick of your shit." He pushed Glen in the chest. The beam from his flashlight momentarily blinded Glen.

Glen's eyes darted back and forth.

Is this some joke?

It's not fuckin' funny.

"Hey, cool it, okay?"

"No," Mark pushed him again.

"What's the *fucking problem?*"

"As if you don't know."

"Christ, I *don't* know. That's why I'm asking!"

"More games, Glen?" Glen could feel Mark's breath on his face.

Another push.

Glen staggered backwards.

"What games? I don't know what the fuck you mean!"

Mark pulled back his arm and clenched his fist.

Glen threw his hands up for protection. "Don't even *think* about it, pal."

"*Fuck!* What's the use?" Mark muttered. "You won't change your mind anyway. It's all about you. Always has been."

Mark turned away from him.

What the fuck was that all about?

Mark walked back to the Jeep.

"You've gone too far this time," he said over his shoulder.

Slowly, Glen followed him.

He must know about the pendant.

He snuck back and followed me and watched me pick it up.

But I checked, he wasn't there.

He must've been hiding to the side of the path or something.

Bastard.

But as Glen walked closer to the Jeep, he realized Mark's anger had nothing to do with the pendant.

The Jeep sat on an angle, lopsided.

For a few seconds Glen couldn't work out why. He didn't remember leaving it like that.

Then his eyes followed Mark's flashlight as the beam travelled down the deep groove in the Jeep and to the back tyre.

Glen shone his flashlight there too.

The tyre was flat.

"Shit," he said as he knelt by the wheel, his fingers running across the deep slash on the side of the tyre.

"That ain't no ordinary puncture," Mark said from beside him.

"You've got that right," Glen said as his fingers curled around the gash and felt inside the tyre wall.

Something's cut right through it.

And deep.

Something sharp.

"Lucky we've got the spare in the back," Glen said.

Mark shook his head. "Think again. Look at the front tyre too."

Glen aimed the flashlight at the front tyre.

Shit it to buggery.

The front tyre was also flat. The same deep scar ripped through the tyre wall.

"Fuck, *no!*"

"Fuck, yes! We're stuck out here."

"Get the cell phones."

"Checked both. There's no network this far out. They're useless."

"Shit, man."

"I hope you're happy."

Glen turned to look up at his best buddy.

"Huh?"

"You got what you wanted, okay? A night at the church? Well done. A terrific plan. I hope we enjoy the fuck out of it."

"What are you talking about? *I* didn't do this."

"Sure, sure," Mark leaned against the Jeep and folded his arms across his chest. "I guess it just happened then."

Yeah, I guess it just did. Somehow…

I turned the corner of the church.

He was squatting by the tyre.

He stood up as I walked closer and started to attack me.

To yell at me.

Like I'd come back too soon.

As if I'd caught him in the act.

Maybe he still had two tyres to go.

Just who's playing the games around here anyway?

Glen stood slowly, and turned to face him.

"Why do you think *I* did this?" he asked in a calm voice.

"Well I don't see anyone else around who could've done it, do you?"

Glen nodded. "Yes. In fact, I *do.*"

Mark's face changed to an emotion Glen couldn't read. Was it shock? Or disgust? Or both.

He stifled a laugh. "You're not *serious?*"

"Deadly," Glen whispered.

"Jodie was right," Mark turned from him. "You really *are* crazy. I should've listened to her when she told me to keep away from you."

Glen grabbed Mark by the shoulders, swung him around and slammed him against the side of the Jeep. The

Jeep shook at the impact and the sound of the clash echoed deep into the darkness.

"Get your hands *off me!*"

"You really think I'd do something like this to my *own Jeep?*"

"Yes."

"Do you *really?*"

"*Fuck yes!*"

"I'm not the crazy one, *you are!* Why would I do something like that?"

"I don't know. You want to stay out here or something. You want to feel like you're trapped out here. Relive the experience. Pretend to be in the novel. I don't know. But you *had* to do it."

"Really?"

"Yes, really."

"What about you?"

"*Huh?*"

"*You're* the one who's been at the church longer. You were here picking through that pile of shit while I left and went looking all around the place. *You* had plenty of time to do it."

"You did it when you left me in the church. You came out here to slash the tyres and then pretend to get lost," Mark countered, trying to get out of Glen's grip.

"That's *bullshit.* I went to the Jeep for my flashlight. That's all. And the tyres sure weren't slashed then. After that I went straight to the tennis court. I wasn't here long enough. But *you,* you had all the time in the world while I was gone. You were poking around in the church just *waiting* for me to leave. *You* did it!"

"Why would I?" Mark looked frightened now, the anger draining from his face.

"To stop us going on to Strangways!"

"*Huh?*"

"You don't want to go to Strangways. You've seen enough and you want to leave here now, anyway you can. You never wanted to be here in the first place."

"You know that's not true."

"It is."

"Glen, I just *agreed* with you we'd go to Strangways. Remember? At the tennis court?"

"You wanted to go home."

"No, I'm here to see this through with you. I *want* to see it all. I *want* to go to Strangways. If I didn't want to be here, I wouldn't be here. And anyway, how does slashing the tyres help me leave this place? If anything, it means we're stuck here for longer. *Why* would I do that if I wanted to leave?"

Glen studied Mark.

Is he telling the truth?

He can't be.

That's the problem.

I didn't do it.

And if he didn't do it, who did?

Tyres don't get slashed like that by themselves.

The barman? Some local fuckers?

His eyes moved along the deep gash down the side of the Jeep.

Just like the gash in my paintwork.

It's almost exactly the same.

The maniac from the General Store?

Possibly.

It has to be. He's followed us out here.

But what if it isn't?

Glen let go of Mark and let him stand. He looked around into the night, then let the beam from his flashlight drop down to the tyres again.

"Fuck," he muttered. "This is just fucking dumb."

"What are we going to do?" Mark asked.

They looked at each other.

The anger had gone.

"We don't have much choice. Do we?" He turned to run his eyes over the dark, brooding church once again. "I don't want to stay here all night."

"Me either."

"So we have to walk."

"You're *kidding!*"

"No, I'm not. We walk. I'm not about to be stopped from finishing this. No local country fucks are going to stop me now. We walk to Strangways. Or you can sit here and wait, I don't care either way."

Glen waited for an answer.

Mark turned to look at the ruined tyres.

"I guess we don't have any choice," he muttered.

"There's always a choice."

"Okay. I'm not staying here by myself. We walk."

Glen smiled. "Let's get going."

ELEVEN

"Intense, huh?"

"What is?"

"What we're doing. Just you and me."

"Yeah, it sure is."

They trekked on through the forest, side by side.

They hadn't said much for quite a while, each of them lost in their own thoughts.

The forest seemed to stretch on forever. But Glen was confident he was leading them in the right direction. The map was the only guide he needed, and he'd made sure they took it with them as they left the church.

Don't want to be wandering out here forever.

They were walking in the right direction, he was sure of it. North. And he estimated that they were about half-way there by now.

Quicker in the Jeep.

Don't think about the Jeep.

Don't think about what he did.

Not now.

Keep focused.

Why would Mark do it? Why would he slash the tyres?

He's right. It wouldn't help him leave here any quicker. Anyway, he wants to be here, I can see that.

Then again…

Maybe he's *the one who's sick. Maybe* he's *the one who wants to feel like he's trapped up here.*

Living on the edge.

Remember how excited he got when he was standing on the tennis court. Calling out to her.

Screaming her name…

Still, it didn't matter. Not right now. No one was going to stop Glen from completing his mission. If they had to walk, then they walked. They'd check out Strangways and then they'd head back. Another walk would get them to Daylesford and they could call for help from there.

It's not like a walk or two is going to kill us.

Glen wanted to break the silence with his buddy. He needed someone to talk to so that time would pass quicker.

"This is pretty neat," he said. "We're actually walking in her footsteps."

Mark smiled and nodded his head.

Maybe I'm starting to break him down after all.

It was darker with the pines around them. While the trees gave them extra cover from the cool night, they also made it harder to see.

"Wouldn't it be amazing if she was still out here?" Mark asked.

Yes, success. He's talking.

"Yeah, *right*, like that's gonna happen," Glen replied.

"They never found the body."

"Don't confuse fact with fiction, man."

"I'm not. They *never* found the body."

"I think you'll find they did."

"You sure?"

Glen scratched his head. "We should've remembered to bring the newspaper file with us from the Jeep."

Mark laughed. "Too late now."

The conversation stopped.

The breeze rustled the trees, and the creaks and groans sounded strange and eerie, like some nearby beast on the prowl, following them and watching their every move.

A chill ran down Glen's spine.

He shook it off.

The forest was densely populated with the pines, their trunks standing tall and bare, with most of the foliage starting on branches more than ten or fifteen feet above their heads. The ground was covered with a blanket of dead pine needles, softening their steps as they walked.

"So, you think this is the way she came?" Mark asked.

Glen looked around them and nodded. "No doubt about it. While the others took the long route, she cut through in this direction. I drew it exactly on this map. We're following her path as closely as I could work out."

"That's how she arrived so quickly?"

"Exactly."

Mark smiled. "It makes this walk pretty exciting."

"Yeah."

"Better than driving there."

Why would he say that?

Unless he always wanted to walk.

Unless he slashed the tyres!

Let it go. It's not important right now.

"Yeah, I agree," Glen said.

They walked on further into the night.

"How much further?"

"Not sure." Glen checked the map with his flashlight. "But we'd be getting close."

"What a headrush," Mark muttered. "Walking in her *footsteps,* pal. Her actual damn footsteps."

"I know."

Glen found his mind wandering to Zoe. He could remember the descriptions of her from the book. He'd read them over and over again, and when that wasn't enough, he memorised them as well. That way, she would always be in his head no matter where he was.

Her face was small but almost perfect in every way. Her eyes were dark brown and her stare was divine. Her nose was slightly bent, as if it had once been broken, but her smile was lively and infectious. She had a small scar running across her left eyebrow and her shoulder length brown-blonde hair fell around her ears, some of it escaping the ponytail whenever she wore one. She constantly wore her hair differently, whether in a ponytail or in braids or in a bun, but it always looked perfect, no matter what.

Her whole body could move in one cat-like fluid movement and her voice was soft, gorgeous and enticing.

Her breasts were small and round, perfect, and delightful to look at. Her stomach was muscled and tight, and her tan seemed to shine in the light, to make her glow. The top of her bellybutton was pierced with a gold ring and hanging from the ring was a small diamond, sitting neatly and comfortably in her bellybutton hole, as if it were a perfectly natural place for a diamond to reside.

And the best part…

She was completely shaved between her legs. Even her tan spread between her dark folds.

She was so beautiful.

Her clothes—when she wore them—left nothing to the imagination. He could remember all her outfits, and how good she looked in them, but he had two favourites in particular.

The first was the black t-shirt with short sleeves and a tight neck. It hugged her body and served as a reminder of what was under the material. Across the front of the t-shirt was a multi-coloured strip divided into four squares. The first square held a picture of a red dog, the second of a white cat, the third of a blue mouse and the fourth of a yellow piece of cheese. Underneath the design were the words *Natural Selection.*

She looked so hot in that.

Then again, she looked good in anything…and nothing.

Her breasts bulged under the t-shirt and the bulges drew the eyes of anyone who looked at her. Along the neck and arms of the t-shirt were dozens of little metal rivets, punched into the fabric to border the whole design. The rivets would shine in the light.

Shine just like her.

I wish she were here now.

He had searched everywhere for a t-shirt like that. But he could never find one. No one had ever heard of a *Natural Selection* t-shirt. He even thought about paying to get the shirts designed and made. There was a killing to be made on the internet for stuff like that.

People on eBay would buy dozens of the shirts.

The discussion groups would too.

You just had to be first and to beat the thousands who followed.

You'd make a killing.

And the beauty was anyone could do it. You just had to be first.

Hell, some guy was even selling mugs with I LOVE ZOE printed on them and he was making a packet.

Easy.

People would buy it.

People would buy anything.

But the second outfit was the one that always got him hard.

It was made of black leather, what there was of it, and it made her look as if she was wearing a large spider's web. The leather straps went over her shoulders and under her arms, as well as around her hips. But between the straps was mostly bare skin.

Strips of leather ran across and under her breasts, pushing them out and upwards, making them rounder and more compact.

A circular piece of leather surrounded her bellybutton, highlighting it and making the diamond sitting there look like a bullseye. The leather circle drew attention to the centre of her stomach, exactly as it was supposed to.

And if you dropped your eyes lower...

Two thin strands of leather ran from the circular bellybutton section and down between her legs.

It left her exposed. Her shaved mound open and in view from almost anywhere.

And those eight inch black leather stiletto-heeled boots... *Fuckin' gorgeous.*

Glen could feel his cock pulsing as he walked.

She looked unbelievable.

No matter what.

Imagine if she were here...

Imagine looking at the diamond in her bellybutton and the moist folds between her legs as I push her thighs apart and lean forward, sliding my cock slowly into her warm centre.

I'd slide right inside.

Nice and easy.

And she'd close tightly around me.

So tight.
Yummy.
So fucking yummy.
Instead of buying the *I LOVE ZOE* mug and paying for the *Natural Selection* t-shirt to be made, he'd decided to give Jodie a replica of the leather outfit Zoe had worn. It'd been expensive and it took him a long time to track down someone who would make it for him exactly to his specifications.

And without laughing at me or looking at me like I was weird.

Fuck them all.

What I do with my money and my time and my cock is my own business.

He'd given it to Jodie on her birthday. He thought it would turn her on.

It didn't.

She just didn't get it.

She never understood.

I only wanted her to be more sexy.

Couldn't she see that?

More like Zoe.

His erection subsided as he thought about Jodie.

Why can't more girls be like Zoe?

She's all a man wants…

All a man needs.

He thought about how many times he'd cum reading the book, masturbating as he read. When Jodie wouldn't put out for him, when she wasn't there for him, or told him she wasn't in the mood, he always had Zoe.

Some of the scenes he played over and over in his head, time and time again.

Whenever something went wrong or he was depressed or he needed time alone, Zoe was always there for him.

Not like Jodie.

He only had to close his eyes and think about her.

She climbs up onto the table and stands above him. She places one foot on each side of his head and lets him stare up her long legs to the folds between them.

"I know what you want," she says. "Why say no to this?"

His erection grew again, faster this time.

"I know you're thirsty," she continues in her deep husky voice as she slowly bends into a squatting position. "And I know what you're thirsty for."

She's just inches from his face now. He can smell her, see every detail of her folds, her labia, her glistening pink insides, and her ass.

Her hand reaches between her legs and unfastens a black stud on the back of her outfit. The leather straps between her legs fall away. She unfastens another black stud on the front and lets the straps fall to the floor.

"You want me?" she asks.

He doesn't answer. He just stares at the beauty before him.

"I know you do. Your cock tells me."

He lifts his head slightly, trying to reach between her legs.

She lifts herself up, out of his reach. Teasing him.

"Uh-uh, not that easy," she says to him.

He rests his head back down.

The oil shines off her lips and folds. He studies the small pucker of her anus. She's so wet and inviting.

"You want me?" she says again, as she lowers herself back down. "If you do, say it."

I have to.

"I want you," he whispers.

"I can't hear you."

"I want you."

"Louder."

"I want you!" he yells.

There's a pause.

Then Zoe lowers herself onto his face.

"Good boy," she says. "I knew you did."

Then he's covered by her folds. Smothered by her.

His tongue shoots forward and buries itself deep in her. He searches inside her, wanting to feel everything; her soft, silky sides, her wet flaps and folds, her dark tangy interior.

He tongues her with passion. Searching out and finding her hard clitoris and rubbing back and forth, swirling around her nub, sucking on it.

She rocks slowly back and forth on his face, moaning deeply to herself, running her hands down his chest and stomach.

Her juices flow quicker, dripping into his mouth and spilling from it, trickling down the side of his face. She's wet and slippery and so good.

Her anus rocks back and forth in front of his eyes, puckering and quivering as her passion builds.

"You shouldn't deny yourself," she whispers to him.

He feels her hands down the side of his stomach, moving towards his hips. They reach further down as she bends forward, her ass tilts more, thrusting her clitoris back onto his tongue. Her nails scrape along the sides of his thighs. Then they trace a path up over his legs and down between them.

She squeezes his testicles and makes him jump.

"I like that," she says as she squeezes them again.

She leans further forward as her fingers grab his shaft and begin to massage him slowly.

And then, her mouth engulfs him.

Warm and wet, her tongue dances along his shaft. Her lips suck hard. Her tongue licks at the tip of his cock and then her head bobs up and down. She starts slowly, but quickly builds faster and faster.

He hears her moaning. He wants to reach out and grab her, to run his fingers up and down her back, to play with her wet folds.

She rocks back and forth on his face as she sucks harder and longer.

He tries to hold his passion back.

He holds on for as long as he can, but he can't stop it. Her tongue and lips and hand in combination are too good, too perfect.

Wonderful.

And he explodes in her mouth.

She keeps sucking, keeps massaging, making the orgasm last; the pleasure is long and exquisite.

She begins to lick him as she bucks faster and faster, rubbing her mound against his face.

Her breathing gets deeper and quicker, her anus tighter. She throws her head back, strands of her hair escape from her ponytail.

She cums as she massages him with one hand, and squeezes his balls with the other. She lets out a long deep moan and she wiggles her hips as he tongues her more.

So wonderful.

Why couldn't Jodie be like her?

Her juices would be smeared across his face, dripping into his mouth and down his throat.

Eventually, she would stop rocking back and forth. She'd just sit on his face, breathing hard, until he stopped licking her rock-hard clitoris. When he did, she would lean backwards slightly, moving her clitoris away from his tongue. He would suck on one of her flaps instead, sucking it deep into his mouth, stretching it as far as it would go.

She would moan and lean forward again, licking the last few drops of cum from the head of his cock.

"That was nice," she'd say as she lifts herself off his face to start sucking him again.

He'd begin to grow hard once more, almost instantly, and the whole scene would repeat itself in his head.

Countless times now he'd played that scene over and over in his mind. It never failed to get him excited. It always got him hard, hot and horny. And it always guaranteed the best jack-off ever. His orgasms felt wonderful, like he was cumming honey and gold. It felt so good.

And I do it for you, sweetheart.

All for you, my love.

Why can't I find someone like you?

His cock was throbbing in his jeans now, the tightness making it hard to walk.

Think of something else. Think of something to take your mind off your cock.

Think of Jodie.
Yeah, that will work.

He'd tried to get her to try new positions, he'd tried to get her to shave her pussy. First he started with subtle little hints. But when they didn't work, he became more direct, even sometimes just asking her, begging her point-blank to do it for him. But she would have none of it.

"Love me for who I am, not for who you want me to be," she'd said.

Yeah, right. Like that's gonna work.

There's no greater waste than a woman who doesn't use her body to her advantage.

Or doesn't want to.

She hadn't even wanted to try. She'd never given it a chance.

She might've liked it.

Stupid bitch.

Put on the leather, shave your pussy, dye your hair. You might've fuckin' enjoyed it.

He shook his head.

His erection was dying.

"Zzzzzzooooooooooeeeeeeeee!"

Mark's voice startled Glen.

Mark turned to face him, a wide grin across his face.

"Sorry, couldn't resist," he said.

Glen laughed. "Yeah, what the fuck. Let's do it."

"Zzzzzzooooooooooeeeeeeeee!" they called together.

Then they listened for a reply.

But the night remained silent.

Glen swung the flashlight in an arc, letting the beam slice across the trees surrounding them.

Come on, he wished.

Don't be fuckin' stupid.

Ain't gonna happen.

Ever.

"Damn it," he said.

Mark turned to face him. "What is it?"

"Nothing. Just thinking."

"About Zoe?"

"Yeah."

"Me too. I'm so fucking horny I think I'm about to explode."

So I'm not *the only one.*

"Come on, pal. Put your cock away and concentrate. We've got to get to Strangways."

"Nearly there?"

"Pretty damn close, I think."

"Cool. Do you think we'll find anything once we arrive?"

"I doubt it. But who cares? Remember, we're the first to do this. We're the ones who cracked this wide open."

"Yeah. We were first."

"All the others will now follow in *our* footsteps."

"Won't be the same for them."

"No way. No one will live this night like we have. We'll be legends."

They walked on together in the dark.

"A-grade fuckin' legends," Glen continued. "And legends never die."

TWELVE

They stopped in their tracks as they came over the hill. Glen looked through the thinning trees, down the slope into the valley.

The beams from the flashlights didn't stretch far enough, but with the half-moon shining above them, he could just make out the two old farmhouses down in the valley, no more than a couple of hundred feet away.

"Is this it?" Mark asked by his side.

"Take a look. What do you think?"

"Sure looks right to me."

"Exactly." Glen folded up the map and handed it back to Mark.

Almost there.

The farmhouses were set away from each other by a distance of about 80 feet. They both appeared identical to each other, except that the first farmhouse looked in much better condition than the second. Each house sat in the middle of a cleared field. The pines thinned out as they reached the properties, where they stopped altogether. A fence divided the area between both houses and Glen could make out the dirt driveway running up to the second farmhouse.

The second farmhouse was old and looked uncared for. From where he stood, there didn't seem to be any front door, but it could've been covered by the collapsed verandah. Some of the roof looked as if it had rotted through years ago as well.

To the right of the second farmhouse, and set just behind it, was a barn.

Just as the book described.

The barn was totally different from the farmhouse. It looked well-kept and newly painted. At least, he thought it did. But he couldn't be certain of anything, not from this distance.

It's legend time.

Glen turned his head to face Mark. "That's it, alright. Just as the book described."

"You sure?"

"Yep."

"And you *really* want to do this?"

Why would he ask that?

Why now?

"I've already answered that, man."

"Just checking," Mark smiled.

"Don't fuck with me." Glen smiled sharply back. "Not when we're this close."

They started down the hill towards the farmhouses, leaving the weather-beaten old sign behind them.

WELCOME TO STRANGWAYS

One event can define a lifetime…

Glen remembered reading that somewhere a few years ago.

Psychological bullshit, he thought at the time.

He never really understood how one event could shape somebody's future and change their entire outlook on life.

Until now.

I've been dreaming about this night. How it would feel, what I would do. How cool it would be.

And I'm in it.

I'm living my dream.

This is it.

Nothing else matters.

Nothing that went before.

Only this.

Right now.

Walking with Zoe…

Being part of her.

Her a part of me.

His hand reached into his back pocket and he ran his

fingers lightly over the half-heart pendant.

She's a part of me.

"Which one?" Mark asked as they walked across the dirt track that connected the two driveways of the farmhouses.

He turned to her.

She was wearing black button-up jeans. Each of the silver buttons glinted in the moonlight and reminded Glen of the diamond positioned snugly in her bellybutton. She wore a black top too, tight and figure hugging. It had no arms, so her muscled forearms and biceps were still on display. The neck of the top was cut into an L shape, showing some of her neckline and left shoulder.

Her hair was in a ponytail, with only a few strands escaping to the side of her face. She wore nothing on her feet and her toenails were painted bright red.

He smiled at her.

Zoe…

I'm here for you.

Her beautiful face smiled back at him.

We're together at last.

"Hey, you okay?"

Your voice is all wrong…

"Stop looking at me like that."

Glen blinked and shook his head.

He stared back at Mark.

"Sorry," he muttered.

"Don't go crazy on me."

"I'm okay."

"You sure?"

"Yeah, yeah…"

"Which one do you want to go to first?" Mark repeated.

Glen eyed both farmhouses again, then turned to look around him.

It was you.

Wasn't it?

I saw you.

Didn't I?

"Let's start with the one on the left."

"Doesn't look like anyone's lived out here for years."

"They were abandoned even when the events happened." Glen tried to shake Zoe's image from his mind. "So it must be quite a long time since anyone's lived here."

"Who'd want to live out here in the middle of nowhere anyway?"

I'd live anywhere with Zoe.

She's all I'd need.

I'd live out here with her forever.

They continued down the dirt track, their flashlights moving left to right. Away from the trees, Glen felt exposed, out in the open for anyone to see. He kept scanning around them, looking for anything out of the ordinary. But there was nothing.

Just us.

No one else.

The night felt colder now they had left the forest. The sky was clear overhead, the half-moonlight helped them see further than their flashlight beams would stretch. The cool night breeze blew in their faces.

They began walking up the driveway.

I'm walking up the driveway.

The actual driveway.

They walked closer to the farmhouse. Glen pulled ahead slightly, the excitement getting too much for him.

Gotta get there.

Gotta get there now.

The farmhouse looked like any other nondescript country shack. The timber frame looked solid, but old and weathered. The heavy wrought iron verandah spanned the front of the house, and the peeling paint on the hand railing showed the house had stood in the valley for quite some time. The rock steps up to the font deck were pitted and pockmarked; they had probably weathered storms and winds like this for countless years.

As they got closer to the house, the beams from the flashlights started to play over the building. The verandah loomed over them like a dark cloak, ready to swallow them in its darkness. The windows looked like the deathly black eye sockets of a long-forgotten skull.

Sitting on the edge of the deck was a dead sunflower poking out from a terracotta bowl. It looked like it had died from lack of water.

They stopped as they reached the front steps.

"Farmhouse number one!" Mark announced in a loud voice, as if he were a tour guide.

Glen smiled. "I know."

"Looks just like it was in the book, huh?"

Glen shrugged. "The author knew his stuff."

The cool breeze gusted around them.

Metal scraped loudly in the distance, the noise echoing through the valley.

Glen snapped his head around, following the noise.

What the…?

He peered into the night and towards the other farmhouse.

Did it come from there?

The wind died and the sound with it.

"Did you hear that?" he whispered.

"Yeah."

"What *was* it?"

"I don't know," Mark came closer and whispered in his ear. "Someone slowly being turned on a spit, roasted alive and dying a horrible agonising death?"

Their eyes met.

And then they both broke out laughing.

Glen shoved Mark away from him. *"Don't* say things like that."

"You *love* it."

"Yeah, of course, but *not* out here. You'll freak me out."

They laughed again, their voices echoing across the valley and into the night.

They walked up the steps and onto the deck.

Mark cupped his hands around his face and peered in the first window.

"Nothing here," he called to Glen. "The place looks empty."

Glen walked to the front door and knocked loudly three times.

"We're out in the middle of nowhere and you *knock?*"

"It's polite."

"But no one lives here."

"It's still polite."

They waited.

Listened.

Nothing but silence.

Then he tried the doorknob. It was rusted and old, but it turned easily. Glen pushed and the door swung inwards.

Easy.

He aimed his flashlight into the house. He could make out the four rooms inside, each of them spanning out from the small entranceway. He took a slow step inside the house and turned the beam to the left. The room was empty, no furniture at all, just a thick layer of dust on the floor and large grey cobwebs sagging from the corners of the ceiling. There was no sign anyone had lived in there for quite a while.

Glen turned and aimed the beam through the door to the second room. He heard Mark's footsteps behind him.

"Nothing to see here," Glen said over his shoulder. "Anyway, it's the other farmhouse that's more important."

"Really?"

"Yeah, don't you remember?"

"Sure I do, but look at *this.*"

Glen swung around and followed Mark's beam into the third room, the one at the back of the farmhouse.

From where they were standing, they could see the red shoes swinging in the air in the middle of the room.

"*Fuck,*" Glen said as his beam met Mark's.

The cool breeze blew in from the front door and all around them. The shoes swung and turned slowly in the air. The dress flapped slightly. The body rotated just above the height of their heads, and in the very centre of the room.

The top of the doorway hid the rest of it from their sight.

Glen took a step forward. More of the body came into view. He saw more of the dress now.

Their flashlights played over the small body and slipped down to the old wooden chairs that were set out in the middle of the room. There were at least a dozen of them, surrounding the body and forming a haphazard circle.

But Glen found he couldn't take his eyes off the small, swinging body.

Mark was right behind him, he could hear his heavy breathing by his shoulder.

Glen could feel his own breathing accelerate.

Another step.

His heart was pounding in his chest, faster now.

Then another.

His eyes moved further up the body.

The hands came into view. The whole body was swinging around slowly, rotating in the night. The dress was old and worn, the fabric eaten away by moths. There were dark red blotches on the front and back, and large tear marks all through it. A small pouch hung from some wire around its neck. The pouch rested against the body's lower stomach.

Another step.

Glen saw the long, dark hair. It was in dirty knots and some of the red blotches were in the hair too. The face was pointing to the ground at a strange angle. It was hidden from view by the hair hanging down in front as it swung away from them.

And the noose was tied at the side of the neck.

Fuckin' hell.

The other end of the rope was tied to a beam that ran the length of the ceiling. They both stood by the doorway, looking up at the small body, waiting for it to rotate one full circle again so they could see the face.

"Christ," Mark said. "Who is it?"

"Fucked if I know."

"It's a *child.*"

"I know."

"How long has it been here?"

"Don't ask me. How the hell would I know?"

The body turned.

They readied their beams.

And the face twisted into view.

He couldn't see all of it, but he saw enough.

It didn't have a face.

No face at all.

Glen turned away quickly.

And smiled.

It was an old sack.

The face was an old, brown sack.

Glen laughed.

Mark looked at him, his eyes wide.

Glen turned and pointed at the hanging doll as he laughed some more.

"It's a doll," he managed between breaths. "It's a *fuckin' doll.*"

Mark's eyes moved from his face to the doll and back again. Almost as if he didn't believe him.

Glen leaned against the doorway, letting his laughter subside and waiting for his heart to stop beating so hard.

Mark walked into the centre of the room, pushing through the circle of wooden chairs, and looked up at the doll.

"Hey, you're *right,*" he agreed.

Of course I'm right.

Mark reached up and swung the doll around. "It's just a few sacks tied together in a dress."

"I know."

"Pretty creepy though," Mark added, pulling at one of the legs. "And so lifelike."

"Well, it's lifelike in the middle of the night with just flashlights," Glen walked over and looked up at the doll. "But it's probably not so scary during the day."

His flashlight focused on the small pouch resting on the stomach of the doll. It took him a few seconds to realise exactly what the three lumpy sacks were.

He pointed his beam at them. "I thought our doll was a girl. But it looks like she's a he."

The three sacks were fashioned to look like a large cock

and balls.

"Weird."

"I know," Glen grinned. "But *sooo* cool too."

He reached up and gave the doll a twist, spinning it fast.

"How's it hangin', girlie?" he smirked.

"These locals sure know how to scare the city guys." Mark turned away from the doll to survey the rest of the room.

"Yeah." Glen aimed his flashlight at the face of the doll, watching as it spun quickly in front of him. "The kids out here sure have a fucked sense of humour. Now we know why the door was unlocked. They wanted us to come in and see this. They wanted to scare us half to death."

"It worked."

"It sure did."

Glen turned from the doll and walked the circle of wooden chairs, moving the flashlight beam from one chair to another. They were all the same, just plain wooden chairs, all facing the doll in the centre of the circle. Finding nothing of value with the chairs, he shone his flashlight across the room, checking all the corners and the walls.

On the wall opposite the door was a crudely painted obelisk. It was painted in red paint that had run badly, but Glen could still make out what it was supposed to represent.

It's an obelisk, alright. Just like the one at Rocklyn.

"That's freaky," Mark said from behind him.

"I know. Too freaky."

"Maybe the barman was right."

He scanned the other three walls quickly, but there was nothing else in the room at all.

Nothing.

Not even dust or cobwebs like in the other rooms.

Mark was in the entranceway again, shining his flashlight into the fourth room.

"Anything?" Glen asked as he walked to him.

Mark shook his head. "Empty. Just like the others. Weird, huh?"

"Very."

Fuckin' locals.

Can't scare us with shit like that.

Even though the chills were rising along Glen's spine, he shook them off.

"Come on," Glen said as he ran past Mark and thumped him on the shoulder. "I'll race you to the next farmhouse."

"Deal."

They sprinted out the door and over the verandah.

The cool breeze blew stronger now, through the open farmhouse doorway and into the four rooms.

The doll twisted slowly in its noose.

THIRTEEN

They ran up the driveway to the second farmhouse, their flashlights cutting wildly through the night.

Mark was in the lead, but only just.

Let him win, Glen thought. *He has to win something, sometime.*

"I'm catching you," he yelled. "Here I *cooooommmmm-mmeeeeee!*"

His voice rose to a yell in the night, a primeval scream that felt so good.

He could hear Mark was doing the same.

Mark reached the verandah a few seconds before Glen. They came to a halt, the screams dying in their mouths, but still echoing around them.

"I won," Mark said between deep breaths.

"Yeah." Glen bent himself over to catch his breath. "You're right. You beat me. Fair and square."

"You're out of shape. Too much time on the internet."

"I'm okay."

"Too much time with your nose in that book."

"I'll survive."

"Too long with your hand on your cock."

Glen laughed. "Don't knock it until you've tried it."

Slowly, they caught their breath.

"Ready?" Mark asked.

"Yep."

They turned and shone their beams onto the second farmhouse.

It was a ruin, almost falling down. Part of the wooden-slated roof was missing, leaving a large hole over half the house. The planks of wood making up the walls were old and dirty. The paint was peeling and some of the wood had come away from the frames, falling to the ground or with one end just hanging in the air. There was no glass in the three windows facing them. The front door was wide open and swinging in the wind and a second door was resting on the ground, having fallen from its rusted hinges.

The verandah, or what was left of it, had collapsed at the far end, completely blocking off half the house with debris. But the area near the doorway was free of rubble. The iron sheeting on the fallen verandah was loose and flapping in the wind, held on only by a few remaining nails.

Weeds and grass had grown up the front steps and through the decking, almost covering it completely and hiding it from view. The brick chimney on the side of the house had fallen over backwards, spilling its bricks into the grass beyond, leaving a huge hole in the farmhouse wall.

"Shit," Mark muttered.

"I know. Not very inviting."

The farmhouse was more of a ruin than described in the book.

They climbed the rickety steps to the decking. Each weed-covered wooden board under their feet seemed to creak and moan and sag under their weight.

"But really cool, no matter what," Glen said.

"Oh, totally."

They walked up to the front door and pushed it aside.

Glen peered into the house, using the flashlight to scan what was left of the interior.

The house was just as badly weathered inside as it was outside. The walls were stripped almost bare, the drywall soggy and crumbling to the ground. Large gaping holes remained in the wooden frames of the walls, allowing Glen to see almost all the way through the house.

There was hardly any ceiling left.

The wind blew directly through the house, entering from where the chimney and fireplace used to be. It blew through to the other end of the house where the only wall consisted of two large sheets of metal, nailed together and sitting askew. There was enough space at the side of the metal sheets for Glen to see out into the night and across to the barn.

He moved the flashlight from left to right, through all the rooms in one quick arc.

And then in the middle of the house he saw it.

The old green door.

It was shut.

There it is!

Just like in the book.

Fuck me.

He nudged Mark and pointed at the door. But Mark was already looking in that direction.

The green door.

And the other room behind it.

Paydirt.

Bullseye.

Eu-fuckin-reka!

This is it.

Glen stepped further into the house.

He looked down at the floor to watch where he was stepping. With the help of the flashlight, he could see that some of the floorboards were missing. There were complete gaps in the floor where floorboards had rotted away, while other areas still had enough flooring to get him to the green door.

Careful, don't do anything stupid when you're this close...

Slowly, he wove his way across the floor, stepping cautiously across the gaps and testing each board he stepped on. Some groaned and some sagged, but they all held firm.

He moved from what was once the entranceway through to what he guessed was the lounge room. Each step took him closer to the door.

He turned to look over his shoulder. Mark was still standing in the entranceway, watching him.

"You coming?"

Mark shook his head. "No way. This is far enough for me."

"You sure?"

"Positive."

"Okay," Glen turned back to continue. "Your loss."

With a few more carefully placed steps, he was in front of the green door.

The fucking door.

Just like the book.

Just like I imagined.

Now I'm living it.

I'm here.

With the aid of the flashlight he could see the paint on the door was peeling, and the old yellow wallpaper that had once brightened the room now sagged and was slowly disintegrating.

Carefully, he reached out to the old rusted doorknob and grasped it. It felt cold and rough to his touch.

"Here goes everything," he whispered to himself.

He turned the knob and pulled.

The door was locked.

Fuck.

He pulled harder.

Fuck, no! It can't be.

He put the flashlight under his arm, grabbed the knob with both hands and pulled.

The door stayed locked.

He pulled. Then he pushed.

Fucking stupid. It can't be locked.

This house is a ruin. It should just fuckin' open.

No!

"Problem?" Mark called from behind him.

"The door's locked."

"*Huh?*"

"The door, it's locked. Damn it." Glen pushed harder, placed his foot on the side of the wall and pulled again.

Nothing.

FUCK!

Why would it be locked?

He couldn't work it out. He let go of the knob and stared at it.

Then it hit him.

Simple.
It's locked.
Well locked.
To stop people like me getting inside.
It made sense.
All this way… And I can't get in.
"What're you going to do?" Mark asked.
Glen thought fast.
There's still a chance.
"Quick," he said. "We can still take a photo."
"Okay." Mark put his flashlight on the floor and pulled the camera out of his jacket pocket.
Glen backed up to the door and crossed his arms in front of him, making sure his right profile was turned to the camera.
"Ready?"
"Fire away."
The flash blinded him for a second or two.
"Hang on," Mark said. "I'll take two more, just in case."
Two more flash explosions left Glen with spots before his eyes.
He blinked.
"So what's the plan?" Mark asked.
Glen rubbed his eyes and blinked again. Slowly, he began to walk back across the floorboards the way he had come.
Retrace your steps and you'll be fine.
He blinked again, the flashes still in front of him.
"The windows," Glen said as he took a tentative step. On the way back, the floorboards all looked different in the flashlight beam.
"Huh?"
"Outside." He blinked some more. "There's two windows in the room behind the green door. If we go outside, we can still look in through the windows."
Another step.
Another blink.
"Good thinking," Mark said. "I'd forgotten about the

windows."

"Well, that's why I'm here." Glen took a large step between missing floorboards, trying to blink the flashes away. "Read the book as many times as I have and you'll remember things like that."

Almost there.

Glen was only a few steps from the entranceway. His eyesight was almost clear again.

"Hey!" Mark called.

Glen looked up at him.

The flash exploded in his face.

Glen stepped backwards, put his foot down.

It kept going.

The white in front of his eyes blinded him.

He couldn't see.

He reached out for something.

Anything.

But there was nothing to grab onto.

And he fell.

Hard.

His back slammed through the floor, breaking through the weathered floorboards, wood cracking and splitting and digging deep into his spine. He cannoned into the ground underneath the house. His head hit hard, jarring his brain and sending small stars across the white flash in front of his eyes.

The breath slammed out of him and pain shot down his back as his body came to rest.

This can't be happening, he thought as his world went dark.

FOURTEEN

He saw the hands first, and then the head and shoulders.

"Glen?"

The voice came through to him.

He blinked his eyes a couple times more.

"Can you hear me?"

Mark.

He was reaching down towards him.

What the fuck happened?

For a moment, Glen couldn't remember.

The flash.

Falling.

Then he remembered it all.

"You okay? I'm *sooo* sorry."

Stupid fuck, taking a picture of me so close. That flash went off right in my face. What did he think would happen?

Glen lifted his hands and ran them through his hair. He could feel the dust, dirt and cobwebs all over his body. He tried to wipe it all off, but it stuck firm.

"Yuck," he muttered as he sat up slowly. "What is all this shit?"

"Don't ask." Mark peered down at him from his squatting position and tried to help wipe some of the cobwebs off his friend's shoulders.

"Don't worry, I *know* what it is. I'm *laying* in it."

Mark smiled, but it slipped from his face. "Sorry."

"What the *fuck* were you thinking?"

"I wasn't."

"I know. I can tell. It's pretty fucking obvious from down here." Glen reached up and Mark took his hands and pulled.

Slowly, Glen stood up, shaking broken floorboards and clumps of dirt and weeds and spiders from his body, the pain of the fall ebbing slowly away.

"I just wanted to take a photo of you walking across the floorboards. You know, to show everyone when we get back."

"Yeah, well, it was just *stupid.*"

"I know."

"The flash blinded me."

"I know."

"I couldn't see where I was going."

"Sorry, Glen. I really am. Truly."

Glen let go of his hands and wiped more of the grime from his body.

"Doesn't matter," he muttered. "I'm okay. I *think.* Nothing's broken, from what I can *tell.*"

He turned around and looked where he'd fallen. His body had created a large hole in the floorboards, cutting off access to the green door.

Unless you're willing to climb down there to get across to it, *he thought. Not that there's much point. It's locked anyway.*

If only I had a crowbar or something heavy...

There's a tyre iron in the back of the Jeep.

Great. Too far to go back for it.

"My flashlight?" he asked.

"I'll get it." Mark knelt by the hole in the floor and reached back into the darkness.

I should push the fucker in and see how much he *likes it.*

After a few seconds of searching, Mark lifted the flashlight and handed it to Glen.

"I saw it fall in there with you."

Glen tried the switch.

The flashlight was dead.

"Shit."

He shook the flashlight and could hear the pieces of broken globe rattling inside.

"Fuck."

Mark's face twitched with a broken smile. "Sorry again."

Glen glared at him. *"Again."*

He threw the flashlight back into the hole and heard it clatter for a few seconds before it came to rest. He reached out and snatched Mark's from his hand.

"Mind if I use *yours?"* He turned and walked out the door without waiting for Mark's reply.

He walked down the steps and marched across the front of the farmhouse, still brushing the cobwebs from his hair.

Better not be any fucking spiders crawling over me...

He looked over towards the barn. He didn't turn back and didn't look to see if Mark was following.

I don't care.

The asshole can rot in hell for all I care.

Fuck him and his stupid fucking camera.

He turned the corner of the farmhouse, walked down the slight decline and past the metal sheets that served as a wall. Further down the side of the farmhouse the old wooden wall was intact. He shone the flashlight along the wall until he zeroed in on the window.

Yes.

Jackpot.

Exactly where it should be.

With the slope of the ground, the windowsill was at chest height. He stopped and shone the light inside the window. Standing on his toes, he used his other hand to cup around his eyes as he stared inside.

Nothing.

Darkness.

Just blackness.

It took a second, but then he realized the flashlight beam wasn't penetrating past the glass in the window. He looked closely at the glass.

Damn it. Damn it to hell.

The window had been painted. Nothing would get past the black paint that had been smeared on the inside of the glass. There was no way he could see anything through it.

Fuck.

Why would this window have glass when none of the front windows do? And why paint the glass black?

Unless they have something to hide.

Just like the locked green door.

They have something to hide.

Oh fuckin' yeah!

They won't beat me like this.

I won't let them.

One last chance.

Turning quickly, he walked further down the decline to the back of the house. He turned the corner and shone the flashlight along the wall.

There.

My last chance.

He walked to the window at the back of the house. But the slope of the ground was too steep. The windowsill was almost three feet above his head.

Shit it to buggery.

He shone the flashlight at the window. The beam penetrated. He could see two large cardboard boxes pushed up against the lower half of the window. He raised the beam higher. It slipped from the box and appeared on the ceiling.

On the ceiling. The ceiling inside the room.

A-grade fuckin' legend.

There was no black paint smeared on this window. He'd be able to see inside if only he could get up there.

I just have to get up there. Somehow.

"Find anything?"

Glen turned to see Mark leaning on the side of the house, his arms crossed in front of him. Glen ignored him and started searching around the back of the house.

There's got to be something here. Somewhere.

"What are you looking for?"

Ignore him and maybe he'll go away.

"Can I help?"

It might take a while, but he'll go. Eventually.

"I said, can I *help?*"

"You've helped enough already, thank you."

There was nothing of use at the back of the farmhouse. No ladder or box or anything he could use to stand on. The whole area was clean.

I've got to get a look inside that window.

"Please?" Mark asked.

Fuck, whining like a girl now.

He turned to look at his friend. He couldn't read the expression on his face. He didn't care.

Glen started to say something, but over Mark's shoulder he saw what he needed.

The barn.

There has to be something in there I can use.

A ladder or table or something.

He smiled and charged at Mark.

Mark put up his hands to fend him away.

Glen grabbed him by the shoulders and pushed him against the side of the farmhouse. His eyes bored cruelly into Mark's.

"Stay here," he whispered.

"Huh?"

"Stay right here. Don't *move.* Don't go *anywhere.* Don't do *anything!* Just stay here until I get back."

"Where are you going?"

"To the barn."

"By *yourself?*"

"Yes."

"Can't I come with you?"

"No."

"I want to help."

"You will, by standing here and doing nothing."

"But, *please?*"

There he goes again.

"It'll be dark here," Mark continued, his eyes sliding to the ground and his forehead creasing.

Scared of the dark like some stupid little kid.

"Should've thought of that *before* you broke my flashlight."

Glen turned and marched towards the barn.

"If it gets too dark, just take some photos!" Glen smiled as he yelled over his shoulder. "The flashes are so bright, you'll be amazed!"

Mark didn't reply.

"Fucking pussy," Glen muttered as the flashlight shone in front of him, lighting his path to the barn.

FIFTEEN

Every step he took brought him closer to the barn and further away from Mark.

Good.

Let him wait and think about what he did.

Blinding me with the flash like that.

I could've broken something when I fell.

I could've been stuck there.

Idiot.

He studied the barn as he walked closer towards it. His flashlight beam didn't reach far enough in the night, but he could make out the details by the moonlight. At first he thought the barn was new, or constructed more recently than the farmhouses. But as he got closer, he realized the barn was probably just as old as the farmhouses. It had just survived the elements much better, and there was no sign of the dilapidation that was present in the farmhouses.

Some things survive better than others.

Like Mark and me.

Some people survive better than others.

He kept an ear out for Mark, just in case he called out or panicked and came running after him.

Scared of a little darkness…

Glen just hoped there was something in the barn he could stand on to look inside the window of the farmhouse.

There has to be.

Please?

It all comes down to this…

He walked up the slight incline and stopped out the

front of the barn. It had two large sliding doors, painted in red with a white sash running diagonally across them.

He stepped closer and reached out for the handle on one of the large barn doors.

It better not be locked…

He turned the handle and pulled. The door slid open slowly, squealing along its rusty old tracks. Glen turned to look behind him, back towards the farmhouse, as the squeal of the door echoed in the night.

He couldn't see anything.

Or anyone.

You're missing all the fun, man.

Serves you right.

Glen turned back and pointed his flashlight inside the barn. He spotted the large bales of hay first. There were dozens of them, lined up along the far wall, some stacked three high. He looked for any farm equipment, but he couldn't see any. In the far corner was a workbench. Nailed to the wall above the bench was a shadow-board, with the outline of a variety of tools drawn onto it. But the tools were missing.

No tools, but maybe I could use the workbench?

He stepped inside the barn and walked over towards the workbench.

As he got closer, his heart sank.

The bench was large and made of heavy wood. There was no way he could drag it all the way back to the farmhouse.

Damn it.

Gotta be a ladder here, or something.

He stood in the middle of the barn, sweeping his flashlight from side to side. The beam bounced from the workbench to the bales of hay, across the barn walls and down the sides. And then his eyes spotted it.

Yes.

Success.

The flashlight shone on an old metal drum, sitting in a far corner. It was black and covered in cobwebs and dinted in a few places, but Glen didn't care. It stood about three feet tall.

That's exactly what I need.

He walked over and squatted by it, rubbing some of the years of grime off its sides with his hands.

Perfect.

Let's just hope it's empty.

He stood and grabbed the lid of the drum, trying to prise it open to see what was inside. But the lid was welded tightly shut. Glen looked around for a crowbar, but he couldn't see one. There was no way he could pry open the lid with just his bare hands. Instead, he grabbed the drum by the far rim. Making sure his feet wouldn't slip on the hay-strewn floor, he pulled at the drum, trying to tip it over.

At first, the drum didn't move. It felt as if it were stuck solid to the ground. He pulled again, harder this time.

Come on. Do this for me.

Slowly, the drum moved. Another pull. Then another. The drum began to tip.

It doesn't feel all that heavy. Maybe it's empty.

Another pull.

Gravity finally took over and the drum toppled on its side, slamming into the ground with a dull metallic thud.

Easy.

So fuckin' easy.

He swivelled the drum around slightly so it faced the open barn door, and kicked at it with the heel of his shoe.

It rolled towards the door, a strange sound coming from inside. Something was loose in the drum, rolling around and hitting against the sides. Glen pushed at it again and the sound repeated.

What is *that noise?*

What's in there?

Glen ran his flashlight beam up and down the rolling drum. The drum was welded shut at both ends. No writing. No label. Nothing to give any clue as to its contents.

No time to find out anyway.

He kicked the drum through the barn door and out into the night.

Maybe we could roll the drum back to the Jeep. Or leave it here and come and get it once we've fixed the tyres. We could take it home and check out what's inside.

Maybe it's something cool.

A body?

Jewellery?

Cash?

Or not.

But he was sure the noise sounded metallic.

Maybe it's just large clumps of sand or rust.

Maybe it's nothing.

He kicked the drum down the short slope outside the barn. He kept his flashlight on it as it rolled in front of him, bouncing and thudding into the night.

Glen looked up at the farmhouse for any sign of Mark, but he couldn't see him.

Hope he's scared.

Hope he's shitting himself.

He kicked at the drum.

It rolled a few feet further.

The noise coming from the drum sounded louder now in the night.

The cool air blew around him as he looked skyward to the half-moon.

Gotta know what's in that room.

Maybe we can break the window and climb in.

Yeah, that'd be something.

Check it out and then get inside.

Take some photos as proof.

Cooool.

It was quick and he only caught it out of the corner of his eye. He was looking down at the drum when it happened. He stopped in his tracks and turned his head towards the farmhouse. The noise from the drum continued for a few seconds until it came to rest a few feet in front of him.

Glen focused his eyes and waited.

Maybe I'm imagining things.

But I'm sure I saw it.

And then it happened again.

He saw a flash light up the night at the back of the farmhouse. Then another.

He grinned.

He must be scared.

Glen kicked the drum out in front of him once more.

Serves him right.

Maybe the sound of the drum echoing in the night has got him scared.

Another flash.

What a fucking pussy.

He better not run out of film…

Glen kicked the drum once more, harder this time. It bounced away in front of him, rolling faster towards the farmhouse. The rattling noise was louder now.

He grinned.

Another flash, then another straight after it.

Glen shook his head.

Enough.

I can't scare him to death.

Even though he deserves it.

He called out to Mark. "It's just *me!* Hang on, I'm almost there!"

No reply.

Still sulking probably.

There were no more flashes.

Glen kicked the drum and walked closer.

He's probably embarrassed now.

I know he got scared.

And he knows I know.

Glen bent down and pushed the drum the last twenty feet up the small incline to the back of the farmhouse. The drum was wet and slippery now, having rolled through the dew on the long grass, and it suddenly felt heavier in his hands.

Not as easy as I first thought.

But he struggled with it.

I won't be beaten now…

He rolled it up to the back wall, right under the window. Exactly where he wanted it.

Almost there.

"No, no!" he called as he straightened himself and used his leg to brace the drum against the back wall. "I'll do it all myself. No need to help, man."

He was out of breath. It was steaming around him. A trickle of sweat ran down his forehead.

No answer.

"Mark?" he called as he swung the flashlight into the night, the beam bouncing off the trees around him.

No answer.

Sulking little shit.

"I *know* you're here. I saw the flashes!"

Glen traced the flashlight beam across the trees and over the back of the farmhouse.

"Come *on,* Mark. Quit this. It *isn't* funny. I need your help with this drum. We'll be able to see in the window now."

No answer.

"Come *oooon!*"

No answer.

Fine.

Suit yourself.

Glen turned and bent down by the drum.

Fuckin' stupid fucker. Let him miss all the fun.

See if I care.

Glen dug his fingers underneath the drum and slowly tilted it back onto its base. It clunked into position right under the window.

Perfect.

They can't stop me.

No one can.

This is it.

The drum sat on a slight angle; it leaned forward, due to the slope of the ground, and away from the wall of the house. Glen hoped the ground was level enough to let him scramble on top of the drum and look inside the window without the drum tipping over.

One way to find out.

He grabbed the top of the drum with both hands and readied to pull himself up onto it.

"Don't."

He heard the voice behind him. It shocked him and he jumped. It sounded like a whisper. He let go of the drum and turned around, the flashlight beam cutting through the trees and all around him.

No one there.

No one.

He tilted his head, listening for any sound. Any movement.

He held his breath.

Nothing.

"Hello?" he whispered back.

No answer.

A chill cut through his spine.

He shook it off and turned back to the drum.

Don't go crazy on me now.

Keep it together.

Almost there.

"DON'T!"

He swung around again, flashlight beam bouncing from tree to tree.

He heard her before he saw her.

The bushes parted directly in front of him as she stepped into the clearing. She stopped walking and stood no more than twenty feet away from him.

He looked at her as she stood there.

She was naked.

Her body gleamed with sweat. His flashlight beam shone off her skin.

What the...?

He could see her breasts rise and fall as she took deep breaths, her nipples erect in the cool night air.

His eyes dropped to the diamond in her bellybutton. It gleamed. The sweat streaked her sides and stomach, as if she too had been covered in a fine layer of dust like the drum.

Glen realized then he was holding his breath, his

mouth wide open in amazement.

It can't be her!

His eyes dropped lower to the shaved mound between her legs. It was wet and slick too, and ever-so inviting.

Glen's cock began to pulse.

Jesus H. Fuckin' Christ!

And then his eyes dropped lower.

To the shovel she was clutching in her right hand.

His eyes darted back to her face.

She was staring at him.

He smiled at her.

She didn't smile back.

She stood there for what seemed like an eternity. Glen waited for her to say something, or to move. But she didn't. She stared back at him, getting her breathing under control.

He waited in the quiet night.

He wasn't going anywhere in a hurry.

My God. I'm not going anywhere.

She's beautiful.

A-grade fuckin' beautiful.

Eventually her breathing returned to normal and her breasts stopped rising and falling so quickly.

She seemed so tall and strong. Her hair was in two shoulder-length braids, one down each side of her face.

He studied her face, trying to read her emotions, but she was a blank canvas. She just stared at him.

"*Zoe?*" he asked as he took a step closer to her. "Is that really you?"

Of course it is.

It can't be.

Look at her.

But it can't be her. It's not possible!

Just like in the book.

No, better. She's even better than she was in the book.

She's gorgeous.

And she's mine.

All mine.

Legend time!

He took another step towards her. Her face tilted, but she didn't move.

"My name's Glen," he called to her as he moved closer still.

Easy.

Don't frighten her.

"You don't know what an honour it is to meet you."

It sounded like a stupid thing to say, but he wanted to keep her at ease and not frighten her off. He needed to make her understand he only wanted to talk to her.

Just one picture.

Please, just one picture, you and me.

One picture, one kiss, one fuck.

They've got to believe me now.

She moved the shovel from her right hand to her left. She said nothing.

They stared at each other in the cool night.

They stared for a long time.

This isn't going well.

Gotta do something.

Gotta get a picture.

Now.

"Mark!" he shouted over his shoulder.

No answer.

"Hey, pal. Where *are* you? You gotta get here quick!"

Come on, answer.

"*Mark!* Get here *now!*"

"No, you get *here!*" Mark called from somewhere behind him.

Yes, success.

Come out, you coward.

She took a step forward.

He saw her.

And she knew he saw her.

He held his ground.

"No way, man. Get out here now. She's *here!*"

"*What?*"

"*Zoe's* here! I can see her. She's right in front of me!"

There was a pause.

No one moved.

Where the fuck is he?

"That's *bullshit!*"

"Huh?" Glen called over his shoulder, tilting his head and trying to pinpoint Mark's position.

"I said that's *bullshit!*"

"No, no it's *not!* She's here, I'm telling ya."

"It *can't* be her."

"Why?"

"Because she's *here!*"

Huh?

What the...?

Glen turned instinctively. The flashlight traced from the girl, across the trees, and further along, searching for Mark.

He didn't find him.

He found her.

Further down the farmhouse, she was standing just outside the bushes and she was staring straight at him.

Fuck me to buggery.

Her hair was in a ponytail. She was naked. Her nipples were erect. Diamond in her bellybutton. A wet and slick ever-so-inviting pussy.

She held an axe in her hand.

What the fuck?

His flashlight zipped back across the night, zeroing in on the girl with the braids. She was standing still, but much closer to him now. He was sure of it.

Much closer.

"What the *fuck's* going on here?" Glen yelled into the night, his beam darting back to the girl with the axe.

No answer.

"Mark!" he yelled again.

No answer.

His beam caught the movement in the trees between the two girls. He held the flashlight as steady as he could, his breathing hard, his heart pounding.

She stepped out into the clearing.

Naked.

Bellybutton diamond.

Shaved.

Her hair was in a bun and she looked just like the others. Except she had a long dark swirl of a tattoo stretching from her neck, across her right shoulder and down her arm. It stopped at her right wrist. She carried nothing in her hands. She turned, head tilting, to stare at Glen.

This is unreal.

This can't be happening.

He swung the flashlight back to the girl with the braids.

She was beside him now.

Right next to him.

Smiling at him.

Glen jumped, the flashlight tumbling from his grip.

Her smiling face was burned into his mind as the night went dark.

Fuck!

How did she get next to me?

I didn't hear her.

FUCK!

He fell to his knees, his hands frantically searching for the flashlight as it rolled down the slope and away from him.

He heard them whispering.

Then he heard a slight giggle.

He looked up at the half-moon and prayed for some light. But only the cool night breeze blew around him.

He blinked his eyes.

All he could see was her smiling face, burned into his mind.

He heard their footsteps through the grass.

Slow.

Methodical.

"Help," he whispered.

But all was silent.

And the darkness engulfed him.

UNCOVERED

SIXTEEN

It was dark.

Silent.

Darker and more quiet than he had ever known.

And he cursed himself for ever starting out on this journey.

How could I have been so stupid?

So wrapped up in my own fuckin' self-importance.

I should've listened.

But I wanted to go to the edge...

He tried to laugh, but couldn't.

To the fuckin' edge...

He breathed heavily through his nose—it was the only proof he had that he was still alive.

He had a soft dark blindfold cutting across his nose and eyes and tied at the back of his head. He also had a hood covering his whole head, which she had put over him and tied off around his throat, just above the dog collar she had placed there earlier. He could see nothing through the material.

Nothing.

The hood was hot and smelt of stagnant breath and air. And all was dark.

His ears were blocked with earplugs, pushed all the way in so he couldn't hear anything other than his own breathing and thoughts.

And his mouth and jaw were held open by a tight ball of wadding which made it impossible for him to close them. The cloth that had been shoved into his mouth was dipped in vinegar, making him want to vomit, but he controlled himself—he had to. He didn't want to choke and die. If the wadding fell any further back into his mouth he could choke on it, and if vomit erupted from his stomach, it had nowhere to go.

His arms were spread above him, tied tightly by the wrists, and his legs were splayed below him, tied by the ankles. He was tilted at a slight angle, the middle of his back resting on cold hard wood and his head leaning on a small soft cushion. He was naked and cold.

And there was nothing he could do about it.

All he could see in his mind's eye was her face.

Her smiling face.

Right next to me.

He could see nothing else.

Her smiling face.

That smiling face.

The face of my dreams.

He had no idea how long he had been standing, tied the way he was now.

Hours? Minutes? Days?

Time meant nothing to him anymore.

Only survival.

His legs were beginning to numb and his arms ached. His body was sagging badly but there was little he could do about it. His arms and legs hurt too much when he moved them.

The muscle cramps spread up his legs and back again. They arched through his whole body, slicing through his shoulders and ramming into his brain. He bit down hard on the wadding in his mouth, squirting more vinegar down the back of his throat. He willed himself not to be sick, and for the cramps to stop.

Eventually, they did.

He was breathing hard through his nose again as he tried to get himself under control.

Come on, you can do it.

He felt a breeze gently caress his body. His eyes moved from side to side, trying to see, even though he knew he couldn't. The silence was total, apart from his rushing heartbeat.

He could feel the cold settle on him.

Should've run, he thought as he stood there, tied on the wooden X that scratched incessantly at his skin.

Didn't have the time.

I couldn't.

She was there.

I couldn't run from her.

Her?

Them!

He tried to move his arms and legs, tried to see if he had any flexibility in his bindings, he didn't.

He moved his head from side to side, as if looking for her.

Them.

But the blindfolds gave nothing away and the ear-plugs made sure the silence was total.

Only his thoughts accompanied him.

He waited for a long time, or so it seemed to him. He stood there tied, leaning back on the X, waiting for their next move.

Not my fault, anyway.

It was his.

All Mark's fault.

Asshole.

Why couldn't he come out when I called him?

Where the fuck is he anyway?

Is he hanging from an X like I am? Is he tied and bound and gagged? Or is he still hiding under the farmhouse like some scared little shit?

Fucking useless scared stupid cunt.

Man, if you were here now I'd—

But he didn't get time to finish his thought.

A hand touched his groin.

Glen's mind froze and his breathing stopped.

The hand was soft and warm. It began massaging his limp cock.

Huh?

Despite the situation, the hand felt so good on him, so warm.

He began to grow.

Within seconds his cock was hard and pulsing. He could feel her pulling on the cock-ring, playing with it.

Yeah. That's it, tease me you sexy bitch.

Glen smiled.

This could be okay after all…

Then he felt her mouth around him, hot and wet.

Oh fuck, yeah.

So good.

She wants me.

Her hand continued to massage his balls as her lips engulfed him and sucked deeply.

Glen tried to relax on the X, but it was difficult to do so.

She's there.

Sucking me off.

Sucking my cock.

A-grade fuckin' legend.

YES!

His breathing quickened and his mind painted a picture of what she was doing to him. After a few minutes he began to reach climax. His body tensed and readied for the moment.

And then her mouth left him.

Huh?

Fuck, no!

He was hard and ready, but she was gone. His cock was wet and pulsing, and left to the cold night air. His balls ached deeply.

No, bitch. I'm almost there!

Come back!

Then the hands rubbed against his chest and down his arms.

Yes! Oh, YES!

He could feel them all around him. Hands on his legs and arms and chest.

They're all here.

All of them!

Hands on his balls and around his cock. Running

through his hair and pinching his nipples.

How many?

There could be dozens.

Dozens of them.

They're all here, watching me.

Wanting to fuck me.

He smiled.

They want me.

Me!

The hands got heavier. They held harder. Tighter.

Hey.

He tried to move. He couldn't.

HEY!

And then he felt the cold steel against his cock.

His body tensed.

The blade slid up his shaft.

His erection quickly subsided.

She pumped him some more. Licking his tip and taking him deep within her mouth. He started to grow hard again.

No.

He couldn't stop it. It felt so good.

No!

She was massaging him harder and faster. His cock was pulsing, the orgasm ready to explode. Her teeth pulled on the cock-ring, her tongue danced up and down his shaft, sucking hard and deep, licking his tip and sucking at the pre-cum that dripped there.

He twisted his head from side to side.

So good.

So nice.

This is all I ever wanted.

All I ever needed.

I've made it.

Man, I'm going to die!

It's soooo cool. Just think about it. My life is in her hands.

This is serious shit. I mean it, I'm going to die.

But what a way to go!

He couldn't hold back any longer. Her tongue was

dancing on his tip, her hand pumping his shaft, squeezing his balls.

The other hands held him down, held him firm. He could picture them all around him, naked and wet and horny and holding him down. Their juices dripping from their shaved pussies, so wet and soft and oh-so-fuckable. Licking each other's nipples and kissing their bellybuttons, their tongues slipping down to the juices leaking from between their legs. Tongues lapping it all up, drinking it down, dancing across hard, pulsing clits and licking deeper and deeper inside.

He started to cum.

He could feel it and so could she.

She pulled her mouth away.

He exploded.

And then the pain sliced through him.

The skin around the base of his cock split. He felt the blade slash right through, he felt the burning sensation as it cut across in one quick movement. The pain rolled down his groin and through the rest of his body.

He could feel the cum shooting into the darkness, the warm wetness on his thighs and legs.

So much cum.

He could feel it spraying everywhere.

Ecstasy turned to agony and his moan of pleasure turned to a scream of terror.

He bit down hard on the wadding in his mouth, squirting vinegar down his throat and making him want to gag.

His balls pulsed uncontrollably. The stump where his cock had been pumped semen and blood into the darkness and down his legs.

He tried to move his arms and legs. He wanted to grab them, hit out at them, kick them. His back arched off the X, trying to squirm out of their grip.

He needed to scream. Tried to.

Anything to stop the pain.

But his bindings were too tight.

And his energy was quickly failing him.

The orgasm ended.

The blood kept flowing.

And the pain continued.

One by one, the hands left him and the coldness returned.

All was still.

The wetness continued to spread down his legs.

Her smiling face burnt into his mind.

He would never forget her smile.

Ever.

A-grade fuckin' legend.

And legends never die.

...AND OTHER STORIES

BROKEN COOKIE

Mummy is pretty. But she won't eat. She's sick. Real sick.

Like I took her tea and food and she just lays there and won't eat like she's not hungry or doesn't want it. It goes cold and yucky and I have to throw it away.

Then I make some more but she doesn't move and she won't talk to me like she used to when I did something good or nice. Thank you Jane she'd say and pat me on the head and smile and say nice things.

My mummy is pretty.

I place the new cup of tea by the bed and make noise but she won't look.

That smell is more bad now, yucky smell like in the bathroom. I climb into the bed with her and show her the cookies so she can eat but she won't. She has dark spots all over her and she needs to eat the cookies. There's no food left in the cupboard.

Mummy is pretty but her hair is all messed.

I say shower but she won't move and I can't help. She's real sick like I never seen before. She needs to eat. I'm hungry but I can't eat 'cause she has to eat what's left to make her big and strong again.

I go and sit at mummy's table and comb my hair and it's messed too. I talk to her and try to be friends but she won't talk back is how sick she is. So I talk and pretend she answers and says yes Jane no Jane I think so too Jane and we laugh and make fun like we used to before the yelling.

Mummy was pretty then too.

I don't like the yelling.

I stare at the mirror and think of the yelling and why

I didn't mean to spill the juice 'cause it just slipped and it fell and spilled and I didn't mean it. Daddy started the yelling and he got up from the kitchen table and yelled loud and called me a stupid fucking dumb kid and he hit the table with his fist and ran at me.

Mummy yelled too and he yelled again and they yelled at each other.

He said the c-word I'm not allowed to say and made Mummy cry.

I don't like the yelling.

I tried to hide under the table but daddy was too fast and grabbed my leg and his fingers dug in hard and it hurt a whole lot. I yelled and screamed and tried to kick him away. He pulled me out and dragged me towards the door and mummy went to stop him and he yelled back some more.

Mummy hit him with one of the pots on the stove and she hit him hard. He dropped me and I fell to the ground and it hurt and he yelled more at mummy.

He hit her on her pretty face. Then he hit her again. His fist made her face red and blotchy. Mummy stopped yelling a second and just stared at him. I think she started to cry again.

I don't like it when mummy cries.

I jumped up and down screaming but he threw me against the wall and pushed mummy out into the hall and down to their bedroom. He slammed the door hard and the pictures on the wall shook and two fell and broke on the ground. I could hear yelling from the bedroom and I climbed back under the table and sat there in the spilled juice and closed my eyes hard and put by fingers in my ears and tried not to breathe.

I stayed like that forever and only opened my eyes once daddy ran through the kitchen and out the back door and didn't say bye to me. He was yelling real loud and I was scared again.

I waited until the sun came back up and then went and locked all the doors and shut all the blinds like mummy said to do if anytime she or daddy were out so bad people wouldn't get in.

I wiped up the juice and got out of my sticky clothes and made some food and waited for mummy to come for breakfast but she didn't so I went up the hallway and she was in bed and she was already sick.

And she's still sick. Mummy's still asleep.

Daddy didn't hurt me this time.

Sometimes he would make me take off my clothes when mummy wasn't there and we were all alone. He would hurt me down there where I'm not allowed to say. But he didn't hurt me this time.

He hasn't come back since then.

Three sleeps ago people knocked on the front door and pressed the bell. But mummy said never answer the door to strangers because they could be bad people. They didn't sound like daddy but they were calling for daddy and mummy so I guess they weren't bad people. But I was too scared to let them in 'cause mummy said not to and she always wanted to look good for visitors and right now she's too sick to see them and there's no food left for them to eat.

I don't know what I'll do when the food runs out.

I leave mummy to sleep some more and go back into the kitchen and I look through the cupboards again but there's nothing left I know. I open up the tins and look in the plastic baskets but there's nothing in any of them and there's only a broken cookie left in the cookie jar.

I'm hungry and want to eat it but I know mummy is sick and should eat it but she hasn't eaten anything so I guess I can eat it. I put it in my mouth and chew but it's soft and old and gooey and it's not nice and I spit it out.

I walk over to the kitchen window and pull the curtain back and the bright comes in and hurts my eyes so I close it again and sit on the stool and wait for mummy to call for more tea.

I wait and think about daddy and his yelling and his hurting and I wonder why he hasn't come back to see if mummy is okay. Why hasn't he been to see mummy? He could go get us some more food and we could all eat and mummy could get better and look pretty again.

I walk to the back door and listen and make sure no bad people are there and I unlock it and open it and look out at daddy. He's sitting on the back steps and his head is hanging down and he looks sorry and sad. I go up to him and sit next to him and smile but he doesn't smile back.

His tea is cold too and he hasn't touched his cookies. I talk to him but he's still mad and won't talk back and so I pretend he's talking back and laughing and playing games with me.

His shirt is all red and it looks like he's been painting but he's got some big sores and cuts on his wrists and body and he needs a shower too or something to make the smell go away. I tell him to eat the cookies but he still doesn't answer so I tell him mummy's real sick and we need more food to get her well but I guess he's asleep and can't hear me.

But he's not yelling anymore and he doesn't want to hurt me so that's good. I leave him and walk back into the house and keep the door open just in case he wants to come in and help me and mummy.

I sit on the stool and look out the back door at daddy and he must be asleep 'cause he doesn't move much only his hair moves in the wind and his shirt moves kinda too. The wind blows the smell into the house and I don't like the smell so I close the door a bit and then start to make mummy some more tea. I wish there was some food that I could give her but there isn't and I feel bad that I ate the broken cookie and spat it out and didn't give it to her 'cause she needs it.

When the kettle sings I make the tea real careful and try not to spill any. I don't want daddy getting mad again and I want to show him how I wiped up the juice after he left but he hasn't been inside so I haven't shown him yet. But the floor is dry now and there's no juice on the floor or in the cupboards.

I watch the cup as I slowly walk down the hall but a big sudden noise frightens me and I jump and spill the tea on the carpet and I know daddy will be mad and I try to stop it from spilling but the whole cup flips and falls and the tea spills as it hits the floor. I kneel down and wipe it up with my hands but it burns me as I try to push it back in the cup 'cause daddy is coming inside and he will see it and yell again and it will start again and I'll get hurt and so will mummy and she's sick and needs to get well.

The banging gets louder and I look down the hall waiting for daddy to come in but the noise isn't coming from there but from the front door. The bell is being pushed and there is knocking and people calling daddy and mummy and it sounds like there's a lot of them. One man is yelling that he is a policeman but he's yelling real loud and a policeman wouldn't yell like daddy. I know it's a trick and that they are bad people and mummy says to keep away from bad people.

I look at their shadows on the glass in the front door and I get scared when they start hitting the door and it begins to move and break. I run back to the kitchen and call to daddy but he's still sitting on the back steps and won't move to help me. I want things to stay quiet, they can't wake mummy 'cause she's sick and she needs her rest.

I call to daddy again but he won't answer and there's a big black bird standing on his shoulder pecking at one of daddy's eyes. Stuff is oozing down his cheek and why won't he stop the bird and make it go away? The bird pulls at daddy's eye with his beak but it won't come out, it just moves around a lot. Make it go away, daddy. Bad people are here and I don't have time to shoo it away.

The noise and yelling gets louder and I run back down the hall and I can see the door will be open soon if they keep hitting it like that. I run into mummy's room and try to be real quiet as I open her wardrobe door. I tell her everything is alright and not to worry but she's still asleep.

She hasn't touched the cookies or the last cup of tea I brought her.

I climb inside the cupboard and hide.

Dark and nice. Safe.

The noise is softer now but I can still hear the yelling

and if they yell daddy will yell and the fighting will start again.

I don't want that to happen.

Mummy's real sick and it can't happen.

I close my eyes tight and put my fingers in my ears and try not to breathe.

I concentrate and I can feel the warmth inside me grow and I can see them in my head now, inside the doorway, walking slowly down the hall.

I'll stop them yelling and fighting.

I'll make them not do it again.

I'll make them real sick.

Just like mummy and daddy.

SCHISM

The phone is dead.
It can't be.
I hang it up.
Still nothing.
The light flickers above me as I stare out into the darkness. The damp aroma of the phone booth fills my nostrils. My stomach turns over and I don't know whether I'm starving or going to be sick. The grimy phone booth windows are smudged with handprints, dirt and grime.

A mosquito buzzes across the glass, as desperate for escape as I am.

Its buzzing fills my ears.

I pick up the receiver once more.

Listen.

Nothing!

It can't be dead!

I shuffle around in the enclosed space, my eyes searching the darkness for any sudden movement. Any sign out of the ordinary.

Any sign of…

Who? What?

I can't remember.

Like the phone call I can't make, I can't remember who or what I'm running from. I can't remember who I'm trying to call.

It's dark and cold and I rub my arms, trying to warm them in the night.

How did I get here?

I can't even remember that.

I hang up the phone once more, turn around and face

the doors of the phone booth. I stare out into the night. My eyes searching the darkness.

The light above me flickers loudly.

The mosquito buzzes.

I search the pockets of my shorts once more.

Still empty.

Nothing.

How could I leave home dressed in only my shorts?

I can't remember.

I have no idea.

The light flickers one last time and then doesn't come back on. The darkness surrounds me and the temperature in the phone booth seems to suddenly drop. I'm sure I can see the breath in the half-moonlight...although I can't be sure.

The mosquito still buzzes.

I have to get out!

There's no other option. I don't want to. I know going out there into the night is even worse than staying here. But I don't know why that is.

Either way, I have to leave!

I pull open the door. It clunks loudly in the night. The cold air enters the booth in a wave as gooseflesh prickles up my arm.

It's the middle of summer! Why is it so cold?

I step forward, my heart sounding loud in my ears.

One step.

You can do this.

Another step.

Yes!

I hear the sound in the distance. Like a high-pitched wail.

And the memories seep back to me...

* * *

My TV dinner had gone cold.

I'd been eating it, I could remember. I'd sat down on the sofa for dinner and placed the dinner on my knee as the clock struck 6pm. The food was hot; I had a mat underneath. Then it was cold and sitting on the coffee table.

But I had just been eating it. I was sure of it!

Shaking my head, I stood and walked from the lounge room with my meal.

I was hungry.

The clock struck 8pm as I reached the kitchen.

8pm?

I'd never fallen asleep that early at night before. In fact, I'd always had trouble sleeping no matter what time it was.

Napped? For two hours?

It wasn't like me at all.

Maybe I'm sick…

Maybe I had one of those new-fangled horrible diseases going around that I'd been hearing about.

I could be dead in hours!

Nah, I didn't panic. I'd napped is all.

The full moon was shining through the window, striking the kitchen wall and filling the room with a faded dirty-white glow.

I walked to the oven, placed the meal back inside and set the timer for fifteen minutes. It would be hot again in no time. As I moved my eyes to the temperature dial, I felt woozy.

I remember that now.

Light-headed, my mouth dry, bile filling the back of my throat.

I had crouched down on the floor, letting the feeling pass and trying to think straight again. I was dizzy for a few moments, but quickly the feeling passed.

Breathe.

Just breathe.

I looked out the window. The moon was higher in the sky, its glow obscured by the clouds. The kitchen was darker. The timer on the oven was set at zero.

Zero…

I pulled the dinner from the oven. It was still cold.

Colder than before.

Huh? What the…?

The clock in the hall read 10:12.
Blackout. Gotta be. I've had a blackout.
No, more than one. Several.
I felt fine but I knew something was wrong.
I'm having fits or a stroke, or something.
I needed help.
The phone!
I reached towards the phone on the kitchen table and picked up the receiver as the clock struck midnight. Its deep tone echoed through the now dark house.
I glanced outside the window.
The moon was higher again, a half-moon tonight. Clouds gone, the moonlight illuminated the kitchen where I stood. The receiver was still in my hand.
But it had been 6pm a few minutes ago!
I couldn't've blacked out. I was still standing.
I stared into the night.
How could this happen?
One moment the moon was low in the sky. Then high. In less than a few seconds, hours had passed!
How?

* * *

I lean back against the cold metal of the phone booth, letting the door scrape shut behind me. I close my eyes and try hard to breathe slowly.
Calm down. Just calm the fuck down!
The cold metal of the booth chills the skin on my back. I tell myself the shivering I feel is from the cold night, not from fear.
I open my eyes once again. I can see further now I'm adjusting to the darkness; the bushes by the side of the road, and even across to the other side. I peer into the trees, looking for any sign of movement. Nothing. I tilt my head slightly, stretching my hearing, hoping to pick out any noise from the silence. But there is none.
Nothing and no one.
My car is parked on the side of the road. The Chevy is

old and dusty, long grooves and dents along its sides and hood. The engine is off and so are the headlights. It's just as quiet as everything else.

Go! Go over, get in and drive away!

I know I should.

But something is stopping me, telling me to keep away.

Go!

I can't.

GO!

I won't!

Go, go, go, gogogogogogogo!

'Noooooooo!' I yell into the night.

My voice croaks and the shout is nothing more than a whimper.

My throat is dry. I need a drink.

And then I remember more…

* * *

I couldn't stay there. Something told me I had to get away.

I had turned, stumbled from the kitchen, searched for a light, knowing one was near, but my hands were trembling and the switch eluded me. I'd run for the door, fumbling with the lock—the bolt was stuck—I couldn't get it to work.

I'd been eager to escape, and I was dying for a drink.

I stood in front of the sink, looking out into the night.

Dark and cold.

No moon now.

Me. All alone. At the sink.

I could hear water, but it wasn't rain.

A chill was dancing along my arm.

The tap was running and I had a glass in my hand. Water was overflowing into the sink, mixing with the blood dripping from the gash along my wrist.

I turned around and looked at my watch. 4:38.

Again!

NO!

I dropped the glass. I had no control, I just dropped it. It rolled from the counter and I heard it shatter loudly on the floor. It splintered into a thousand pieces.

Just like me...

I turned and ran.

I found the door easier this time; it was unlocked. I smeared blood all over the silver door handle.

Outside in the cool night, I felt better.

My head was no longer spinning. My stomach was calm.

The night was bright. I looked up into the sky and gazed at the full moon. But it wasn't the moon. It was so colorful. Magnificent.

I was in awe. I couldn't move.

So colorful!

I felt better. Calm. Warm and safe.

Everything will be alright...

I remembered climbing into the car and turning on the ignition. The engine had spluttered and sounded loud in the night. The sweet aroma of lemon filled my nose.

Calm. Just keep calm. Everything's going to be alright.

I checked my watch.

5:01.

It's crazy. It can't be 5am!

I looked through the windscreen at the all-night restaurant.

Company.

People.

That's what I need.

People.

I need reality.

I rushed inside, not caring who saw me or what they thought. I found a corner booth and sat down, trying to get my breathing under control again. I was sweating, but I didn't know why. I looked down and saw the sweat rolling down my arm and over the long scab across my wrist. It was only then that I realised I was wearing just my shorts.

Where are my clothes?

I wished I could remember.

I was hungry, so hungry. And I needed a drink.

People were staring. I didn't try to stop them. Let them stare all they want.

A woman came up to me. She was dressed in a uniform and she gave me a weird look; like there was something wrong with me. I tried to ignore her, but it was hard. The way she looked at me made me feel uneasy, like I was some kinda freak or something.

What the hell would she know?

Then she was gone.

It's 5:23.

The food was in front of me, half-eaten.

I don't remember one mouthful, but I dabbed at my lips with a napkin.

I still felt hungry. I still wanted more.

Why can't I remember?

My thirst still wasn't satisfied after four cups of strong coffee.

Gotta have coffee. It'll keep me awake. Need coffee. Need to keep awake and aware.

Then I'm at the register, paying the bill. The girl smiled at me a plastic smile. The same smile that was printed on her plastic nametag.

Hi! I'm Sue, the nametag read…

Fuck you, Sue. And your fake little smile.

I didn't care.

She said something. I nodded.

She didn't care either.

I'm in my car, turning on the ignition once again.

I checked my watch.

3:01.

I looked out the windshield but I couldn't see anything other than the reflection from inside the car.

It was dark out there.

I need to get somewhere.

I knew that much.

Somewhere…

I needed food and drink too. I was hungry and thirsty and had to get away.

Quickly.

I drove into the street, but I didn't know where I was going.

I turned on the headlights, but I couldn't see anything.

It's so dark.

I rubbed at the windshield.

No help.

Too dark.

Way too dark.

I stopped the car and rubbed the windshield harder.

This is crazy!

I could see a small bright light further down the road. So small…

What the hell is it?

And then it had disappeared.

No, not disappeared. Just closer.

And getting closer.

A big light now. A lorry? Something larger than that? A rig?

It was going too fast.

Way too fucking fast!

I raised my hands in front of my face. It was a reflex, even though I knew it wouldn't help, I did it anyway.

The light bathed the car in its glow.

It's gonna hit!

I squeezed my eyes shut, but it was no use. It was still blinding me.

A high-pitched wail surrounded me. Deafened me.

And then nothing.

The light was gone. So was the noise.

No, not gone.

I could feel it. I could feel the presence beside me.

I didn't want to look. I didn't want to know.

I was shaking.

It's beside me!

I tried not to turn. I couldn't do it.

No!

I couldn't. But at the same time, I had to!

No!

I resisted. I gritted my teeth and I squeezed my eyes tighter.

No!

And then I felt it leave me, slide past me. I felt it leave the car.

I was still shaking, the sweat beading and rolling down my body. My breathing was hard and the aroma of lemon was all around me.

Yes!

I knew I'd won. I knew I'd beaten the urge.

Yes!

And then I'd opened my eyes…

* * *

I reach back and grip the side of the phone booth as the events play over in my mind.

I'm going crazy. There's no doubt about it. Crazy!

But I know there's no turning back. I know the thoughts are spilling now, pouring back into my consciousness. There is no stopping them.

I sob into the night as I let my legs buckle.

I slide down the side of the phone booth as the final memories return…

* * *

Its face was pressed against the window.

It had moved from sitting by my side in the car and was staring in at me through the windshield.

Those eyes!

Large and dark.

Round, lidless, empty eyes.

Its lips were moving.

What? Is it trying to speak?

I tried to hear, to listen, but I could hear nothing. I

didn't understand what was happening. But somehow I knew.

I won't!

I will not talk. It can't make me.

'Not now, not here.'

I didn't say it. But I did.

I don't know how, but my mouth didn't open and I spoke no words. But I said it. I know I did.

My hands fumbled for the keys. I turned on the ignition.

Gotta get away! Leave! Gotta leave! Gotta leave town!

No. Go back to the house.

I can't!

I sat numbly behind the steering wheel, not knowing where to go. The engine revving around me.

Just go! ANYWHERE!

It was still there. Peering inside. As if it had control over me.

Does it?

Go. I had to.

Just go!

The car was glowing. The blinding light was filling it again as the high-pitched wail returned.

Go! GO! Gogogogogogo!

It was gliding around the car and towards me. Towards the car door.

I shrank back from it.

No!

It reached out for the door handle. Its long, slender fingers quietly grasped the handle.

Its face was getting bigger, bigger.

Closer.

The eyes large and unblinking.

No!

It was coming towards me. Right up to the window!

I'd fumbled with the gear-stick, put the car in first, and pressed down hard on the accelerator.

But the engine had stopped.

* * *

I crumple up into a ball at the base of the phone booth. I place my head in my hands.

No! This can't be happening to me. I won't let it happen. It CAN'T!

The earth below me is warm, comforting. I could lie here forever.

I wish I could.

But then I remember.

* * *

It was in the car with me again, its head by my ear. I shielded my eyes from the light as it got brighter still.

The high-pitched wail was deafening. It was so loud I tried to scream above it, tried to fight it off as the fear rose inside me.

In the car with me again. Right next to me.

It reached out for me as it tilted its head. I looked into its eyes and it seemed to smile.

Slowly, it opened its mouth. I thought it was going to speak to me, to say something, but no words came out.

Then I saw the teeth.

Long, sharp, pointed and bloody.

It lunged towards me, pain tore through my neck.

I tried to scream again.

But everything went dark and quiet.

And then I knew.

* * *

The phone is dead.

It can't be.

I hang it up.

Still nothing.

The phone booth light flickers above me as I stare out into the darkness. The grimy windows are smudged with handprints, dirt and grime.

A mosquito buzzes across the glass, as desperate for escape as I am.

I pick up the receiver once more.

It's dead.

I shuffle around in the enclosed space, my eyes searching the darkness for any sudden movement. Any sign out of the ordinary.

Any sign of...

Who? What?

I can't remember.

There's something in the back of my mind. A dark patch, no, a blockage. Something I can't touch. When I think my thoughts are deflected.

But I do remember. And I don't.

I do, but I don't!

Fragments of memories skirt across the edge of my mind.

The sofa...dinner...cold...the night...the moon...the restaurant...the car...lemon...blinding light...teeth... pain.

I just can't quite reach them.

How did I get here?

I can't even remember that.

I hang up the phone once more, turn around and face the phone booth's doors. I stare out into the night. My eyes search the darkness.

The light above me flickers loudly.

The mosquito buzzes.

It's trapped here.

Just like me.

I don't know what I meant by that.

I glance at my watch.

10:46pm.

Strange, I thought it was much later than that.

I stare into the night and open the phone booth doors.

The mosquito continues to buzz.

It's trapped here.

Just like me...

CELL CANDY

There she goes now, right past my window, but no one even notices I'm here or that I'm watching. This is so easy and so simple, I can't believe I'm doing this.

I wait for the cars to go past and then I rev the engine and pull out into the traffic. There aren't many cars around. Not really. I've seen plenty more along here at other times of day. It's overcast. The clouds are heavy and it looks like it could rain. Everyone's probably staying inside.

Inside.

Nice and warm.

I follow at a safe distance, so no one gets suspicious. It's been a while since I've done this, but I don't think anyone is looking out for me. No one knows. No one cares. At least not on the sidewalks or in their own cars or in the stores I drive past. They have their own lives, their own problems, and the last thing they're thinking about is me.

I'm cool and calm. My hands aren't shaking as I hold the steering wheel. They were earlier, but not now.

She's in front of me, about eight cars up now. It's a big long black car, and it's slipping through the traffic. Almost like those limousines you see all those famous rock stars getting into on tv before they drive off in a rush.

It's in front of me, slipping in and out of the lanes, people wondering who's inside.

But I know.

I know she's in there. I saw her. But she didn't see me.

* * *

So, let's work it out. This is the fifth time I've done this. Only the fifth. But each time has been as good as the last. Well, almost...

Not the third time, though.

She caught me on the third time. That's what got me into all this trouble in the first place.

I was stupid, I know that now.

I was over-eager.

I wasn't thinking straight.

I'd made too much noise and she caught me in the backyard.

Damn it, I didn't even have a chance to get to the lock on her back door. Not even close. All the plans I'd been working on, what I'd do to her, how it would feel, and *how* I would do it, all fell to nothing when she heard me and found me that night.

How could something so good turn to nothing so quickly?

And there I was, hiding like some scared animal in the dark, hoping she wouldn't notice me.

Cowering. Wondering what to do next.

Because it had all gone so wrong.

And I hoped she wouldn't see me half-hidden in the dark.

Who the hell was I fooling?

Of course she did.

And she called the cops.

Damn her.

It didn't take much time to all fall apart after that.

Assholes.

It was so unfair.

* * *

And now I'm driving behind her again. It's raining now. Raining hard. And it's cold, but the damn heater in the car is broken. That's the problem with cheap little shitty cars. Everything in them is weak and shitty. Should've got something else, something better. Something like the one she's in now.

That would be nice.

But I don't care. It doesn't matter.

I'll follow her anywhere.

Anywhere…

Nothing else matters anymore.

And I *will* get my revenge.

And it's weird, you know?

Sometimes it's hard to blend in; to make myself feel like no one is watching me. I try to stay cool and not to be nervous—like I am now, this is easy—but I'm always wondering if someone, somewhere is watching me. Even if I can't see them, someone must be watching me from somewhere.

Or that's what I think, anyway.

But today, I mean, it's been such a busy day for her today, so I guess no one has really noticed me. I don't stand out. I tend to blend in. No one notices me. At least, I hope not.

Her family was all around today. And she was there, her smile and her gorgeous face, the centre of attention as always, her glow shining like a radiant light. Everyone else fluttered around her, drawn to her, like moths to a flame. And I know how they feel.

I just wish I could get so much closer.

So beautiful.

So much closer.

I will.

I know I will…

I stood far enough away so no one would see me. I just watched and smiled and stayed out of the way in the corner. I just watched and let the events happen around me. It was like I was a part of it, even though no one noticed me.

This time I won't get it wrong. This time no one will stop me.

* * *

But how can someone so nice turn on me and call the cops? I mean, call the cops on a complete stranger? She knew nothing about me. Didn't even give me a chance to explain! Of course, I was dressed in black and had a screwdriver in my hand and I was hiding in the bushes in her backyard, but I still think she over-reacted.

Didn't give me a chance.

She called me names.

Struck out at me.

And then to top it all off, she called the cops.

Bitch.

But none of that matters now. I have my plan. It's foolproof. And I'll be with her tonight. Nothing will stop me.

* * *

Her car turns the corner in front of me.

I'm still a few cars back, but I can see it in the distance. Black and sleek, it's hard to miss as it glides around the corner, even as it glides through the rain.

I can still keep track of her even this far back in the traffic.

I follow her path. I turn the corner only seconds later.

And I look around every-so-often. It's force of habit now. I do it instinctively.

I'm sure someone will notice me or someone will wonder what I'm doing. But the road is filled with cars and I'm not doing anything wrong. I just look like every other motorist. Calm and collected on the way home.

The way home…

No need to panic.

No need to worry.

Hell, even my screwdriver and hammer are both well hidden. I've learnt that lesson the hard way. The screwdriver is down my sock and covered by my trousers. The hammer is tucked into the belt of my pants and my jacket hides it so no one can see it.

I even checked it out in one of those big mirrors at the department store she works at. I checked tonight on the way over, even though I knew she wouldn't be working there today.

Force of habit, you know?

I stopped by and made sure there was nothing suspicious about me. The jacket didn't bunch around my hips, my trouser legs were straight and unwrinkled. You couldn't see or notice anything.

Perfect.

Everything was perfect.

* * *

That's where I first saw her, you know. All those months ago. How many now? I have no idea. Just can't seem to remember dates and times like I used to. I don't really have any need for them, not anymore. That's one of the first things you lose anyway.

I saw her in the department store. She was working behind one of those shiny glass and metal counters, selling perfume. She cast a little lost smile at me as I walked past her and she reeled me in perfectly. I couldn't help but smile back. She's got one of those faces, you know? And a smile that's like honey on your lips.

"Care to try a new fragrance?" she'd asked me.

I went to say no, thinking it was a woman's perfume or something, and I certainly wasn't about to try it. But it wasn't that anyway. It was cologne. Male cologne. Sounds like perfume to me. But she smelt so nice and her smile was so warm and there was something about the way she stood with her hip pushed to one side and her hair back on her shoulders and that figure-hugging suit she was wearing that made her look all professional and sexy at the same time.

She wanted me there.

And she smelt nice.

Real nice.

All those perfumes and colognes danced around us

both and I got high or drunk on it all or something.

We talked and she showed me some fragrances and I bent forward to smell them but I was really trying to smell her. To capture her scent. To breathe her in.

To know her.

I tried to be charming but I think it all went downhill pretty fast. It felt like we talked for an eternity, but I'm guessing now it was only a few minutes, tops. I mean, she must talk to about a hundred or more people every day in her job, so I couldn't have been there for hours.

She wanted to know if I wanted to buy any of the cologne.

Of course, I didn't. *She* was what interested me, not any stupid bottle of high-priced liquid. I wanted *her*.

I told her I didn't have the cash, couldn't afford the stuff and, anyway, I don't use it.

Her smile disappeared in a second, wiped from her face like a passing shadow.

But I didn't care. Hell, I don't think I even noticed her change in attitude straight away. It didn't concern me much, to tell the truth. I was still looking at her and wanting her and needing to get to know her. She was all I wanted.

I mean, don't get me wrong, I never wanted to follow her.

It wasn't the plan.

I never really thought about it.

I didn't think then and there that I had to follow her.

"Stalking," they call it now.

"With intent," the cop had said. Whatever the fuck that means.

I wasn't just following her. I wasn't stalking her, with or without intent. They just didn't get it. Didn't understand. I wanted to get to know her more.

Better.

That's really all there was to it.

So she could get to know me.

So we could be together.

How could she possibly judge me from a few minutes

in a department store? Hell, she didn't even *know* me. And how could she unless we got together more? It makes perfect sense if you stop to think about it, but they just didn't understand.

Christ, hasn't anyone ever been *in love* before? Have they *forgotten* what it feels like? How you live and breathe each other the same way I was drowning in those fragrances swimming around her?

Couldn't they *see?*

Anyway, she wasn't hard to follow.

She left the department store at about 5:10, stopped on the way home for a hot chocolate at a roadside stall and smiled and laughed with the guy serving her. He knew her and she knew him. So she must've stopped there every night.

She sat and read a book, some romance novel with a badly battered cover—so she must like it—for about twenty minutes before walking the five minutes to her bus stop.

I'll never forget that walk. Her stride. The way she moved.

Her blonde hair would bounce as she walked, trailing behind her ears and off her shoulders like threads of gold. She walked with such an upright gait, almost like she was marching to a beat in her head, and she always looked straight ahead with her chin raised and strong.

Like she had a purpose.

She knew where she was headed. She was in control.

But she never turned around.

Never checked what or who was beside or behind her. Never.

Almost as if she were ignoring the rest of the world.

Never turned around.

You really should, you know. You should always check all around you, no matter what. Three-sixty degrees is the key. Never let your guard down for one minute. From any direction.

So, following her home was easy.

I walked behind her, sat four rows back on the bus,

got off at the same bus stop and followed her right up the street and to her front gate.

Easy.

She made it so easy.

The confident ones always have a weakness. A blind spot even they've overlooked.

Of course, I didn't follow her inside. Nope, not that night.

I was smart. Just in case someone saw me.

I waited. Played it cool.

Waited a whole week, I did. And I kept away from the department store and her home too.

You can't play it too risky. You've got to take your time. These things can't be rushed.

I knew where she lived and I knew what time she'd get home.

I visited her house during the day, that very day I decided to do it. Yep, I walked right up the street in the daylight and looked around. I checked out everything. The front and sides of her house, the neighbours, and then I walked around to the back of her house.

The cops said I was casing the joint. But I had no idea what they were talking about. I told them I wasn't. I was just looking at it.

I had to know where everything was during the day-time so I knew where it would be at night. It pays to be smart like that. And I was.

Or at least I thought I was.

But I wasn't too smart at all.

At night, the backyard looked the same, but I couldn't remember every feature or detail. I should've stayed longer during the day, but I didn't want to be caught, so I left quickly.

Maybe I panicked a bit. Who knows...

Anyway, I climbed over the back fence that night and everything was going so well. But she'd put some empty bottles on the back step. I don't know, rubbish collection or something. But the bitch put them there sometime after getting home that night and I walked right into them, didn't I? Knocked them off the step and watched as they fell and tumbled and broke on the paving below.

So damn stupid, now I think about it. Should've taken a flashlight. But I thought at the time someone might see the beam.

Anyway, it was late at night, real quiet, and those bottles tipped and tumbled and fell away from me and there was nothing I could do. The bottles sounded so loud in the darkness.

I held my breath. I waited and prayed and hoped that no one heard. But then I saw the light go on inside and I heard the running feet.

She wasn't scared, that was for sure. She knew what she was doing. She would meet this head on—no matter what—like she did when she walked.

I hid in the bushes nearby. I didn't have time to hide properly and I certainly didn't have time to escape. I just hid and hoped and prayed that she wouldn't see me and wouldn't come after me. I wasn't really doing anything. Jeez, I hadn't even made it to her doorway!

But I forgot I had the screwdriver in my hand.

And I was scared. I didn't know what would happen. I'd run my plan through my mind countless times and each and every time it all worked absolutely perfectly. I never had a Plan B. Never thought she would catch me or that there would be any trouble.

And the door opened.

And she stepped outside and turned on the floodlights.

And she saw me.

And I saw her.

She was standing there in a long blue night-dress. The light came from behind her and it shone through the fabric. I could make her out. All of her. I could see it all.

Her long legs.

Her hips.

Her breasts.

Her nipples were erect and I wondered if that was because she was scared or because it was cold.

Or was she really turned on?

Did the breaking bottles scare her and make her wonder who was out there and whether they were here for her? Did she get all excited and wet thinking about being taken by a stranger and fucked and raped? Some girls like that, I hear. Or did the sound of the breaking glass stop her from laying in her bed, naked. Did I interrupt her as her fingers massaged her hard, wet clit?

I didn't know if it was any of these things.

But I'm sure I could make out the fuzzy outline of her pussy between her legs. The light didn't really shine there, but I'm sure in the shadow I could see her pubic hair.

It looked nice.

She looked nice.

All of her.

I licked my lips and couldn't take my eyes off her. And I think I might've groaned just a little.

And the night was quiet, remember?

That's when she swung around and saw me. That's when her eyes grew wide and her mouth turned to an O.

She saw me.

And she knew me.

The recognition was there in her face. There was no denying it. Her face turned into the same expression she wore when I told her I didn't have the money and wouldn't be buying the cologne.

She'd turn and panic and lock the door and scream, right?

Wrong.

She came at me.

I thought about running as she yelled and abused me. I thought about fighting back. But I couldn't. I just sat there, scrunched in the corner, wishing the bushes would swallow me and make me invisible from her tirade. I watched her breasts bounce as she pointed at me. Watched her nightie slide across her legs and wished to a-god-if-there-was-one that I was the one sliding all over her.

She was naked.

Except for that thin piece of material.

Standing there naked in front of me.

I tried to talk. I couldn't.

I put up my hands, but that just showed her the screwdriver. Made it look like I was trying to attack her even though I wasn't.

Why would I attack her?

Damn it.

And with all her noise the neighbours were soon outside and two large old guys with sweaty hands and smoky beer breath grabbed me and held me until the cops arrived.

I tried to explain it to them too, but they just kept yelling me down and calling me names I didn't like.

I wasn't the pervert they thought I was.

I *knew* this girl and she knew me. Why doesn't anyone mind their own business? They're always sticking their noses in. Every single one.

They just didn't understand.

* * *

And then there was the trial.

That was a mess too.

I didn't help myself either. Pleading to her to let me love her and be with her. Even in the courtroom I kept looking at her, trying to catch her eye, waving to her and calling out to her during the testimony. The judge yelled at me a few times too, told me to shut my mouth. I told him I'd shut his for him, permanently, if he didn't mind his own business.

She never looked at me though.

Not once.

There was never any doubt about the outcome.

But at least I *did* find out her name. That was in the trial. The lawyers kept using it over and over again.

Her name was Candy.

As sweet as Candy.

But she never smiled that smile at me again.

Never.

Until today.

But, of course, she wasn't really smiling at me today. I mean, her family and friends were there, so I guess the smile was for them. But I saw it. I saw it as they moved about her and talked to her.

She could keep them enthralled too. Just like she does me. That's the kind of girl she is.

Maybe she *was* smiling for me.

Maybe she's had a change of heart and she was really smiling now for me. Secretly excited that I was there with them all.

It's possible, I guess. I have no idea, really, but it would be nice to think so.

* * *

She's inside now and I'm waiting out the front. I've got to go through this one more time in my head, make sure I've got everything clear and that I don't make the same mistake this time.

I can't afford to.

This is my best chance and I won't get another.

So make it good. Make it great.

I've been out here for a few hours, waiting for the darkness to settle and for the rain to stop. I have to make sure it's dark and no one is around. Darkness is most important as it gives me the edge. At least it's not raining anymore.

I wait and wait and listen to the radio and keep my head down and try to find a station that isn't just talk-back and news. There's got to be a radio station without talk-back and news. Nothing's worse than talk-back and news. The world is full of news and stories about car crashes or tornados or lunatics on the street or rising crime rates or taxes or whatever and it's just all so damn depressing.

Everyone's depressing now.

But not Candy.

My Candy.

Tonight she's mine.

All mine.
All night.

* * *

Okay, it's dark enough now and I think I'm finally ready. Well, as ready as I'll ever be, I guess. It's now or never.

I pull the screwdriver from my sock as I get out of the car. Quietly I close the car door, check both ways to make sure the street is clear, and walk as calmly as possible across the road.

Keep calm.

Nice and easy.

Simple really.

The screwdriver makes quick work of the chain on the gate. Not strong enough to hold a gate like that. I guess they didn't reckon on me coming around for another visit.

This wasn't as nice as her old place, but that wasn't going to stop me.

I found out she'd moved when I got back into town and came looking for her. I knew the old address, could never forget a thing like that, and went straight there.

No luck.

But it was weird that as I drove back into town, she was walking down the street in the opposite direction.

I mean, that's like Fate or something!

Think about it! How lucky could you be? And I was mighty pissed too, because I was hoping she was still at the old place but I could tell from the mail in the mailbox that my Candy wasn't the "Bob and Ruth Tanner" who lived there now.

So there, just as I'm driving back into town and I'm wondering how the fuck I'm gonna find her, there she is walking away from the department store and crossing the road in front of the park to go for her lunch break.

I know it's simple now to think she'd be at the department store, but I wasn't thinking clearly and that idea hadn't entered my mind. Funny how the simple things can slip off your radar now and then. I just knew I *had* to get to the house and I *had* to pay her back. Never even thought about the store.

But it didn't matter, because there she was and I knew then that everything would be alright.

Even after all that time, she was still walking straight and still with her chin proud and true, and she was smiling that wonderful gorgeous smile and her hair was flowing behind her like it does in those shampoo ads that are just too good to be true.

I smiled then too. Smiled for the first time in months.

* * *

So the gate was just way too easy.

I'm walking slowly up this concrete path, keeping my wits about me and watching all around me.

360 degrees, remember?

Candy should've.

Even though the gate was a cinch, I know I'm going to have to work harder to get inside. I know that. And I'm prepared.

I have to slip inside and finally be in there with her and do what I should've done all those months ago.

* * *

I thought I'd be able to handle where they sent me. But it wasn't easy. All these people yelling at you, ordering you around, telling you what to do, when to do it and how to do it.

It's inhumane really. I deserved better treatment than that.

I got used to it eventually, of course, but it wasn't easy. I was the new guy for a while and I was the one to be picked on until some new sucker arrived and they picked on him. Then I could pick on him too.

Slowly you learn…evolve.

You learn lots of things in there.

And you learn about trust. Who to trust and who not to trust.

I learnt a whole lot.

Like how to get out of locks and how to open secured doors and windows and stuff. And that's going to make it much easier for me to get inside this time, even though she's got better security here.

She won't stop me.

Not now.

Not ever.

* * *

I'm wiping away the sweat because I had no idea it would be that hard to get in. But it doesn't matter. I've learnt well and I'm inside now and I didn't make a sound. No bottles this time either.

Not here.

Haha. Wouldn't that be funny?

I'm here and she doesn't even know it.

This place isn't as big as her last one. I don't have any trouble finding her and it takes only a few seconds to be standing by her, even though it feels like forever.

Everything has to be perfect so I'm putting the hammer and the screwdriver on the ground. Nice and gentle. Not making a sound.

Perfect.

She doesn't stir at all and I remove the covers and place them on the ground, carefully and quietly.

See? I've learnt well.

She's still smiling that wonderful smile and I'm wondering if she's thinking about anything. If she's thinking about me or her life or her dreams or her family or her big day today.

Such a big day…

I lean over to kiss her, trying hard not to breathe, not to make any sound. I don't want her to hear me.

But it's not enough. I can't just kiss her. I need more. I'm hard.

I *want* more.

This is my dream. She is my dream. And this is my chance. My cock is telling me it's now or never. No matter what the consequences, I have to give it to her. I have to slide inside her and feel her and empty myself in her.

I've waited long enough.

Slowly, as slow as I dare, I climb up to be beside her.

Even though I'm careful and I'm watching what I'm doing, my foot nudges her as I slide next to her.

Damn it! NO!

My eyes dart to hers.

But she's still smiling. She's not moving.

I knew it!

She wants me here.

The bitch actually *wants* me here!

It's all part of her game. And she's not giving anything away.

She wants me here!

Candy wanted me all the time.

Slowly, my hand falls to her breast and I stroke it. It's cold and the nipple is hard.

Is she turned on? Does she want me?

Did I see her smile twitch just then? Did I?

It's a game to her, just a game…always was.

I understand that now as I slip my hand under her nightie and feel the smooth roundness of her breast.

All that crying in the courtroom and talking about the psychological terror I put her through was all bullshit. It turned her on as much as it turned me on.

I know it for a fact now.

So she was turned on and all horny that night she found me in the backyard.

It's all just some kind of power trip or something.

Bitch.

I'll hurt her just the same.

She doesn't know that yet, but I will. I'll have some fun while I'm at it. The tables have turned.

She still hasn't moved and I know she won't now. She's mine and she's smiling and she's ready.

I'm pulling up the nightie and I can see for the first time real close the gorgeous mound of dark hair between her legs.

I can't resist that so I'm slipping my fingers between her cleft and pushing hard and deep inside. She's dry in there. Not completely dry, but too dry for my liking. So I slip my fingers out of her and I put them in my mouth, slicking them with my spit before I plunge them back inside her.

Yes, that's more like it. All soft and wet and ready now.

And she still hasn't moved.

And she won't.

I climb on top of her and I take off my clothes. My shirt and jacket come off quickly, but I have to manoeuvre slowly and carefully to pull down my trousers and boxers. My cock pulses with my rushing heartbeat and it's hot and hard in the cold night air. I lean forward, grabbing my cock in my right hand as I trace it around her tits and feel the soft nightie on and around my glands.

I tear off her nightie in one quick violent movement and throw it to the ground. She rocks with the force, her breasts jiggling and her hair pluming, but she soon settles again and returns to her sleep. I run my tongue across her lips and around her nipples and trace the jagged scar of the autopsy incision down to just above her pussy.

The stitches used to sew her up are hard and coarse on my tongue, but the soft insides of her pussy more than make up for it.

I work away deep inside her. She's tight inside. Tight and clean. Just the way I like it.

I push my tongue inside as far as I can reach, my neck and jaw muscles straining to reach inside her as far as possible. Her body welcomes me, sucks me in. Wants me to stay.

The tip of my nose pushes higher, seeks and finds her wonderful small nub of pleasure. I move further up and lick at it, swirling it around in my mouth, then biting down on it. Teasing her, driving her wild.

After some time I stop licking her and push her legs further apart. There's not a lot of room in these cramped confines, but I manage to wedge my hips between her legs and I line up my cock with her lovely folds of flesh.

I can't wait to be inside her and feel her.

Finally.

And then I slip inside and she's all around me.

Inside.

Nice and warm.

Surrounding me.

Wanting me.

And I'm pumping away and I can feel myself climaxing quickly.

This is all I ever wanted.

I push forward and kiss her hard on the mouth. Her lipstick smudges and her smile is mushed.

Some of her top lip slides from her face and I can see where the mortician has sewn her mouth closed. He's done a good job with the makeup and the wax, but the more I kiss, the more it smudges and disappears and slips.

How could something so good turn to nothing so quickly?

The bruising is starting to show now too, as are the gashes.

Am I fucking her too hard?

She isn't complaining.

She's still smiling.

So I fuck her harder.

I can even see the fracture in her skull as I pump faster, harder. And some of her hair has moved to the side.

That was where she hit.

It wasn't the impact of the car hitting her that did all the damage. It was hitting the ground hard and sliding into the gutter near the park.

That's what killed her.

She hit hard and never moved again, sprawled in the gutter, her blood streaming down it and into the sewers.

It took an awful long while for the cops and ambulance to arrive and for them to clean up the scene. And such a crowd had gathered too. But that was a good thing. It meant I could hide in with everyone else and pretend to be just an onlooker.

Little did they know…

And even though she's starting to fall apart as I pump harder and harder, I don't care.

Not now.

Not during these wonderful seconds as I melt into her.

As I cum inside her.

I flood her pussy with my juices, my life essence. I give back what I've taken from her.

And slowly as I deflate and slip from her, I collapse onto her and hold her tight. Her cold, still body is against my hot, hard, sweaty, heaving body. I hold her and tell her I'll never let her go.

I'm inside her now, way inside. I'm filling the cavities and the arteries and the veins she no longer uses. My sperm is inside her, swimming through her. Life continues. Life is inside her again.

And I gave her that life.

It's all worth it. The time in the hospital, the escape, the killings to get here. The hiding and the terror.

All worth it because I'm here now.

By her side.

In her coffin.

In her crypt.

Finally Candy is mine and we're together.

Me and her.

Together.

Candy and me.

Us.

My soul and her soul together.

My cells and her cells dancing and intermingling.

Becoming one.

I am her and she is me.

My life in what is left of hers.

I'm flooding her.

Taking her over.

Making her mine.

Cell by cell.

Me and her.

My cell.

My cell.

She'd never come to my cell.

No matter how many times I wrote and asked. Or pleaded.

Never even answered. Not once.

But I'll cum.

I'll come in hers.

Her Cell.

I'll cum all night and all day…flood her more and more, until she's seeping from every hole, from her cunt and mouth and ass and ears and nose. To the large jagged sewn-shut Y ripped into her chest and stomach. I won't stop until my seed spills freely from her and covers her.

Her cell.

My cell.

My cell.

Is now.

Her cell.

And she is mine.

She is my CellCandy…

DEAD OF NIGHT

"Did you see that?"

"What?"

"Out there, in the bushes?"

"Out where?"

"I'm not sure, I thought I saw something."

Andrew sat back in the driver's seat and looked through the windshield, out into the dark night.

"There's nothing out there," he said.

"I'm sure I saw *something*," Fiona whispered as she pointed out in front of them.

Andrew narrowed his eyes and focused outside the car. It was so dark he was only just able to make out the bushes and trees that surrounded the car park. He turned to look out the side window, but could see no one at all. The car park was empty—exactly why he chose it—and secluded as well. He didn't think they would be disturbed here, halfway up a mountain in the middle of the night.

"It's just your imagination," he said as he turned and leaned back over to Fiona. His eyes dropped down to her exposed breasts. Even in the half-light, he could make out the beautiful white skin and the dark dollops in the middle of each.

He ran his tongue across her left nipple, which was colder now, having lost the warmth from his mouth. But it was rigid. She was scared, he could tell. Maybe that was part of the fun.

Even though his ears were still ringing from the concert, Andrew could hear the wind blowing through the trees outside in a slow ebb and flow, like deep breathing.

This place is perfect, he thought to himself. *Just right.*

He noticed then that Fiona was perfectly still, her hands no longer danced along his naked back or ran through his hair. He took one last lick of her nipple and pulled away, his eyes rising to face hers.

She looked scared.

"What is it?" he asked.

"I'm *telling you* I saw someone out there." Her eyes locked on his.

"There's no one out there!"

"There *is!*"

"I just checked, honey," he said in a quiet voice. He smiled at her and his hand reached up to brush the blonde locks away from her forehead. "There's no one out there. There never is this time of night."

"I know what I saw," her voice became cold and hard.

Like her body, he thought.

"Don't worry about it," he said as he reached forward to kiss her.

Fiona pushed him away. *"No!"*

"Come on," he continued, fighting with her.

"NO!" she yelled, pushing harder.

Shit.

Andrew gave in and let her have her way. He slumped back into the driver's seat and sighed deeply.

Sitting in silence and staring out into the night, Fiona covered up her breasts with both hands.

Andrew watched the trees and bushes directly in front of the car. There was very little distance between the hood of the car and the tree-line, and no one in their right mind would be out there at this time of night.

She's imagined it, he thought. *It's that simple. Imagined it all. And now we're sitting here doing nothing.*

The silence stretched.

Come on, he thought. *Do something!*

The wind rustled through the trees and the limbs danced together in one fluid movement.

Andrew turned to stare out the driver's window. His eyes darted in the night, checking out the empty car park, looking for anything that might be out of the ordinary.

No one.

Nothing.

He looked up into the sky and watched the heavy clouds move overhead, skirting across the moon and obscuring the moonlight.

We can't sit here all night, he thought. *Although it would serve her right if we* did!

He knew he had to do something, he had to break the silence somehow.

I've got to have her.

He turned to face Fiona again.

She was still staring out through the windshield.

"Do you see anyone, honey?" he asked in a soft voice.

She shook her head, not taking her eyes off the trees in front of the car.

"Well, maybe they've gone," he suggested.

She didn't move.

"I mean, if you can't see them now, they must've gone, right?"

Fiona nodded and slowly turned to face him.

"What if it's him?" she whispered.

"Who?"

"You know, the Mountainside Murderer."

Andrew rolled his eyes.

"You're not *serious?*" he asked.

"He's killed *five* people." Her eyes burnt into his. "It's been in all the papers and on the news. Five people he's killed. Brutally stabbed them all to death on nights just like this. Five in two months."

"Honey, he's not out there."

"He could be."

"Trust me, he isn't," Andrew smiled.

She paused and then worriedly smiled back.

"You know I'll take care of you, don't you?" he asked in a soft voice.

"I'm sorry," she muttered, shaking her head slowly. "I've ruined everything, haven't I?"

Andrew leaned closer and reached out to place a finger on her lips.

"Sssh," he said. "You haven't ruined a thing. Everything is still fine."

"Really?" she smiled more.

He reached forward and removed her hands from her breasts.

"Everything will be fine," he whispered as he took her left breast back into his mouth. He leaned closer and let his left hand slip down her thin, smooth stomach to her jeans.

He sucked long and hard and her nipple rose with his tongue. He slipped open the button on her jeans and undid the zip.

He could hear her breathing quicken, become deeper and more rhythmic, and she moaned out loud as he slipped his fingers into her warm, tight, wet pussy.

Her arms surrounded him and he felt her hands slide up his back once more, rising and combing through his hair. He bit down hard on her nipple and heard her gasp in surprise.

Yes, he thought. *Yes, finally.*

His fingers slid in and out of her easily, her wetness all the lubrication he needed.

She wants it too. She's so horny she's almost wetting herself.

He pulled away from her breast, his mouth leaving her skin with a slurp. Tracing up to her neck with his tongue, he bit her chin before continuing upwards and kissing her hard on the lips. Her tongue danced with his, their breathing joined, deeper and faster now. She was squirming underneath him, pushing her body hard against his.

She wanted it. He could tell.

He pulled away from her kiss and climbed closer, keeping his fingers moving inside her wet folds, rubbing her and feeling it swell as he did so. He licked at her right breast, biting at her nipple, before continuing down her so soft and gorgeous belly. He circled her belly button with his tongue once...twice...a third time, teasing her as his fingers slipped faster and deeper below.

She was rising and falling with his rhythm, letting out soft groans and whispering his name.

He could smell her juices now, rising from her and mixing with their breath and sweat. She smelled good.

Good and ready.

He lowered his head further, his tongue skirting her pubic hair and his nose taking in her scent. His fingers were sticky and wet. He couldn't wait to taste her. He couldn't wait to be in her, so tight and ready.

His eyes traveled down her jeans and long legs to the white cowboy boots she was wearing. They were white embossed leather with silver frills and they stretched halfway up her calves.

Man, those boots are sexy, he thought.

His tongue cut down through her pubic hair and headed straight for the beautiful folds of her pussy.

That's when she yelped.

That's when her hands clawed his back and started pushing him away!

"No!" she cried. "No no! *Nonono!*"

Andrew fought her off as he was pushed back into the driver's seat, the harmonica in his back pocket digging into his skin.

"Hey, hey," he yelled as he hit the driver's door. "Calm down! What the fuck's the matter with you?"

Fiona was staring out the windshield and into the night again. One hand covered her breasts, the other was struggling to zip up her jeans.

Andrew followed her gaze, but the night was too dark and he couldn't see anyone.

"What?" he asked.

"I saw it again," she whispered.

"Huh?" Andrew couldn't believe what he was hearing.

"I saw him again," Fiona repeated. "The Mountainside Murderer!"

"You're not *serious?*"

Fiona's eyes darted to him. "I'm *very* serious. I know what I saw."

Andrew ran a hand through his hair.

What game is she playing? There's no one out there!

He turned and looked out each car window.

No one.

Nobody.

Zilch.

"I don't want to stay here any longer," she whispered as her eyes moved back to the front of the car.

Andrew stared at her. He couldn't believe what he was hearing.

"Please?" she asked again. "Can we go?"

I know exactly what she's playing at, he thought. *Get me all the way up here, get me hard and horny for a fuck, and she thinks she can just go all frigid on me? She thinks she can lead me on and then just say no right when we're finally about to do it? She knows we came here to fuck. Why else would she hang around the stage door after the concert? She wanted to be picked, she wanted to have me. We both know that! Hell, she's horny too! She's leaking juice everywhere! She's not gonna fuck with me like this.*

He stared out the windshield again. Then he turned and checked every window one more time. Just for her benefit.

We're not leaving here that easily, Fiona, he thought. *Not until I've finally got inside you.*

"Honey," he said in a calm voice. "I don't see anyone."

"Well, I can," she replied.

"Where?"

"Out there, between those two trees," she pointed straight in front of the car.

Andrew craned his neck, playing her game, and focused on where she was pointing.

"I don't see *anyone* there," he replied, trying to stay calm.

"Well, he's not there *now,*" she replied. "He's gone."

"Oh," Andrew nodded his head.

Bitch. Fucking with my mind when I should be fucking with her pussy.

"Well, if he's gone, he won't—"

"He came *back* after disappearing the first time," she interrupted him.

"I don't think he'll come back again," Andrew replied as calmly as possible.

"How can you be so sure?"

"Well, I can't."

"It's the Mountainside Murderer."

"No, it's not." He shook his head. "Anyway, he's only ever struck on the Westside. Nowhere near here."

"I want to leave," she whispered.

He sighed.

Not that easy, Fiona. Not yet, anyway.

"Please?" she asked as she turned to face him, her eyes melting him.

God, she's beautiful, he thought.

He didn't want to say no to her. But he deserved something, something in return. He was hard and ready to explode, and he wanted to explode inside her.

Gotta call her bluff, he thought. *Make her stupid excuse go away. I can't let her win this one. I have to prove to her she's wrong and then I can get what I deserve. I can't let her win like this.*

"No," he replied. "Let's stay."

Her face fell and suddenly she looked very scared.

Quite the little actress…

"Please, Andrew. I *want* to leave."

"There's no one out there!" he heard his voice rise.

"There *is!* I saw *him!*" Fiona repeated, staring back at the spot she had pointed out.

"Well, I don't!" Andrew couldn't stop himself, he was yelling now. "There's no one out there. You just said so yourself! There's no one there, so there's nothing to worry about."

"I want to go." Fiona began to cry.

"You're not going *anywhere* until we're finished *here!*"

She turned to stare at him, the tears starting to fall from her eyes.

"Please," she begged one more time. "We can go any-where else. *Anywhere!* Just not here. He's out there and he's watching. He'll *kill* us!"

Fucking Jesus Hell fucking Christ, Andrew thought. *She's not gonna drop this story! She's gonna stick with it no matter what!*

"Fine," he said as he sat back in his seat and picked up his shirt from the floor of the car. "If this is how you want to play it."

He climbed back into his shirt and began rebuttoning it, looking out the driver's window as he did so. He couldn't look at her right now. He didn't want to, anyway.

I warned you. I fucking warned you.

He could hear her sobbing begin to slow and then she blew her snuffled nose. He finished with his top button and realised he could still smell her juices on his fingers. He wished he were tasting her right now.

Then he felt her hand on his shoulder and he turned to look at her. She was kneeling on the seat and smiling at him. The tears had made her mascara run and her wet cheeks glistened, but she still looked beautiful.

"Thank you," she whispered. "For understanding."

"Oh, I understand alright," Andrew replied.

"I don't care where we go, just not here."

"We're not going *anywhere,*" he said in a level voice. "I already told you that, we're staying right *here!*"

Her face fell and she slumped back in the seat. Her eyes darted back out through the windshield before returning to stare at him. Her mouth opened, but she didn't say anything. Suddenly, tears began to fall once more as she shook her head back and forth.

"Please," she whispered. "Let's leave."

"No, Fiona, I've already told you. *NO!*"

He reached forward, shoving her further into the seat. She squealed and grabbed at him, but he pushed past her and reached down to the glove compartment. His fingers slipped under the flap—

they were slipping into HERS just a few minutes ago

—and pulled hard. The glove compartment sprang open and the light inside illuminated the contents.

She screamed as soon as she saw the revolver.

He grabbed it with one hand and slammed the glove compartment with the other. Slowly, he climbed back into his seat, making sure the gun was in view at all times. Not that he had to bother, as Fiona's eyes never left it for even a second.

She was shaking now, cowering back in her seat, trying to stay as far away from him as possible.

He reached forward with his free hand, trying to calm her down, but she wouldn't listen.

"No, no, no, *no no no,*" she was saying over and over again.

"Hey," he kept his voice calm and level, "don't worry. Calm down. Hey, *calm the fuck down!*"

It didn't work.

She was becoming hysterical.

"Don't, please, just don't hurt me. Please, *no!*"

"QUIET!" he yelled at the top of his voice.

That got her attention. She quickly shut up.

He waited a few seconds for Fiona to regain some control. He watched her, stared at her, counting to ten to give her time to get a grip.

"There's no need to panic," he finally said, making sure he sounded calm and level-headed. "I'm not going to hurt you."

"Please don't," she whispered.

"You've got nothing to fear," he continued. "I guess I just have to prove something to you."

He dropped his eyes from hers and checked the revolver.

Yep, loaded. Good.

"Just be a good girl," he whispered. "And no one will get hurt, okay?"

Fiona nodded her head as she began to chew her bottom lip.

Andrew smiled and leaned towards her. She still cowered in the seat, but he managed to kiss her hard on the lips anyway.

Her eyes never left his as he leaned back into his seat. She smiled a nervous smile at him.

I'll show her, he thought. *Fucking bitch playing head games with me.*

His finger curled around the cold, hard metal.

He smiled as he watched her.

Then he pulled hard and fast.

She screamed a short, sharp scream as he pushed open the door and climbed from the car. He let go of the car door handle and bent down to look at her again.

"Don't go *anywhere,"* he told her.

"What?" she looked surprised.

"I said, don't go anywhere."

"Where are *you* going?"

"To see if there really is someone out here," Andrew replied.

Fiona's face changed from surprise to terror. *"No!"*

"I'll only be gone a minute."

"No!" She climbed over into the driver's seat and stared up at him. "Don't go, don't leave me here all alone."

"You'll be fine. Just lock all the doors. I'll only be gone for a minute, two minutes tops."

"No, Andrew, *please!* It could be dangerous out there! He'll get you!"

Andrew smiled down at her. "Don't worry, I've got this, remember?" He pointed to the revolver.

But it wasn't enough. Fiona was shaking again now, the tears beginning once more. *"Please,* Andy, let's just leave here. Let's go anywhere else and we'll be safe and fine. *Please!"*

She was begging him.

She looked cute when she begged.

No way, sweetheart. You've played this hand and we'll see it all the way through. I'll prove to you no one's out here and then I'll come back and take what I deserve.

"It'll be fine," he said as he reached down and kissed her. "Back in a minute."

He turned and walked away from her.

"No, Andy!" she called after him. "No, *please!* Don't leave me here alone! I've got no protection! What if he comes for me while you're gone? What if he *kills* me while you're gone?"

Andrew stopped in his tracks and stared into the dark woods. He smiled.

Gotta give her credit, she almost got me there!

He wiped the smile from his face, turned around and walked back to her.

"You're right," he said. "I should've thought of that."

He held out the gun to her.

"Here, take it."

"What?"

"Take it for protection. If he comes for you, you'll have some protection. Just pull the trigger and I'll come running."

Afterall, I won't be needing it. There's no one out here anyway. But I'll play your little game, darlin'.

"You *can't* be serious?" she said as she eyed the gun being handed to her.

"Of course I am! I'll only be gone for a minute or so anyway," he replied. "Here, take it."

Fiona reached out and took the revolver.

"Good, now shut the door and make sure they're all locked. I'll be right back."

"He'll *kill* you!"

"Hey," he replied with a shrug. "I'm lead guitar in *The Graveyard Diggers!* No one is going to kill me. He probably just wants an autograph."

Andrew smiled as he turned from her and walked to the front of the car. He heard the car door slam and looked over his shoulder just long enough to see Fiona scrambling over the seats to lock all the doors.

Ha, he thought. *I'll show her who's the master of games around here.*

He stopped in his tracks and looked through the trees in the direction where she had pointed. He crouched slightly and then tilted his head, as if he'd heard something.

This'll be scaring the shit out of her, he thought. *Serves her right. I'll fuck her yet.*

Then, slowly, he stalked through the trees and into

the darkness.

When he'd counted out fifty steps, he stopped, turned around and leaned against the nearest tree. He was far enough from the car that he couldn't see it.

And that means the stupid bitch can't see me either.

He placed his hand in his back pocket and pulled out his harmonica.

"Wish I had my guitar," he whispered, as he placed the harmonica to his lips and began to play the chorus from *Deadshit,* the Graveyard Diggers Number One single.

Number One with a bullet, he thought. *And I'll shoot you full of love yet, Fiona.*

The cold settled in all around him. As did the darkness of the night.

I wonder how long I should wait?

Then he smiled as he reached into his front pocket and felt the car keys nestled against his leg.

I can wait a while. She's not going anywhere tonight.

He crouched down at the base of the tree and closed his eyes, his lips touching the cool metal of the harmonica, his tongue wetting the comb and probing the holes.

His smile widened as he thought about how wet Fiona's pussy was and how easily his fingers had slid right inside. He felt himself growing hard again as he thought about going back to the car and sliding his cock deep inside her.

Inside her tight, warm pussy. It'll be the best damn fuck ever.

He knew he would have to thank Fiona for this little game, because this was like nothing else he'd ever experienced.

He paused for a moment, listening to the night, then placed the harmonica back to his lips and quietly played the bridge from *Corpse Marker,* and waited.

I'll soon play a pretty tune on her…

* * *

Fiona stared out into the night.

She was sure it was getting darker out there. The more she stared into the area where Andrew had disappeared, the less she could see.

Her hands held the gun tight. She was shaking, but there was nothing she could do about it.

Her eyes double- and triple-checked the locks on all the doors. She was safe.

*For now…*she thought. *Could get risky later, though.*

She stared back through the windshield.

Come on, come on…come back, Andy. I need you here.

She wanted to do something. She *needed* to. But she had no idea what. She didn't want to get out of the car—too risky—but she didn't want to just sit there either. The night seemed to be getting colder, and that made her shake even more.

She continued to stare through the trees. She focused her eyes, praying they would discern something new.

Nothing.

Dark. Blackness. Nothing.

She realised she was biting at her lip.

Come on, come back.

She stared down at the gun in her hands.

"Just pull the trigger and I'll come running." That's what Andrew said. If I fire the gun, he'll come back.

She smiled and nodded to herself.

Yeah. He'll come back.

She reached for the door.

Slowly unlocked it.

Pull the trigger. "Just pull the trigger."

Opened it carefully.

He'll come running.

And then she saw the movement.

She let out a short, sharp scream as she slammed the door and locked it fast.

Fiona looked out through the window again, her breath fogging the glass, but she could see no one.

I know what I saw, she thought. *It was out of the corner of my eye, but it was a movement, I'm sure of it.*

She stared off to the right of the car, where she was sure she'd glimpsed something.

Or someone.

So she sat and waited.

Too scared to move. Too scared to do anything.

Gotta wait this out.

Just gotta.

Please, Andrew, please just come back.

Please let there be no one else out there. Don't let tonight turn out all wrong and bad. Not tonight. Please.

The wind blew through the trees. It was getting stronger, she was sure of it.

I can't sit here all night. He has to come back soon.

Turning her neck, Fiona checked out the back windows of the car.

Nothing.

No movement. No life.

Maybe it's just the wind. Maybe I am *just making it up. I'm too nervous, maybe that's it. I need to calm down and try not to panic.*

Sitting still and holding her breath for what seemed like ages, Fiona strained her eyes, darting from the front of the car to the side, looking for anything or anyone to prove she was right.

She ran a hand through her hair and rested the gun on her lap.

Why's he taking so long? Why hasn't he come back?

And then she realised exactly why Andrew hadn't returned.

No, no! I won't believe it!

But she knew she was right. Andrew should've been back by now. It wouldn't take long to scout in the bushes and come back to the car.

Unless…

Unless whoever was out there got to him first.

Fiona felt the fear jag down her spine.

Fuck. I knew he shouldn't've gone. He should've stayed here. We should've stayed together!

Her eyes darted across to the ignition.

No keys. Fuck! He took them with him!

She placed the revolver on the driver's seat only long enough to zip up her jeans and check her boots were on. Grabbing the revolver again, she unlocked the door and opened it quickly.

I can't stay here by myself any longer. I can't just wait for him to come and get me. I have to try to save Andy. I have to stop whoever is out there!

She climbed from the car and stood in the cold night. A shiver passed through her as she turned her head and checked to the side of the car once more.

Slowly, Fiona took a step towards the front of the car, closer to the trees.

Her boots sunk slightly in the wet underbrush.

They'll get all muddy and need to be cleaned again. I should never have bought a white pair, she thought. *Still, as long as they're comfortable and functional.*

Her eyes tried to slice through the darkness, but she couldn't see anyone.

The trees moved in the night, swaying with the wind.

Fiona listened carefully for any sound, any hint as to where Andrew was, but the wind swallowed it all.

"Hello?" It came out in a whisper, so she tried again, louder this time, "Hello? Andy?"

Nothing.

"Andy? You out here?"

She knew it was a stupid question, but she didn't know what else to say.

She walked to the front of the car and leaned back on the cold hood.

"Andrew? Where are you?"

Her voice disappeared into the night.

She tore her eyes away from the trees for a few seconds to check she still had the revolver in her right hand. She could feel her fingers gripping the handle, but she had to make sure with her own eyes.

She shivered again. The wind messed her hair.

I should never have agreed to come up here. I don't know this area at all. It was a stupid stupid idea.

"Bitch."

She jumped at the voice. It was close. Somewhere in front of her. Somewhere just on the other side of the trees.

Fiona's eyes darted from side to side. Her mouth opened to say something, but nothing came out.

"You fucking lying *bitch.*"

It was a deep, hateful voice and it filled her with total fear.

"I'm going to make you pay for all the *fucking lies* and the games you play. I'm going to *cut you deep,* cut you and make you *hurt.*"

Fiona wanted to run, but she was frozen to the spot. Only her eyes moved back and forth, trying to pinpoint the voice in front of her.

"I'll cut the ears, cut the nose, and cut the *tits* off your body. I'll make you beg for mercy and make you wish for death. I'll *gut* you wide and *slice* right through that little *cunt* of yours."

"No," she whispered first. And then her voice rose with her panic. "No, no, please no! Don't hurt me, leave me *alone!* DON'T HURT ME PLEASE!"

Her whole body was shaking, her eyes darted in the darkness, the wind blew and the trees swayed. She tried to move, but couldn't. She wanted to, but couldn't.

"Just before you *die,* I'll cut out your *clit* and make you eat it."

Then he was laughing. She could hear it loud above the wind, a guttural, deep, manic laugh that didn't stop. It seemed to be all around her now.

Stop it, stop! Leave me alone!

Fiona put her hands to her ears and closed her eyes, willing and praying for the sound to stop.

But the laughter continued, as did the wind and the sound of the trees all around her.

"Time to die, bitch!"

She opened her eyes just in time and saw him running towards her, out of the darkness from between the trees.

She fumbled with the revolver, took aim and squeezed the trigger.

The sound was loud and shattered the night.

She watched him jerk to a stop and then stagger slowly backwards, as the blood quickly grew on his chest. Her eyes met his as he reached out to her before falling backwards.

Andrew hit the ground hard, partly disappearing back into the darkness between the trees.

No!

Fiona dropped the gun.

Oh, Andrew! Oh fuck! No! Please no!

The silence returned to the night. The wind continued its dance with the trees.

And Andrew lay dead in front of her.

All she could see were his feet and legs. The rest of him disappeared into the darkness.

What have I done? Andrew, oh shit, I didn't know it was you. I didn't know. I'm so sorry! I didn't want it to happen like this. Oh, Andrew, I'm so fucking sorry.

She found herself standing, no longer leaning on the hood of the car. Slowly, she took a step closer towards him. Carefully, she moved further into the night.

Andrew's body jerked for a second.

Fiona let out a short shriek and stopped in her tracks, but Andrew lay still again.

Oh Jesus, what have I done? It can't have happened like this!

She crept forward another step, and then another.

No no! Please no, don't let this happen. No!

With every step, she could see more of Andrew. His hips, his blood-soaked t-shirt covering his stomach and chest, his arms flung out to the side of his body, his harmonica half buried in the dirt.

Tears filled Fiona's eyes as she crept closer. She was shivering more now, the cold night making her teeth clatter, the trees swaying over Andrew's body.

She fell to her knees.

"No," she whispered as she reached out to try and stop the blood pumping from his chest.

She leaned forward to kiss him on the lips. But

his blank expression stared unmoving back at her. She couldn't kiss him. She just couldn't do it.

Fiona threw herself backward, away from the corpse, and tried to stand. But her legs just wouldn't work, none of her limbs would.

She filled her lungs to scream, but a hand slammed across her mouth and cut off any chance.

She was pulled backwards by her hair and dragged until she could stand. She was leaning against someone, she could feel the body behind her, hear his breathing and feel the rise and fall of his chest against her back. She could also feel the large erection digging into her from behind.

"I told you I'd gut you wide and slice right through your sweet little *cunt,*" the voice whispered in her ear.

She tried to struggle, but he was too strong, Andrew's blood on her hands making her grip slippery and loose.

"And your little hero boyfriend ain't gonna stop me now."

She wanted to turn around and look into the eyes of the man who held her, but he wouldn't let her. She felt a sharp pain in her side, just above her hip. She wanted to scream, but couldn't. His left hand was still across her mouth, she had to breathe through her nose.

His right hand appeared from behind her, holding a large hunting knife. Blood smeared and dripped from the blade as he brought it closer to her, running its edge down through her cheek, slicing it in two.

Tears spilled down her cheeks and across his fingers. She could feel her skin part, flare outwards, the blood flowing down her neck and shoulder.

"Time to die, princess," he whispered.

And she knew he was right.

The knife traveled down her body, slicing her shirt and quickly sawing through her jeans. She tried to struggle, but it was no good. In seconds he cut the jeans away from her legs and tore her panties from her hips. Her eyes caught a quick look at the wound near her hip. It looked deep and jagged and pulpy. She could see her own hip bone glistening in the moonlight.

"Now, my sweetness, if you scream, I'll slice the skin from your body, piece by piece before I plunge this knife right through the back of your skull," he whispered. "If you don't scream, you'll only feel my cock, and then I promise I'll kill you quickly and with little pain. Deal?"

Fiona nodded her head slowly.

Carefully, he removed his hand from her mouth.

Fiona gulped in the air, forcing herself to think clearly and not to panic.

His hand traced down the side of her body, feeling her soft, cold flesh, stopping only for a few seconds to caress the hole he'd torn there.

"Mmm," he continued. "You'll be a fine fuck tonight. I'm going to enjoy every inch of you."

He bent her slowly forward, the pain in her side more than doubling. But she knew there was nothing she could do. She could feel the bouncing head of his cock between her butt cheeks.

He pushed her down and kept one hand on her back, making sure she stayed folded in two. She grabbed her ankles for balance as blood dripped in front of her eyes from the gash in her cheek.

"Who are you?" she whispered.

"Who do you think, bitch?" he asked as the tip of his penis rubbed against her anus. "I'm the Mountainside Murderer."

Fiona's body tensed at his words.

"You would've heard about me," he continued as his cock began to force its way into her. "I've killed five people."

"Nine," Fiona whispered, grabbing her ankles tighter and readying herself for the pain.

"Huh?"

"You've killed nine people," she said again.

His low, guttural laugh filled her ears. "You're wrong, girlie. The newspapers say five."

"They haven't found the other four yet," Fiona replied, her right hand slipping into her right cowboy boot.

"Shut the *fuck* up!" he said as his cock rammed hard. "I'm the Mountainside Murderer, so I should *fucking* well know!"

"No, you're not," Fiona said, her fingers sliding around the handle of the knife held snug inside her right boot. She lunged away from him in one movement. His cock slipped from her with a loud slurp as she spun around quickly, diving forward and burying the blade of the knife deep into his right eye.

She smiled as he fell to his knees screaming and clawing at his face, blood and white-milky eye juice flowing from around the blade imbedded in his skull.

"You're not the Mountainside Murderer," she whispered. "I am."

JUNGLE

Each weekday afternoon I'd see one particular girl walk in front of my car at the traffic lights on the corner of Hulme and Groden. She was a school girl with long dark black hair, and she was dressed in her blue and white uniform; blazer, skirt to her knees, long white socks and black shoes. She'd walk right in front of me, her chin held high, backpack slung over one shoulder, pulling her blazer back, showing me her small but firm breasts, her hips working from side to side.

I couldn't get this girl out of my head.

And as I was currently "between girls", the more this girl taunted me with her good looks and great body, the more I wanted her. I couldn't help it. It was almost like it was on a primeval level—I wanted her so badly.

She was pretty young, and I knew she would still be a virgin.

Every day I would be there at the same time, and she would walk past, head high, breasts on show, never knowing I was watching her so intently, wanting to reach out to touch her.

Some days her beauty would infuriate me. I didn't know whether to drive straight over the top of her, or seduce her; she was so innocent and so sexy. But she knew what she was doing, she knew how she looked and was damn proud of it.

I'm hot and you can't touch me, is what she was saying to the world.

Her looks and the local laws conspired against me. Jail bait.

I'd taken to parking nearby, watching her walk across the street. I even started to follow her to and from school. I knew where she lived, I knew what time her parents came home from work, I knew she rode her bike to the local grocer on Tuesdays and Thursdays.

I thought many times about running her down, accidentally hitting her, taking her home to look after her, making her better, washing the wounds, undressing her, tying her up and gagging her, kissing her naked, soft flesh all over. Making love to her.

I knew I couldn't do it, couldn't get away with it, and I wished like hell I was a paramedic or even a police officer—something that gave me the opportunity to take her right from the street. And part of me wondered if that's exactly what she wanted. What she needed.

Maybe I could make it work with her. Maybe she was the right girl for me.

There had to be a way.

I just needed to work out how to snatch her without her parents and the school panicking and calling the cops. I stressed so much on her, wanting to take her and make her mine. Scenarios and ideas played out in my head, but I couldn't see a way to do it… not without going to jail.

It got so bad, she was so much in my head, in my thoughts, my fantasies, that I missed my deadlines at work, my sales figures suffered and I couldn't sleep at night. Hell, I couldn't even eat, I was thinking about her too much.

I'd been doing this for almost seven weeks, following her and thinking of her, wanting to be with her and to make her mine. Each night I would sit in my darkened apartment, looking at the photos I had taken of her with my digital camera. With a click of the mouse button, I had image after image of the girl flashing across my computer screen; walking to school in her uniform; going home, laughing with two of her classmates; going out with her parents to the restaurant on Troughton Avenue; cycling to the grocery store with her iPod clipped to her jeans; sitting cross-legged in her backyard dressed only in a singlet and track pants, reading a book with her hair braided; sitting on the porch, doing her math homework; sunbaking at the local park; hanging out at the mall by herself, twisting a braid of her hair around and around in her fingers as she waited for her Subway order.

So many images in which to lose myself.

I'd spent all these weeks fixating on a school girl I knew would never be mine. I would never be inside her, never feel her above me, her most inner barrier giving way to me as I impaled her for the first time. No matter how much planning I did, I couldn't have her, she wouldn't want me. She wouldn't come with me...

Unless I made her.

* * *

I sat across from her house, a couple of doors down, not right out the front...I wasn't stupid. I had a good view of the front porch and driveway, and I could see all the way up the street, just in case.

The bottle had only a few drops of GHB left, but there was more than enough to work its wonders.

At the local nightclubs you could get almost anything, as long as you had the right amount of cash. Uppers, Downers, Ice, Heroin, they could all be bought for the right price. But I was never interested in anything like that. I never wanted my senses dulled by any drug. I wanted to be able to experience everything; to feel it, taste it, and remember it. I'd be alert, even if others weren't. GHB was all I needed, I'd done my research.

Over the past few months I'd become an expert in judging exactly how many drops to administer into a drink, depending on the size and build of a woman. And also by how much she'd already had to drink.

It was tricky at first. I'd been a bit heavy-handed with the first few, and that meant they were usually knocked out within ten minutes or so. On a couple of occasions I had to apologize to nearby patrons as she fell flat on her face or needed to be carried out of the bar or dance club.

But an unconscious fuck was still a fuck, no matter what. And sometimes they were the best, as the girls never complained or stopped you from exploring each and every one of their holes. The next morning they'd wake up sore and bruised, and not remember a thing. If they did, they'd be too embarrassed to let their friends know they got so drunk they'd let a stranger fuck them to oblivion.

What can I say? It's a jungle out there. Fuck or be fucked. Pure and simple.

Once I got the hang of GHB, the rest was easy. Anyone was mine. All I had to do was choose them. I've fucked girls who, back at school, would've turned their noses up at me. Those with rich dads and ex-model moms, who thought they were the best and most beautiful creature to walk the earth.

But with a few sips, they're gone and they're very suddenly all mine.

I'd fuck them, pull on their long blonde hair until it broke away at the dyed roots, bite their pussies and flaps until they bled, cum all over those snooty mouths and turned-up noses, rubbing the head of my cock all over their lips and down their chins.

I'd used the drug sparingly, of course, making sure I would never take anything too far or get myself into something I couldn't get out of. Last thing you need is a corpse on your hands. But there wasn't much left in the bottle, just the one or two drops that I'd been saving for a very special prize.

She walked down the street, backpack slung over her shoulder, blue blazer flapping in the wind, long dark hair reflecting the rays of the sun and blowing across her face, those clean white socks pulled up all the way to her knees. There was just enough skin between her socks and her skirt, just enough to promise so much, and to reveal enough. I knew she'd never been touched there, and that made me want her even more. I would be the first to slide my hands up above those socks, around her thighs, higher, to that forbidden fruit that no one had licked, sucked or tasted.

She was coming home from school, walking the same path she walked every school day, her head held high and her breasts poking proudly forward. That look on her face of *I know I'm hot and there's nothing you can do about it.*

My Princess was coming home.

And I was waiting for her.

I hadn't really planned any of this. I'd just driven out to her home and sat, waiting for her. I knew I wouldn't do anything, not without much more thought, or at least a damn good opportunity, but as I rolled the bottle of GHB around in my hand, I could feel myself growing hard at the thought of what I could do with her. A little drink, some GHB and she'd be mine.

But it wouldn't be today, no matter how turned on I was.

Not yet. It will happen, but not yet.

And then I got the idea.

I turned the key in the ignition and let the engine roar. I leant over to the passenger side and opened the glove box, dropping the bottle of GHB inside. Reaching into the back of the car, I grabbed my street directory and quickly opened it, finding the right map for that neighborhood, and placed it on the seat next to me. I pushed the button to lower the passenger-side window and checked my appearance in the rear-view mirror. I flattened my hair down a bit, and checked my smile. I looked fine.

Then I drove along the street, nice and slow, enjoying every moment as I closed the gap between me and my Princess.

She didn't notice me as I approached, didn't look my way as I pulled up just a few feet in front of her. She only turned and looked when I called out to her.

"Er, excuse me, Miss?"

She stopped, turned.

I smiled.

"I'm a little lost. I was wondering if you could tell me where Elm Avenue is?" I knew I was close to Elm, and I knew she'd know where it was. "I'm from out of town and

I just can't find it."

She walked over towards the Cherokee, putting her hand above her face to shield her eyes from the sun, getting a better look at me.

"Elm?" she asked.

I nodded, holding up the street directory and smiling. "It's here on the map, but I'm hopeless with maps."

She stepped closer.

That's it. Closer. Closer.

"You've gone past it. Ah, I think it's a couple of streets back," she said. Her voice was light, delightful. She had a Southern accent that just drove me insane; a sing-song slow drawl that sounded like an angel. I could feel my cock pushing hard against my jeans, wanting to break free.

"Oh, really?" I turned to look out the back of the car, making sure I furrowed my brow.

"Don't worry," she smiled then, a beautiful grin, perfect white teeth, red luscious full lips. "The signs aren't too good around here. It's easy to miss."

I leaned forward, across to the passenger side, holding the map out so she could see it.

"So, if I'm here, I just have to…ah…do a u-turn or…?"

She stepped up then, right up to the car. I could touch her if I wanted to.

Do it, do it now!

I glanced out of the windshield, checking the whole street.

No one around. No one near.

Grab her and just go!

She smiled at me, actually *at* me this time, not just a polite smile. It was a personal smile, from one friend to another. It had feeling, I could tell. Her green eyes were so sharp and vibrant. So full of life. The greenest I'd ever seen. Young, fresh, and all mine.

Her hand reached out to the map and her eyes dropped to focus on the page. She tilted her head slightly and her hair shifted, strands falling across her face, her chin, her throat and shoulders. She bit at her lip just a little, as she concentrated on finding her place on the map, her top teeth holding her lip against the bottom ones.

She pointed to where I was pointing, and the nail on her index finger touched my finger for a second, then she withdrew it slightly. Her perfect hand, manicured nails, soft skin, small fair hairs, just inches from mine.

Grab and go.

NOW!

"You're here," she said, bringing me out of my thoughts with her sweet voice. "You just need to turn around and go back two blocks. Elm is there."

She moved her finger to point to Elm.

I leaned over further, wishing I'd taken my seatbelt off. It was cutting into my side but I didn't care. I wanted to get as close to her as possible.

I could smell her now, smell her hair and her scent. Whatever she was wearing made me harder than I'd ever been. It was a mix of flowers and lavender and coconut or something. I wasn't sure. But it was intoxicating nonetheless. I wanted to taste her lips, lick the juice from her pussy, right then and there.

She stepped back. Sudden, and quick. My Princess took a step back away from me. I panicked slightly, thinking she must have sensed something. What had she noticed? Had I given myself away? But she was still looking at me, still smiling. She'd just stepped back and removed her hand, having answered my question.

"There's a 7-Eleven on the corner, you can't miss it."

I nodded, like I was taking all this in, but really I was just hoping to catch another whiff of her scent so I could remember her, so my mind could conjure her wholly and totally, so I could think of her later, that night, tomorrow, next week, when I was alone, or in the shower, or whenever I needed her.

"Thank you," I finally said. I straightened back into the driver's seat and smiled at her one last time. "I think I should be okay now."

"No problem," she replied. "I hope you find what

you're looking for."

And with that, my Princess was gone.

I did a slow u-turn, watching her continue down the street, walking up her driveway and onto the porch. I drove past as she unlocked the door to her house and stepped inside. Her long black hair disappearing into the darkness inside, her long white socks swallowed one by one.

I drove down to Elm and turned left, no real reason why. I just did what she told me to do. I followed Elm, not thinking about anything other than my Princess, her look, her touch, her smell.

She touched me.

I wanted her.

Smiled and talked to me. Such a radiant smile, such a beautiful accent.

"I hope you find what you're looking for," she had said.

I smiled to myself.

Yes, Princess.

I certainly had.

* * *

After our meeting, I couldn't get her out of my system for any longer than a few minutes. I couldn't stop thinking about her. How we'd talked, how she had touched my hand, her accent, her smile, her *smell*. I wondered what she was doing, how she'd spent her Thursday, Friday or Saturday night. Did she go out and party? Was she curled up in bed, tucked in and all warm, sleeping soundly? Was she at the dinner table with her parents, head bowed and saying Grace over that night's meal?

And more and more, I thought about how I could get even closer to her.

She liked me, that much I could tell. She would probably welcome seeing me again. After all, I was polite and charming. Probably most guys didn't dare talk to her, intimidated by her beauty...but I dared, and I'd been permitted. She would see me again, she'd want that much. I just knew it was something we both wanted.

I smiled.

Soon…

* * *

I checked the GHB was still in the glove box and that the battery of my digital camera was charged.

It was Monday afternoon and I'd left work early on the pretense of visiting a client on the east-side, but I was sitting outside Lansdale High instead.

I'd timed it just right. School was finished for the day and the kids were spilling onto the street, filling cars and leaving.

My eyes danced across the boys, the girls, the colorful mix of young faces, the blur of movement, the sound of laughter and yelling. Then I saw her, walking down the path, talking in a group of four other girls.

Hello, my Princess.

She was in the middle of the pack, two girls on either side of her, and she was talking to them all, her smile wide. She was laughing, and I realized I hadn't heard her laugh. I imagined what she was saying, her voice, that accent, and as I did, my eyes dropped down lower, down her shirt and past her breasts to her skirt, the flash of leg she was showing, her long white socks pulled up to her knees.

I grabbed my camera and looked around me, making sure I was far enough away from everyone that I wouldn't cause any suspicion. I watched her in the viewfinder, placed the cross-hairs over her heart, pressed the button and took photo after photo.

She was frozen before me, laughing, turning, talking, walking, bending, checking her backpack, wiping the hair away from her eyes, handing a book to another girl.

The other four were pretty too, but not like my Princess. I looked at them only momentarily. They were nice—three were shorter than her, only one was taller—

but they were all listening intently to her. My focus was on my Princess, and so was theirs. She was that kinda girl. She could stop anyone in their tracks.

She stood at the school gate just long enough to say goodbye to her friends, pecking each of them on the cheek with a goodbye kiss. Then she turned and started walking home, taking the same route she did every day of the week.

I waited until she was around the corner and out of sight before I started the engine and drove after her. I was breathing hard and my cock ached from being restricted in my jeans.

I stopped the car at the corner and looked down the road that ran by the school. She was walking away, her backpack slipped over her left shoulder, her hair on her right side blowing in the wind.

I turned into the traffic and slowly followed her, edging ahead of her by the time I reached the next set of traffic lights. I pulled over and turned around in my seat, watching her as she walked towards me.

She walked as straight and as proud as usual. She didn't see me. She didn't have to. The world saw *her*, that was what counted.

I picked up the camera again and focused on her. But before I could take another photo, she stopped walking, turned around and waved.

What the…?

A boy ran up to her side and stopped to talk to her. He was slightly shorter than her, had spiky brown hair and ears that poked out. He seemed around her age, but at the same time he looked so much younger; his socks around his ankles, his stance slumped slightly forward. They talked for a short while and I used the zoom on my camera to get a better view of what was happening.

He was talking fast. Her head tilted and she laughed at something he said. He looked surprised for a second, but then he laughed too.

My Princess turned around and started walking down the street again, and this time, the boy walked with her.

He kept talking, telling her something that clearly interested her. She nodded and laughed again, this time running a hand through her lovely long hair. And still the boy talked.

Won't he ever shut the fuck up?

I'd stopped taking photos. I didn't want this boy spoiling any shots I had of her. As they reached the traffic lights, she bent down and slipped the backpack from her shoulder. It was obviously heavy, and he leaned forward to pick it up.

Don't you dare…

She was still holding the top strap, and that's the same strap he reached for.

"No fuckin' way," I whispered as their hands touched.

It was only for a second, and maybe no one else noticed it, but their hands touched and stayed touching for way longer than was necessary.

Then my Princess let go, withdrew her hand slowly, and he took hold of the backpack for her.

"You little asshole," I said, as I seriously thought about going over there and yelling at him, telling him he had no right to do that, and to tell her he was only after one thing and if she wasn't careful he'd end up raping her.

But I sat there and just watched them cross the street and stop at the other corner to talk some more.

My erection died away quickly.

He smiled and so did she, then he handed her the backpack once more. They said a couple more things and then she turned and continued walking. He watched her go and I watched him. Eventually he turned around and headed back the way he had come, a huge smile on his face.

Little fucking prick. Asshole. Think you deserve her? Think again, ass-wipe. Think you're going to pop her cherry? You wouldn't know how to you little fucking fucker.

I turned the car around and headed for home. I didn't even want to think about her right then. I couldn't imagine what he was saying to her, but I could easily work out what he was trying to do.

Creepy little shit. He'd cum before he got his pants off.

Even worse was the thought that she might be interested in someone like him.

He's just a boy! Why would she want him?

It didn't make any sense. She knew better, she could have better. She could *have* the world and she didn't need him sniffing around, wanting to break her, fuck her and make her bleed.

Touch her, and I'll break you in two, pencil dick.

By the time I got home, I'd calmed down somewhat. I'd reasoned through events a bit more, had time to make sense of it all. I mean, he was probably just a friend. He was probably in her class, they were probably talking about some assignment they had to do.

Homework, yeah, that's it.

There was nothing suspicious in what had happened. It was just my mind magnifying every little event. I'd never seen him before and I'd certainly never seen him at her house, or followed her to his. So, there was obviously nothing going on between them. I was just over-reacting. She probably didn't even like him. She was just being polite.

My Princess would always be polite. Saying please and thank you.

"Please fuck me. Yes, oh, thank you," her beautiful southern accent filling my ears. "Fuck me harder. Fuck me again. Break me and make me cum, please. I wanna cum with you. Make me, please."

I smiled to myself as I sat down by my computer and looked at her beautiful face on my computer screen. My growing collection allowed me to sit back and watch my Princess over and over again, whenever I wanted.

Perfect.

Connecting the camera to the computer, I started to transfer the new images across to my hard drive. I looked at each of them, one by one, taking in every detail, looking for things I'd missed while I was taking them outside the school.

She was smiling, talking, pointing at one of the other girls, turning to listen, kissing, waving goodbye.

Her uniform looked so crisp, so fresh and new; her

socks a vibrant white in contrast to the darkness of her black hair; and that hint of flesh, the browny color of her tan, stretching up towards her thighs and even higher.

I went back to the start of the photos again and looked at the other girls who had been with her. They were pretty, but not so striking or naturally beautiful. One had too much makeup and she looked like a vamp, another had ratty hair that made her look like a kid's doll, but suddenly I found myself imagining them all together, in a room, my Princess and all her friends, naked and waiting for me.

Each of them naked, on all fours in front of me. I'd smudge the makeup of the vamp and pull on the doll's ratty hair until she squealed like a pig. I'd move from one to the other, smelling them, running my hands lightly along their waxed clefts, licking them, tasting them and then fucking them in line, one by one.

They'd want more, of course. They'd beg to be fucked again and again. They could take turns sucking me off, in pairs, making me cum, swallowing me whole and tasting my goodness while I ate each of them out, ordering them to sit on my face and squirm on top of me, their juices dripping down my throat and chin and their musky scent filling my nostrils, drowning me in virginal delight.

I smiled again, all the thoughts of the boy who had bothered her gone from my mind.

Slipping my hand down the front of my jeans, I pulled down the zip slowly, releasing my hard cock from within… just as she would when she kneels before me.

Yes, Princess, you and I, we have nothing to worry about.

I spent hours flicking back and forth between all the photos I had taken, looking at each of them over and over again, remembering each day I took them, remembering how she sounded when we'd talked and touched.

I wanted more.

To touch her all over, lick her, kiss her, fuck her all night, teach her how to be a woman, bring her to womanhood.

The more I looked, the more I thought, the harder I became. My cock pulsed between us.

I watched the photos as a slide-show and rubbed my-self, imagining that it was her who was sucking me off. Hard and fast, just how I liked it. When the photo flicked on the screen of her on her bike, riding to the grocery store, the wind through her hair, her nipples hard in her tight aqua top, her leg raised on the pedal, allowing me to see up her thigh into the darkness where her fruits awaited…

I aimed well and splattered her picture with my cum.

It ran down the screen, some down her face and over her breasts, some more slowly rolling across her skirt and down her legs, one long strand heading for the darkness between them.

I would have my Princess. I would fuck her and make her a woman. *My* woman.

Not soon. Not some day. Not when I had the chance.

No, she was too pure, too good to pass up.

I would have her, I knew.

I could wait no longer.

* * *

It's past two am, but no one is around, no one saw me enter the house. The backdoor latch was simple and although the wire door squeaked a little, breaking the little pane of glass and unlocking the deadbolt from inside was easier than I expected.

I started to sweat as I stood there in the darkness, having never been inside her house before. It was quaint, not quite what I'd imagined, and the décor was a little too 60s for me. But her parents' tastes didn't concern me.

Only her taste.

It took a little while to work out the layout of the house, especially in the darkness, but once I found the hallway and the stairs up to the bedrooms, the rest was easy.

I was sure my breathing was loud in the darkness, but no one stepped out of the bedrooms to confront me, no one stopped me as I crept down the hallway. I was ready, on edge, just in case someone came out from somewhere in the night, but no one did.

Her mother didn't scream as I stabbed her father through the heart.

He jerked around a bit in their big queen-size bed, but she didn't really seem to notice anything was wrong until I slit his throat and the blood started spurting over her back and shoulders. That's when she sat up and fumbled for the light, trying to turn around and see me at the same time. I slashed at her hands and punched her hard across the jaw once…then again. Her head cannoned into the bedside table and she just kinda flopped over like a leaf half-caught on a fence.

Yeah, there was a little noise, but nothing that caused my Princess to come running. She probably didn't hear a thing, tucked up all nice and warm in her own bed further down the hallway.

I made sure her mother was out cold and double-checked her father was still bleeding to death in the bed. She was breathing, he wasn't. Neither were going to stop me now.

I used the sheets to wipe the blood off my knife and hands, wiped the sweat from my brow too. I checked my appearance in her mother's mirror. I flattened down my hair a bit, and checked my smile. I looked fine. I had to make sure I made the right impression.

And now I'm standing outside her bedroom door.

It has a little name-plate on it, one of those cheap tacky things you pick up at jumble sales. It says BECKY'S ROOM.

Underneath, someone's written ENTER AT OWN RISK.

I smile as I wipe the sweat from my brow and take a moment to try to calm down. I double-check the bottle of GHB is in my trouser pocket. I've saved it for so long, but now I really doubt if I'll even need it.

She's mine, GHB or not.

I glance down the hallway once more, just in case her father or mother has made a miraculous recovery.

But I know they haven't.

I'm in control and everything is going exactly to plan.

I place my hand on the doorknob and grasp it tight. It feels cold in my grip, the silver knob almost searing itself to my skin.

Every second, every moment, every sight and sound and smell is magnified a thousand times.

I focus hard on her name on the door.

BECKY.

Holding my breath, I turn the knob slightly and the door opens inwards without a sound. My eyes dart around, now accustomed to the darkness, and I can make out a bookcase, a wardrobe, her desk and her backpack laying flat on her desk chair.

"Mom?" I hear her whisper sleepily, the sound of her voice filling me with joy. She sounds groggy, tired...or maybe just not quite awake. "Is that you?"

"Becky?" I whisper softly, the door swinging open fully so I can see her and she can see me.

"Yes," is her automatic reply. "What is it?"

And now is my moment, now is my reward. My cock is hard and throbbing, pressing desperately against my jeans, willing me on, wanting me to continue, aching to be inside her.

She sits up, reaches slowly for her bedside light.

I don't stop her. I won't.

This is it. Our time together.

Becky will be pleased.

It's a jungle out there, Becky. Fuck or be fucked.

Now it's your turn...

WHITE CHRISTMAS

"Thirty-nine, ninety-five," she said.

I smiled at her, but she didn't smile back. She just stared down at my hands, waiting for me to produce cash or a card.

She had nice blue eyes along with full and luscious red lips. Her blonde hair was in two pigtails and dark roots stuck out from underneath. She looked pale – her gray uniform probably didn't help – but the black eyeliner ringing her eyes and her bright red lipstick made up for that.

"Last minute gift," I said to her, smiling as I did so.

She nodded but didn't lift her eyes.

"Thirty-nine, ninety-five," she repeated.

At this time of year, you'd think she'd be full of Christmas cheer.

I slowly pulled my wallet from my jeans, still watching her intently and trying to remember everything about her, to capture her fully in my mind's eye before we part. Her thinly plucked eyebrows, the barely noticeable blonde down on her top lip, the way her forehead furrowed as she waited impatiently for me to pay. I took my time, hoping she would look up at me.

But all too soon I had the cash out of my wallet and I was handing it to her, taking a moment to look around at the long lines of people at the registers, some ten or twelve deep. I hardly noticed a smile on any of their faces either.

So much for Christmas good will.

I thought about turning around and throwing my arms out wide, yelling at the top of my voice, "It's *Christmas* people! Where's your festive spirit?"

But I didn't. I'd spotted the security cameras at the front of the store, one by the entrance and the other in one of those black domes attached to the ceiling right above the check-out lines. You couldn't see inside the dome, so you never knew where it was focusing.

Stay cool, look normal, pay cash and leave.

She quickly took the cash from me, letting our hands touch only for a brief second, and started the transaction. My eyes chanced a glimpse at the name-tag, pinned above her left breast.

Shandi it said in big black print.

"Hi Shandi!" I thought about trying to start the conversation again. *"Looking forward to Christmas?"*

But I knew what the answer would be.

She's probably counting down the hours until the store closes.

"Not long now," I said, still smiling.

"Huh?" she asked, her voice flat, her eyes focused on the register.

"Until closing," I replied, pointing at my watch. "A couple of hours and you're done. So hang in there. Not long now."

She handed me my change and pushed the box towards me, then gave me a smile that was all lie.

Lips like that should be put to better use.

I muttered a quick goodbye to her as I lifted the box, but she was already reaching for the merchandise of the person behind me.

"Merry Christmas how are you today," she intoned in one long monotonous breath.

Nothing merry about it...

I tugged the rim of the baseball cap down lower on my forehead as I pushed my way through the crowd. Everyone was doing exactly the same thing, panic shopping on Christmas Eve and looking for that one very special gift for the love of their life.

I smiled as my eyes dropped down to the box I was carrying.

This is perfect.

Just like Christina.

This would be our fourth Christmas, and I knew this would be by far the best yet, as it would be the first time we'd spent Christmas together. Our families had always got in the way the previous years; she'd have to visit hers, and I'd always end up visiting my folks out of State, or suffering through my sister's food and booze-driven Christmas extravaganzas.

Not this year.

No, this time, everything had worked out perfectly.

I walked out of the mall to be greeted by darkness and rain, and I carefully dashed to the car park, my cap keeping the rain from my face, and my free hand searching my pockets for the keys.

Working at the factory at this time of year usually meant long hours and double-shifts. The extra money was good, but this year I wanted it to be different. This year I wanted everything perfect for Christina and me. I'd managed to swap most of my shifts with Sam and Peter, and Ken said he would cover for me on the days I couldn't swap. So, in the end, that gave me the next week off, and time enough to properly enjoy Christmas for the first time in years.

I found my keys as I reached the Jeep and quickly unlocked the door, bending forward and placing the box on the passenger seat before climbing in behind the wheel. I shook the rain from my coat and started the engine.

The rain was heavier now, but I didn't care. Three days it had been raining, but nothing would dampen my festive spirit. It could rain for the next forty days for all I cared, as long as Christina and I could spend the whole time together.

I smiled as I drove out of the parking lot, knowing everything had worked out perfectly this year.

* * *

I wanted the Christmas tree to be perfect, that was the first thing, so as soon as I got home I pulled it out of its box and set to work. Sure, it was plastic and fake and too small, but with all the baubles and tinsel wrapped around it, along with the flashing lights, no one would really know. It was the effort and the thought that counted, and I knew this was going to be the most exciting Christmas Eve I'd ever had – even more-so than when I was a little boy.

Because this year, I was in control.

When you're a kid, you're excited and get lots of presents, but in the end it's an adult day and you're pulled from one family to the next, watching as your mom and dad slowly get drunk, start to yell and… well, that's when the fighting would usually begin. My sister and I would take our new toys and head to another room to play until both our parents passed out or walked out, door slamming behind them.

Not this year. No, I would never be like them.

I placed the angel on the top of the tree and climbed down the ladder, standing back to look at my handiwork.

"She'll be impressed," I said to myself as I hurriedly cleaned up and hid the Christmas tree box behind the sofa.

I wanted everything to be just right.

I checked my watch. I had it all planned and wanted to make sure everything was ready.

I rushed to my bedroom, took off my baseball cap and climbed out of my work clothes, throwing them into the laundry basket as I passed by on the way to the bathroom. I had a quick shower and shave, and then climbed into my best suit. I hadn't worn it for a couple of years, and kept it only for special occasions, and I was pleasantly surprised that it still fit me pretty good.

I walked back to the kitchen and took the champagne from the refrigerator and set it on the bench, next to the two long-stem glasses.

Chilled, but not too cold.

It was then I noticed the mistletoe resting on the hall-stand by the door.

"Shit," I muttered.

How the hell did I miss that?

I grabbed it quickly and rummaged around in the hallway closet until I found the hammer and a couple of nails. Everything needed to be just right. I hadn't planned this for so long just to have it go wrong now.

Quickly, I slipped down the stairs to the basement, opening the door quietly and heading towards the middle of the room.

The ladder was still upstairs by the Christmas tree –
Shoulda brought that down with me. Damn it.
– so I used a couple of crates and stacked them on top of each other. They were just the right height to allow me to stand on them and nail the mistletoe onto the wooden beam overhead.

And that was when Christina woke.

Her head moved slightly to one side, and I saw her arms tense.

Of course, it was stupid to have nailed the mistletoe into the beam right then, because it had woken her, but I had little choice if I was to have the night exactly as I'd always planned.

Her head rolled backwards and she looked up at me, her eyes trying to focus as her hands balled into fists.

She hung there, strung up and hardly able to move, watching me as I nailed the mistletoe in place above her head.

"Almost time," I whispered to her. "Sorry, didn't meant to wake you."

She shook her head and tried to say something, but the gag in her mouth wouldn't let her. I knew I really should loosen it a little for her, or take it off for a while, as it was tied very tightly around her head and scrunched up her pretty features. But the last time I did that, she screamed way too loud, and I couldn't risk anyone hearing her cries from outside.

"You know what happens under the mistletoe, right?" I asked her.

She shook her head, but I was pretty sure she knew exactly what happened.

"Tonight's going to be so special, Christina," I said as I checked the knots in the rope binding both her wrists.

"This is what we've both been waiting for, my love."

I climbed off the crates and pushed them to one side, leaning the hammer against them.

"I've got a very special present for you upstairs too, I just know you're going to love it."

She shook her head again, this time much harder, and her whole body swung slightly from side to side. I took a moment to check the ropes around her ankles as well, but they were holding tight too. I'd learnt my lesson last night when I'd brought dinner down to her and she'd kicked it out of my hands.

I still had to clean up that mess; broken plates and spaghetti bolognese in a cold lumpy pile over near the furnace. But it could wait. If she didn't want to eat before Christmas dinner, I sure understood.

"I'm all dressed up," I said to her as I switched on the portable floodlight to show her my suit. I stood there, arms wide, and spun around for her a couple of times. "What do you think?"

She didn't say anything, didn't even move this time, just watched me. Her eyes narrow and dark, peering at me through her messed red curls.

"I bought you a dress and everything," I continued. "It's blue and backless and I think you'll like it. It's very you, at least I think so. It was on sale in October. I wasn't planning on buying it, but when I saw it I said to myself, yes, that's perfect for Christina."

I smiled, but it didn't work.

"If you're good, I *will* let you go," I continued. "Let's just have Christmas together and then you can go, alright?"

Her expression changed then, her head tilted to one side and I could see that she was really listening to me now.

"It's true. I'm not going to keep you here forever. I'm not that kinda guy. I just want to have Christmas with you and then you can go. We'll have a great time, I promise, and then you can leave and we can keep this our little secret okay? If you like it enough you might even want to stay, maybe."

I knew I was talking too fast, but she *did* seem to be

listening.

"I'm sorry you're all dirty and grubby… and I sure didn't want to leave you down here with no clothes on. If you're good, I'll give you a bath and help you get into the dress and we can go upstairs and see the Christmas tree I've brought and you can open your present and we'll drink champagne and talk and laugh and see in Christmas Day getting to know each other and having a wonderful time."

We stood there in the basement, no more than a few feet apart. I wanted to look down at her breasts, to kneel before for and touch her cleft, but I knew this wasn't the time. I'd stolen a few glances when I'd undressed her, but she was unconscious and it didn't feel right then, it was as if I was prying… spying on her. So I'd tried very hard not to look, to touch, taste or explore.

I would save myself for later.

And then, she nodded.

Just a slow dip of the head, once…then twice.

"*Really?*"

She nodded again.

I took a step forward, my wildest dreams coming true sooner than I expected.

I knew she would understand if I had a chance to explain myself to her. I knew if she calmed down and got over my initial actions she'd understand why I did what I did.

As neighbors we didn't talk that much. We'd nod and wave whenever we saw each other, like normal neighbors would on any street around the world. But it was Christina's husband who always scared me. He drove a truck and wore cowboy boots and smoked cigars and I knew there was no way I would have a chance with her while he was around.

He often took the truck on long trips out of State and across the country, and I'd fantasized countless times about breaking into her house, pinning her down, making love to her and giving her the passion I just knew he couldn't provide. But I never took the risk, never dared chance my dreams, just in case he came home and discovered us.

But two weeks ago when I drove up the street after

work and saw the removal truck in front of their house, and saw him drive off with a parting, "Fuck you, bitch! She's better than you ever were, you useless cunt!" I knew that I now had a chance.

It *would* work out. My dreams *could* come true. I'd waited over four long years for my chance with Christina, and nothing was going to ruin this evening.

In retrospect, going over there late last night and asking to borrow some sugar was dumb. Just plain dumb. I'm awkward at the best of times, but to head over with an empty jar to borrow sugar from the girl of your dreams is never going to work.

But time had been running out. I wanted to spend Christmas with her, so I *had* to make the move when I did.

If anything, I was just lucky that she knew me by sight as her neighbor and probably thought I was safe. She might've turned anyone else away, but she smiled and invited me in.

She was in a bathrobe and I apologized for getting her out of the shower.

"Don't worry," she said, her voice light and beautiful, her red hair still wet and clinging to her shoulders and arms. It was the first time I'd heard her voice and she sounded so happy, so carefree.

Probably thrilled to be rid of her asshole husband.

"I spend way too much time in the bath, anyway," she continued over her shoulder.

She had one hand on her robe, keeping it closed as we walked into her kitchen. But I could tell from her chest and legs that she was naked under it.

As she knelt down by a cupboard and reached inside for the sugar, I wrapped the rope around her neck and yanked backwards hard.

They make it look so easy in the movies, but she didn't pass out after a few seconds, or go limp or faint. Instead, she fought and twisted and made horrible gurgling noises as I dragged her out of the kitchen, down her hallway, through her house and out into the backyard, pulling her down the back stairs and dragging her across the concrete, through the rain and the grass and wet slush and mud and whatever.

She almost got away when I had to turn to open my back gate and drag her into my backyard. I never use the back gate, so the bolt was rusty and stuck – *should've checked that earlier* – and I had to take one hand off the rope and lean against the gate to force the bolt free.

She picked that moment to spin around to reach for me, her sharp fingernails scratching at my pants and shirt, tearing at the material and trying to tear into me.

So much strength for someone so pretty and so slight.

That's why I'd made sure I'd cut those nails of hers down to the quick once I got her into the basement.

Even though I thought I was going a good job at cutting off her supply of oxygen, she still hung on, still fought and still made way too much noise.

I panicked a little when things weren't going as I had planned. I kicked at her plenty of times, maybe too many, and in the end I just got real frustrated and let go of the rope so I could walk around and kick her in the stomach. She tried to crawl away across my lawn, but after a few of those well-placed kicks, she didn't move anymore, didn't fight. She just spit up a whole lot of blood and laid there limp and quiet.

From there, it was easy. I could concentrate on dragging her down into the basement without worrying about her fighting back or screaming for help. Her bath gown had been lost somewhere, but I found it later at her back gate. Luckily, I'd found it before anyone else. I'd thrown that into the furnace and burnt it, just as an extra precaution.

People get tripped up over the smallest details.

Once I'd tied her up for her own safety, I went back upstairs to clean up. I didn't want her seeing me all muddy and covered in sweat. I needed to look my best for her. Then she'd understand and we could both start off on the right foot. She'd forgive me for my little indiscretion because she'd soon see the real me.

I heard her screaming the moment I stepped out of the

shower.

The gag wasn't part of the original plan, but I couldn't have her acting in such a way. She'd ruin everything, so I had to think on my feet.

I tore my shirt into strips and ran down to the basement, yelling at her to be quiet, but of course that had no effect. The punch to the stomach did, though, and her screams vanished along with the air from her lungs. That gave me plenty of time to tie the gag tightly into place.

I wanted to clean her up, and I told her I'd get her some dinner, but every time I came near her, she would try to scream through the gag and would pull on the ropes and try to escape.

I went upstairs and turned on the radio, forcing myself to ignore her muffled cries as I made dinner. After half an hour, I went back down with dinner nicely prepared, a rose resting on the side of the plate. I should've been more careful, I guess, but I was excited and wanted to share the meal with her. I didn't notice she'd managed to slip her left leg out of the rope that had been holding it.

I held the meal out to her. "For you," I said.

And she kicked the plate from my hand, my spaghetti bolognese flying through the air, all my good work in the kitchen unceremoniously swiped aside and dumped at our feet.

I'd doubled the rope and retied all the knots after that, even though her thrashing made it difficult for me.

This wasn't how it was supposed to be.

For a while, I honestly thought my dreams weren't to come true.

So I'd left here there last night, and ignored her muffled cries this morning as I readied for work.

Now, it seemed as if she'd had time to think about things, to reflect, and she was acting much better.

Absence makes the heart grow fonder.

I was pleased.

"If I take off your gag, you won't scream?" I confirmed, just to be absolutely sure.

She shook her head.

"Promise?"

She nodded.

"Then I'll untie you and take you upstairs for a bath, okay? You're probably dying for one, right?"

She readily agreed.

"Okay, then."

Slowly, I walked closer towards her, being careful and watching her every move. But she just hung there, her eyes now full of hope.

Maybe I *had* made a breakthrough.

I reached out with my left hand and gently touched her face, feeling her soft, warm skin. My fingers closed around the gag and pulled it out of her mouth and over her chin.

She let out a big gasp, and I watched her breasts as her chest lifted and fell, over and over again.

I gave her the time she needed, letting her catch her first real breath for almost twenty-four hours.

"Thank you," she whispered, in a dried, cracked voice.

"My pleasure, Christina."

"Can I…. have s- some water?"

"Of course!" I nodded. "You can have anything you want. You name it, it's yours."

I saw a smile slip across her face, then quickly disappear. I could tell she was enjoying this too now.

I turned to get her some water from the sink in the corner, then I changed my mind.

Maybe I can make her earn it.

I turned back to face her.

"But, you *are* still under the mistletoe," I said. "And we really *should* be very traditional this time of year."

She stared at me, chest still heaving, her eyes narrowing once more.

"I removed your gag, so you could return a favor, don't you think?"

I waited and watched as she watched me.

"Okay," she whispered finally.

"*Really?*"

"Yes," she added. "You deserve it."

She understands! She feels exactly the way I do! I knew it.

It was like a dream – like all my fantasies and plans and hopes suddenly appeared before me.

Here was Christina, tied up and naked in my base-ment, *wanting* to kiss me. Actually *aching* to be with me, and so soon in our relationship! Maybe she wasn't out of breath at all, perhaps she was just *lusting* for me.

Hot and horny and wet and wanting me as much as I want her.

"You can't hide it, you know," she said, her eyes drop-ping down to my groin. "I can see how turned on you are by all this."

And she was right. I was hard and throbbing, my cock pushing against my pants. I wanted her more desperately than I thought possible.

So I stepped forward… leaned out towards her – hop-ing and praying – and she leaned in towards me.

She understands! She knows what I want, what we both want!

Our lips touched and her warmth and softness flooded through me as her tongue darted into my mouth and I closed my eyes and let her passion flood over me. I stepped closer, kissed her harder, wanting more and more and more.

Our tongues danced together, touched, probed deeper.

We were one.

Then her lips were gone.

In a flash they left me.

And I felt the pain shoot along my nose as she bit down hard, her teeth breaking skin and gristle and muscle as she wrenched and tried to tear through.

I wanted to scream, to pull away, but I couldn't. Her teeth held tight and hard and the pain made me weak and woozy and I just wanted it all to stop.

No no nonononono! Not like this.

I could taste the blood in my mouth, could feel it spill-ing down the back of my throat.

I lashed out, my knee connecting hard with her stom-ach. I felt her breath on my face as her teeth let go and she yelled in pain.

I pushed away from her, overbalanced, fell backwards and hit the ground hard.

"You *fucking* loser," she spat at me, blood and skin and stuff handing from her mouth and slipping from her chin. "Who the *fuck* do you think you are? How dare you keep me here like some fucking dog, tied up to do whatever you want to me. Do you really think I'd want *anything* to do with someone as deranged and *fucking stupid* as you? Get me the fuck out of here or I'll scream this place down."

As I picked myself up, I used one hand to hold my throbbing nose, trying to stem the flow of blood, and the other to reach out and grab the hammer from the side of the crates.

"You think you're some kind of big man? God's answer to women? What the fuck is *wrong* with you? Are you *crazy?*"

I couldn't speak, I just shook my head as I stepped towards her. I just wanted her to stop talking, to stop screaming at me, to be quiet and to not call me names like mommy did. I just wanted her to be nice Christina from next door again, and to want me and love me and kiss me and hold me and make this Christmas special.

Special, damn it!

"I just got rid of one fucking *retard*, and I was *married* to him. Why the *fuck* would I get involved with another?"

She just wouldn't stop.

Not until I made her.

I lashed out once with the hammer, aimed it at her foul bloody mouth, watched as it took out her front teeth and snagged on her jaw, pulled it back hard before striking again and again.

And again.

It didn't take long.

She stopped making sense, didn't say much else that I could understand. Didn't have the chance.

Even her whimpering eventually ended.

And the basement was silent once more.

* * *

I stood there for some time, just watching her, counting the slow rise and fall of her breathing, watching the blood flow down her face and onto her breasts... then slip lower.

This hasn't quite gone to plan.

I pulled a handkerchief from my pocket and used it to dab at the blood running from the bridge of my nose. The bite hurt like hell, but there wasn't a lot of blood. She hadn't done as much damage as I thought.

It still hurt like hell, though.

And my suit was ruined, along with Christmas Eve.

I didn't know whether to be angry or sad.

I thought Christina was the one for me, and I was sure we'd really connected, just in those last few seconds before she attacked me and tried to bite off my face.

She'd looked at me....*differently.*

I was sure there must've been a way to show her what I was really like, how I could be there for her, to love her and protect her.

She had to understand.

I looked up at the mistletoe, hanging crooked on the nail above her head.

That was stupid.

No wonder she got so upset, waking up all tied and bound and cold in the basement, and then with me trying to kiss her.

Dumb. Why did I even think that would work? Just stupid.

She coughed then, a glob of blood falling from the hole where her mouth used to be, dropping to the floor with a loud *splat.*

Her legs tensed and she muttered something I couldn't understand as she slowly came back from unconsciousness.

She lifted her head slightly, just enough for her eyes to meet mine. I felt uncomfortable standing there as she stared at me, the bloody gash in her face resembling a possessed sneer, like she was holding me in contempt, as if I was some disgusting primitive animal.

Who's the animal?

I wasn't the one tied up and all bloody, covered with dirt and piss and blood and spit and whatever.

I was the one who was free, able to move around and go about my normal day-to-day existence. She should've been *thanking* me for looking after her, for caring and making her at home in *my* house, showing her *my* hospitality.

Loving her.

Quickly, I took a step forward, keeping the hammer in my hand, just in case she somehow managed to attack me again. But I wasn't stupid this time, I kept my distance and made sure I didn't get too close.

"Look at what you've done to *me!*" I screamed at her. "How could you? After all I've done for you?"

She spat at me, mucus and a blood-covered tooth landing at my feet.

"I *tried* to give you a nice Christmas, I *tried* to show you I could care, and this is how you *repay* me? I thought you were different, not like the others. I thought we really *connected.*"

She just stared. I could see the hate in her eyes now. There was no doubt about it.

"I didn't want it to be this way, I never dreamed this would be the outcome. I only wanted us to spend Christmas together and finally get to know each other. Is that so much to ask? Four years we've known each other, but we've never really taken the time to be friends. You're lonely and so am I. I just thought we could be together."

Clearly, what I was saying wasn't helping. And I guess I could see her point. Arguing about who was to blame wasn't going to get us anywhere.

Hell, it's Christmas. Peace on Earth and goodwill to all men.

And women.

Especially Christina.

I tried a different tack.

"Look, I don't want us to fight," I said as I smiled at her and took a step backwards, trying to look relaxed and okay with all that had happened. I wanted to let her know

I wasn't going to strike out again. "I don't want us stuck down here for all of Christmas. I'm sorry I hit out at you and I'm sure you're sorry for what you did to me."

I leaned closer and pointed to my nose so she could see the damage.

"See? We both got hurt. So why don't we just put it behind us and start again. What do you think?"

She said nothing, but I could tell I'd probably convinced her. Maybe showing her my own wound had made her see sense that neither of us were going to win by arguing and fighting.

And then I had a terrific idea.

"I know," I said, my smile growing as I placed the hammer in the sink, hoping that would win her trust. "What if I go upstairs and bring down your present?"

She coughed a little more and I could see the ropes digging deep into her wrists, the strain on her arms must've been enormous by now.

She's getting tired.

"Stay here," I said to her as I moved away, the excitement rising inside me. This idea was too good to wait any longer. "I wasn't going to let you have the surprise until Christmas morning, but I guess under the circumstances, you can have it tonight and we can forget about all this trouble, okay?"

I didn't wait for an answer, instead I dashed upstairs and grabbed the box. It wasn't wrapped, I hadn't had the time as I'd only just bought it, but in the dim light of the basement, I guessed she wouldn't see much until I presented it to her anyway.

I carefully walked back down the stairs with the box hidden behind my back.

I can't wait to see her face.

And I stood in front of her, happier and more excited than I'd ever been before.

Ever.

"Which hand?" I asked her.

She didn't reply.

"Go on, guess which hand?"

We stared at each other, neither willing to give in. But I couldn't wait any longer.

"Alright, I'll show you." I brought the box out from behind my back and held it out to her. "What do you think?"

I watched her eyes dance across the words printed on the box, saw her forehead furrow and watched as she thought carefully – first denying, then understanding exactly what I'd bought for her.

"Want me to open it?" I whispered.

Her eyes darted back to mine, and what was left of her mouth tried desperately to formulate something meaningful through the blood and missing teeth. But she only let out one small, pathetic word.

"No."

Then she was shaking her head back and forth, blood and spit flying everywhere as she wrenched once – then twice – on the ropes holding her.

"Christina, *don't*!" I said.

But that didn't stop her. She pulled harder, her wrists darkening, bruising more, her legs trying to kick out at me, a primeval growl forming from somewhere inside her.

I put the box on the ground next to me and held out my hands.

"Christina, please, don't! Don't stay mad at me. I'm no longer angry at you."

But she wasn't looking at me, wasn't listening now, she just kept trying to tug and pull and break her bonds. To escape me, to leave me here all alone.

Like everyone else.

I studied the ropes holding her wrists. I was sure one was loosening under her weight and the prolonged attack.

I knew I had to act fast.

She didn't notice when I moved away from her, heading to the sink to retrieve the hammer. She was thrashing back and forth, the growl getting louder and turning into a scream.

She didn't try to stop me as I crept closer to her, making sure I was out of her reach, but she not out of mine.

My first blow missed, hitting her on the shoulder and

glancing off. I'd been aiming for her head, but she was moving too fast for me. Still, she felt the pain as the hammer hit, and that stopped her struggling right away.

She looked up at me one last time, opened her mouth either to say something or to scream again.

I didn't wait.

I brought the hammer down on her skull.

My second attempt was a bull's-eye. So was the third.

She slumped finally, her body giving way, only the ropes holding her upright now. Her pretty red hair was dark and matted, her breasts no longer rose and fell with her breath.

I threw the hammer to the ground after the fifth blow and just stared at her until I got my own breathing under control.

"You've ruined everything now," I said to her as I turned away and knelt down next to the box.

The Matco Tools Jump Starter Cables were some of the best cables around, or so the guy at the hardware store had told me. The clamps were heavy duty metal and perfect for connections on any kind of battery. The 28 inch flexible cables were excellent in cold weather, and they even came equipped with reverse polarity protection – according to the box – just in case you accidentally reverse the clamps.

No chance of that happening.

I carefully unpacked and unraveled the cables.

"This was meant to be a surprise," I said to her, but she didn't answer. "It won't be as much fun now."

I quickly attached the cables to the box I had built last weekend. It had taken me a while to work out how to attach the cables to the mains electricity running through the basement, but a quick Google or two had given me all the information I needed.

My workmates Gerard and Shane had given me some pointers too. Even though we all worked at the abattoirs, Shane had been an electrician when he was younger, and Gerard knew a whole lot about cars.

I soon discovered that it was deceptively easy to wire the jumper cables into the mains. A couple of visits to Radio Shack and the hardware store and I was all set.

I reached over to the switch on the wall and turned it on. The LED on the front of my home-made converter glowed softly into life.

Perfect.

I expected her to cry out in pain and try to kick out at me again as I attached each of the clamps to her breasts, but she just hung there like a rag doll. She didn't even move as the metal teeth squeezed and took hold, pushing and disfiguring each of her nipples, turning them blue and puffy.

I knew then that the struggle was truly over.

I could still hear her shallow breathing as I knelt before her, watching the blood slowly flow down her, and I knew our time together was quickly running out.

All my plans – ruined. It wasn't meant to end like this. Not now. Not so soon.

I leaned towards her, felt her warmth and smelt her sweat and piss. I was so close to her and she was so inviting, so totally at my mercy.

For anything.

I leaned closer, licked at the blood pooling in her belly-button and then ventured lower. My lips met hers, and I dared to kiss her there for a few seconds, then a few more.

When she didn't move, didn't try to resist, I knew for sure she was mine.

My tongue darted out and I tasted her insides, a sweet sticky taste of desire and blood, of funky willingness and fear, of total surrender. I rolled myself around her clit. Felt the firmness, the nub of her very essence.

And she let out a moan.

I threw myself backwards, hand across my face to defend myself, but she didn't move, didn't try to attack.

Her head still hung there, the two gaping holes in her face and skull not bleeding like they had been.

In the end, she had enjoyed it, I was sure.

I checked my nose in reflex, wiped it with the handkerchief again, just to make sure, but my bleeding had stopped too.

"I'm so sorry," I said as I reached over to the switch on my converter. "I'd really hoped you'd have been a part of this."

I flicked it on, and she danced before me.

The dank, stark aroma of burning flesh intoxicated me even more than her spasms. I watched as the burning dark patches of skin quickly grew outward from her nipples to cover her breasts, then spread towards her throat and stomach.

My hand slipped down the front of my pants and I grabbed my throbbing cock, jerking it as she jerked, twisting and turning and pulling as she did. As the electricity charged through her, I could feel her life force – her love – charging through me.

She spat some more blood, and I watched as her head was thrown backwards, her eyes rolling back in her head and a shuddering low moan emitted from the place where her mouth had been.

I watched and tugged harder as she convulsed, until the white foam spewed from within her, over the holes where her lovely teeth had once been and dripping down her bloody cheeks. Crimson and white ooze joining, running together, mixing.

And I came as she came, my inner soul flooding me as the electricity flooded her.

A very White Christmas indeed.

For those few seconds we were together as one. As lovers should be.

She choked on the white and red and chunky vomit that erupted from her, drowning her, taking her from me in a matter of seconds.

And finally she was still once more.

Eventually, I turned off the power and just sat there, wiping my hand clean with the handkerchief and watching what was left of her life drip and flow away from her.

The burning smell disappeared quickly, as did her breathing, replaced by the heavy and intoxicating miasma of vomit, shit and cum.

After a while, I stood and walked towards her, reaching

out to remove the clamps from her charred nipples. Next, I nudged her shoulder with my finger, making sure she was dead. She didn't move, other than to swing limply on the ropes for a few seconds.

No breath. No sound.

"Christina?" I whispered to her, tilting my head towards her mouth, listening for a reply.

I didn't get one.

"I wish we could've made this last a little longer," I said to her. "I'd planned great things for the next few days. You would've had a ball. We *both* would've! But it's all ruined now."

I turned away from her and walked to the light-switch, flipping it on for the first time since I'd brought Christina down to the basement. The florescent lights flickered into life overhead.

I picked up the Polaroid camera from the shelf near the sink and walked back towards her.

"Smile one last time, my love," I whispered as I squatted down and took a photo of her face, then of her vagina, and then one long shot of her whole body resting in all its final glory.

I stood there and waited for each of the photos for develop, watching as she came to life once again, this time on paper – captured now once and for all.

As a keepsake.

Mine forever.

I smiled at her again and ran my fingers over the photos, remembering how she felt and tasted. I lifted the photos to my face, kissed them, pressed hard against her mouth and licked her stomach and cunt once more.

Remembering.

Not letting go.

Even though I was disappointed it had all ended so quickly, the result was still exceptional.

Sometimes relationships don't last as long as you'd expect. That's just a sad fact of life.

But we'll always have the memories of our good times together.

Putting the camera aside, I walked over to the back wall and picked up the staple gun. Slowly, I positioned the Polaroids down on the final row. I made sure each was straight, and directly under the ones above it, before stapling the final three into place. Then I wrote the date underneath each.

Christmas Eve.

I stood back and surveyed the whole wall, counted each and every one of the sixty-seven Polaroids I'd taken of Christina.

The first day I saw her.

That time in her backyard.

When she was out front talking to Mr. Worcester from across the road.

The time I followed her to the gym.

Getting into the car after shopping at the mall.

Her birthday last year, when the party was held at McGovern's Bar.

That time I followed her to the park.

The mall again.

The hairdressers.

Her work.

Her mother's house.

In the bath, taken through her bathroom window.

Last week.

Saturday.

Two days ago.

Yesterday before I went to visit her.

And now.

I turned to my left and looked at the other wall. I had eighty-two photos of Nicole, and another twenty-nine photos of Joanne, but she'd moved neighborhoods before I could do anything to her.

I sighed deeply and turned to look at the photos of Christina one last time.

We'd been good together.

I just wished we'd made it through to Christmas Day.

Still, I'd received my present early, so I couldn't complain.

"Anyway," I said to no one in particular, as I turned to my right and walked over to study the seven Polaroids stapled to that wall. I reached out and ran my fingers around her bright red lips, and caressed her two lovely blonde pigtails. "There's always New Years, Shandi."

I smiled.

What a happy New Year it would be.

DOWN ON KATIE THE NINTH DAY

An extract from
The Modern Days of Sodom

The storm continued unabated outside throughout the night and well into the morning. Waking early, as I'd become accustomed, I found work continued even through the storm. No man-hour was spared, with teams working day and night, erecting the tents, unpacking trunks and unfurling the long purple sails.

Breakfasting on the meager rations provided, I sat in my usual position on one of the high benches at the side of the arena, watching the colorful spectacle play out below me in ritualistic fashion, just as it had on every morning of my time here. I didn't interfere or speak to anyone - it wasn't my place - as explained to me by Madame Duclos upon my arrival.

Instead, I waited until beckoned by young Montserrat, who took me down the nearest walkway and to a satin-draped doorway. Once there, she smiled politely as she did to me every morning, still refusing to look me directly in the eyes. She leant forward and touched me lightly on the shoulder, her lips quickly dancing across my ear as she whispered to me, curtseyed and then left me alone.

I nodded to her, although I knew she did not see it. I wanted to say something, anything, acknowledge her in some way, but I knew that would not be allowed.

Pulling the satin curtains back across the doorway, I walked into a small alcove lit by candles and filled with a musky aroma. The pillows were the colors of deep reds and blues and were arranged in one large circle on the floor, not unlike the formation of the ones from yesterday. Except, this time, there was only one girl lying across them.

She was naked, her cleft hairless and glistening in the candlelight, and she was beckoning me forward. There were four large X-frames positioned near the cushions, the one closest to me bore deep, long scars of frequent use.

"Welcome," was all she muttered as I stepped towards her, already hard and throbbing inside my trousers.

I guessed that she was probably in her mid-teens, still developing, but more than enough of a woman for me.

She wore only a collar, coloured deep green, which labeled her as more experienced than the girls from yesterday. I could smell her juices and her scent; her unfulfilled desires.

She knelt before me and unbuttoned my trousers, pulling down my underwear as well, her eyes and mouth widening as she examined my cock.

"Nice, Sir, if I may say so," she said as she reached forward and massaged my shaft.

I nodded to her to continue and unbuttoned my shirt, throwing it to one side. Now, I was as naked as she was, and I wanted her just as badly.

"Is Sir hungry?" she asked me.

I nodded my head, staring deep into her blue captivating eyes. Her hair was tied in a bun, streaks of blonde and brown and red and blue fighting the bun's tight grasp.

"Dessert," I whispered to her, repeating the command Montserrat had whispered to me.

She giggled and turned away from me, stretching over to a small metal trunk and quickly opening it. As she rummaged inside, I let my hands drop down to her small, pert breasts and I took one of her hard nipples in my fingers, twisting it and pinching it, feeling it grow harder.

Soon, she straightened up and held out a bowl of whipped cream to me.

"Does this find your agreement, Sir?" she asked. "It is fresh today."

I nodded, letting her nipple fall from my fingers. I let my hand slip behind her head, to the bun of her hair and grabbed it roughly.

She gasped, but I also saw the smile play across her features. She placed the bowl of cream between us before she leaned forward and, at my guidance, began kissing my cock, taking it into her mouth. I was hard, throbbing as her tongue sucked and licked, her lips warm and wet and ever so inviting.

She soon stopped and looked up at me, a mischievous grin on her face. She placed her hand in the bowl of cream and then tilted her head back, opening her mouth wide. She lifted her hand above her mouth and let the cream drip into her mouth – one dollop, then another - filling it quickly.

She stopped just long enough to swallow the mouthful of cream and lick her lips before she did it again, filling her mouth once more.

As she swallowed again, she used her other hand to grip my cock, keeping me hard and ready.

Another mouthful, another swallow.

She swallowed again. More cream. More swallows. White streaks slipping down her cheeks, running down her neck and over her breasts, dripping from her nipples in a slow rhythmic beat that could not match the steady pounding of my heart.

She only stopped once the bowl was empty. And when it was, she threw it to the side and wiped her lips.

"Delightful," she whispered.

I had no idea if she was speaking of the cream, or of my cock.

Bending low, she took me into her mouth again. She was sticky and cold now, her tongue dancing across my shaft as she pumped faster and faster. Slowly, she gestured for me to firstly kneel, then to recline on the cushions, until I was lying on my back, in the position she required. All the time, she sucked me harder and deeper, her tongue dancing across the head of my cock, her fingers playing with my hardening balls. I leaned back, stretching out on the cushions, feeling myself building, knowing I would soon succumb to her.

And then she pulled away from me, leaving my cock

to throb in the cool morning air, sticky and with traces of cream and spit.

I looked up and saw her bending over, on her knees at my side, with her young, tight ass now pointing high in the air, her face and chest pushed into the cushions away from me. Her hands worked quickly, feverishly, even with her contorted in this way. The folds of her vagina so close to my face, I could smell her, could see the juices awaiting me. But my eyes were drawn higher, to her tight, hairless anus, where she worked with a rubber water bottle and some flexible hose.

For a moment, I couldn't fathom exactly what she was doing. But soon I did.

She was inserting one end of the hose up into her anus, pushing it further and further inside.

I watched wordlessly, as the small puckered mouth greedily ate as much hose as possible. Then she made a grunting sound and stopped momentarily, letting the hose hang from her like some bizarre female sex tail. She lifted her head and reached out for another container hidden nearby under one of the cushions. She pulled at the lid and, as she did so, she turned to smile at me.

"Mousse," she whispered to me. "I do hope Sir likes chocolate flavoring."

She straightened herself up as she scooped the mousse out of the container, dolloping it into the top of the water bottle, pushing it down the neck with her still-white creamy fingers. During this time, I remained comfortable on the cushions, watching as she emptied the whole container into the water bottle.

When she was done, she shook the water bottle vigorously and I could hear the mousse sloshing around inside. Then she felt around for the hose, now hanging between her legs, and attached the free end to the mouth of the water bottle and hung it upside down on a nail protruding from the nearest X-frame.

"Is Sir prepared?" she asked. I nodded, not wanting to stop her. Even though I was unsure of what delights were awaiting me, my cock was still awaiting service.

"Then you must assist me," she said, giggling with delight. She pointed to the hanging water bottle. "Please, squeeze?"

I sat up slightly, bracing myself with one hand while I reached for the water bottle with the other. I unhooked it from the X-frame and drew it closer. As I did so, the hose grew taught between the water bottle and her ass. My eyes met hers and she nodded, as once again she knelt on all fours and beckoned me to continue.

Slowly, I squeezed the bottle, and as I did so, I could see the dark sludge of the mousse quickly traveling down the flexible hose towards her.

She wiggled and jiggled her sweet young ass in my face as the mousse got closer. She could sense it was coming, getting more excited with every passing second.

She had done this before, knew exactly what we had to do, and she clearly trusted me with the task. She knelt there, awaiting the mousse I was pumping slowly into her, her ass and cunt so close, so smooth and inviting in the candle-light. I was truly spellbound.

The mousse reached the end of the hose and quickly slipped inside her. The hose opening her perfectly for access.

"I will take it all," she whispered to me. "Eat it all up."

I was still massaging the water bottle, getting every last drop of mousse through the neck and traveling down the hose. I don't know how long it took; five, maybe ten minutes. But I didn't want the spectacle to stop. My cock was still bobbing and pulsing, and truly I had never felt so captivated in all my life.

Watching the girl open herself up in such a way, to have mousse forced into her anus, to readily and so eagerly accept it, was something I found to be very satisfying indeed.

Eventually, I heard her whisper, "Full now, Sir."

I placed the water bottle on the floor and she reached behind herself and carefully removed the hose from her ass.

I watched the small pucker of her anus close quickly,

and she farted a little - due more to the release of the hose and some air than anything else, I'm sure – and a small dollop of mousse escaped her, quickly rolling down towards her eager vagina. After a few seconds, she climbed up from the floor and turned to face me, kissing me lightly on the cheek and pushing me back down onto the cushions.

"Thank you, Sir," she whispered.

She stood up above me then and showed off her swollen stomach, rubbing her hands all over it, caressing herself and smiling as she did so.

"Am I acceptable to you?" she asked. "Am I what you desire?"

I was speechless, and just watched her. She looked as if she were pregnant now, her belly large and bloated, almost as if she were at full term.

"You requested dessert?" she asked.

I nodded.

She smiled widely. "I thought Sir looked hungry."

She knelt down once more, but slower this time, as if she was enjoying every new sensation. Her stomach ballooning out in front of me.

"Sir should be aware," she said as she did so, "that time is of the essence. Being so young and inexperienced as I am, I can hold my current state for no more than five minutes."

She climbed over me and squatted, straddling my pulsing cock. Then she let herself slide down onto me.

She felt tight – hard inside – her added load allowing little space for me. It took me a moment or two to get comfortable with the feeling.

Once I was fully inside, she started sliding up and down on my cock, quickly getting wet and extremely slippery. She rubbed her hard nipples and moaned deeply as we fucked, her expanded belly close to my face and large in my vision.

She rode me for a short time, but I soon became aware of a strange new wetness between us. It was warm and sticky, and dripping down over my balls and between my legs.

She was leaking.

The mousse was slowly sliding out from her anus. But at that moment in time, this did not concern me. If anything, it was heightening the whole experience.

As I neared orgasm, she slid off me and knelt as best she could by my side, taking me into her mouth and sucking me hard and fast, rubbing the head of my cock against her lips, licking it like a young child devours a candy. I glanced down to see the mousse smeared over my groin and cock. She was licking me clean, enjoying the taste of it all.

She sucked more, longer, again, faster now. I exploded in her mouth and she sucked harder, swallowing all my goodness, sucking my balls dry, taking every ounce of me until I could give no more.

Then she gargled in front of me, my semen splashing upwards over her cheeks and lips and down her chin, across her breasts and swollen stomach, mingling with the drying strands of whipped cream. Eventually she swallowed.

"Is Sir full?" she asked, licking her lips clean.

I knew there was more to come. And I told her so.

"I want more," I said.

She nodded and smiled at me once again.

Wiping my cum from her chin, she stood up and over me, repositioning herself so one leg was on either side of my stomach. Then she squatted, facing away from me this time, and I watched as she parted her ass cheeks with her hands and let her anus open up wide. The mousse slipped from inside her is one messy, long, lumpy waterfall of a fart. It slapped down onto me and spread a warm wave across my chest and stomach, splattering my face and arms and the surrounding cushions as well.

Once she was sure it was all out, and all that was left was her passing wind – her anus mutely blinking its single eye – she turned around and asked, "Warm?"

She looked so proud, and as she stood up, she began fingering herself, spreading the mousse in and around her cunt, rubbing hard her clit and sliding two fingers deep inside herself.

I nodded. "Perfect."

"You will be requiring cream."

It wasn't a question this time, it was a statement in a little girl voice. Her eyes surveyed me as an artist would inspect an incomplete work on canvass. She smiled as she nodded to herself.

She took a couple of steps back, her feet now on each side of my chocolaty-brown knees. She leaned over me, her face above the mess of mousse across my stomach and chest.

She stuck her dark-stained fingers down her throat.

And vomited.

Expelled from her was the whipped cream, along with strands of stomach juice and white globs of my cum that she had just swallowed. There were chunks of other food as well, dark brown and grey and orange and yellow. It all splashed down onto me, the white goop and colorful chunks mixing with the dark chocolate mousse, finishing off my dessert with a riot of color and sickness.

She vomited again, making sure her stomach was empty, just a bit more liquid this time. And then she vomited again, or tried to, as nothing came up, other than a terrible sound of a dry-retch, which proved she had given her all.

Eventually she knelt down next to me and ran her fingers through the steaming concoction on my stomach and chest. She swirled it around, making patterns and mixing the cream and cum with the mousse, the chunks with the chocolate, licking her fingers clean, then licking me.

She dragged a handful of her sick down over my hard cock, smothering it in the still-warm dessert, massaging it along my shaft and around my balls, before taking me into her mouth; taking my cock and my cum, her mousse and cream and vomit inside her once more. She moaned deeply as she did so, pumping fast and faster until I gave myself to her again, adding more of my topping to the dessert we had both so willfully celebrated.

After that, even though she played in the mousse and with my deflating cock, we both knew that I was spent for some time. I lay there with my eyes closed, trying to commit to memory every second of the events that had taken place. I smiled, knowing that truly this had been the best day of my time here.

When I did open my eyes, she was gone. Montserrat was kneeling beside me, rubbing me clean with towels and smiling down at me through her red locks of curls.

She didn't say anything. She didn't have to.

She dressed me and provided me with some water, and sat with me until I was ready to leave. Then, together, we left the room and headed back up the hallway towards the arena.

The morning was still crisp, but not cold, and I could feel the heat leaving my body. Three people were fucking on the ground just inside another doorway, and I could still hear the storm in progress above us.

Montserrat guided me back to my lodgings and left me to shower, but I didn't want to wash away any of the memories. My skin was still sticky and stained from the dessert, and I spent most of the afternoon reclining on my bed, reading, and running my hand along my body, remembering her and how wonderful she felt.

Only come evening did I shower and decide to write down the events, to properly savor them in the weeks and years to follow.

I decided that I would endeavor to seek out the maiden from today with a mind to spending more time with her.

Retiring into bed for the night, I wondered if Montserrat would help me with my plan, or whether enlisting her in partnership would lead to events like those from my second day here, the outcome of which I dare not think about again, let alone commit to paper.

For while this journal serves to capture tales and events I never wish to forget, some things I've seen here I shall never wish to remember, although I know in my very soul that I am cursed to remember them until my dying day.

* * *

PREY

KEP AWT

I smiled to myself as I first saw the words, written large and jagged, in blood red scrawl, dozens of feet high across the side of the Sydney Opera House.

Or what was left of the Sydney Opera House.

The jet boat steamed through Sydney Harbor, taking us underneath the Harbor Bridge, its rusting coat-hanger style frame towering above us, and the broken skeletons of dozens of dead swinging in the wind underneath, all hanging from their broken necks.

It was the first sign of life, or death, that I'd seen for days. The first indication of what could happen to us if we weren't careful.

I turned to Worcester and Jenkins. Even through their visors I could see they were staring at the dead too.

The writing and the hanging corpses were a sign, a warning to us all. We had to be careful. We had to be on our game.

Worcester turned to me and I smiled. He gave me the thumbs-up.

Can't fuckin' wait, his voice came through loud and clear on my headset.

We'd read about what could confront us here; all heard the stories. The media were one to sensationalise, but we'd done this before.

Africa. The Middle East.

White Rhino. Elephants. Gorillas.

Been there. Killed that.

But this was always the ultimate dream. Money and

the right friends can make any dream a reality. This proved it.

And now here we were, sailing up Sydney Harbor, heading for what was now known as Death's dock. Where our adventure would begin.

We'll be there in five.

Crothers was piloting the boat, and I turned to him and nodded. Watched as his visor nodded back.

'Bout fucking time. I could hear the gruff voice of Dawson, still below deck, sleeping off the hangover from last night's party. We'd celebrated hard and long – knowing within less than twenty-four hours we'd be landing in Sydney – united in one cause. The ultimate hunt.

Worcester and Jenkins were from the US of E, and they'd been hunting together for over twenty years. Their kills included pandas in Tokyo and even the Tassie Tiger, one of the seven brought back to life through DNA cloning. They'd broken into the San Diego Research Institute specifically to take them out.

To be honest, I admired their balls for that.

Dawson was from the Republic of Texas. Fought in the final three years of the Great Southern War of Independence. He bragged of taking out Senator Ballard with just one shot from that railway car, but I thought he was full of shit. His hands shook too much to be a marksman of that caliber. And everyone knew Trevor James Cruden was in jail for the assassination.

Crothers owned the jet boat, and ran the tour. He'd made a killing (literally) smuggling people like ourselves onto the island and off again. He'd hunted over a dozen times and said he never tired of the buzz, the thrill of it all.

The thrill's the key, he'd said as we climbed into our suits and tested them last night. *Nothing else you do – ever – will be as good as this. You've reached the peak. You've made it guys. It's time to be Gods!*

As the jet boat arced gracefully in the harbor and turned to prepare to arrive, I could make out the old wooden dock, covered in coiled barbed wire and skeletons. Rusting signs warning of radioactivity and Zs were everywhere.

Keep away. Turn back now. Do Not Enter.

A smile crossed my lips and we neared the dock. We were arriving in the same harbor as the early explorers over three hundred years ago. How the place must've changed since then.

I turned to look at the remaining grey wings of the Sydney Opera House. Burnt and looted, it was far from the tourist attraction it had once been. Now, it only served as a reminder of the violent and devastating events of the past.

Terra Australis was now the last place on earth you'd want to go.

Unless you were us.

It was 26 years ago now since the Zombies had over-run the country. No one's quite sure why, but some kind of genetic mutation brought on by the Great Flu Panic a year earlier, so they said. Others thought it was some weird government conspiracy gone wrong. Someone always thinks that...

Others thought it was Texas, trying to release some kind of biological agent to take out the rest of the Old USA before the Great Southern War began. I guess we'll never really know for sure.

But they came from Mexico, spread across the Old States and further. Within a year, the Zs were everywhere. Spreading across the world via jet boat and sonic jet and causing destruction wherever they went.

Bush Labs were the first to invent the taser to take them down. "The Zaser" they called it. Stupid name, but it was effective. It would knock the Zs cold for hours.

And with it, the tide turned.

The UN Zombie Trails debated mass extermination. But those who wanted genocide were drowned out by the bleeding heart liberals who said the Zs were still alive, still people, still entitled to *rights*.

And that's when the decision was made. The roundup began, and they were transported to Australia. No other place on the earth was so large, so distant and surrounded by so much water.

With such great expanses of desert – millions of miles worth – it made sense to drop them out in the middle of nowhere, in their camps, and let the bastards kill each other.

So, once again, after almost three hundred years, Australia was a prison colony.

Of course, the Australian government welcomed the relocation with open arms. The amount of money poured into the country by governments around the world was extraordinary. The problem was solved, swept under the carpet, and Australia reaped the rewards.

But then something went wrong.

The Zs stopped fighting amongst themselves. They got a little smarter. The eastern side of the Australian Wall in the Northern Territory was breached, and they moved en masse, in their thousands across the desert heading east – straight for Sydney.

There was panic and bloodshed, hours of shocking live video coverage of the coming Z-wave. And no one stood a chance.

They reached Sydney before the Government could rally their troops, before the international community could send help, and they commandeered sonic jet flights out of there – heading once more for every corner of the earth.

It happened so very fast; a bloody red wave of death and destruction.

Most of the flights had been shot down before they landed, of course. And very few made it out. But still, the threat was real, and no one wanted to risk it again.

Flights to Australia were cancelled. The world watched, captivated as Sydney burned for over a week. Then Melbourne, then Brisbane.

Those Aussies smart enough to flee did so quickly, heading west to Perth, where the Western side of the Wall still held. The borders were closed in two days, and as the Zs moved west through South Australia, laying waste to Adelaide, the wall thwarted their attempts to spill into Western Australia as well.

Looking back, it was inevitable. But at that time, they thought they had the situation covered. How wrong they were.

Over there, look!

It was Jenkins. I followed his pointing hand and turned to survey the Harbor Bridge. I could see them too. Probably a dozen or more. Just standing there, watching us as the jet boat docked. They hardly moved. Just stood bolt upright and still.

Scary fuckers, Dawson's voice cracked in my ear.

"Not half as scary as us," I replied.

We climbed from the jet boat onto the old rotting deck and carefully grabbed our supplies.

The sun was beating down on us, magnified by the mandatory full body suits.

One backpack each was all we could take. We'd soon be on our own and, if we ran out of anything, we'd be in trouble.

The comms sets inside our suits were our only connection to each other.

Last chance, guys. If you don't want to do this, tell me now, Crothers said as he took out his remote.

But we were all silent. No one was going to lose face now. Not after so long and considering how much we'd paid.

So Crothers set the jet boat on its automatic course to safety in the middle of the bay.

Just us now, team, Jenkins said. *Scary, huh?*

But I wasn't scared. I was ready. Nervous, for sure, but excited as well.

I'd waited a long time for this experience.

You've all got your GPS and designated sections, yes? Crothers double checked.

We all nodded.

And we meet back at Redfern on Friday, 21:00 hours, correct.

We agreed quickly. We didn't need reminding of trivialities we'd all known for months.

Gibson, this is your last opportunity. We won't mind if you come with us.

Crothers was talking to me. And I knew what he meant.

"No, it's fine. I'll be okay."

I was the only one heading off on the hunt alone. I'd paid an extra five million Euros for the pleasure, and I wasn't about to change my mind.

I'd picked Melbourne, and Worcester and Jenkins were taking Brisbane, while Crothers and Dawson were staying in Sydney. I was pretty sure Worcester and Jenkins wouldn't be interested in me tagging along with them, and I didn't really want to stay in Sydney, as it was a little too close to the reactor for comfort.

The brochures said it was fine now, that the levels were low, but you could never really tell.

No, I was heading to Melbourne to hunt by myself, because that way, no one would know what I would do.

No one of importance, anyway.

The hunt is the hunt. By any means. By any way.

Okay, then if everyone's ready, we'll head over to the warehouse and get the jet bikes.

We followed Crothers along the dock. The electrified fences on either side were covered with the burnt and rotting remains of corpse upon corpse. In this state of decay, it was hard to tell if the Zs had been trying to get in, or whether we were walking past humans who had failed to escape. Either way, they were dead now, and left there as warnings to the Zs to keep away.

Within minutes we were in an underground bunker and picking our jet bikes. I picked a sleek black one and set my backpack and rifle on the back. I threw my leg over the main body and sat on the seat, leaning forward to place my hands on the handlebars.

This was it.

I smiled.

Within four hours on this baby, I'd be in Melbourne.

On my own.

On the hunt.

* * *

The protective suits were a pain in the ass, but necessary.

I did seriously think about taking mine off once I arrived in Melbourne, but thought better of it. Radiation can travel and, even though I was well away from ground zero, I didn't want to risk it.

They said keep the suits on at all times, so I decided I should.

I was here to kill, not to be killed.

Plus, the comms were hard-wired into the helmet, so taking off the suit meant that I'd lose contact with the others, and we'd all agreed that was a golden rule not worth breaking.

I was in Melbourne by late afternoon on Monday, with just enough time to set up camp. I'd initially planned to have my base in the old Flinders Street Station. As a kid I'd seen InstaPics of an old disused ballroom from the nineteenth century, rumored to be housed somewhere in the rubble, still untouched to this day. But a quick scan with the Z-scanner showed that this was a base for hundreds of Zs.

Instead, the GPS recommended Southbank, so I holed up in the dilapidated Crown Towers.

Zs didn't like water, so there were locations near the Old Yarra River that were considered a "green zone" on the GPS screens inside the visors. So at Crown Towers I stayed.

A king in his Crown Towers.

I'd laughed out loud.

Something funny? Worcester asked in my head.

"No, not really," I'd replied.

Worcester and Jenkins had arrived in Brisbane an hour earlier than I'd arrived in Melbourne. And Crothers and Dawson had set up their basecamp in Redfern where we'd all meet again on Friday.

We checked in every hour and gave our status, as agreed. Although we could hear all of our conversations, the other groups rarely said anything. Everyone had just one thing on their mind. Conversations were few and far between – only the hunt mattered.

I scouted around the Crown Towers once I'd set up camp and used my scanners to check for any signs of life. Z-scanners were purposely built to track the bastards down, and had been created by Bush Industries back when the fuckers roamed the Old United States. They were expensive then, and even more so now, but some ex-military guys still had dozens of them from the initial fighting and would sell them for the right price.

Researchers now said Zs regularly hunted together and formed their own communities, with a hierarchy and worker Zs. It was as if they were almost human. Some said they still *were* human… and the debate still raged on and on.

I didn't care one way or another. I was here for one thing. All my life had been leading up to now, to here, to this hunt.

Some blamed the purposeful detonation of the Lucas Heights Nuclear reactor just shy of 20 years ago. At the time, it seemed like a good idea. The Zs had broken free and had amassed in Sydney. Why not use the Nuclear reactor to take the fuckers out?

Why not indeed!

A perfect solution. And possibly the final solution.

In doing so, they might turn tail and head back to the interior of the country. And, if not, we'd take out enough of them to be able to send in international troops and wipe out what was left. The mission would be accomplished in a mere few weeks.

So they sent in the jet, they opened fire on Lucas Heights, and the reactor did what we knew it would do.

But the resulting explosion and fallout did nothing to extinguish the lives of the Zs. If anything, it helped them adapt and evolve. At least, that's what the scientists say.

They thought they'd hit the most populated area and the fallout would wipe them out like Chernobyl did over a century ago. And, sure, it took some of the bastards out, a whole lot in fact, but it just made those who remained smarter. They adapted somehow. Evolved. They understood that as a group, they were an easy target. So they spread out around the country.

Like ants from an overturned ants nest, they fled, fanned out and left destruction in their wake.

The old US even considered bombing the shit out of the place, like they did Vietnam, but they decided it'd have the same effect.

Fuck all.

The best defense was a natural one – water. Zs just couldn't survive water. Once the sonic jets were banned from flying to Australia, plenty of the Zs had tried to swim their way to freedom through sheer desperation, but none made it.

They just couldn't compete with the distance.

No one could work out why, but it was as if they couldn't understand why they hadn't found dry land. The bastards would just stop swimming mid-stroke and sink. They'd drown themselves instead of going on, all within an hour.

And so here they all stayed. Contained. Packaged.

For us…

I didn't hunt that first day. I concerned myself with fortifying my basecamp and making sure there would be no surprises in the night. The best way to stay safe was no sound, no light and no fires. Zs eye-sight was good in the day, but even sharper at night. You had to blend in, to be hidden from view, and not give your position away.

If you showed yourself, they'd strike for you. But if you kept quiet and hidden, they could walk right past you and not even know you were there.

Crown Towers had been a casino and hotel back in the day, already falling into ruin before the rise of the Zs. I scanned it floor by floor, taking the stairs, and once I was sure there was no activity, I took a room on the fifth floor and set up camp.

The place was wrecked. It had been overturned several times, but the dust on everything was a sure sign that it hadn't been inhabited for years.

All the windows were broken, and the pile of burnt wood and springs told me a bed had once been set alight here. But I didn't need anything. I'd roughed it before and would do so again.

Occasionally I could hear shouting and screaming from the other side of the Old Yarra River. Someone was beating on some metal, a monotonous drumming over and over again, every few seconds. But I kept my scanners live and checked them religiously.

There were no Zs on this side of the river. I was safe, of that I was sure.

I made my bed and ate my protein bar, and watched the sun set over the city.

B Base safe, Jenkins reported in a few minutes later.

S Base secure, said Crothers.

I thought about not replying, to give the guys a scare. But that really wasn't how these games were played.

"M Base fine," I replied. "Any kills yet?"

I got a fucker, Dawson said. *Tried to lunge at my jet bike. But I gutted him.*

None here, Worcester said. *Early night and we'll head out early.*

"Agreed," I replied. "I'm doing the same."

Make sure your PBA is set, replied Crothers.

The PBA monitored your breathing. If for some reason the Zs got you during the night the PBA would let the others know you wouldn't be joining them for the return voyage.

I watched darkness fall across the city, then laid back and closed my eyes.

Tomorrow the hunt would begin.

* * *

I watched the morning sun reflect off the destruction of the Melbourne Central towers; the glass in every window blown out and smashed, the window frames and supports rusting and rotting in the light breeze.

The Rialto Tower was the same, burnt out and soulless in the still morning air. It was hard to imagine this was the city that had once housed 30 million people. From my vantage point, I couldn't see the Eureka Tower, but I had a good indication of where it had once stood. My plan was to cross the river, and head down towards what was once the Melbourne Cricket Ground; its old sporting grandstands would be a perfect location for a sniper.

I'd then hunt through the old gardens, heading around the Myer Music Bowl and aim to visit what was left of the Eureka Tower, its shards and twisted metal apparently still smoldering according to the InstaPics.

This would take more than a day to achieve, but that was okay, I had everything I needed in my backpack, and it was never a good idea to stay in the same place for too long.

I slung my rifle over my shoulder and slowly headed down the stairs and out into the street, stopping only to check my jet bike was still well hidden in the Towers basement.

I always kept my scanner on, and made sure I checked it every minute or so. While my hunt was – by necessity – a slow and patient one, I knew the Zs could move fast. You couldn't second guess what they were thinking or what they would do. Your scanner may be empty one minute and swarming with the fuckers the next.

We'd learnt that much, as least.

There had been a time when everyone got a little complacent. The western section of the Great Aussie Wall had held back the Zs for a year or more. They seemed content to riot through the eastern part of Australia and live in the radioactive fallout that covered Sydney. They showed no real signs of wanting to invade Western Australia and get to Perth.

Those Australians who had survived the initial wave set about rebuilding their lives in Perth, and the Government tried hard to rebuild what was left of the shattered country. The international community felt partly to blame, especially as they'd dumped the Zs there in the first place, so the money and support continued to pour in.

Fuck, it seemed crazy now you look back on it. Was everyone so blind? Did we all think we could handle it?

Couldn't those in power see what *could* happen?

But no one did.

Australia died on the day of the Perth Olympic Games tragedy.

No more. No second chances, no half measures. They got as many humans out of the place as possible, on boats and aircraft carriers…anyway they could. Thousands upon thousands made the escape before the Zs overran Perth too.

It was almost as if the Zs had waited, biding their time, like they *knew* the Olympics would be the center point.

"Australia, Open to the World!" was the slogan.

It would be they country's epitaph.

The Zs used the event to prove they were in control.

They were smart. They would win.

Zombies eating the arms of athletes and decapitating swimmers was not the kind of opening ceremony the Olympic officials had in mind.

Total disaster. No other words for it.

And the second wave of Zs spilled from the western side of the Great Wall, and the destruction of Australia was complete.

The country was closed and renamed Terra Australis: Z State… Forbidden Territory.

Except to us.

Except to me.

B camp on move.

Yep, S camp too.

"M camp up and at 'em," I replied. "Good hunting, gents."

I walked along the bank of the Yarra River, heading for the half-cracked shell that was all that remained of the Melbourne Cricket Ground. It was a cool fall morning with some low-level areas of fog, but I kept one eye on my scanners and another on my surrounds.

On the other side of the river, near the old Flinders

Street Station, I could see individual Zs lurking and scavenging, grunting and foraging. I was sorely tempted to take a couple out at this distance, but I held my nerve.

Patience was needed.

Once I shot at them, I'd signal my presence to every Z within a mile radius or more.

No, I needed to be in a safe area, high and hidden, so they'd be confused as to exactly where I was located. I wasn't a Z massacre kinda guy. No skill in hunting like that. No... finesse. I much preferred the kills to be up close and personal. Sniping is purely a clinical approach, but I'd be satisfied with that if it was too dangerous for a close kill.

You don't shake hands with a white rhino. You respect it and kill it when the opportunity arises. I know. I've got the five tusks to prove it.

I took my time, walked slowly, quietly. Nothing was to be achieved by giving myself away.

I passed a broken and beaten down sign that read DED FUKA, written in a shaky and child-like hand.

So they came onto this side of the River, or had at some stage. I turned and surveyed the whole area. The damn suits made it hard to use your periphery vision, and even though outside sounds were relayed into the helmet speakers, I'd much rather trust my own ears.

Still, I'd play the game as instructed. Radiation poisoning wasn't something I wanted as a souvenir. The suit stayed on. It just added to the challenge.

Three of the Cricket Ground's large light pylons that were still standing were decorated with skeletons in varying states of decomposition. Some still had hair and flesh, others were missing arms and lower limbs. The bodies twisted slowly in the light morning breeze, being picked bare by the Zs and ravens.

A chill passed through me then, as I looked up at the bodies. There'd been reports of people who came here, scientists to begin with, then the pro-Zers who wanted to try to communicate with what they called the "unfortunates." But none of them ever returned. And even the hunting parties...tales of those who'd paid large sums to come here and never returned.

But Crothers proved it was done successfully, and often. He was a multi-player with the trophies to prove it.

I walked on, passing rotting corpses and destruction, heading closer to my first vantage point.

Fuck yeah! Catch of the day!

It was Dawson. He'd managed the first daily kill.

You asshole, Worcester replied in my head.

Extra points for me. Right through the head with one kill shot. Man, you shoulda seen this fucker's head explode. He didn't know what hit him. These Z-tip bullets are terrific.

Where are you? Jenkins asked.

Manly. Heading to St George.

Congrats. We're tracking a group of three right now. One's a woman.

Coooool. Get her first. Right in the pussy.

Hahahaha.

Good luck.

We don't need it.

I didn't say anything. I didn't want to. The fact Dawson beat me to the first kill just spurred me on. I picked up my pace, knowing there were only five of us in the whole country, and I sure as hell wasn't leaving here ranked any lower than number one.

A whole friggin' continent to do with as we pleased.

To enjoy the hunt. To kill our prey.

I was more than happy to take on Melbourne alone. I'd always hunted that way.

No one needed to know what I did, or how...

I passed another sign, this one hanging from an overhead tree branch at the entry to the Cricket Ground's car park.

MUTHA FUKA

Who knew they could almost spell? They were smarter than I gave them credit for, that was for sure. The myth that they moved as a mindless wave of...well, zombies, was just wrong. Left to themselves (and maybe because of the fallout) they'd managed to forge out of the destruction some kind of civilization, to survive out here in the middle of nowhere.

Are they smarter than us? Smarter than *me*?

That thought chilled me. But I shook it from my mind. Don't lose your grip now, not when you've come so far.

Still, the fact Dawson had struck first – and so early in the day – had pissed me off.

This wasn't just a personal hunt. It was a game as well. A competition.

Everyone had downloaded the unedited *Zombie Hunt* episodes. It was a worldwide sensation, but no one really believed what they saw was real. Some said it was fake, others said it was Hollywood trying to make a comeback after the '53 CalQuake. Either way, it was nothing like this. This was real... this is it.

Real reality.

The best that money could buy.

We'd worked out the scorecard as soon as we'd got onto the jet boat in New San Francisco. Ten points for the first kill of the day and five points for each subsequent kill. As we were separated by location, proof was needed for every claimed victim.

Male kills required a scalp. Female kills a nipple or full breast. Extra points for a full breast, of course.

So general sniping wasn't going to win the game. Proof was only easily obtained with an up close and personal kill. And the only problem with *that* was that once there's a gunshot, the Zs spill from their hiding places and come after you. So, the more silent the kill, the more chance of bagging the proof you needed.

"That's fucked up, man," Dawson had complained. "I just wanna shoot the fuckers, mow them down if I have to. But you want me to get in there and bring proof as well? That's *crazy*!"

Worcester had just shrugged at him as we sat at the jet boat's bar. "Up to you if you play or not. If you want to hunt and play like a coward, go for it. Or do you want to put your balls on the line and live a little?"

In the end, Dawson had reluctantly agreed. And now, so far, he had the first two kills of the hunt.

Worcester and Jenkins had kept to themselves and chatted quietly together on the boat. I had no real idea what they were doing, or plotting. It wouldn't surprise me if they didn't report their kills via the comms units and come back to Sydney with proof of all their kills.

It wasn't a bad plan.

So I'd play their little game too and keep nice and quiet. Surprise them all with what *I* come back with. Stun them all with my scalps and tits... and more.

Anyone can lop off a titty... I planned to go further down, grab something more prized.... more... personal.

Zcunt.

Even if it hadn't been used for years, I didn't care. I'd give it a good workout before slicing off the folds and throwing them in my backpack.

A cunt to show...

...and maybe three or more to keep.

So many years I'd laid awake at night thinking of this journey. Being here. Doing this. Finally on the hunt. The things I'd imagined I'd see. The things I'd hoped to do.

I'd take a tooth and maybe a tongue. A piece of ear as well as a tit. A finger or a toe. Anything to remind me of my success. Each and every one pleasurable for so many reasons. Each and every one taken with my own hands.

And even though we'd all agreed on the boat that the young ones were off-limits, I knew without a doubt that if I encountered a little boy, that kill would be one of the sweetest.

Unless it was a little girl.

I'd hack off the little shit's cock and keep that one just for myself. And if it were a little girl...well... the pleasure would be indescribable.

But I wouldn't tell the others, as some acts remain frowned upon.

For today, the focus was the top of the grandstands of the Cricket Ground. It was a perfect viewing platform giving a 360 degree vantage point of the land below. I'd sit and watch...and wait.

I'd choose my prey carefully and with precision. I'd

line him up in my sights and then I'd shoot. Once, twice and then again.

But it didn't matter if I hit him or not, not this time. The sound would bring them running. And as they ran, I would watch.

Where do they come from? Where are they hiding? And do they leave anyone behind?

I would then have an indication of exactly where they lived, how the acted and how they reacted to my presence.

Taking a life requires study.

It requires... refinement.

It deserves understanding.

I'd put money on the majority living in the station, and I was gambling they'd come streaming from there, along the old city roads and towards the stadium.

When panicked, the adults would run, ready to fight. That much I'd learnt from Zombie Hunt and the early research papers. They'd leave behind their homes... and the children.

I'd shoot some more, take a few of the approaching hoards out, and whip those who remained into a frenzy. Then, over the walls of the stadium, I'd drop the raw meet to the ground below.

While they fought over the small amount of raw food, I'd sprint to the other side of the stadium and make my exit... heading back towards Flinders Street.

And the kids.

Little kids are easiest to round up - no matter what you hear, it's true. Once you take out their mother or father, or they're left behind by the adults, they seem lost, unsure of their leader or what to do next. They're like young animals, completely alone and without any real survival instinct.

The younger the better.

I've been told you can walk straight into their midst, just walk straight up to them, and they'll just assume you're an adult Z, and won't even pay you any notice...for a short while at least.

Maybe it's your smell – or how you react – but you've only got a few minutes to make your move from inside their camp; to take advantage and make your play before they do eventually work out you're not one of them.

It would be easy to stroll in there with the incendiary device and set it in place, taking down what remained of the station and the kids within. Dozens, if not more would die. And I have to admit seeing them fly apart was quite appealing. Some might survive the blast, but most wouldn't. Watching them flail about is infinitely more satisfying than a bullet to the skull. And there would be enough time in the ensuing chaos to pick off any who were injured and lame, and let my knife do its work.

I could kidnap a girl too…take her with me. One fierce blow on the bridge of her nose would be enough to send bone shards into her brain and then she's mine. Or maybe one would already be unconscious. Either way, I'd take one with me, and have her as mine.

Until I got what I needed.

Live prey is always more fun that dead prey. Even Z-prey.

The doors to the Cricket Ground were barricaded, but it took me no more than a few minutes to push some of the obstructions aside and enter the stadium. Even some of the flimsiest of barriers could keep the Zs out, as they saw the blockage but few ever thought too hard about trying to move it. Instead, they'd push against it, screaming and yelling, achieving nothing.

This talk of their evolving intelligence was just bullshit.

Scientists were on record as saying the Zs had started to evolve after the Lucas Heights Nuclear disaster. But did they really know? The scientists sent down here very rarely returned and for every pro-Z scientist, there was a Z-change denier.

But from what I'd seen so far, Noble Savages?

Hardly.

Just A-grade fuckin' Zs.

True, out there in the wastelands some had worked out how to use hammers and axes and such, but only to cave in a skull and lop off an arm.

Intelligence?

Fuck me. No way.

Blind fucking luck, more like it.

I walked onto the turf of the cricket ground and took a moment to survey the area all around me. There was no one in the stadium. No one alive, at least. Bodies and destruction, yes, seats torn apart and goal posts thrown through stadium boxes, but nothing else. The weeds had long ago taken over what was once a manicured and curated lawn.

I walked across the playing surface and headed to the far side of the stadium. Once there, I began the long walk up the steps to the highest vantage point I could find.

Four days to go… most kills win.

Most *proven* kills is champion.

And that would be me.

* * *

I checked my night vision. This was my last night on the hunt, and I wanted to see as much as I could, to remember it all, every single moment. I wouldn't be coming back, so the more I saw, the better.

Carefully and quietly, I left my lookout position in the bent and decaying metal spire of the Arts Centre, walking back towards my base while scanning the Yarra and surrounds for any Zs still on the hunt.

There was no doubt about it; the last few days had been an experience of a lifetime...

While I'd initially thought there weren't many Zs in the area, my first few shots had seen them come from every direction. Thousands of them, all sprinting towards my location at the cricket ground.

And since that moment, they'd been altered to my presence, and bands of Zs had begun patrolling. Night and day.

For me.

Just who the hell was being hunted here?

I hadn't slept much in the past few days as I had to keep aware and on my toes, always moving. I'd almost been discovered at the Myer Music Bowl when I'd arrived there late on day two. Almost walked straight into a campsite overflowing with Zs. I'd been tired, been lax, not concentrating as I should have been.

But they hadn't heard me, and I'd managed to use the twilight to slowly back out of there and get away.

The bomb in Flinders Street Station worked like a treat on day three. I'd taken out more than just kids, adults as well. And as the survivors fled, I was able to climb the rubble and find more souvenirs than I thought possible.

"Pay dirt," was all I'd said.

That you, Gibson? Jenkins had asked.

"Yes."

We thought we'd lost you.

"No such luck."

I scalped one of the males and forced my knife through the throat of a female wheezing near me.

When she stopped her unholy cry, I cut her open and took her left breast.

Her heart too.

It was cold and smeared with rotting blackness.

I bit into it and tasted her very essence. Her soul, if she had one.

I was King.

No, no…. God.

I had won.

I managed to take three more souvenirs before I could hear the Zs returning from their patrols.

I stabbed a boy in the side and ripped him open. My hands fumbling around the ball sack and cock, my knife cutting deep and hard, even as he screamed at me. Within seconds I had his cock and balls in my hands, and they went straight into the backpack.

I fled the scene and was lucky enough to find an unconscious young female face down in the rubble as I made my escape.

I couldn't see her face, but it wasn't her face I was interested in. I grabbed her by her long brown hair and dragged her with me.

She slowed me down, but when I was far enough away from the station, I stopped and picked her up, slung her over my shoulder and carried her instead.

Now, she lay next to me, in Crown Towers where I had returned for my last night. She'd died earlier in the day, as I'd enjoyed a little too much the games I had planned for her.

But I'd found her quite suitable for my needs, and quite tight no matter where I explored.

It was the final pleasure that had been the most rewarding. Slipping my knife into the side of her eyes and watching each of them pop. her own white liquid ooze running down her cheeks as my own white liquid filled the sockets where her eyes had been.

I knew then that I would be the ultimate champion. No one would beat me at this game, because I had no one holding me back.

S Base reporting. Crothers voice sounded loud in the darkness.

B base here. It was Jenkins.

"M base too" I replied.

What's our tally, gents? asked Dawson, still sounding supremely confident.

32 kills here between us, Jenkins replied.

Is that all? Dawson replied.

Asshole, I thought.

53 here between us, Crothers chimed in.

Hope you can prove that, Worcester replied.

Oh, we can. We can, Dawson added. *What about you, Gibson?*

"Enough," I said. "You won't be disappointed."

To be honest, I didn't really care that much about their game. Not now.

I turned to look at the girl.

I knew I'd won.

Even if I couldn't tell them.

I'd stopped counting once I'd carried her away from the station. The others didn't matter now I had her.

Just remember, gentlemen, we're meeting at 21:00 hours

tomorrow at Redfern. Crothers was saying. *Have a safe trip back. The jet boat docks at 21:15. We leave at 21:30 with or without you.*

And that was it.

I scanned the night vision and checked the scanners once more. The Zs were out in the street, no doubt still looking for me. But none had ventured onto this side of the river, and there was no sight of any life in the Crown Towers.

Not any more.

I lay down next to her for one final time, turning on my side, I placed my left arm on her cold body, my hand resting in the gaping hole where her vagina had once been.

"Goodnight," I whispered.

But no one heard me.

* * *

S base here. S base. Emergency!

Crothers voice was loud and crackling in my ear.

"Whatthefuck?" I screamed back, his voice had startled me. Riding the jet bike at these speeds, the last thing you need is a voice screaming in your head.

I looked around me to make sure I wasn't in any danger of hitting the treetops below me.

Redfern is out, Crothers was saying now. *We're here at Redfern, but so are the Zs. There's a fucking camp here. They've set it up in the last few days, while we've been hunting further north!*

A camp? I could hear the incredulous tone in Worcester's voice.

Believe me, they're massing here for some reason. So we need to change our final meeting place. We'll meet in Mosman instead, okay? I'll punch through co-ordinates now.

"Fine by me," I replied as the co-ordinates for Mosman flashed up on the visor.

Okay, whatever, Jenkins replied, sounding pissed.

I set the new directions on the bike and glanced at the time. It was almost noon and I was tracking well to arrive before 21:00. All would be fine.

And as I rode, I thought about her.

How I'd left her there in Crown Towers. My princess.

I'd propped her up against the windows, so she could look out and survey her kingdom with her missing eyes forever. I even fashioned a little crown from some wire I'd found, to place on her head.

Stupid, I know. Sentimental too.

I fixed her hair and made sure she would be confortable. Left her there, with one final kiss on her cold, scarred cheek.

My Princess in her Crown Tower.

I said goodbye to her, turned and I never looked back.

Within minutes I was on my jet bike and heading away from Melbourne, leaving my dream hunt behind me, but with enough memories and souvenirs for a lifetime.

And while I'd told myself I didn't care about the others and their stupid little game, part of me wanted to tell them everything. To knock the cocky smile off Dawson's face, to show the old hands in Jenkins and Worcester that a new guy could better any hunting take of theirs, and to give a reason for Crothers to remember me above every other hunter he'd have on his tour from now until his retirement day.

But I knew I couldn't tell them everything, even though I wanted to.

My hands tightened on the handlebars and I kept my head down.

I couldn't afford to relax now. Couldn't slip up at this late stage.

Sydney was just five hours away.

* * *

I arrived early, just before sunset, so took a detour to the bay and saw the jet boat heading towards the dock on its predetermined route. Soon we'd be aboard and heading back to New San Francisco.

I spotted a Z scaling the Sydney Opera House and

took a moment to secure my last kill of the tour. He was clambering up the sheer wall with a garbage can lid in one hand, banging it against the tiles and screaming at the top of his voice. I blew him away at long-range, my rifle on target again, as usual. There'd be no souvenir from him, as his head exploded and he tumbled end over end down the once-white sails of the Opera House, but it had been fun nonetheless.

The last kill on the last day.

Our final basecamp filled me with excitement and also a little sadness. I'd be returning home, leaving the thrill of this place behind. Leaving my kills, my memories, my sport.

My Princess.

"I'll be there soon," I said.

No problem, Crothers replied. *We're waiting for you.*

"Worcester and Jenkins there already?" I asked.

Yes, we're here, Jenkins replied. *You're lucky last.*

"Hope you're ready to welcome the winner," I replied.

You're cocky, Dawson replied.

I couldn't wait to wipe that stupid smile off his face.

"No, just victorious," I countered.

* * *

I drove up next to the other jet bikes as night fell, and turned off the engine, surveying the area as I did so.

I checked my scanner and then peered about me, my eyes running along the perimeter fence. No holes, no tears in the barbed wire. Just body upon body piled up on the other side. We were definitely in a secure area, but it never hurt to double check.

The floodlights ringed the area, and their bright light made me squint.

The Zs didn't come near bright lights, something to do with their eyes, or so they say.

My backpack was heavy, heavier than when I'd started. The supplies and rations had been replaced with my trophies, and I'd already sent a comms back home to the guy who mounted all my kills. He never asked any questions, no matter what trophies I brought him.

We had an agreement, and that was all the mattered.

I walked towards the tattered red tent, the signpost of our final basecamp, knowing that within half an hour we'd be on the jet boat and heading home. So many stories to tell, I felt like I could talk for days. But I knew once we got back home, the secret had to remain with us.

We had to keep quiet.

As quiet as this night.

I stopped by the tent and dropped by backpack to the ground.

Turning to bend down, I rummaged inside and quickly decided what I could show, and what I couldn't.

I had make an entrance to remember.

I stood upright and glanced around me once more.

The night was dead. Just floodlights and devastation, nothing more.

Maybe we'd finally killed all the fuckers.

I smiled.

Imagine being part of the team that rid the world of this menace forever. Imagine being the one who put the final bullet into the final Z, to remove the menace of these animals from the world once and for all.

To eradicate them to extinction.

We'd be heroes.

I'd be a hero.

I walked to the tent and threw back the flap, taking a large step inside.

"To the victor, the spoils!" I called as I spread my arms wide, four scalps in my left hand and two breasts clasped tightly in my right. "Which of you fuckers think you're going to beat me now?"

I stopped in my tracks and my trophies fell from my hands.

They turned to face me, and they smiled.

My eyes danced across Worcester and Jenkins, Dawson and Crothers. They were strung up before me, arms and legs wide, the wire clamps holding them rigid, just a few feet off the ground. Their eyes stared back at me, blinking, pleading.

But I was too stunned to do anything but look.

They were all naked, their chests opened up, skin peeled back and rolled down their abdomens. I could see wires and cables and tubes linking their stomachs and lungs.

And two large piston-looking attachments plugged directly into each of their hearts.

The hearts that still beat, ever faster now, upon my arrival.

I wanted to say something, to call out and let them know I could save them. But I was struck dumb, unable to move, to understand, or do anything other than look.

Their necks had been ripped open too, like sardine cans, skin rolled to one side and clamped into position, more wires and tubes attaching to their vocal chords and tongues, large mesh devices clamping their jaws into half open positions ensuring they couldn't move.

Welcome.

It was Dawson's voice in my ear and my eyes darted to look at him. But he hadn't spoken. Or, rather, his mouth hadn't moved.

We have been waiting for you.

As I heard the voice, I saw the vocal chords move, saw his voice-box react to the stimulation of the wires attached to it.

It was horrible. Unspeakable.

How could they do this?

And then the rage filled me. Uncontrollably so.

"You fuckers," I said, as I dragged my eyes away from my companions long enough to look at the Zs who were surrounding me.

All of them.

Dozens of them. Standing around me. Watching me. Looking at me like I was some kind of animal on display for their twisted enjoyment.

"How dare you!" I spat at them, but they said nothing in reply.

I'd walked into an ambush.

But the fence wasn't breached. The spotlights were on.

"You shouldn't be here," was all I could manage to say.

Neither should you, said Worcester. Or whoever was controlling Worcester.

As one, they all took a step towards me.

I had no choice, I ripped off my headgear and flung it to one side, as I had to see clearly and know what and who I was up against.

All of a sudden radiation poisoning wasn't my biggest concern.

I turned to look behind me, but the fuckers were everywhere. They were blocking my only chance of escape.

I glanced over at Worcester and Jenkins, Crothers and Dawson, for any sign of help, any possible way they could make me understand. Jenkins had closed his eyes and Dawson was crying. Crothers was shaking his head but Worcester was just watching me, unblinking, as if he knew what was to come.

Fuck it.

I knew I'd been outplayed. Out positioned. Out smarted.

The Zs took another step. Then another.

My eyes zipped along their ever-enclosing circle, looking for a leader, for someone who was controlling the situation. If I could take him out, maybe they'd panic. Maybe there'd be just enough time to push through their ranks and get back to the bike and head back to the boat and get away from here.

Or to Melbourne.

Yes, that's it, escape back to Melbourne and my Princess. Return to her in Crown Towers.

Game's over, I heard Crother's voice crackle into the headset on the ground.

And then, as one, they advanced.

I only had time to grab my rifle and place the barrel under my chin.

"You're not beating me," I screamed as my fingers fumbled blindly for the trigger.

I'd win after all. I'd blow my brains out on my terms.

Beat them at their sick fucking game.

But then the hands were on me, pulling at me, tearing at my clothes, ripping the rifle from my hands and dragging me away.

I'd lost.

Beaten by a fucking Z.

The assholes were smarter than we gave them credit for.

They truly *were* evolving.

And I was destined to be one of their trophies, pinned to a wall and opened up, wires and gauges attached, my heart kept pumping, my blood replaced with some kind of black ooze so I could be prodded and gawked at.

My own voice used against me, out of my control, sound and thoughts of others being piped through me like I'm some kind of entertainment for them.

To be a thing of amusement for these fucking savages.

To be displayed as they shuffled by, looking and pointing, laughing and shaking their heads.

Fuckers.

Each and every one.

My life in their hands, to do with as they wish. Crucified but kept alive at their very whim.

Animals, fucking animals. Each and every one.

They may think the game is over, that they've won, but I'll wait. Wait and pray that someday another tour will arrive, another group of humans on the hunt. And somehow I'll let them know, I'll manage to control my own voice once more, and I'll warn them and plead with them to get us out of here.

And they'll come, and they'll blow these fuckers away.

And the game will start anew once more.

I'll be ready.

No A-grade savage Z will beat me.

No animal will ever win.

Not ever.

AMBER RISING

A short sequel
to *Lake Mountain*

The sound was loud in the night and it startled me. Then it repeated, louder this time.

Thud thud thud.

Three loud raps on the door.

"Hello?" came a gruff voice from outside. "Anyone in there?"

I sat frozen for what seemed like ages, but another round of thudding shook me out of it. I put my sewing down on the bed and stood silently.

I thought about blowing out the kerosene lantern on the bedside table, but then quickly decided against it. He could see the light from outside, of that I was sure, and if I put it out now, he'd know for certain I was in here.

"Can you *help* me?" he called. "I need some help."

As quietly as I could, I walked out of the bedroom and shut the door behind me. The hinges were old and rusty, and they moaned loudly in the quiet of the night. I'm sure he could hear me, probably hear my footsteps on the old creaking floorboards as well, or my heavy breathing…or the pounding of my racing heartbeat.

I crossed the lounge and crept towards the window as he knocked hard on the front door again. I made sure the lantern in the lounge room didn't throw my shadow across the window or by the gap under the front door.

"I know you're in there, I can see the fucking light. Help me, please!"

He rapped harder. The door shook under his fists and I wondered for the first time whether or not it would hold under his constant battering.

I held my breath as I reached out to the curtain and slowly pulled it back far enough to look outside.

The night was dark, and it took my eyes a few seconds to adjust to the patchy moonlight. I could see him hunched over by the door, dressed in a black leather jacket, jeans and boots. He was crouching down, facing away from me, focusing on the doorknob. Both his hands were fumbling, trying to turn it.

"Help me, *damnit!*" he screamed once more. Then he used the full force of his body to lunge against the door, his shoulder like a battering ram. "I fucking *know* you're in there!"

I moved away from the window and quickly scanned the lounge room. All of a sudden I wished I was back in the valve house, safe and sound in that small, warm cocoon that kept me safe for so long, and hidden away from people and the world.

I knew I couldn't stay there forever, I knew I would outgrow it, and with more campers and visitors to the dam and the surrounding area at Lake Mountain, I had to leave when I did, just to stop from being discovered.

I'd been so lucky to find this place. I just came across it one day when I was out walking in the woods. Yes, it's old and falling down, but I'd had plenty of time to make repairs; to fix up the holes in the roof and the gaps in the windows. While it may have looked like a deserted old shack in the middle of nowhere, it was proudly my home. A place to hide. To be safe again.

He hammered against the door once more, and my eyes darted to the doorknob. It was twisting back and forth. He was trying to work the latch, but luckily for me, he didn't realize that it was the deadbolt at the top of the door that was keeping it tightly shut.

For now.

"I'm not going anywhere," he called. "Just let me in. Come on, *please*. You don't understand."

I edged closer towards the door, my hands nervously running through my long hair.

"Look, I'm sorry," he called. "I'm *hurt*. I came off my

bike down the road a ways. It's a dark night, wet road, I didn't see the turn. I'm injured and need your help. That's all."

I *almost* believed him.

The roads around Lake Mountain were old and worn, many just tracks really, and Devil's Bend was aptly named due to the number of bad accidents that had happened on that sharp turn. Real bad, real dangerous, especially at night. And it *had* been raining earlier.

But I'd seen him through the window and he didn't look injured to me. He looked as if he just had one thing on his mind.

And I wasn't about to give him *that*.

I tied my hair back in a ponytail to keep it out of my eyes. I needed to be alert now.

He had scared me to begin with, shocked me and destroyed my solitude, and it was obvious he wasn't going to leave without getting what he came for.

I was wearing jeans and a shirt and I thought about covering myself up, but that would be an admission that his reach - his fear - had extended inside my world, making me feel uncomfortable and self-conscious, even though he was still outside. I wouldn't let him ruin *my* home, *my* place. It was a stupid thought, because he was already doing that, he already *was* inside…just inside my head. And soon he'd be inside other areas.

No fucking way.

"I've called the police!" I yelled.

I didn't think about it, I just did it, yelled back at him without thinking, both giving away my location and confirming that I was inside. *And* that I was female.

Good one, girl. Nice fuck up.

I stared at the door and waited. He was silent for a few moments, and then I heard his deep sigh.

"You *what?*"

"I called the police! If you're injured they'll be here in ten minutes to help you."

"Jesus," he muttered, probably to himself, but I heard him through the door. "You don't *need* the cops."

Even though I was staring at the door, I was trying to look through it, picturing him hunched over on the other side, knowing his thoughts, knowing what he wanted. He could probably smell me, smell my fear, and couldn't wait to fuck me and kill me, his cock hard and pressed against his jeans. He probably had it out now, in his hands, rubbing it, preparing it for me as now he knew I was female and alone, and all his to do with as he pleased.

Terrific, Amber. You might as well just open the door and say, "Fuck me."

"I'm hurt. I need attention *now*. I'm just asking for your help," he said as his fists pounded the door once more.

The force of the attack this time caused me to take a step backwards, as the door shook and the dead-bolt looked as if it was about to snap. I'd attached the deadbolt to the door, and I knew the screws weren't holding as well as they could be. I didn't have a screwdriver so I'd used what I could find to screw them in. Those short screws in the old timber had to give way eventually.

"I can't help you!"

"Yes, you *can*. I need some water, and a place to lie down, that's all," he called to me. "Don't you *understand*? My leg's beaten up real bad... I'm losing a lot of blood."

"You managed to walk here okay," I called back.

"*Huh?*"

"If you're so badly busted up, how did you walk here?"

There was silence from outside, and I watched as the door handle turned slowly one more time.

"And how did you find me?" I knew I was winning now. His story was falling apart. "Why come out here if you're hurt when you could stay by the side of the road and flag down a passerby?"

"It's 2 am in the morning. There are *no* other cars!"

"There could be. Eventually someone would drive along and find you. But you came up here instead. Why?"

"I saw your light!"

"Dragged yourself up here with your busted leg."

"*Yes*, goddamnit."

"Well, I don't believe you! I'm *not* helping you and I've

called the cops and they'll be here soon to deal with you. So you better fuck off unless you really *are* hurt because they'll get you and I'll tell them everything."

With that, I turned away from the door and moved across to the lantern. I lifted the glass housing and blew out the flame. Then I walked across to the bedroom door, opened it and did the same to the lantern in the bedroom.

Now, the whole house plunged into darkness.

Quietly, I crept back to the middle of the lounge room and stood facing the door once more. I hoped that I'd shown him I wasn't scared, that he couldn't fuck with me. I stood strong and proud, staring at the front door, almost daring him to make his next move so I could prove I wasn't going to take his shit.

The pounding on the door had stopped and he didn't say anything for a long time. I could still hear his breathing though, so I knew he was still there.

He was doing something, but I couldn't work out what. The clouds that had brought the rain earlier were now also obscuring the moonlight, so I had no hope of clearly seeing him in the shadows. I relied on my hearing, once I got my breathing under control.

If anything, the darkness made me feel much better. I liked the darkness. It was like a warm blanket, a good friend. It enveloped you and protected you. Saved you.

Just like she did.

I think it was all that time I spent in the blowhole, hiding out from the cops after it all happened, I got used to the darkness then, welcomed it, knew that it would protect me. And now, standing my ground in the lounge room against an unknown outsider, I felt safe and confident again.

He was on *my* patch, and he wasn't getting what he wanted.

"You know," he said slowly, in a quiet voice. "Your shack doesn't *have* a phone line."

I didn't say anything. His words took the breath from my lungs and I just froze to the spot.

"You've got no utility lines out here at all. No power,

no phone. That's why you're using lanterns."

How did he know *that*? Had he been watching me through the window before he started knocking on the door? Had he been watching and getting all hot and bothered, horny and hard?

Fucker.

"I've got a mobile," I called too quickly, my voice wavering and betraying my fear.

He laughed then. Actually *laughed* at me.

"Sorry, sweets, no network coverage out here either. I know that because I tried to use my phone when I came off the bike."

"I have access and I've called the cops," I yelled at him, but it was clear he wasn't believing it. And the fear in my voice made it clear that even *I* didn't believe it.

"Nice one," he replied. "Now open the *fucking door!* Please." The please was tacked on as an afterthought.

I turned and walked over to the cabinet beneath the window. As quietly and slowly as I dared, I bent down, pulled out the top drawer and let my fingers fumble around inside until I felt cold steel.

I smiled as I lifted Tyler's revolver from the drawer and held it in my hands. I'd long ago run out of ammunition for it, but I kept it just in case, for bluff, for situations just like this one.

I straightened up, and as I did so my eyes met the window.

And looked straight into his.

I pulled back quickly, a gasp of fright escaping me. He was peering in through the window, but it seemed like he hadn't seen me. The moonlight was patchy, so perhaps that's what saved me.

He was staring through the curtains, looking around, trying to see any movement I guess, but the curtains probably hid most of the lounge room, and me.

He had dark slicked back hair and a small goatee. His face was thin and gaunt and his eyes looked beady and too close together. His lips were lopsided and sneering.

He didn't look too beaten up from an accident to me.

I raised the gun and pointed it at his head, knowing that if I only had a bullet, just one *single* bullet, I could end all this now, without him even knowing, just by placing one single bullet between his eyes.

But I couldn't. I'd used the last of the bullets trying desperately to shoot a rabbit for dinner some months earlier. The little fucker kept hopping away whenever I got too close. It had won that battle and I'd gone hungry again.

He cupped his hands over his eyes and pushed further against the glass, his nose squished and deformed against the glass, his breath now fogging it.

I prayed for the clouds to swallow the moonlight once more.

"Look," he called. "I understand how this must seem. And I really don't *mean* to be a pain in the ass, and I certainly don't mean to scare you Miss, but I *am* injured and need your help."

I didn't reply.

"Is there someone else in there who can help me?"

Nice try, asshole.

"Maybe your boyfriend or husband?"

Like I was going to answer *that*! He already knew the situation, it was confirmed for him the moment I'd opened my big stupid mouth and gave myself away.

He turned away from the window for a second, looked down and seemed to wince as he tried to do something.

Maybe he is hurt.

"I tell you what," he said as he disappeared from view. "I'm going to slip my license under the front door, okay? You can read it and take down my details or something. Then you can let me in."

Like *hell* I was! Just because he was passing me his (probably fake) license under the door, didn't mean I was going to let him inside. I mean, what as I going to do? Write down the details for the cops so that when they found my raped remains they could go after him? How *stupid* did he think I was? Obviously he'd destroy any details I copied down or take them with him after he'd fucked me, killed me and buried me in a shallow grave somewhere.

I didn't say anything, just listened as I followed his movements from the window back to the door. Seconds later, his license slid under the door and landed at my feet.

I bent down and picked it up. I'm not sure why, but I wanted to see the name of the man who was trying to end my life.

Slowly, I walked back into the bedroom and closed the door behind me. I sat on the bed in the darkness, placed Tyler's revolver by my side and felt for the matches by the lantern. I struck one and let it burn only long enough to read the man's name.

Vaden Collins.

I blew out the match and slipped the license under my pillow.

I sat there for a short time, saying his name over and over in my head.

Vaden Collins, Vaden Collins, Vaden Collins, Vaden, Vaden, Vaden Collins.

Then I heard the glass shattering.

I turned and for a second had no idea what to do. But I knew I had to act fast. My hands flew out, fumbling for the revolver in the darkness. I felt it next to me, thought I had it, but as my fingers closed around the cool steel it slipped from my shaking hands and I heard it fall to the floor and slide along the floorboards to god-knows-where.

Fuck!

I didn't have time to get down on my knees and search for it. I had to move *now*!

I bolted to the bedroom door, not worried now about the sound of my footsteps or letting him know where I was hiding.

I swung open the door and looked towards the front door. The deadbolt was still firm, the door was still on its hinges.

Out of the corner of my eye I saw the curtains puff outwards and I turned to see a hand, then a leg reach through the window.

He was climbing inside. He'd broken a pane, unlatched the lock and was now hurriedly trying to climb through.

I ran to the fireplace and grabbed the poker - the one with the sharp hook on the end for pulling logs around in the fire - and turned, ran towards him, lifted the poker high as his shoulders and head lunged through the window.

Saw him as he saw me.

Screamed as he did.

And brought the poker down hard on his head.

Once.

Twice.

And then again and again.

He fell forwards, towards me, taking out my legs as he hit the ground, and I went tumbling too, the poker jarring from my hands as I landed heavily on top of him.

My scream lasted longer than his. And once it ended, the darkness surrounded us both, and all was quiet, and I was safe again.

* * *

Vaden Collins really *had* been in an accident. His left leg was broken up real bad. I'm not sure exactly where it happened, but if it took place down at Devil's Bend, he must've put up with a lot of pain to make it all the way to me.

I sat in the darkness, not daring to move for so long, until I was convinced he was really unconscious and not just playing dead.

I could hear his breathing, so I knew he was alive and I figured either my blows with the poker had been enough to knock him out, or it was the awkward fall onto his head as he fell through the window.

Anyway, he was unconscious, and that gave me enough time to regain my composure and work out what I was going to do.

I dragged him into the bedroom and relit the lantern. It was then I could see the smears of blood that trailed all the way back to the window. His leg was pretty messed up. I could see bone and muscle and grit.

Bad accident for sure.

Still, he didn't look nice. He had some weird tattoos on his arms and one of a snake around his good leg. I found this all out when I took off his jacket and cut away what was left of his jeans. He had muscles on his arms that proved he must work out too much, and his cock was uncircumcised and a little on the small side.

When I had him naked, I made sure I tied him down to the bed good and proper. I didn't want him giving me any trouble, not now. After all, people can get the wrong impression. And those muscles of his worried me, so I made sure he wouldn't be able to escape.

So, I bathed his wounds; his leg and forehead, where the poker had done some damage near his left temple. I'd aimed well with the poker and the wound was deep. There was a lot of blood, and I had to make sure he didn't lose too much.

Then I set to work.

I sewed up the forehead gash first. It didn't take too long, only a dozen or so stitches.

The leg was another matter.

I did what I could, which wasn't setting broken bones or anything. I just sewed as quickly and as expertly as I could to help stop the mess that was still oozing away.

It took some time, and a whole lot of patience, but I finished him and made him whole again.

I was pretty pleased with the results, and I knew he would thank me eventually. In the end, he'd got what he wanted. I *did* help him out and save him.

I was halfway through sewing his mouth closed when he began to regain consciousness.

I panicked a little, and tried to rush the job, and I think it was my fumbling hands and the fact that the needle jabbed into his tongue and gums a couple of times that probably brought him back to reality sooner than I hoped.

His eyes shot open and he stared at me.

"What the fuck?" he mumbled out of the corner of his mouth, as he pulled on his bindings, trying to free his arms and legs.

But he wasn't going anywhere; he was tied too tight for that. Even the ropes double knotted around his head and neck meant that he couldn't move his head from side to side.

"Shhhh," I whispered to him. "It's all right. I'm looking after you."

He struggled in vain for a couple of minutes, crying out of what was left of the opening in his mouth, but I knew no one was around to hear him.

I took a step back, sat down in the chair by the bed and continued with the sewing I had been doing earlier, before he had interrupted my solace.

It seemed so long ago now, but I knew only a couple of hours had passed.

He struggled and strained, but not for long. He soon realized he wasn't doing anything except exhausting himself further.

I could see him turning his head ever so slightly, watching me out of the corner of his eye. I knew he could just see me, and I waited a while, continuing with my sewing, making him wait until I had sewed the arm closed.

Eventually, I placed the arm on the table by the bed and walked back over to him.

"My name is Amber," I said, smiling. "You never asked. I know you're Vaden. Or at least you *say* that's your name."

He nodded vigorously. "Yes," he said, the word falling spastically from the side of his mouth.

"I'm sorry I didn't believe you were in an accident. But a girl can't be too careful."

He nodded again, faster, oh-so-ready to agree.

Agree with a girl to get what you really want.

"I don't want you to worry," I said as I leaned closer with the needle. "I'll be kind. I'm just making you better."

He tried to recoil from the needle, but there was nowhere to move.

"I can't have you yelling like this. It gives me a headache and annoys my friends."

I threaded the loose fishing line that was still hanging from his top lip through the eye of the needle and continued working where I had left off.

He wasn't fighting now, wasn't trying to escape. He was just staring at me. His eyes were pleading; tears slowly leaking at the edges. He whimpered every time the needle slid into the skin, sounding like a lost dog about to give up hope.

Within a minute I had his mouth nicely sewn shut.

He was breathing fast through his nose now, non-stop and quick. In time he would reconcile with himself, think about all the things he had done, the good and the bad, and what he had planned to do to me.

We all need that time, the quiet time where we can fully evaluate ourselves, to understand what life and death is all about. My time had been hiding in that blowhole, thinking about everything that had happened, Tyler and Raven, Duke…everything.

I'd come out of the blowhole reborn. It sounds silly, I know, but it's true. The day I walked out into the sunlight once more, I knew what my future would bring, and how I could make it happen. Knowing the cops had gone, and that all the events that had led me here were in the past. They had made me what I am.

The new woman. The new Amber.

Reborn.

I left him alone then, to have time for that self-discovery, and I walked over to the dressing table and sat down to look at myself in the mirror. I picked up my hair brush and undid my pony-tail, letting my long hair cascade down my back, the long dark locks shining in the lantern-light, the two purple strands running down each side of my face, like a ribbon.

I played with my fringe, brushing it forward over the scars on my forehead, and brushed along my long locks until I counted to one hundred.

Then I put the brush to one side and smiled at the three faces reflected in the mirror. I turned around and smiled back at them.

Vaden's breathing was much slower now, and I knew he was at peace. He would listen now, and understand.

I stood and walked towards him, quietly kneeling by the side of the bed, so I could whisper in his ear.

"I know you can see them," I said. "And they can see you."

He didn't say anything, his eyes just looked at mine, then slipped over my shoulder, so I knew he was looking at them now.

"They're my friends, and soon they'll be yours as well." I continued. "I've always had trouble meeting new people, I just can't quite relate to them. You know what I mean?"

He nodded slowly, but didn't look at me.

"But Devil's Bend is a dangerous place, and I find it much more interesting meeting people this way."

I turned away from him and sat down on the floor, leaning up against the bed and looking over at my boys.

"Peter's the one on the left. He's my oldest and dearest friend. I met him before I even moved in here. Then there's Julian. He's the prettiest of the bunch, and the newest. You can thank Devil's Bend for bringing him here too. You can both discuss your accidents, although he was in a car. And the guy on the end is Nathaniel. Sorry about his arm, I'm still working on the repairs. I should have that re-attached by the end of the week. Still, he doesn't like to complain. Do you, Nathaniel?"

I smiled at them and they smiled back.

"Everyone, this is Vaden. Say hello."

It's good to have friends, friends you can trust. Those who don't cheat on you or betray you, turn their backs on you when you need them the most.

I looked down to my hands, turned them over so I could see the scars on my palms, the rough and callused and ugly reminders of those days so long ago.

"I'm sure you'll get to know them," I said as I turned and stood up once more. "They're already very interested in you."

I picked up the needle and threaded some more fishing line. He was watching me now, intently, eyes wide. His breathing started to accelerate again, but I didn't care, I'd let him take as many breaths as he could, because now they were limited.

I started with his left eye, and even though he scrunched them up tight, that didn't stop me. In fact, it kinda helped. He struggled as much as he could, but I'm very good at this now, and had his eye sewn shut within a few minutes.

He struggled more as I worked with his right eye. I guess the whole finality of it all had dawned on him by now. Maybe he was a little slow, or he'd just refused to believe. I had to reach over him to continue my work. No amount of soothing would stop him trying to escape, and he put every effort into his final attempts.

It wasn't really my fault when the needle skewered his eyeball. He let out a huge muffled scream when it did, as the white ooze dribbled away from under his eyelid. I even thought for a moment he might break his bonds, or the scream might tear through his sewn up lips. But both held, and after this final scream, he fought no more.

I sewed shut the remains of his right eye quickly and easily. With no struggle and little eyeball left, the chasm left behind was easy to stitch. I could always fix that problem later anyway.

His breathing was low and slow as I started on his left nostril. I thought he would struggle one final time, would show some kind of valiant hopeless resistance, but even as the needle pierced the flesh, and dug through the gristle of his nose, he no longer struggled. It was gone, released from within him.

Vaden was mine.

"Don't worry, baby," I said as I tied off his left nostril and started work on his right, his final breaths slipping in and out of the quickly closing gap.

How narrow the avenues between life and death really are. How close we all walk to our final moments every second of the day. How quickly death can descend upon us all.

"Your eyes may be closed now, Vaden," I whispered to him during those final, belabored breaths. "But don't worry, I'll see for you as I see for all my friends. Because my eyes are forever open."

STEVE GERLACH: ON THE EDGE

*A Confessional with a Rising Star
in Horror and Suspense Fiction*

(This is an expanded and updated version of a much shorter interview published in Cemetery Dance magazine, issue #51, 2005)

Australian Author Steve Gerlach seems inevitably poised on the threshold of universal Big Name success. Having risen quickly and dramatically through the ranks of the genre's small press in both Australia and the United States, his horror and suspense fiction has for nearly a decade systematically captured the imagination of readers not only in those two countries but worldwide. His work also caught the eye of the New York publishing establishment, resulting in a 2004 mass-market paperback release of *Rage* that expanded his reach to bookstores everywhere. In this extensive and definitive interview with Ron Clinton, Gerlach fields questions on life, writing and the woman he can't get out of his mind…

* * *

RC: Over the last few years, you've garnered a considerable amount of publishing success that has allowed your work to reach a significantly larger audience than before. That must be quite gratifying, both creatively and financially, particularly after more than a decade of self-publishing or writing simply for the love of the craft.

SG: It is gratifying to finally see your work reaching a larger audience. And, in a way, I have to thank the core group of readers who have been with me since the mid-nineties and who tirelessly recommend my works to others. Certainly, the Internet has made this much easier to do, and being the webmaster of the official Richard Laymon site has helped too. But writing is still the key and still where those thrills are for me. Creating a story, a setting, a world and delving into interesting (and sometimes bizarre) characters are the core reasons I write. Getting to know these people I create, working out what they would do and how they would react—that's where the biggest buzz is.

RC: Before we delve too deep into the more recent successes that have expanded your popularity beyond that core group of readers you mention, let's talk about the early years. You've previously worked as an editor for an international crime magazine and an Australian roadbike magazine, a researcher and columnist for an Australian daily newspaper, and have held various positions within several technical corporations. Since 1996 you've operated the *Richard Laymons Kills!* website and were also the historical advisor for the film *Let's Get Skase*. Give us a peek into your background and how you feel these divergent ventures helped shape, or hinder, your creative passion and talent.

SG: I guess I've been blessed in having a chance to work in every field of writing. Whether that be non-fiction articles, editing, proof-reading or in the film world, it's given me a very well rounded view of the whole publishing industry. And I think that can only help you as a writer.

RC: Specifically, how so?

SG: I can see book publishing from an editor's point of view, also from marketing and distribution. My editors know I'm keen on marketing and PR, and I like a hand in working out positioning and design of my novels. I don't know if that's a good thing for *them*, though *(chuckles)*. As a writer, everything you do is important, because it may come in handy one day as you're writing fiction. I know the contacts I have made in the film and technical worlds are of great importance to me now, as I have people I can contact to answer questions and scenarios that I may need help with.

RC: You're a fellow with two young children and a full-time job — and yet you've also managed to release two or three novels in about as many years, edit a couple anthologies, write introductions to others' work and, of course, run not only your own author site at http://www.stevegerlach.com but the *Richard Laymon Kills!* website as well. This juggling act must pose quite a challenge at times.

SG: Let's just say it can get very hectic indeed. Yep, two kids, webmaster and author. It can be very hard and taxing at times, and sometimes it can mean I have to lock myself away for a couple of weeks to get the basic structure of a novel down on paper, but I have a system that works very well. Who knows, I may patent it one day *(laughs)!*

RC: Along with all that, I understand you've also constructed— and still maintain—several fan websites for your other interests.

SG: Yes, that's correct. But they haven't been updated for years. Those who have the time and the inclination can probably find a few secret Steve Gerlach sites out there in cyberspace.

RC: But one site, I believe, uniquely contains a Gerlach screenplay.

SG: Ah, that's true. It's a screenplay—well, teleplay actually—for a BBC science fiction program called Doctor Who. The script was submitted for Season 27 of the show, but the show was cancelled before season 27 began. A damn shame too, because it was a great script. But you're right, it's out there on a Who site I created. It's entitled "The Emissary of Death." Sounded like a good title at the time. Now, I'm not so sure *(laughs)!*

RC: Have you written any other scripts that escaped the curse of "Emissary?"

SG: You know, now I come to think of it, there *is* another Doctor Who script in a drawer somewhere. It's called "Madhouse." I must give that one a look someday. I really liked that one!

RC: Okay, let's get back to the novels. Give us an idea of your writing schedule.

SG: Well, it varies for each book. But basically, each book has a very long lead time from when I first get the idea, then I research it, plan, outline and then finally sit down and write it. For example, *Lake Mountain* was actually something I planned to write before *Love Lies Dying*. But Zoe Barber from LLD came along, and I just *had* to get to know her more. So *Lake Mountain* was shelved until LLD was complete. *Lake Mountain* was actually conceived way back in 1998. 2003 saw me researching this novel for about 6 months (around about the same research time as LLD) and I spent a couple of months getting the story and characters together. So that's, what, 5 years from inception? Jeez, that's a scary thought.

RC: It sounds as though you're as studious and conscientious about your writing duties as you might be about any regular job. How about the daily grind—what's your writing schedule from day-to-day?

SG: When I sit down to write, I *have* to treat the novel as a job. If I don't, I'd sit around and procrastinate all day. So, when I'm not at work with my day job, my routine starts at 7am to read the previous day's writing. Then I write until about 12 noon. I stop for lunch and go for a walk, shop at the mall or something. Anything to get me out of the house. Then I edit what I've written from about 3pm til 5pm. Dinner, then news. Then a damn good movie to finish off the day. Go to bed, sleep, get up the next day and start again. This type of freedom mostly occurs when I'm on vacation from work, or weekends, public holidays and so forth; otherwise, I just simply try to make as much time for writing as I'm able.

RC: Since your writings have settings and a style that is distinctly American, many of your newer readers may be surprised to know that you've lived in Australia your entire life. Why have you opted to tailor your stories to an American audience—is it a personal preference or an obligatory requisite for publishing success?

SG: Yes, I'm Australian born and bred, although I've visited the US on three occasions. As far as tailoring my stories, I try to write in a "your world" style. That way the events and people and places can translate to any-where—specifically, the world of the reader— your world. The thriller / horror market in Australia is not particularly large, nowhere near as large as the US, so I have always tried to write with that market in mind. *The Nocturne* certainly took place in the US, but the rest could take place anywhere in "your world."

RC: Do you find it difficult translating your cultural influences to fit a generic universal flavour?

SG: Actually, it's not that hard at all. The world's a big place, but we're growing to be more and more alike these days. Especially in the case of the US and Australia. I always write the first draft using Australian terms and words I'm familiar with. Then as the edits go along, I pull it closer to the US, swapping terms here and there. Plus, of course, my US editors are always on the ball, changing words they feel need to be changed for an American audience. I keep a list of those and make the changes accordingly in any new work I write. In the end, not much is different.

RC: We mentioned before your involvement with the *Richard Laymon Kills!* website. This began in December of 1996, I believe. What prompted you to design this acclaimed site that, nearly from the start, had the integral involvement of its namesake—and what drives you to continue its updates years after Mr. Laymon's tragic passing in February 2001?

SG: I've been reading Laymon now for about 20 years. My first Laymon was *The Woods Are Dark* and I was hooked from the first chapter and never looked back. I always pestered publishers and bookstores about the next Laymon release, but they never seemed to have any details—or they didn't care. When I first connected to the Internet in 1996, my first search was for a website dedicated to Laymon. I was pretty disappointed when I couldn't find one. So, I thought, it was up to me to become the one-stop-shop for every-thing Laymon. So, that's how it started. Luckily, the planets were all aligned and not only did I get the publishers' support, but also Richard's support as well. The site continues, and will continue, to be the place Laymon fans can gather to discuss his work. Also, with Laymon releases becoming more frequent in the US, I'm finding readers new to Laymon are logging on and saying hi, and finding out all the information they need to continue their Laymon collection. It's an honor to keep the site up and running at full steam in Dick's memory.

RC: Let's talk about Richard Laymon a bit more since he is so clearly an inspiration for your own work. Tell us a bit about the man you knew as Dick, and how he influenced your life and your writing.

SG: He's influenced me quite a great deal, no doubt about that. As you find when you read my novels, they have the same cut-to-the-bone style as Dick's. I like the way he wrote, and I like reading that sort of style. So, I also like to write that way myself. I'm not one for pages and pages of description or exposition. But he's not my only inspiration. Robert Bloch, Richard Matheson, Rod Serling, Jack Ketchum have all influenced me over the years. But it was a huge shock to all of us when he died, and I'm not sure if the ripples of his passing have yet subsided. It took us all quite a while to recover from the news...and I can still remember exactly what I was doing when I first heard. And, of course, I thought it was a joke at the time. Now I just wish it were.

RC: What do you feel is ultimately Laymon's legacy when it comes to horror fiction, the genre he helped champion and popularize?

SG: I think Richard's legacy (to both me and the genre) is twofold. One: always push the limits, both of the genre and yourself as a writer. He went to extremes, sometimes to sickening effect, but it always worked and he always managed to pull it off. It always works if it's Laymon. And the same goes for writing as a craft or art. Always push yourself. Always trying something new. Always grow as a writer with your next novel or short story. I try to challenge myself with every novel I write, to do something new and different. That's what makes it exciting to write and tell these stories. I love doing something I've never done before and making it work. *That's* the excitement in writing, *that's* what keeps me going. His second legacy is: don't take it all so seriously. Richard was always happy, always willing to share a joke, always willing to go the extra mile for someone. In the end, this isn't rocket science, lighten up and enjoy it...you'll go crazy otherwise.

RC: Along with the authors you mention, who were some other writers who influenced your writing—and what in particular do you feel you've learned from each of them?

SG: Well, Bloch, Matheson, Serling and Ketchum each have their own very unique style and are able to tell a damn fine story in clean, defined prose. And, of course, dialogue is the key as well, and they're each masters at that. But I could mention a handful more, including Bentley Little, Charles Beaumont, F. Paul Wilson and more. In fact, I still have a letter Robert Bloch sent me and it's framed on my wall. He wrote it just before he died and I read it probably once a week.

RC: A couple of the authors you mention have previously acknowledged that research is an integral part of fiction writing, a necessary evil to enhance the fictitious reality and avoid simple factual errors; other writers may claim it's unnecessary and can stifle free-flow creativity. Where do you come down in this debate?

SG: Oh, research is key, no doubt about it. As you can tell from the lead-times for my novels, I take research very seriously. In fact, I do too much, and most of it is not used in the novels. But it can be the little things, the small often overlooked details, that give the story its strength. In *Love Lies Dying*, for example, it's very important that a piece of rope in an S&M scene is tied a particular way. While I did copious amounts of research into S&M for the novel (including visiting a house of domination and talking to some of the Mistresses there) it really came down to the minute details, and the mind-set of one of the characters that made the novel work on a much stronger level. And *that's* why research is so important. It makes it more real, because it is. It's time consuming and sometimes confusing, but it has to be done for this kind of novel. Any information that can make the novel more real is very important indeed, even if it's only for the author's use!

RC: Okay, let's dive into your published works thus far. *Rage* (WildRoses Productions, 2003, 26-copy signed/limited HC; Bloodletting Press, 2003, 300-copy signed/limited HC; Leisure Books, 2004, mass-market paperback), while not your first book published, was the first written—back in 1992, I believe. How did this slim novel find its way out of the proverbial trunk and ultimately into a mainstream New York publishing house?

SG: Well, *Rage* has always been my dirty little secret. When I wrote it in 1992, I shopped it around to the publishers down here. One of them wanted to publish it, but the marketing department didn't know how to market it, and they were worried it would be banned. So, I shelved the novel, threw it in the filing cabinet, and let it gather dust. After the success of *The Nocturne* and *Love Lies Dying,* Troy Taylor from WildRoses Productions, a small publisher down here in Australia, wanted a "Gerlach Original." I told him there weren't any, and that *Lake Mountain* was at least two years away. He said that I must have something somewhere, and that's when I mentioned *Rage.* He wanted to read it, and I said no. But he kept at me and eventually I told him *I'd* read it and let him know if it was any good.

RC: And what were your initial impressions upon re-acquainting yourself with it?

SG: That it's amazing that a novel can really mature in 10 years. I mean, the issues I was dealing with back then are just as relevant today, probably even more so with the Columbine and Virginia Tech shootings and tragedies of that ilk. So, I gave it to him to read and he snapped it up immediately. It was printed as an ultra-limited down here and sold out before publication. And that's when the US publishers became interested and got involved. So I'm proud my "black sheep", as it were, has finally found a place in the world.

RC: Do you foresee any of your other trunk novels shaking off their dust to appear anytime soon?

SG: No, I don't think so. There're two still gathering dust, *Unforeseen Circumstances* and *Injustice,* but I don't think I'll ever wipe the cobwebs off those. Although, I said the same thing about *Rage,* so who knows...one day, maybe.

RC: Fair enough. Well, let's talk about *Rage* a bit more, and the person who actually authored it. Written fifteen years ago, *Rage* tells a simple, linear tale of a man's disintegration of self-worth and self-control, one who finds himself increasingly unable to cope with what he construes as constant rejection and betrayal by the female gender and, indeed, the world at large. It was penned by an individual who, like his protagonist, is in his early twenties...a person, I'm sure, much different than the man you are today. What were you feeling when you wrote that work, a book of such angst and, yes, rage?

SG: There's no doubt that at the time I lived the part of Ben. Don't get me wrong, I *wasn't* Ben and the things that happened to him didn't happen to me—well, not on that scale, anyway—but for the period of time when I was writing the novel, I lived Ben's part. I dressed like him, I moped like him. My family could tell you some interesting stories about my "dark" period.

RC: And if you were to go back and speak to that young man—or any of today's budding twenty-something authors who often find the road to publication strewn with obstacles—what advice about writing or life would you offer?

SG: Hmmm, tough one. I'd probably say to stick at it, to keep writing, because it all will pay off in the end. Everything you write, every mistake, every victory, makes you smarter and stronger for what comes along next. Keep at it. Believe in yourself. That's the most important thing. Believe that what you are doing is right and have the balls to push yourself further than you've been before. Go to the edge every time.

RC: Sage advice. Well, let's get back on track. *Rage's* protagonist, Ben, delves deeper and deeper into despair and rage over the inequities he feels heaped upon him, the pressurized control he has kept his smoldering emotions under begins to loosen and comes steaming closer and closer to the surface, climaxing ultimately in raw, hideous violence. It's a strong, character-driven novel that pushes the constraints of political correctness, particularly in this age when, at least in the United States, there is a very potent sensitivity on matters of school-age violence and guns, even more so than back in '92 when the book was written. Did you have any concerns about a political-correctness backlash once this book hit the shelves at the local Barnes & Noble, and do such outside matters in any way impact what you choose to write?

SG: You can't worry about things like that when you write. You write the story that is in you, you watch it unfold as the reader does. You can't sit there and think, "Oh no, that's going too far. I'm not going to do that." I'm not here to censor myself. If others want to do it, that's their problem. I push to the edge each time, and there's no doubt that some of the imagery in *Rage* had some people staggering from their comfy chairs, but that's the whole point really. If you can't confront tough issues and if you can't get people to think and consider what you're trying to say—the message of your novel—then why bother? What the past 15 years prove is that *Rage* is an even more important novel now than it was when it was first written—but the message is still the same. P.C. backlash? Well, if it got people talking about the book, about the issues of drugging our children instead of dealing with their issues, and about violence in media and for entertainment, then I'm all for it. Bring it on.

RC: On a gentler note, setting aside the psychosis, violence and other mature themes contained within the book, *Rage* is—at its core—a love story. Humor and horror are often labeled as opposite but complimentary sides of the same coin, as demonstrated best perhaps in the short works of Robert Bloch. But horror and love...one would imagine that's a more difficult hybrid to write.

SG: Yes, it is a love story. The saddest love story of all. Ben is so close, so close to having everything he wants, but a few small events that could change everything just don't go his way. It's about fate and love. And it's dark and ironic. Remember Burgess Meredith in that Twilight Zone episode?

RC: Sure—the one where he's the last surviving human being, and his thick glasses break just as he's about to, for the first time in his selfless life, finally have the time and opportunity to simply *read*. Great stuff.

SG: That's the one. The episode was called "Time Enough at Last" and written by Rod Serling. Excellent, heart-wrenching stuff. Ironic. *Rage* is like that. But difficult to write? Actually, no more difficult than any of the other novels. Just different for a whole stack of reasons.

RC: *Rage* is, perhaps more than any other of your novels, a character-driven novel; it's all about Ben and his personal, inner drama. Do you find novels of this type easier to write than more plot-driven narratives, like *The Nocturne,* for example, or more difficult—and why?

SG: Each novel comes with its own unique difficulties and problems. I don't think any of them are necessarily harder than another to write; they are each unique and come with advantages and disadvantages. The advantages with *Rage* were that it was a simple linear story, where the characters take center-stage. Really, it's a character study, just like *Love Lies Dying*. Whereas novels like *The Nocturne* and *Hunting Zoe* are more plot or story or "chase" driven. *Lake Mountain* is a bit of both.

RC: I understand the signed and limited hardcover of *Rage* from Bloodletting Press contained edited portions deemed too extreme for the earlier Australian hardcover and Leisure paperback. Do you personally see yourself as an author who enjoys "pushing the envelope?"

SG: Yes, that's true. For the Aussie release, I removed the scenes that had the Aussie publisher back in 1992 all worried about it being banned. I reinserted them for the US edition after discussions with Larry Roberts, the publisher at Bloodletting, who believed they should be reinstated. And I agree with him on that. And yes, I have to push the envelope both for myself as a writer, and for my readers. Pushing characters and situations to their extremes, watching how they react and what they do. That's what "pushing the envelope" means to me.

RC: The novel you wrote next—but the first actually published— was *The Nocturne* (Probable Cause Productions, TPB, 1999; Bloodletting Books, signed/limited HC, forthcoming), a horror/sci-fi thrill ride. I can't help but notice there was quite a time lag between the writing of *Rage* at the beginning of the '90's and *The Nocturne's* publication much later in the decade.

SG: Yes, and no, I guess. I finished *Rage,* probably, in 1992. I then shopped it around for a year or so down here. I was then planning and working on the outline for *The Nocturne.* But I was working for Australia's biggest newspaper at that time, so my novel writing time was cut drastically. By the time I got to writing *The Nocturne,* then editing it to my liking, it probably gets us to 1995 or 1996. Can't quite remember the exact dates now. But while there's a large gap between actual novel completion dates, there's a whole lot of behind-the-scene stuff going on.

RC: More research?

SG: Yeah, in fact I traveled to Arizona specifically for that novel. Even though it ends up taking place in Washington State! *(Laughs)* Best laid plans and all that...

RC: The contrast in both pacing and structure between

the two divergent works is quite marked. *The Nocturne* comes off as a much more accomplished, confident novel, resounding with a clear maturity of style and ability. Upon completion of the work, what was your sense of the book?

SG: Well, to begin with, I'd buried *Rage* away in a cupboard, thinking it was too extreme and too violent for anyone to read. So with *The Nocturne* I took another track. I pushed myself in another direction, wanting to see if I could write a chase novel that starts at 100 miles an hour on page one and doesn't let up until the final page. That was my goal, and I was very happy with the results. At the time, I felt it was my best novel, and it certainly was to that date. The style had improved, as did the plotting and characterization, which is what you'd hope for coming a few years after my last novel. I was very proud of *The Nocturne*, that's for sure.

RC: The full-throttle, staccato pacing of this novel is extreme and, at times, almost exhausting; your intention was obviously to create a work that was pure and undistilled suspense of the highest order. In both its aforementioned pacing and its skewed outdoor survival theme, it may be the closest in both style and content to the writings of Richard Laymon. As indicated before, he was clearly a huge influence in both your life and art. Was *The Nocturne* essentially your homage to the man you consider your mentor?

SG: Certainly, in lots of ways, I think so. *The Woods Are Dark* was the first Laymon novel I read. It pulled you in on page one and didn't let go until the story was complete, and that was something I was aiming to do with *The Nocturne.* I wanted to create the same pace and suspense, not let the reader go for one second, so they would be as exhausted as the characters by the end of the book. And I think the novel succeeds like that. I can think of only two sections in the novel where I actually give the reader a chance to, well, "breathe."

RC: Did you receive any feedback from Mr. Laymon, either before or after publication?

SG: Once I'd completed the novel to my satisfaction, Richard gave it a read and suggested a few things—one being to move it from Arizona to Washington State. Which is what I did. His comments and influence made the book much leaner and starker, for sure.

RC: While your other two novels tend to focus on a central character, this plot-driven book was drawn on perhaps your largest canvas yet, with a huge cast of characters whose actions and motivations in the narrative were sewn together beautifully to form the whole. Were you intentionally attempting to stretch your creative abilities when writing this book after *Rage*, to take your talents "to the next level"? Was this the book that confirmed for you personally that, yeah, you know what, I *can* do this!

SG: It was certainly make-or-break time. With *Rage* being much more character-based, I then had to try a larger novel. More characters, more settings, more violence. In *The Nocturne*, the characters escape from Hell and arrive somewhere worse. That was the tag line, and I had to make sure I lived up to that. There are probably half a dozen main characters in the novel and an ensemble of, literally, thousands. They all had to come together and face impending doom, more than once or twice. It was a tough slog, back then. I had people and events everywhere, tragedy, love, death, and escape. And it had to all start from chapter one and not let up in intensity, suspense or drama until the final page. For me, back then, it was a big task, a big creative push to get me on the edge again—but I got there, and the results speak for themselves.

RC: Now, for those who haven't had an opportunity to read *The Nocturne,* tell us a bit about this novel.

SG: *The Nocturne* deals with a motley group of people, fleeing a fire that is destroying their whole town. They are detoured onto a side road and into uncharted forest where they come across another town where people are... well, not as they first seem. They have to band together to fight for their lives, while also trying to escape the firestorm that is coming their way. They have limited time and resources, and every step they take could lead to death, one way or another. It's lots of fun.

RC: There seems to be a consistent overlying theme in your work, that of the individual struggling against a maelstrom of inexplicable violence and injustices, more often than not succumbing to its dark promise. While *The Nocturne is perhaps less fatalist in that regard than your other works*, the ending might suggest otherwise. Do you hold a generally pessimistic view of the world and, if not, why do you believe this view tends to insinuate itself into your writing?

SG: Hmmm, I don't think I'm overtly pessimistic per se. But I do like dabbling with the dark side of human emotion and psyche. The enjoyment for me is finding characters and people, getting to know them, creating their likes and dislikes and idiosyncrasies and then placing them into situations that are extraordinary and very dangerous indeed. So, that leads to good fighting evil, light fighting darkness. But good doesn't always win. You can never be sure. And sometimes good crosses the line too far.

RC: So that preference for the darker elements of human nature then simply finds an organic extension in your writing.

SG: Right. And that's what I find so fascinating about the whole novel writing experience. That's where the buzz is for me. What if he goes there? What if that happens next? How would he react if... Now, there's not much interest, in my view, if the story is "What if he falls in love and everything works out okay?" Much much better if the story is, "What if he falls in love, and she's abducted and every day he receives a part of her body in the mail." Now, *that's* entertainment! *(laughs)*

RC: Along with exploring the dark side of humanity, *The Nocturne* also had a bit of a science-fiction flavor to it. Do you plan on revisiting that genre in part or whole anytime soon?

SG: Ooooooooooh, but did it? That's the big question, isn't it? I was heavily influenced by Bentley Little's *The Mailman* at the time, and that's a novel with no real answer in the end. The readers have to fend for themselves on that one. And the same is true, to an extent, with *The Nocturne*. Was it sci-fi? Was it government conspiracies? Was it? *Was it?* I had a hell of a time deciding whether or not to include the epilogue that is now part of the novel. I originally left it out, but I think it's good to have there now, as it does give some closure to the novel. But the other questions you have to work out for yourself. But I do believe that sci-fi and Steve Gerlach don't ordinarily mix. At least, that's what I think now, anyway. Who knows, in the future, maybe. I don't rule anything out. But there're no plans right now.

RC: The original version, an unsigned trade paperback self-published under your Probable Cause imprint, was limited to just, what, 200 copies or so? However, I understand that it's due to be reprinted in a signed/limited hardcover soon by Bloodletting Press, who also reprinted *Rage* and *Love Lies Dying*. I imagine it must feel quite gratifying to have your backlist reprinted to such popular demand.

SG: The good thing about Larry Roberts and the guys at Bloodletting Press is that they have always had a dream of a "Gerlach Library" of hardbacks, available uncut and in full glory, for the US market. From the very beginning with our discussions, Larry always had that vision. And I like a guy with a marketing edge and a grand plan. So it will indeed be very nice to see *The Nocturne* joining the others as part of the Bloodletting Press "Gerlach Library!"

RC: Will *The Nocturne* be revised in any way, or will there be any extras offered, as in the case of *Rage?*

SG: No, I don't think so. For many reasons, but mostly because I believe a book is written at a particular time, in a particular place, in my career. I don't believe in rewriting or revising novels that are already complete. These days, with modern technology, that's all too easy to do. I believe a novel shows your skills and where you were at a particular time in your career. And that's how it should stay. It's the same with movies. They shouldn't be tampered with, recut or reshot. They need to stand as they were, on first release.

RC: Although *Rage* was edited several times over for its various releases, correct?

SG: Well, yes, *Rage* had the scenes deemed too strong for Aussie audiences re-inserted in the Bloodletting version (and then deleted yet again for the Leisure mass-market paperback). But that's slightly different. And, of course, typos and the like should be removed as well. But that's as far as it should go. There are a couple of scenes in *The Nocturne* I would *like* to change, but I don't think that's the point. They stay, as they are, because that's how it was when the novel was first released. Call me crazy, but that's what I believe.

RC: Editing aside, what about any extra bonus material?

SG: As for added extras, well, I'll need to head on down into my archives to see if I can pull out some old character sketches or maps or something...but there *will* be a nice little surprise or two in one of those releases that my readers will really love. But my lips are sealed for now.

RC: Your next novel, 2001's *Love Lies Dying*, was the second and final one published by your Probable Cause Productions (and later reprinted in a signed/limited hardcover by Bloodletting Press in 2006). You earlier mentioned your research into S&M fetishism for this novel— you clearly did your homework, so to speak, as many of the intimate activities portrayed between the two central characters could make even the most jaded reader wince. This erotically-charged novel was, again, quite a departure from the novel that preceded it.

SG: As each novel should be! No reader wants to read the same story twice. Each novel needs to be as vastly different as the ones that preceded it. But, again, this is where the characters are so important. John Murdock and Zoe Barber are totally different to Ben and Christine in *Rage* or Jeff and Donna in *The Nocturne*. And, yes, there was quite a bit of research that went on for *Love Lies Dying*, including a visit or two to a house of domination. What I learnt there, and from talking to the mistresses at the house, was absolute gold for LLD. And, once again, it was the little things that became important. The style of a tied knot, the smell of sexual sweat, the way a keyring is carried and so on.

RC: As erotic as it is brutal, how difficult was it to achieve an effective narrative balance between seduction and horror?

SG: Really, I leave it up to the story. I don't outline sex scenes, thinking "this sex goes here and that sex goes there." The story tells itself and I let it. I don't force sex on the characters (no pun intended); I place it where it needs to be. In fact, and this may be hard to believe, there were a few sexual practices that didn't make it into LLD, mainly because there was nowhere they would flow easily and realistically into the story. Yes, there were other ideas and scenes that could have been added for effect, but I left them out as they weren't necessary and would've come across to the reader as forced. And I feel the balance was perfect in the end, because what starts as every man's wet dream suddenly swings around into every man's worst nightmare. True, real, ball-shriveling horror.

RC: *Love Lies Dying* is the story of John Murdock, an everyman tangled in a bizarre and horrifying web of events. John comes home to find his wife, Helen, missing, and a rather cryptic—and very possibly psychopathic—young female lying naked on his sofa. The woman turns out to be Zoe Barber, who leads John on a desperate journey to locate his wife...with plenty of masochistic and violent detours   along the way. But LLD is more than just a two-person drama. Much of LLD's story structure revolves around the lead male character's interaction with an omnipresent "inner voice", a voice that remains an integral yet enigmatic presence through much of the story, one that serves both to berate and enlighten him regarding his motivations. What was your impetus for including this plot vehicle which, in lesser hands, could prove cumbersome and awkward?

SG: Basically, *Love Lies Dying* is a book of threes. It has three sections, three words in the title, three main characters, three main settings and...well, I won't spill anymore for those who haven't read it. The "inner voice" was necessary as I knew I would have an extended period of time in the middle of the book where one of the main characters would be alone and, well, tied up for a while.

RC: *(Chuckles)* So to speak.

SG: My readers will get that one. Anyway, the character was needed to help the main character work through issues and to relate his plight at that moment. I always pictured that "inner voice" as a very real character in the novel, the third main character, who plays a very important role. It will surprise some readers exactly who the character is, and how his story ends in the novel, but I won't spoil that either. Surprisingly, the "inner voice" didn't seem at all risky to me at the time, as I had read many years ago a John Farris novel called *The Axeman Cometh* that uses the same literary device for a character who spends the novel stuck in an elevator. There were lots of risks in LLD, for me, but the "inner voice" wasn't one of them. I always felt it would work well. Treating it as a real character probably helped make it work in the end.

RC: LLD's lead female character, Zoe, is one of the most intriguing and beguiling femme fatale antagonists in recent genre fiction. Her motivations and history remain tantalizingly unclear through-out most of this spare, fast-paced novel, adding an eerie puzzle to a novel already drenched in gut-wrenching suspense and sexual savagery. Tell us a bit about how this woman who could haunt men's dreams—and their worst nightmares—came to be born, and what inspirations you perhaps drew on for her character.

SG: I knew Zoe Barber. It's that simple. Well, okay, not really Zoe Barber, but the Zoe on the dedications page of the novel is the Zoe in the novel. Of course, she wasn't that extreme. In fact, she'd die of embarrassment if she read the novel, but she's her. No doubt about it. I knew her for a fleeting moment of time, and I miss her still. But not as much as I miss Zoe Barber! *(laughs)* When working on the outline for *Lake Mountain*, Zoe Barber entered my head one day, and wouldn't leave until her story was told. So, I had to put aside *Lake Mountain* and focus on LLD. The story contained in LLD is her story, as told to me, and she herself is an amalgam of a few girls I knew. Her backstory is real, if pumped up a little; her experiences are real, if skewed a little...and the face and body of Zoe are even more real. In fact, they're exact. Right down to the little scar across her left eyebrow.

RC: It sounds as though the fictional Zoe became quite real to you during the writing of LLD.

SG: Yes, it's difficult not to have that happen when you have such an intriguing character, one who seems so real because she's tied in so inexorably to my past, but I wouldn't say I'm fixated on her or anything…

RC: Guess I shouldn't mention then the red Jeep Wrangler—identical to the one Zoe drove in *Love Lies Dying*—you cruise around in.

SG: *(Laughs)* Okay, okay…guilty. After writing LLD, it *did* take a long while for Zoe Barber to leave my mind; it was time for her to vacate, but she wouldn't. She's mostly gone now, though. My mind's filled now with the characters of my current project. But every so often, Zoe pays me a visit. I'm glad when she does, because she has a hold on me like she does every guy who comes across her path.

RC: Perhaps more than any of your other novels, LLD exemplifies the timeless thematic wellspring of which Richard Laymon drew on so often: the practice of plunging a naive character deeper and deeper into turmoil of their own misguided making. John Murdock, the lead male protagonist, was pushed, pulled and, yes, even punctured far beyond the limits of most individuals, yet his own obsession and questionable trusting nature drew him in further still. Going back to the old noir standards of film and publishing—and further back still—this is a theme that's always enjoyed popularity. Why do you think its appeal is, and continues to be, so universal and timeless?

SG: I think it's the edge. The danger. It's where none of us would ever tread. I've had many guys who have read LLD say to me, "I'd love to do it with Zoe Barber, but of course, I never *would!*" And that's the whole point. Here's a guy who knows he's in above his head, he knows things are spiraling out of control around him, but he goes on, deeper and deeper, because Zoe is there with him. He does what we would (hopefully) never do. We'd back out much earlier. Or would we? And that's the key. In the same way urban legends teach kids not to go down that dark lane to make-out, maybe LLD has the same effect for men who want to obtain the unobtainable. John Murdock gets that chance, takes it, and just look what happens to him! Maybe it teaches us all to be wary of the blonde bombshell.

RC: Along with that, obsession is also a clear, underlying theme in LLD—John's obsession for Zoe, his obsessive quest for his missing wife, Zoe's own secret obsession that ultimately explains her motives—and, in each case, it's this obsession that effectively blinds each of them to the truth and reality of their respective situations. Did you start out with a distinct intention to create a work of fiction that would so singularly examine the explosive and devastating ramifications of one single human emotion?

SG: I always try to write the back-cover blurb for each novel before I start writing. It's a foundation for what is to come and keeps me on track. The original blurb for LLD is much different to the final story. So, it's clear that I didn't set out to write a story dealing with obsession as such. That is, however, the story it became. And you can thank Zoe for that. She was a strong girl on the page, and in my head. There are twists and turns in that novel that even I was surprised about. She was telling her story, and I was along for the ride too. But, yes, LLD did become about obsession. Everyone's obsession, in the end. And that included the author's obsession with Zoe. The real Zoe. But it also deals with the lies in everyday life, the cover-ups, the personal histories people create about themselves to hide the hurt and the anger in their past. The lies they tell eventually become the truth, even to them. So, where does the truth stop and the lies begin? Not just for Zoe and John, but for you and me...for all of us?

RC: I understand the movie rights have been sold for

Love Lies Dying. Is this your first rights sale to a production company, and, if so, why do you believe *Love Lies Dying* was the first of your books to achieve that distinction? How is the production progressing, and do you have any personal involvement with it?

SG: Yes, an Aussie film company has the rights to *Love Lies Dying* and an option on *Rage.* I think they decided on LLD because it's a very character-based thriller with a few main settings, so it's easy to contain. It's early days yet, as they're still completing the screenplay, but I think it's really exciting to see what needs to be changed or tweaked to help a film version take life. But film production is fraught with dangers and unseen catastrophes, so I'm not getting excited until I'm walking down the red carpet on opening night!

RC: Furthering that seemingly inextricable link between Zoe Barber and obsession comes the novella *Hunting Zoe* (Wild Roses, S/L HC, 2004; Bloodletting Press, S/L HC, 2008 (reprint)). For an author whose previous backlist would indicate a reluctance to revisit familiar characters or settings, this novella comes as a considerable departure. As you mentioned, that aura of obsession, of near compulsion, which seems to radiate from the Zoe Barber character apparently extended even to her creator.

SG: Well, she had a hold over me, for sure. I'll admit it. And I know a lot of people who read LLD wanted Zoe to come back. Ironically, a novel dealing with obsession caused many readers to become obsessed with the main character. She's a powerful girl, is Zoe Barber. But I originally said no to a sequel. I don't like them and never wanted to write one. Yet the more I thought about it, the more another story surfaced. And Zoe came back into my head to help me on the way with it. So, yes, *Hunting Zoe,* is the result. But it isn't a sequel as such—it's a side trip, a campfire yarn, that brings more of Zoe's story to the readers who wanted to learn more.

RC: *Hunting Zoe,* the lead novella in this very collection, had an interesting road to publication. It was first published by Wild Roses in 2004 in a signed/limited hardcover run of only 200 copies. As I understand there were some distribution problems shortly after release, it must be gratifying to see this work released in larger numbers to your readership.

SG: Yes, finally *Hunting Zoe* receives the release she deserves. The original printing was fraught with problems from the get-go. In the end, I think the majority of the copies were lost at sea somewhere between Australia and the US. "The Curse of Zoe," I guess you could call it. That particular edition is very rare, as there were very few who actually received a copy. So, it's very nice to have Bloodletting step up to the plate once more and follow their release of *Love Lies Dying* with its follow-up, *Hunting Zoe.*

RC: This work is an intriguing, almost existential spin on the concept of a sequel, blurring the division between reality and fiction and examining what it means to be 'real.' It continues the legacy of Zoe, your female protagonist from *Love Lies Dying,* while at the same time taking a wry look at fanaticism and celebrity worship. It features two obsessed young male fans following Zoe's violent, bloody trail step-by-step as it was described in the original novel, hopeful that what they've read in their favorite book is in fact true and that Zoe, the object of their obsession, actually exists. What they find is somewhat what they'd hoped—and yet altogether different from what they may have expected—to find. And paralleling their quest, this novella is very much, and at the same time very different than, what one might expect of a "sequel." The puzzling duality of what's real and what's not, of what's imagined and what's only feared, is one that not only advances the furious pace of this admirable work but also makes this sequel much more than just a simple follow-up. What were your literary ambitions and goals when writing this novella, both for the work itself and Zoe in particular?

SG: Once *Love Lies Dying* was complete, I thought that I would be free of Zoe. She was gone from my head and I thought I would be able to easily move on to my next project, which was to be *Lake Mountain.* But I found I couldn't shake her, she kept returning and telling me tales…late at night. It sounds crazy, I know, but she was still with me. Add to that the feedback I was receiving from my readers who loved *Love Lies Dying* and—strangely—seemed to want to know all there was to know about Zoe in the novel and the *real* Zoe who she was based on. Many of the conversations that ended up in *Hunting Zoe* were actual conversations some readers had with me. So I thought I would use them to create a new slant on the LLD world. I mean, when it comes down to it, LLD is based in fact. The places exist, the people exist... hell, even the backstory exists! So I decided I would play on the blurring of fact and fiction in LLD. I'd play on that story, or the author's "lies" if you will, to create a side story, a fictional account of two fans, hunting down the facts of their favorite piece of fiction.

RC: Clever. Hunting down lies to find the truth, perhaps only to discover what they've assumed all along to be lies and truth are just the opposite…or blurred so much that the terms no longer have any meaning.

SG: Exactly. What is truth and what are lies anyway? Where does one start and the other finish? That's the focus of *Hunting Zoe* as well as *Love Lies Dying.* So with this approach I was able to write a side-trip (not a sequel) to LLD that would answer a whole lot of questions, while also playing on that blurred line of fact and fiction. And, hopefully, I've succeeded.

RC: It sounds as though reader response was the primary impetus for writing this novella.

SG: Absolutely. I found myself amazed that this one

character could create so much interest and, because of this interest and also the fact Zoe was still with me, well, *Hunting Zoe* was just the next natural step. It was fun to write and, I think, it also allowed me the freedom to twist some things and comment on society's fascination with stars and so-called famous people. Why are they famous? And why are we intrigued so much by them? I try never to really push a political or social line when I write my novels. I write fiction and it should be fun to read. But because of its very structure, *Hunting Zoe* allowed me to say some things, and have a laugh or two along the way.

RC: Do you now feel as though you've finally exorcised her hold on your creative mind, or do you suspect she will at some point appear yet again?

SG: Is she completely exorcised from me? I don't think she ever will be, somehow. Will she appear again? There are no plans right now, but I'd never say never. Yes, I have an idea or two, an outline here and there…even a title if she should return. And I know she wants to, she's got plenty more to say yet. Time will tell.

RC: Your most recent, original full-length novel, *Lake Mountain* (Bloodletting Books, signed/limited HC, 2005), was a frenzied hybrid of classic noir and dark deviancy, a chilling road trip featuring two women plagued by madness and desperation. This particular novel seemed to many to be a true turning point in your writing, a visible maturation of both style and content, exuding a hitting-all-cylinders confidence of craft and complex story structure. Did it seem that way to you as well upon completion, and what is your view of *Lake Mountain* in your overall body of work?

SG: Each novel—hopefully—pushes my limits as a writer and I learn from the experience. There was a lot happening in *Lake Mountain,* a lot of background research and a real focus on trying to get the female narrator's voice right. It had to sound right to me, and also to the readers. I was very proud of *Lake Mountain* and, of course, you always are proudest of your latest novel, but I set high goals for that novel, and I think I reached them all, from both character and plotting standpoints, and also voice, pacing and imagery. It's different to everything that I've written in the past, and pushed me out to the edge yet again. It's a harrowing tale of love, betrayal and maggots. *(Laughs)* It's a road-tale, a chase book and contains some very interesting characters indeed.

RC: Since Zoe in *Love Lies Dying* was an integral but still supporting character, *Lake Mountain* was your first book to feature a female as your main protagonist; in fact, it featured two very distinct female characters as the book's leads, each with very diverse emotional turmoil that was central to their characters' plight. What were some of the unique challenges in writing from a female perspective?

SG: Voice mainly, but also trying to capture the way females think. I'm male, I think a certain way, and here I was writing a novel about *two* female characters—one of whom we'd be privy to her internal thoughts, the other we had to observe objectively but closely. Add to that the fact that they both take up a good deal of the first half of the novel, before the main male character arrives, and it's fair to say it was tough going there for a while. I found myself eavesdropping on conversations between women in the street or at cafés, reading a fair bit of...I guess you call it... chic-fic, and generally trying to think like a female. It's a subtle change and luckily for me I had a few women read the novel before release to make sure the internal logic and external voice were correct for both characters. From what I hear, I seem to have got it right.

RC: Because of the novel's storyline, the landscape itself was a central character in *Lake Mountain,* perhaps more than any of your preceding works. It became nearly as important and fleshed-out as the living characters themselves.

SG: Yes, this novel was very location specific. Actually, everything in this novel was very specific. I drove the roads the girls traveled down; I visited the places they stayed. For this novel, I wanted to be able to "walk through" the scenes if I needed to, and on some occasions I would stop writing and jump in the car, head to the locations and actually *be* in the novel. It certainly helped focus my mind on the sights and sounds that were unique to these places, but it also drew my eye to some of the subtleties that existed there as well. Sometimes the very locations themselves brought to light some plot twist or idea that was later used in the novel. That beats just drawing a map on a piece of paper and thinking, "They go this way." I even made a little trailer for the novel which can be viewed on my website, www.stevegerlach.com—you can see the very locations used in the novel as I take you on a little tour of them. I've even taken a few Gerlach fans on what is now called the Gerlach Tour, which includes driving through some of the locations used in this novel and *Rage* and *Love Lies Dying* as well.

RC: I've seen the six-minute promotional trailer for this novel and I must say I was quite impressed—not only by the tantalizing Hitchcockian homage but the infectious enthusiasm you obviously have for your work and, as well, the marketing aspect of it. Do you feel in this age of dwindling midlist-author rosters that it's contingent upon an aspiring writer to make themselves stand out from the crowd, to show a wary publisher that not only can one cook up the proverbial steak but also understand the importance of selling the sizzle?

SG: It's a tough world out there these days and everyone's thinking of their bottom line. The days of publishers having the money and time to spend on advertising and marketing materials have long gone, if they ever existed in the first place. Sure, if you're a King or Koontz, it's there for you, but if it isn't, you need to be the face of your book. It's that simple. It's your book, your work, you have to publicize it. Me sitting back in the pool and waiting for the magic to happen is a sure road to failure. Musicians can't release a CD and then take the next eight months off. They have to do interviews, go on tour, all those things to make the CD sell. It's the same with books. And, seeing as I've had a background in marketing and PR, I like to be involved in the publicity and the marketing of my novels. I'm always looking for something quirky and different, something that pushes the novel out in front of readers who may not know me and makes them think, "Yeah, I'd like to try this guy." So, with the Bloodletting Books version of *Rage*, the lettered edition is signed in my own blood, and for *Lake Mountain* there's that six minute video trailer. Prior to *Lake's* release the trailer went out on cd-rom—along with a *TeamGerlach* cap—to publishers and media organizations.

RC: How were these PR goodies received?

SG: Oh, they were both a big hit. So, I'd have to say the experiment worked, and I have Alfred Hitchcock to thank for that! I've been a Hitchcock fan for years. I love all his movies, his style, his ability to create great stories, characters, tension and suspense. And I think his visual style permeates my novels as well. I know when I'm writing the novels, I write with a very vivid image visualized in my head. I see the novel visually, as a movie, as I write it. So, it was a great honor to be able to pay homage to Hitch in the *Lake Mountain* trailer. If only he was still around to make a movie of one of my novels...

RC: Never one to shy from extremism in your work—and, in fact, having somewhat of a reputation in some circles as an 'extreme horror' practitioner—there was a mortuary scene in *Lake Mountain* that eclipsed anything you'd previously written, though each had their own extreme moments as well. Is your intention by the inclusion of these scenes to simply shock, to satisfy reader expectations with a 'money shot' or two—or do you feel they serve a greater purpose than simple titillation?

SG: Nothing appears in my novels just for titillation sake. That's cheap and a quick thrill that doesn't last. In each novel I set up three or four key scenes, and these scenes turn the novel around or cause there to be a paradigm shift for a character or characters. But, these key scenes have to make sense and have to be realistic and work with the internal logic of the storyline. The morgue scene is extreme, yes, and was very hard to write, but it's not impossible and, thanks to my research, I knew *could* and *has* been done in the past. It serves to show the extremes of the character. It was meant to shock and surprise and disgust, but at the same time, it hopefully has the reader thinking, "Hey, I knew this character was a bit out there, but she's lost it now."

RC: Yet these types of shock scenes appear without exception in each of your novels and often push—some might say deliberately—the envelope of what's deemed acceptable in standard horror fare.

SG: I guess they do, but only because they are the key scenes that I *need* to visit during the journey. If they were just for titillation, it would be—for me—just like painting with numbers. There's got to be a point, a context, and it has to make sense. And I think that's why that scene is memorable to a lot of people. It wasn't just a quick money shot to get the reader's attention…it's a scene that shows the lengths this character would go to, and sets up the spiral of disaster that is to come. *That's* why it's memorable, because it's a turning point.

RC: *Lake Mountain* is the first novel of yours to be picked up by a UK publisher, where in 2008 it will be released as a paperback through Screaming Dreams Press. Why was *Lake Mountain* chosen as the first of your work to be reprinted, and will your other novels follow?

SG: I'm very excited about the Screaming Dreams line of Gerlach paperbacks. I think because *Lake Mountain* was the latest full novel of mine to be available, the guys at Screaming Dreams felt this would be the best to start with, and I agree with them. I think *Lake Mountain* is a great tale, and a terrific showcase for what I can do as a writer. It's a terrific way to launch the Gerlach Paperback Library. I'm looking forward to seeing this novel in paperback form, and to the release of my other novels as paperbacks in the following months and years through Screaming Dreams.

RC: Tell us a bit about *A Thousand Mettle Folds: Cut 1, The Fall* (Bloodletting Press, signed/limited HC, forthcoming). I understand it's the first in a series of five historical horror novellas co-written with Amanda Kool.

SG: Yes, that's certainly the plan. It's the chance to write some period pieces, steeped in history and detail, while also running a thread of a very disturbing storyline through them all. It's very interesting to work on and quite a challenge, really taking me out of my comfort zone. But that's all part of the fun. I'm really enjoying the research and learning about certain periods in history that, until now, I'd been a little hazy on.

RC: When do you anticipate its release, and how soon are each of the subsequent novellas expected to follow?

SG: I think Bloodletting is releasing the first book in 2008 sometime. And I'd certainly expect to see the others follow maybe annually from there. There's no set deadline, as each takes quite a lot to research, but we'll get there. The complete story is outlined and ready to go, so they'll all appear eventually.

RC: Normally a solitary venture, writing collaboratively traditionally requires a seamless meshing of voices and styles to be effective and successful. Since this is your first experience with co-writing, how have you found the experience, and how do you split the writing duties?

SG: I said I'd never co-write, but sometimes a project comes along and it's clear that two heads are better than one. The devil really is in the details with this series and it'd be a daunting project for just one person to work on. Plus, I always like to be confident in knowing what I'm writing is correct, and with two writers those details can be checked and double-checked. As for the writing duties, we generally write a chapter each, letting the other edit it and add to it before we come together to discuss and strengthen what's already there. On this occasion, a well plotted outline is mandatory to make sure we both stay on the path we've already decided upon. It's weird writing with another person, but also quite exciting at the same time.

RC: Let's move away from your longer writings and get acquainted with your shorter work of which, until this volume, little has been seen. While I understand Bloodletting offered a free promotional chapbook of *"CellCandy"* with their signed/limited hardcover of *Rage* and you have a short-story in *In Laymon's Terms* (CD Publications, signed/limited HC, forthcoming), you clearly seem to prefer the novel form. Why?

SG: You don't see many Gerlach short stories because I really don't write them much. I like the larger canvas and the extra time a novel can provide for story elements and characterization. It's much more enjoyable to construct a novel-length story or situation than to write one limited by the constraints of the short story medium. Of course, this is all just my opinion, and there are some terrific short story writers out there. But I do write short stories occasionally. When a cool idea hits me or I think of something that is suited to a short story, I'll write it, but usually my mind is filled with plot elements and characterization for novels. But, occasionally, yeah, the magic happens. So, a

Gerlach short story is a rare find indeed.

RC: I imagine that inclination toward longer works then makes this definitive volume of short stories one that may not see a companion volume for quite some time.

SG: That's true. I've picked only the short stories I'm particularly fond of for this collection. I don't see there being another collection of my shorter work for a long time. The stories contained in this volume are the ones I'm proud of, as proud of as my novels. Two of them, *"Dead of Night"* and *"Jungle"*, have never been published anywhere before; they're the newest of the batch.

RC: With its aforementioned previous release as an individual promotional chapbook—and now demanding an impressive sum on the collector's resale market—*"CellCandy"* is the story that has had likely the widest exposure of all your short tales, and may arguably be the most extreme in content. Tell us a bit about the gestation of this story, and perhaps a bit of background on each of the other four tales in this volume.

SG: Well, if we work chronologically, *"Broken Cookie"* is one of my earliest pieces and certainly remains fond to my heart. *"Schism"* is another early piece, and I guess you can see in both stories that I'm playing with inner voice and characterization. In fact, it's probably true that most of my short stories are really experiments with a voice, or a situation or a premise, probably because I want to use it in a longer form and want to make sure I can do it well in a short story first. *"CellCandy"* came about as I was writing *Lake Mountain,* and you can see the influence on the subject matter there. I wanted to use some of the ideas, some of the internal thoughts, that wouldn't have worked in *Lake Mountain* and put them to use with a male character. So, the subject matter is along the same lines, but twisted ever-so-slightly to another point of view. People seem to like this short story, it certainly is nasty! *(Laughs)* They're just dying to get their hands on that one! *"Dead of Night"* was written exclusively for a German anthology which, to my knowledge, never got off the ground (although a different version will appear in *In Laymon's Terms,* once that is published.) This short, along with *"Jungle,"* are mainly for the fun of writing. The joy in a set-up and a quick *gotcha!* ending. *"Jungle"* is the most recent, written only a few months ago now. That one still makes me smile.

RC: With a good number of published novels or novellas already under your belt, you would seem to still have a very long and prosperous writing career ahead of you. What direction do you see your writing taking in the immediate future, and what career goals would you like to have accomplished in the next, say, 10 or 15 years?

SG: Well, every new novel is a step in the right direction. In the next 10 or so years? I'd like to see more of my work out there. I don't know how many novels will be published in that time, but there's certainly a few more already cooking in the pot, as you can see from everything we've discussed. *Harmony Chokes* is what I am working on right now, and have been for the past year or so. It's my rather extreme take on the old noir Gold Medal classics of the '50s and '60s. The hardest part is keeping true to the style and length of those old classics. That's the challenge with this novel, and sometimes it's harder than it looks! If I succeed, I'll be very proud of the results. After that, *Dead of Night*—same title as the above-mentioned short story, but a completely different work—will be next and from what I can tell you already, it'll be urban warfare. The city as jungle. And one small boy's fight for survival. There's also an Armageddon-style novel...but that's a whole other story. I write for the thrill, for the enjoyment, for the buzz of telling a good tale and having readers enjoy what they read. That's the clincher for me. So, in 10 to 15 years if I'm able to write another, say, 5 novels or so, I'll be more than happy. Obviously the goal is to break into the US market even further, so let's hope it continues to gather pace. I'm working with some terrific people at my various publishers, so I can only hope our beneficial relationship continues.

RC: Sounds as though your readers have a great deal to look forward to.

SG: You bet. It's going to be one hell of a ride…

(Ron Clinton's interviews and fiction have been published in Cemetery Dance Magazine, Mystery Scene Magazine, *the anthologies* In Laymon's Terms *and* Tales From the Gorezone, *and numerous on-line venues. He lives with his wife and two daughters in the Seattle area of Washington State.)*

Steve Gerlach is one of Australia's few thriller writers. Born and bred in Australia, Gerlach's fast-paced, cut-to-the-bone style is a refreshing voice in the dry, barren Australian literary scene.

Steve's background includes many varied roles. He has worked as an editor for a book publisher; as the editor-in-chief of an Australian motorcycle magazine; editor and publisher of an international crime magazine, Probable Cause; a researcher and columnist for a major Australian daily newspaper; a Technical Publications Officer in the security industry; marketing executive for an international telecommunications software company; a writer for Australian Defence training and software producers; and currently works as a freelance writer.

He was also the Historical Advisor on the Australian film, Let's Get Skase.

Steve Gerlach lives in Melbourne, where he is currently working on a new novel or two.